My Husband's Girlfriend

My Husband's Girlfriend

A NOVEL

Cydney Rax

THREE RIVERS PRESS
NEW YORK

For Christina A. Pattyn,
the ultimate *sister/friend.*

Thanks for being there, for listening, for introducing me
to Mitchell's Fish Market in Birmingham, Michigan.
And most of all, thanks for being you—strong,
knowledgeable, supportive, and funny.

Part 1

Anya & Neil

1

Anya

A celibate husband and wife are the two most dangerous people on earth.

That's what my husband, Neil, told me—one year ago—when our nightmare began. I guess at the time I didn't believe him. But right now, sitting by the phone waiting for Neil to call me from the hospital and tell me the gender of the baby he's having with *her*, well, I believe him.

Lack of affection and regular sex within a marriage is like having a ticking bomb strapped to your body—you only have so much time before something explosive shatters your whole world.

How did we get to this point? Approximately two years ago, I'd be at home slumped on the couch. Lost in a zone. Neil would swagger into the den looking like a taller, thinner, less insane version of Mike Tyson. Beautiful chestnut complexion, intense eyes, and fine in his own kind of way. Neil would stand next to me starting stuff, swaying his hips back and forth, singing low. And then he'd sit down, getting close enough to press his lips against my neck. I'd beg off, claiming, "*Soul Food* is on right now." I'd wave at Neil, inviting him to chill out and watch the show with me, but he'd yank his lips from my neck and storm away. And, feeling guilty, I'd look at the show a few more minutes, then follow him up to our bedroom. We'd start out giving each other a dry kiss on the cheek, something you'd offer a casual friend. Then Neil would rub me between my legs, trying to generate a fire that would need a whole lot more to ignite than those little matches he was using via his idea of foreplay. Next he'd order me to lie on my side. His goal was to take it from the rear.

"I saw two people doing it in this flick," he remarked the first time we tried it. "We can handle this."

Talk about awkward; this position didn't even sound like something an animal could manage, let alone humans. Protesting was useless. So I lay on my side, body stiffening up as if I just heard a strange noise, too terrified to move.

Neil pushed into me so rough it felt like someone tried to shove something hot, hard, long, and round inside my one good nostril. I could barely breathe. I yelled, "Ouch, ouch, ugh." But to Neil it was like I screamed "Hallelujah," because he kept jamming his huge, happy thing inside my tense butt. I'd reach behind my back and grip him. I bucked. Cursed. Pressed my half-inch nails into his sweaty thighs. Dumb jerk thought I was having a helluva time, not realizing how much I ached to escape back downstairs to try to catch the end of my show. But I said nothing. I let Neil do his business. And on a few occasions after that night, I'd continue to do my duty. Letting Neil have an ample supply of sympathy sex. Until the last time we did it; until the day we officially became celibate.

Neil and I were spread out on a huge colorful rug on the floor next to the bed. I was lying on my back. My legs were like a clothes hanger curled around his neck. He was jumping around and slapping my behind, having a jolly good time—until he noticed that I had seized the nearby cable guide, perusing it for a worthwhile pay-per-view movie. He scrunched up his face. "Screw it; screw this mess." He physically slipped out of me. Left me alone on the floor. I wondered if I'd eventually slip out of his heart and his mind, too. I became terrified. That's when I knew something had to give, that our marriage was in the balance. Things might never be good again if I didn't figure out what to do.

Intimacy. Closeness. Feeling each other. Little by little, all those necessary acts disappeared from our relationship. Yet I loved Neil. Couldn't imagine being without him. When Neil wasn't in the room with me, I wondered where he was. When I thought of his spellbinding fragrance, his infectious smile, and how proficient he was at taking care of his family, that and more kept me drawn to him in spite of everything.

Fast-forward to now. These days I have to keep myself from stressing about the new addition to the family. If it weren't for Sharvette, my sister-in-law, I don't know what I'd do. She's Neil's half sister, and ever since their sixty-year-old mother pointed at their front door and told the girl to "get the hell out," she's been living with us here in Houston. It isn't too bad. Sharvette is great company; plus, she has my back, which is imperative because that's the only way I would allow her to live with us.

She's sitting here with me right now. We're in the downstairs den. This room has lots of tall windows, and normally that means sunshine fills it from one wall to the other. But today is cloudy, so the room is dark. But given the circumstances, the darkness kinda complements the mood.

I'm rocking back and forth in my seat. My right hand is clutching the portable phone like it might run away. Sharvette is patting my left hand. She's stroking my skin, rubbing me gently, and acting like I'm the one about to give birth instead of Neil's other woman.

I can't stand the thought of *her*. Neil's mistress. I guess because, like a dummy, I've created her. Because of me, she is. If I hadn't encouraged my husband to find a sex partner, he wouldn't have done it. I know he wouldn't. He's a good man, and he loves me. In spite of this other baby that's about to enter the world, I know Neil Braxton Meadows loves me.

Right now Sharvette is grasping my hand and shaking her head, stopping and shaking it again. I can't stand to look at Vette, which is her nickname. Sometimes her body language speaks as loud as her voice. So I stare at my lap, looking inwardly at my life. I don't like what I see.

"Well, I don't care what gender this little bastard turns out to be, Reesy is gonna always be my favorite niece. And that's all I have to say."

I smile. Sharvette is astounding. She's family. My higher ground. A reliable anchor.

"Because the Negro shouldn't have been messing around on you in the first place. I don't care if y'all drew up that little sex contract. I don't care that both of y'all signed it. He should've known better to even consider that dumb shit. 'Cause if my brother really loved you, he—"

She hushed like her conscience kicked in. But I hadn't done anything to give her a reason to shut up. I know a man can love his wife and still do foolish things. Like making passes at other women while he's standing two feet away from his wife. Or visiting a woman who lives in the same apartment complex as him and the missus. Or telling his lover he isn't happy at home, but at the same time telling home he's not happy having a lover. That's what some men do. I know this. And outrageous as it sounds, that's why I pressured Neil into trying something I thought might work.

The deal is this: In addition to balking whenever Neil wanted to experiment with these painful new positions, I was struggling with a couple other issues that further complicated our sex life. For one, I was prescribed with having FSAD, an acronym for female sexual arousal disorder, which basically means I have a low sex drive, about as low as a dead person's. If you're lucky, you *might* be able to generate some sexual desire, but the drawback is you rarely get satisfied because your body won't lubricate. Orgasms are as rare as a San Antonio blizzard. And you can also suffer from deep dyspareunia, which means sex is too painful to enjoy.

I've found out I'm not alone. FSAD is a condition that affects 47 million American women for a variety of reasons. And to date there is no approved drug to treat this disorder. So even if my delicious-smelling hubby fondles me and gives me the eye, my interest in getting it on fades many nights. Sometimes my lack of desire rattles me, but the truth is I don't terribly miss having orgasms. If I have them, fine; if I don't, it really doesn't matter. Of course, this isn't fair to Neil, but my hormones don't seem to care.

To make things worse, I've gained a good twenty-five pounds in the past five years. I'm thirty-seven years old and my transformed body seldom lets me forget. But yes, I've signed up for state-of-the-art fitness-center memberships. I've bought the useless Paula Abdul workout tapes—useless because two weeks after being gung ho about exercising and getting my fried-chicken-loving self back in shape, the only sit-ups I do are when I sit up in bed so I can grab a decadent chocolate-chip cookie that's calling to me from a nearby table. And although I don't consider myself the most unattractive woman in the world, I really feel uncomfortable when Neil takes long looks at me. I'm afraid he'll see my imperfections, like I'm not everything he expects me to be.

So about a year ago, I walked into our home library unannounced. Neil looked up, eyes enlarged, and yelled, "Anya, not now, not now." He was sitting on the edge of the sofa, naked from the waist down, his dick clutched in his hand, with an unbridled look in his eyes. He grabbed his slacks and clumsily spread them across his lap. I backed up until I was no longer in that room witnessing what I'd driven my husband to do. I felt bad but not bad enough to let him make love to me whenever he was in the mood, which was often.

When I realized our sexless streak had stretched to two years, I thought about what I could do to help the situation. And one day I took a deep breath and blurted, "Neil, why don't you find a partner? Find a woman you can have sex with up to two times a month, no strings attached, but if you agree to do this, you've got to promise me something."

"What's that?" Neil asked, stunned.

"Promise me you won't fall in love. That you're in it only for the sex."

"Are you *crazy?*"

"No, baby, not crazy. I love you," I told him sincerely. I loved him enough to trust him to do something that didn't seem like a big deal at the time. Sure, encouraging your hubby to have sex with another woman is something many wives wouldn't do. But I thought if I controlled that situation, as opposed to letting him take charge of an affair, maybe the outcome wouldn't be as disastrous. Plus, I knew that even if Neil didn't totally understand me, I was certain that he loved me. He was a great, reliable husband, thoughtful, and a superb father. And since mostly everything else in our marriage was decent, why break up just because of sex? So I asked Neil to give this arrangement a try. I reasoned that as long as he didn't grow attached to the woman, and we stuck to our promises, the arrangement could succeed.

The Marital Arrangement of Neil Braxton Meadows and His Wife, Anya

1. Neil should seek and find a single, unattached female sex partner.
2. They should only have oral sex, no penetration; giving and receiving are permissible.
3. No falling in love with her. If she falls in love with Neil, he should end the relationship quickly and respectfully.
4. Anya will never accuse Neil of committing adultery *because this entire plan was her idea.*

I made up numbers one, two, and three. And I made up the first part of number four, but Neil insisted I mention in italics that the idea was mine. I thought it was unnecessary to add that part, but I didn't argue. I gave in so he could feel better. So we could move on.

Neil and I stuck the unsigned arrangement in a drawer for one week so we could both think about it. And we debated the issue until we agreed that oral sex isn't true sex. Whether middle schoolers, college guys, or senior citizens, plenty of men get blow jobs. The act means nothing to them. Besides, are there any stats on how many men fall in love with blow-job-giving women? I thought Neil could share his body without handing over his heart. So we retrieved the document and signed (I signed first) and I locked it inside a file cabinet located downstairs. My biggest concern at the time was making sure Neil believed I was serious. I was, and I still am.

"Damn, what's taking my brother so long?" Sharvette lets go of my hand. I now feel abandoned but understand her anxiety. She stands up, walks across the length of our den, and comes right back and sits at my feet. Vette has recently added blond highlights to her brown hair. Her hair is teased and wild looking, the long strands touching her shoulders and making her look older than twenty.

"These things take time, sweetie," I assure her. "The lady's only been at the hospital six hours. He'll call." My voice sounds light and airy, me trying to be positive and mature. Who the heck am I kidding? If it weren't for the fact that in Texas, murder means a trip to death row, I'd have already handled that fool. But I need to stay in control. I cannot kill my husband or his mistress just because he broke our contract. Even if he couldn't keep his word, at least one of us should.

"I don't see how you can take it, Anya," Vette whispers. She looks at me long enough to force me to stare into her light green eyes. Her skin is glowing, bronze-toned, and blemish free. I hope this young woman can look at my marriage and learn from it. Learn what not to do. Learn that marriage ain't nothing nice; that even if things are shaky within the marriage, a legally bound relationship isn't easy to terminate. Not as easy as some folks (the naive ones) think.

"If I ever get married, which I don't plan to, first I want to live with the Negro for at least five years, just to see where his mind is. Just to see if he's faking it with me or not."

I laugh and cross my legs at the ankles. I have on a cute white blouse, a long blue-jean skirt, and some strappy sandals that I haven't worn in years. I just feel like trying to look sexier for a change.

"Oh really, Vette? And what if the dude fakes it for five years, you two hook up, and then he starts tipping out on you soon after he's made it legal?"

"Don't worry. I have a tight game plan in mind, sister-in-law. 'Cause see, I ain't as desperate as some of these single women out here, doing anything and everything to get a man, to catch a husband. They catching more than husbands these days."

"You right about that. Marriage ain't no joke."

The phone rings and hums against my hand. I just stare. Breathless. It rings again.

Sharvette's eyes grow wider and she snatches the phone from my grip.

"Yeah?" she says. She puts her hand on her hip. "She's right here, what you got to tell her?"

I look at the ceiling.

"Uh-huh, okay, all right, bye."

I look at Vette.

"They just had a seven-pound, five-ounce, nineteen-inch boy. Neil Braxton Meadows, Jr."

I couldn't sleep at all last night. I'd go lie down for a few minutes. Sit up in bed. Turn on the lamp. Cut on the TV, go to the refrigerator, and pile a bunch of chilled white grapes in a porcelain bowl. I slid back in bed and tried looking at R. Kelly music videos. When I couldn't stand looking at that anymore, I turned to TBN and watched a religious program.

"Jesus cares about you," this fifty-something white guy said. He stared straight into the camera. His hair was greasy looking and slicked back, like he was a movie star instead of a soul winner.

"Jesus doesn't know me," I said to the TV, then turned it off when the man started talking about sending in a thousand-dollar donation so God could bless me even though God has way more money than me.

If Jesus knew me, He'd see what I was going through and get me out of this situation. So I don't wanna hear anything Preacher Man got to say.

I knew my thinking wasn't the most divine. People always blame the Lord for things that go wrong in their lives. If there's a war, God started it. If people get killed in a senseless tragedy, it's the Lord's fault because guess who had the power to stop things but didn't? If anybody is going through anything they don't like, well, blame it on the Lord. He's used to being the fall guy, I thought. Pointed fingers shouldn't bother him. And although I freely believed these things, I felt justified but scared at the same time. I didn't believe that saying about how God strikes people with lightning. If that were true, a whole lot more people would be burned to a crisp on a daily basis, and it would probably be raining every single minute of the day, and people would be too afraid to go outside.

But I did have some level of fear, that if I thought inappropriate things, the Lord knew and He'd punish me somehow. I wondered if my troubles were His payback.

Vengeance is mine, I will repay. I recalled that Scripture. And I thought that if God was paying me back, then maybe I'd luck out . . . and He'd pay Neil back, too.

The morning after the baby is born, Sharvette cooks six large pancakes, scrambled eggs, and turkey sausage, and pours two tall glasses of pure orange juice, sets everything on a tray, and brings the food into my bedroom. I am so surprised and touched she's thinking of me, I nearly lose my appetite. But that feeling doesn't last.

I start digging in. "Here, you have some, too." I pat the spot next to me. Sharvette slides in the queen-size bed with me. She's shoeless, sporting red short shorts and a white halter top with a red bra and one strap showing. It looks so silly but that's just Vette. She picks up a turkey sausage and holds it in front of her open mouth like she's about to suck something. She smirks at me, then chomps the meat like she's starving. Oil glistens her lips, making it appear like she's wearing clear lip gloss.

We eat in silence for a minute.

"You actually gonna finish decorating that nursery, Anya?"

I wince but nod.

"I don't know about you, girl."

"Look, Vette, I'm not a young single woman, you are. You don't understand."

"Then explain things to me. Help me understand, Anya. Because I'm starting to think you're somebody's fool."

"It doesn't surprise me that you think that I'm a fool, but that's fine because you are not walking in my shoes." I have eaten two pancakes and I sip some orange juice, not that I'm terribly thirsty, but the pancakes are so thick my throat feels crammed, like I'm choking. I slide the plate to Vette's side of the bed. I get comfy by lying against several pillows.

"Sure, things are tough," I say, "but I'm not going to up and leave Neil. I'm as responsible for this situation as he is, so . . ."

"Bull, Anya. Creating a nursery for your husband's other baby is out there."

"Look, Vette, it's Reesy's old room. It's small, not being used for anything except storage. It'll take no time to do a little paint job, apply some decorative wall border, and pull out Reesy's crib. I doubt that Neil will bring his son over here that much, anyway. It's just in case."

"Yeah, yeah, yeah." Vette is starting to get on my nerves. She acts like she's the wife instead of just the sister-in-law. She's never been married before. How can she possibly understand?

A few weeks ago Sharvette voluntarily informed me that I am a fucking wimp. Those were her exact words. And I just looked at her and laughed and she made this disgusting noise, then exclaimed, "See my point?"

"Nope," I told her.

"Any other person would've cussed me out in both Chinese and Ebonics, but you just let me call you names. Why would you do that? Do you agree with them? Let me know."

Her words stung like a sharp needle puncturing my skin, so I didn't say anything. Vette started rolling her eyes and talking to herself. She could roll those eyes until the whites disappeared. I didn't care about her being mad. I get tired of people mistaking my silence for weakness, thinking I'm a stupid, defenseless wife who never fights. I've learned to pick my battles, and I guess Vette couldn't understand that, just like she couldn't understand my wanting to create a nursery for Neil's son.

"If we have a room here," I explain to her, "then Neil won't have an excuse to go over there with *her*, right?"

"There you go again. Why can't you just say her name? *Danielle.* Her name sounds a little like *Neil.* How cute," Sharvette says sarcastically.

I jump up out the bed and balance a tray in my hand that holds my glass, a fork, and an empty plate.

"Oh, so you wanna go wash dishes now, huh? You're a real trip." Sharvette hands me her juice glass and I stare into its emptiness.

"No, I take that back, Anya. You are a journey."

2

Neil

When my son was first born, I stared at him like he was a newly discov-
ered treasure. And he was. I love my daughter, Reese, but fathering a
son makes me feel like I've done something right for a change. Now, I'm
not so stupid that I think having a son redeems me from my sins, but his
birth was the most positive thing that's happened in a long time.

So many stressful events have gone down, sometimes I feel like I'm
living someone else's life and I've been looking through their window. If
anyone would have told me I'd be skanking it up with a young project
secretary and we'd eventually have a baby together, no way I'd believe it.

But sometimes instead of watching the movie, your life becomes the
movie. And here I am, thirty-six years old, graduated from high school
at age sixteen, supposedly intelligent (MBA from UT-Austin), gainfully
employed (fourteen years' experience at Texas Medical Center, pulling
in six figures a year), a member of a well-known church called Solomon's
Temple, and I have so much anguish, I fear being around firearms,
butcher knives, or large skillets. Things that are already dangerous look
more menacing. So everything around me becomes suspect even if I
don't want it to be.

Overall, Anya seems to be holding up well. She hasn't said a lot lately. When she's not rearing our daughter, she stays busy vacuuming, dusting, Windexing, cooking, washing and folding clothes, and even doing gardening (and she hates getting her hands dirty). But I know my wife. She only cleans when she's livid. She takes to a broom when she's upset. All nervous energy. It's either clean or scream, and I'd rather come home to a spotless house than a woman who has her mouth wide open and is shouting profanities as loud as she can. Don't get me wrong. Our getting into it doesn't happen every day, but it's happened enough for me to detect that thick level of tension inside our home.

At first I wanted to run from my problems, just up and leave Anya, quit my job and start all over, maybe in Atlanta or someplace where there's so many people that I'd feel invisible. But I've decided to stick around. I want to "be a man." Not turn into a loser who takes to a bottle seven days a week, crying in my beer, and living inside my pain.

Call me idealistic, but I also want to be a good father to my precious new son and try to balance things with Danielle in a civilized manner. What helps me cope is the fact that Dani is so chilly, so cool. She's sweet, smart, and most important, she'll kiss but won't tell.

When she got pregnant and started wearing maternity clothes at work, I told her I could act happy for her, but she shouldn't expect more than that. I could play the concerned-coworker role around the office, but no, I didn't want my supervisor or colleagues to know I was the daddy. That would be suicide without the gun. And I was relieved when Danielle said, "Sure, no prob." She never hemmed me up for money, didn't ask for a commitment; she never begged for much of anything. Being there when our son was born was the least I could do. Plus, I am proud of him. He's a healthy, attractive little tyke, my mini me. I can't abandon him.

Now, as far as still having sex with Danielle, who knows what's gonna happen? Could recent events inspire my wife's sex drive so that she's willing to do what I want when I want? After everything that's gone down, I can't picture Anya rushing to dive under the covers with me now. We'll just have to wait and see how things turn out on that end.

Lord knows I have too much to deal with to be worried about every single detail of mi vida loca.

Two nights after my son is born, my wife and I have the house to ourselves. Vette asks if she can go hang out at a mall. I toss her the keys to my SUV and tell her to have a good time.

"I always do," she says, then actually thanks me for the keys, which is a shocker.

After Vette leaves, I call Anya into our library. It's the most peaceful room in the house. Hundreds of books line the shelves from floor to ceiling. There is no TV, or phone jack. Just quietness, escapism.

"Have a seat," I tell Anya.

Her eyes are red and eyelids swollen, but I pretend not to see.

"You look whipped," she tells me.

"Yeah, it's been a tough few days."

"I can imagine."

I flinch. I know Anya isn't being sarcastic, but sarcasm is what I hear. She could smile and say "Have a nice day" and to me it would sound like "Go fuck yourself and die."

"I think it's time for us to deal with a few things here," I tell her.

"Mmmm."

"And, uh, thanks for setting up the nursery. That's very sweet of you, Anya. I hadn't thought of that."

Anya grunts. I start whistling and shuffling papers. Doing this is as uncomfortable as going through my performance evaluation at work.

"Look, Anya, I think things may get better for us. We're going to give it our all, right? We've gotten through the pregnancy, the birth, so maybe we can also get through rearing two kids."

Anya's baggy eyes widen.

"I–I don't mean that you're gonna be like a stepmom, I mean—I don't even know what to call this. But I do want to be in the kid's life. Let's face it. Having sex and getting Dani pregnant is already a done deal."

Her eyes widen even more.

"I know the situation feels awkward to all involved," I explain calmly, "but I refuse to let my kid grow up not knowing who his daddy is. If that happens, it's not going to be because I want it to."

"I know you want to be in his life, I appreciate your honesty," Anya says. Her voice sounds gentle. I thankfully exhale. Anya's a rare woman.

"I realize it's been hard on you, babe," I remark. "You've gone through a lot, much more than any woman should ever have to—"

"Every day I blame myself," she says, her voice rising. "But you're at fault, too. If you would've stuck to just eating her pussy instead of—"

"Anya, please." I stand up and take one step toward her. "I'm sorry, so sorry, Anya, okay? I don't know what else to tell you except I messed up. Don't forget how long it had been since I'd been inside of you."

"You're right, Neil. Now I know it's unrealistic to think a man can stick to just kissing a woman, letting her give you a blow job every once in a while, and leave it at that. You blew it, Neil. And it's hard to get past that."

"Well, Anya, as hard as it is, for our sake you might have to. I'll admit I've made mistakes, but do I really have to hear about them every single day like this? I'm scared I might do something I regret."

"As if there could be anything else?" Anya laughs sarcastically. I guess she thinks that's a zinger that will put me in my place. I don't feel like fighting her, so I pick up the day's newspaper and read the headline out loud.

"'Father Brings Kids into the Basement, Shoots Them, and Commits Suicide.' Hmm, wonder what brought that on . . ."

"Neil, don't even try it. Things between us will never be that bad. I don't have a gun, and I hope you don't, either. Black folks don't do things like that, anyway."

"It's not a white thing, Anya. Pain doesn't have a color."

She doesn't say anything.

"The man was in deep pain," I explain.

"Look, if you are in pain, I don't see how. You got a fabulous, adoring sex partner and a brand-new kid from the deal, but what have I gotten?"

Now Anya is off the couch and in my face. I sit back down. She points a finger, something she knows I can't stand. If she weren't so petite, her weight would look sexy. But because she's barely five-foot-three, her weight gain makes her look pudgy.

I stare at her, having nothing to say. Now she's waving her hands in wide circles. Her head is moving back and forth. When a woman succumbs to irate mode, it's pretty much over.

I let my wife scream obscenities she swore I wouldn't hear again. I am tempted to get a broom, shove it in her hand, and push her toward the kitchen so she can use her energy to clean up instead of mouthing off, but my actions might make her angrier. So I pretend that I'm listening, making like I care about her ramblings.

She goes on and on until her voice becomes a moan, until the weight of her world causes her to collapse on the sofa, until her face is a swollen river, and my heart is a deep hole that overflows with our despair.

That night after Anya blows up at me, I sleep in the library on the sofa. This is nothing new. It's been more than two years since sofa and I have become well acquainted. Sofa is always there; it doesn't avoid me when it's mad. Sofa stays silent when I need to talk about things out loud.

Sure, I can run over to Dani's when Anya breaks into her hissy fits. But many nights I resist. Running is easy. Staying is hard. If I force myself to do things I don't want to do, then I'm developing character. And the older I become, the harder it gets to develop. That's why so many forty-, fifty-, and sixty-year-old men still act like twenty-year-olds. As long as they've been on this earth, they still lack the patience required to be a person of integrity.

Every day I've tried to be a perfect man. And after trying hard and failing, I now realize I'm not without error. Who is? But as bad as things seem between me and Anya, I know I do many things right. Going to work every day, paying bills on time, mowing the lawn, and keeping my fists from making contact with Anya counts for something. At least I pray it does.

I wake up to the feeling of water being sprinkled on my cheeks.

"Get up, sleepy head."

I shift on the sofa and turn toward Sharvette's annoying voice. For someone who hates me, she is always in my face.

"Vette, stop playing, okay?" I yawn. Using my hands, I rub lukewarm water off my cheek. "What time is it?"

"Six-forty-five. You're gonna be late."

"Oh, okay." I sit up. Maybe there's hope for Vette and me. Waking me up shows she can watch my back. I actually did oversleep, and I want to return to work because I already took two vacation days this week.

Now more than ever my job becomes important. I don't want anything to happen—not even being late—to threaten that.

I make it to work on time, relieved to return to an environment in which I have some measure of control. I am a business manager in the facilities department at one of the colleges in the Med Center. My job is to oversee construction, project management, and budget-related matters for capital projects.

All incoming calls are routed through our receptionist, Kyra. She checks in with me a few hours after I get to work.

"Hi, Neil. Welcome back. Please hold while I forward this call."

"Thanks, Kyra."

"Neil Meadows here," I answer. I don't hear anything at first. It sounds like someone is handing another person the phone.

"Hey." Her voice is gentle yet firm, strong yet weak.

"Hey, you." I take a moment to close and lock my office door.

"Sorry about the slight pause," Dani says. "I had someone else ask for you."

"Oh . . . I understand." I clear my throat. "How're you doing?"

"Fine. Could be better, though."

I hear cooing in the background. My heart is torn. I can sniff and imagine how my baby smells like fresh powder. I envision his tiny hands, remembering how humbling it felt when he seized my finger his second day on earth.

"You got anyone helping you? Your mama—"

"Yep, she's still here. I wish she'd fly back to Long Beach, though. She's about to drive me crazy. Mama's either talking too loud or asking me questions while I'm trying to sleep. And she holds the baby too much."

I grin and visualize the scene I haven't been able to witness. "Dani, it's her first grandson. Let her play grandmama, okay?"

"I know but . . . I wish *you* were here. With us. Right now." Her voice, thick with desire, makes me feel I *am* there.

I swallow deeply and rub my forehead, which is coated with sweat. You know some hair-raising thing is happening when a person's sweet voice alone arouses you. Although it feels good, like healing warmth passing through me, I hate that this woman can stir me this way. I wish I could control what should not control me.

"How 'bout this weekend?" I ask softly. "Can you wait till then?"

Dani remains quiet. But her unspoken thoughts engulf the silence. I think about how rapidly kids develop. Even six-year-old Reese is growing and gaining in knowledge. She's learning about Argentina, and how to mix yellow and green watercolors to create blue. Reese can even pluck out a few recognizable tunes on our piano, the same piano I used to practice "Chopsticks" on when I was a boy.

Seeing the kids grow up is important, especially since my dad passed when I was four. If it weren't for the photos my mom has squirreled away in a cabinet, I'd barely remember his face. It seems odd to ache for something you never had. But I missed having my father. His absence makes me more determined to do right by my offspring, especially since my mother's been acting flaky, first by treating my sister like she's a burden and then by asking her to leave. And once my mom heard what Dani and I did, she wearily threw up her hands, distancing herself from more stressful family drama.

The combination of no father and Mom's recent antics makes me resolved to stay on top of my newborn's progress. I love him already, so why wouldn't I spend time with him, rock him in my arms, and let him know I'm his daddy?

"Neil," Dani says, "if I have no other alternative than to wait, then that's what I'll do. But I also called to say thanks. You didn't have to show up at the hospital. I was shocked when you did. When you told a couple of coworkers you were there out of support, I almost cracked up laughing. I wonder if they believe you."

"I don't care what they believe."

"Oh, but you do in a way, Neil, you do, right? Right?" She pauses. "I guess you're still not ready to—"

"Dani, please." As keyed up as her sweet voice makes me feel, I'm ready to get off the phone.

She sucks in her breath. "I know, so sorry. Guess my postpartum worries are kicking in."

"Postpartum or not, you promised not to go there, that we'd make this work, be mature with no drama, remember?"

She sniffs. I hear more cooing, cooing that sounds like it's coming from an adorable kitten.

"Yeah, Neil. And I am mature. You'll see. I'm going to be different than these other silly hos out here. I can handle my business. I'm gonna handle it," she promises, sounding like she's trying to convince herself as much as she's attempting to convince me.

"So," I tell her, "I'm gonna have to run, but you don't need anything today, right?"

"No," she says in a quiet voice. "Don't need anything today."

At the end of that week I stop at Sam's Club before going home. After standing in a long line and finally being handed my purchase, I drive home and pull into our two-door attached garage. I walk into the house, quietly stepping on the carpet, and hiding the package behind my back. My wife's in the kitchen, dishrag in hand, wiping crumbs off the island counter. This room is her usual spot after five o'clock in the evening. We have an open kitchen, wooden shelving, double stainless-steel sink, and a rug placed near the refrigerator decorated with red-and-white lettering that reads *There's No Place Like Home.* Tonight the first level smells like baked chicken, collard greens, pinto beans, mac and cheese, and homemade cornbread.

When Anya sees me (or rather, the box), she throws down the dishrag. I wave the box at her as if to say, *Yes, it's yours.* She grins and covers her mouth with shaking fingers. Then she removes the ring from the box and lets me place it on her right hand. It's a ring she's seen and admired a while ago. Eighteen-karat gold with three sparkly diamonds, it reeks of elegance. This piece set me back three thousand buckaroos. MasterCard handled it for me, though. Thank God for MasterCard.

"Ewww, I love it!" she shrieks. "But why'd you get this, Neil?"

"Uh, love."

"Love?" She bursts out laughing, her perfect teeth showing. My heart wants to melt at seeing her smile. I know she deserves this and more.

"Dang, Neil. That sounds so corny, but oh well . . . It's mine, it's mine, and I'm not giving it back." Anya holds out her hand, waving it back and forth for more stunned looks. She laughs, then presses her soft lips against my mouth. Her lips haven't touched mine in months. I'm not sure if I should act surprised, or enjoy it.

I just turn and walk away.

Sunday morning, I am adjusting my necktie. I ask Anya for my black leather oxfords. I'm upset because I couldn't convince Anya to come to Solomon's Temple. Her church attendance is spotty and that bothers me.

We're in the master bath, which has a wide mirror and a strip fixture of lights. Anya stands in the doorway and sets my shoes on the floor.

"Anya, you sure you don't want to come?"

"Nope, uh-uh. You go on and go. You need Jesus way more than me."

I look in the mirror and start to say something so evil it would cause me to repent, but instead I slip on my shoes. The doughy leather feels like a blanket covering my feet. I brush past Anya and stand next to the bed. I stuff my wallet in my back pocket and grab my little black Bible with the frayed ends.

I turn to my wife. "What will you be doing while I'm at church serving the Lord?"

"I'll be right here waiting on you when you get back. If the spirit of the Lord touches you during the service, I sure hope I can recognize you when you walk through the door." She laughs, waves, and leaves the room.

Listening to her cutting remarks makes me feel like a fool, like I'm a grape she's stepping on.

During my drive to church, I wonder what price I can pay that will make her forgive all my mistakes. Because if we're going to have a reasonable chance to move forward and rebuild our marriage, Anya will have to stop always bringing up the past.

I enter church, feet treading softly, trying not to be noticed. I settle into my padded seat in a row at the back of the sanctuary. I am about thirty minutes late and the front sections fill up fast.

Pastor London P. Solomon is dressed in a majestic purple robe. He's standing in the pulpit, but not for long. He steps down onto the floor clutching the microphone, paces down the center aisle, and stares people in the eye.

"In the new millennium, there's far too much compromise. And these days in America, the new standard is 'Don't adhere to any standard.' Mmm-hmm. Remember the seventies and eighties? I know you do. We're kinda reverting back to that mentality. Do what you wanna do. It's your prerogative. If it feels good, do it. Well, I'm here to tell you I did it, it felt good, and now I wish I could get rid of it."

I shift in my seat and thump my Bible against my leg.

"Tell the truth, have you ever had the urge to do something you knew in your heart wasn't good for you, but you convinced yourself to do it, anyway? Maybe you thought it would be cool because your homeboy does it? You say if your boy Cedric can drink and drive without getting into an accident, then you know you can hold down a few forties and drive down to Galveston without getting pulled over. Is anybody in the house today? Don't act like you don't know what I'm talking 'bout."

I chuckle along with everyone else, but there is little to laugh about. I know where this is going and wonder why I even bother to show up for church. Sometimes I go to worship service because I *need* my soul to be cleansed. I want to wash away my flaws, to be assured that no matter how many problems I have, the Lord is going to magically work them out. And sometimes when Pastor Solomon preaches, we get dessert—a feel-good message that assures us that things between us and God are A-okay. But other times our spiritual daddy feeds us those nasty vegetables. They're beneficial for us, but they sure don't taste all that great.

"The devil is subtle. Like a dripping faucet, he slowly pushes off his destructive ideas onto society. His main tool of doing his dirt is the media: TV, novels, music, movies, newspapers, and magazines. Think I'm lying? He has people going from saying 'Homosexuality is a sin' to 'These people can do whatever they want to do as long as they don't mess with me.' And now we have all these new-fangled shows airing on prime-time TV. We got gay cruises, gay bookstores, gay weddings, gay bubble gum, and act like just because hordes of people are doing this, then it's normal and acceptable, but I'm here to tell you there's a better answer."

I want to jump up and run out the church. I'm not a homosexual or anything close to that, but when the preacher starts talking about sin, any sin, I feel like he's talking about me. I wonder if the dark things I'm doing will be brought to light. I dread Pastor Sol walking down the aisle, stopping at my pew, pointing and saying, "Come up here." By looking at me, no one in that church can even guess I've committed adultery and have fathered a baby with another woman. Sometimes I wonder if I should quit going to church altogether. If I simply stopped going, would anyone even notice or care?

"Don't get me wrong, church. The Lord does love us, He is merciful and long-suffering, but we can't throw away His standards just because a million marching people claim something is acceptable. We can't start listening to judges who enact laws that support immorality. Nooo, church, we cannot allow man to declare what is right, when man is not the true determiner of what's right or wrong."

I shut out my pastor's voice. I begin daydreaming, doodling on the church bulletin, and thinking about what I'm eating for dinner. The door of my heart sounds like it's closing, and I am too scared to listen for the final slam.

3

Neil

I'm standing in the dining room reading the newspaper when Anya says, "Neil, what the hell is this?"

"Huh? Oh, this is what I wanted to talk to you about the other night."

"I see." Anya stares at the typewritten sheet of paper. It reads, "Amendment to the Marital Arrangement of Neil Braxton Meadows and His Wife, Anya."

"It's blank, Neil."

"I know. I want to discuss some additional clauses with you before I actually put them in writing."

"Oh, really? I don't like how this sounds."

"Don't be scared." I pause. "Anya, you may add one or two of your own, if that would make you feel better."

"I feel like this just isn't working, anyway. We agreed to other things in the past and only a few of those worked."

Anya's referring to the fact that we have other contracted aspects to our marriage. Like the ones that say she'll cook for me five days a week, I'll take the family out to dinner twice a week, and I'll buy her a nice present once a month (something gift wrapped, and not just an item in a shopping bag). Sometimes we stick to that arrangement, other times we don't.

Sighing, I lay the newspaper on the dining-room table and take a seat. Anya's eyelids are puffy, like she's been up all night. I now realize jewelry can't extinguish a woman's worries. Why couldn't I learn that before going in debt by three grand?

"Neil, I'm sorry, I shouldn't have said that. But why're we doing all this? What are we trying to prove? That I'm the noble and long-suffering wife and you're the responsible father who made a mistake but wants to do right by his son? Who are we doing this for, Neil?"

"What are you trying to say?"

"I think because we're trying so hard to get it right on paper, we're neglecting who we really are, what we really feel on the inside."

"I'm not following you."

"Neil! If I write down 'I love Neil Meadows' a hundred times, but treat you like dirt every day, would my declaration mean much to you? What's the point of the words if they're not lining up with real-life actions?"

"Anya, I'm trying to do the best I can. I don't want to get a divorce, I don't."

"Who said anything about a divorce?"

"Okay, scratch that. Poor choice of words."

"Is that what you're thinking, Neil? That we should end this?" Her voice is shaky, like as bad as things are, she's never contemplated divorce and wouldn't know what to do if things went there. Sometimes I feel like she hates to be hurt but doesn't know how *not* to hurt. The fact that she sometimes dwells on the negative aspects of what happened makes me think she enjoys the torture of pain, something I don't understand.

"No, baby, if I wanted to end this, I wouldn't be here now, would I? I wouldn't bust my tail every day at work, trying to make enough money so you can continue to stay at home and raise our daughter. A lot of wives would kill for that. They say they're happy they're working and bringing home a second paycheck, but women are dead-dog tired. I see them on my job. They have the long, fancy titles, are driving the luxury cars, but you're going to see frowns on their faces seven out of eight hours. They're popping Prozac trying to cope with the stress of being in the corporate world, raising their kids, and wanting to please their man. So I hope you appreciate all that I do—"

Anya stands up. Her eyes are blazing so bright I want to cover *my* eyes.

"No, you did not say that, Neil. Sometimes I just can't believe you. I guess you want a freaking award or something?" She takes a full walk around our dining-room table and stops at my face.

"You know what? The award I really want to give you hasn't been invented yet. Process *that*."

When a man loves a woman, the world seems brand new. Sounds cliché but it's true. Ten years ago when I first started dating Anya, I didn't want to talk to anyone else (male or female) except her.

"What are you doing?" I'd ask her on the phone.

"Going away for the weekend."

"To?"

"Fort Worth."

"With?"

"Nobody," she'd murmur.

"Stop joking, Anya."

"I'm not joking. I'm driving up there just to hang out with a cousin. No big deal."

Her independence captivated me. I was impressed she wasn't sitting around waiting for the phone to ring. And when she'd come back from her weekends, she never called me the minute she got in the house. She waited for me to call first. I liked that.

"So, Anya, if a guy wants a date with you, does he have to call like a month in advance?"

She laughed. "If a certain guy plays his cards right, he might not have to wait a month to see a certain woman."

"Is that certain woman available this weekend?"

"Depends on what that certain man wants to do."

"Well, Keith Sweat, Gerald Levert, and Johnny Gill will be in concert—"

"Ahhhh, ahhhh, ahhh!" When she started screaming on the phone and not caring that she might sound stupid, I knew I made her happy. And making her happy made me happy, so we hooked up.

Back then Anya let me be the chaser. We'd go to a restaurant of her choice, but she'd trust me enough to order for her. She relinquished the trust to see how much I knew her. To see if I was listening when she told me, "I love salmon, omelets filled with mushrooms, tomatoes, and sausage, and clam chowder." I'd smile, jot down mental notes, and be pumped when I'd pass her little tests. Every woman tests her potential man at some point, to see where his head is, and to identify his priorities.

Now, back in the day, Anya's body was stacked. Not so huge that she needed me to help her step out the car every time, but not so skinny that you'd wonder if she were strung out on crack. No, back then Anya was just right. She had a little wiggle in her jiggle, her waist was smaller, but she was too modest to go around exposing her belly and wearing form-fitting clothes. And her hair was longer, too, before she let Phyllis the hairdresser convince her to get a shorter, more sophisticated cut.

"Neil, do you like how this looks? Be honest." She smiled and cocked her head. At first I zeroed in on her yummy-tasting lips, but then gazed at her pixie cut.

"Sure, sure, you look good."

She *did* look good, even if I preferred longer hair.

"You bet not be lying, Neil."

"Could you tell if I were?"

"If your eye starts twitching, yeah, I could tell."

After that, whenever she'd ask me one of those "damned if you do, damned if you don't" questions, I'd close my eyes and answer.

"Neil!" she'd scream and playfully hit me on the shoulder, but then she'd laugh and not make an issue out of superficial things. I loved that. Loved her. And even though things have gotten way bizarre, I still love her.

Why?

Anya Meadows has some old-fashioned things about her. When we sit down for dinner, I know nothing I'm about to eat is from a box or a can. She loves the feeling of raw vegetables, and she enjoys flavoring up a dish with all kinds of extras—like vanilla powder for my hot chocolate, or lemon peel for my fish, or ground sassafras that she'll throw in a large pot of stew.

When we first started dating, she'd invite me to her small apartment. I'd sit at her tiny wooden table reading the newspaper, until she appeared beside me holding a spoon.

"Here, Neil. Eat this."

"What is it?"

"Just eat it."

"How do I know if you're trying to poison me?"

"You won't know unless you eat it."

I'd hesitate but my willingness to trust her would make me open my mouth. One time Anya shoved a large plastic spoon dripping with a thick brown sauce, some meat and mushrooms (that girl loves mushrooms), and I started chewing.

"How's that taste?"

I closed my eyes, patted my belly. "Tastes great, Anya."

"Neil."

I opened my eyes, burped. "It's the bomb. You did good, baby."

She smiled and blushed, which was pretty easy to make her do back then. All I had to do was call Anya *baby* and I'd get a nice smile.

These days I wonder if roping in the carefree loveliness of the past will be enough to get Anya and me over this hump. In my mind, little Neil and Dani are just humps. They are issues that are potentially life-changing yet don't have to be. Not if Anya and I can handle this right. And if I have to pay her a compliment to lift her spirits, or call her *baby* five times a day, it would maybe bring back a little bit of the past, and I hope it will be effective enough to ease us into a smoother future.

4

Anya

Every day we try to stick to a routine. I wake up at six, put on the coffee, and throw together some breakfast. Neil is out the door by six-thirty. Sharvette gets up, eats, showers, and gets dressed to attend a few courses she's taking at the University of Houston's main campus. Sometimes I wake Reesy and, because she doesn't do Metro, I'll drive Vette to school. Other times she may have someone swing by and pick her up.

But by eight, I want everyone gone so I can begin my day with Reesy.

Our daughter looks like Neil with a dress. Her eyes are wide and large like she wants to take in everything around her. Her face is beautiful and round, and her hair is mounted with braids. Let's face it: Braids for little black girls are just easier to deal with. Reesy squirms and complains that braiding "hurts like hell," but I overlook her silly comments.

We start our day belting out a little prayer.

"Dear Lord, bless this day, protect us from harm, let us be grateful and not complain, lead and guide our steps. Amen." We say this Monday through Friday, no matter how we feel, no matter what has gone wrong the day before.

"Each day is a brand-newww day," Reesy will say. She says it because it's what I've instructed her to say over and again no matter what. Not that it's a total lie, but neither is it something that's necessarily true merely because I proclaim it all the time.

This morning I walk in Reesy's room and tickle her bare feet with my fingers. She sits up, rubbing her crusty eyes with brown fists.

"Hi, Mommy."

"Hey, baby."

"I'm not a baby." I look at her, wondering if she realizes what she said. I wonder if she knows about her little brother. Nah, I can't see Neil telling her something she couldn't begin to understand.

"Right, you are not a baby. You're six—"

"Going on twenty," she giggles. Reesy has no idea what that means. She just repeats what Vette says, what anyone says.

"After you get dressed and eat breakfast, you can start working on your letters, okay, sweetie?"

"Mommm. I already know letters. Can we do something else? Something fun?"

I don't say anything.

Later we're in the kitchen. A corner of this room is designated for Reesy's lessons. Although I am tempted to run off into the laundry room, the den, or back to bed, I've promised myself that between eight and one, most everything we do will center on this cubbyhole.

She has a tiny red desk, a computer, a box filled with toys and books, art supplies, and other learning tools.

"Mommy, why can Tamika go to the real school and I hafta go to the fake school?"

Tamika is our eight-year-old neighbor who has a big, fat mouth.

"Mika doesn't know what she's talking about, sweetie."

"Will you tell me why?"

"You're special, Reesy."

"I don't want to be special."

I feel guilty. Again. I can't make my daughter understand that I am trying to impart to her what Argyle Elementary might not. And it's days like this that I wonder if I should re-enter the workforce and return to my job as a tourism specialist. But when I think about how people go postal in the workplace and can kill folks over nothing, or when I consider how a child can be sent home for bringing a butter knife to school because it's against HISD policy, that's why I choose to be Reesy's mother *and* her teacher. I can nurture my own daughter and instill in her the values that are missing from public school. Moreover, I believe Reesy and I are better off at home, the supposed refuge.

So I get this eerie feeling when the phone rings mid-morning and this woman's voice is at the other end.

"Anya, in spite of everything that's happened, I really am a nice person."

My ears prickle. "Who the hell is this?"

I hear this breathy sigh like the caller is frustrated and has no more words. Then there is a click and a dial tone.

Caller ID indicates the number is unavailable. "If she's unavailable, why can't I be, too?" I say out loud.

Even though I haven't heard her voice in a while, I feel it was *her*. I wouldn't be surprised if it was. When two women have stakes in one man, a confrontation is always inevitable.

I pick up the phone and dial Neil's job. Kyra patches me through to him. He isn't at his desk. I leave a message after the beep.

"Neil, handle your business. What's-her-face called here. I don't know what she wants, but she should be dealing with you only 'cause I doubt seriously that she'd want to deal with me."

It isn't the first time she's called. When she was pregnant, she'd call. I'd be on the other line and this woman would dial our house and ask to speak to Mr. Meadows. I was neither impressed nor fooled. She could've saved that. Because once she let Neil put his dick inside her, they'd long crossed the formality line. I wondered what she called him when he was on top of her. I doubt it was Mr. Meadows.

So I'd be talking on the other line, and this woman would ask for my husband. I'd say "Hold on." I'd terminate my call, click back to her, and hand Neil the phone. I'd stand right there looking at him and listening to their conversation. What? Fucking my husband isn't enough? She has to make house calls, too?

If I'd known what was going to happen, maybe my insight would've stopped me from encouraging Neil to get his rocks off with someone other than himself. Maybe I should have steered him to Main Street, or Calhoun Boulevard in the Third Ward, to find some tantalizing prostitute he could lay up with and then go home. Get some loving and don't be worried about being in the whore's face anymore.

But *nooo*. Sensible, naive Neil has to find some clingy young thing who works in his office. He didn't volunteer this info up front. He dodged my questions about her, reminding me that although this wasn't in the arrangement, I'd verbally promised not to press him for details about his lover.

Even though I pushed him into this, I resented that he had a secretive something he wasn't eager to share. And I'm human. Who is she? I already figured she wasn't overweight. No the hell way. That would defeat the purpose. At the time, I believed he'd probably found some weave-wearing, 115-pound, leggy thing who had a big, fat booty and some jiggling tits. Sooo typical. Not many respectable men go out of their way to search for a dog, so fault me for that one. I set this up all wrong. I put Neil on a chain but the chain was a little bit too long. Now I'm paying big-time.

Open-mindedness costs. There's a huge price to pay when you love a man, tell him you'll do anything for him, then watch your whole world crumble because you're forced to prove the actions behind your words.

5

Neil

By the time my son marks his third week of life, I decide things between me and Anya have settled down enough for me to make a little trip over to Dani's. This is the first time I get to see him since he's been born. I wanted to visit sooner, but Reese got sick with the flu and I didn't want to spread her germs.

After I arrive at Dani's place, I notice she's lost a few pounds already. She looks relaxed; her long brown wavy hair is bound in a thick pony-tail. She's sporting a pair of distressed stretch jeans and a white cotton blouse that shows off her belly button.

"Well, look who decides to show up." Her voice is gentle, so I don't take offense.

"You know the deal, Dani. I don't want the little man getting sick. He knows his father's gonna be more than a ten-minute daddy. We've formed a strong bond already." I grab the baby's finger. He is asleep, eyes shut tight, and managing to look peaceful in a world filled with conflict. I want to climb in his crib, lie down, and cover both of us with a warm blanket. I bend over and stroke his soft forehead with my lips.

He smells good, clean and powdery. A big knot expands in my throat, but I know better than to surrender to my emotions.

"Can you believe we did that?" Dani says. Her eyes are large and unblinking. She keeps shaking her head.

"I want him to have the best of everything," she continues. "But he shouldn't be totally spoiled. That's why he hasn't slept with me in my bed. I don't even want to start all that."

"What do you do when he cries?"

"I'll wait awhile to see if he keeps it up. If he does, I go check on him, let him see my face. But I resist picking Braxton up."

I flinch. A few days after the baby was born, Dani and I agreed to change his name to Braxton Frazier (Frazier is her last name).

I gesture at Dani that we leave the baby's room.

When we settle in her kitchen, I notice a dozen wicker baskets. There is colored tissue paper, oils, scented powders, tiny bottles of jam, plus a whole bunch of other items covering the entire table. Dani creates gift baskets as a side business. She likes making beautiful things and is good with her hands. Her initiative is one of the things I admire about her.

When we first agreed to hook up, and once we got past the initial sexual attraction, I tried to see her for what she is: a beautiful, vivacious woman who gets testy at times, but is loyal. If she takes any missteps, they're not taken willfully. She's blessed with a decent heart and I didn't want that to change.

"I see you've gotten some orders here," I say, lifting a gourmet coffee packet and inhaling the strong, intoxicating aroma of coffee beans.

"Yep, the closer we get to the holidays, the more the orders pile up—usually more than six hundred. I don't mind at all even though I am aching to get back to work."

"When are you coming back?"

"I'm supposed to be there in four weeks, at the end of October, but I might come back a week early. I'm kinda looking forward to it, but some parts of me wish I could put in for a transfer."

I don't respond. At times I wish she'd put in for a transfer, too. I don't know how long we can continue this charade. The way Dani used to come to work every day with a protruding belly but never mentioning the identity of her child's father. Me trying to avoid her around the office, something I'm not sure my colleagues bought—not when they remembered how friendly Dani and I had been in the past. We'd do lunch, sometimes dinner, and always on the pretense of work. But no one ever saw me sliding my arm around her or ogling her in an inappropriate manner. During staff meetings, we sat on opposite ends of the conference table, and we didn't arrive at after-work functions together.

Even though it pained me to play these roles in front of others, I always tried to make things up to her. Sometimes I'd go to her place in the evenings and rub her feet for a half hour. Or I'd offer to go grocery shopping or pick her up a hot meal, making sure she had everything she needed—anything to help ease the awkward situation. She never asked me to do this, I just did it.

And when we got to the core of our relationship, that's when we were able to relax and be the way we felt we wanted to be. Our little trysts would take place during the lunch break. She lives a few miles from work. Every weekday, she'd show up at the office wearing her business apparel and my favorite string bikini underneath. A few minutes after noon, we'd meet at her apartment, go to her bedroom, and kiss and fondle each other. She'd let me partially undress her, removing her jacket, blouse, and skirt. Then she'd spread out on the bed with her legs open. She'd smile and untie the string so I could see part of her vagina. I'd stare at her for a moment and it would take no time for me to get heated up. When I couldn't stand it any longer, I'd yank off her bikini top and bottom, and Dani would pull me against her breasts and let me bang and pound and thrash around wildly inside of her until I felt like I was losing my mind.

It was easy to hold Dani—a joy to squeeze her tight in my arms. Her flesh felt right to my skin, like we were body parts that fit precisely without awkwardness. She'd tell me I was hung like King Kong, which would make me blush every time. Sometimes I'd make love to her and imagine she was Anya. Other times I was happy Dani was just Dani.

One time, after we'd both climaxed and were too worn out to jump out of her bed just yet, Dani nudged me.

"Are we falling in love?"

She continued talking as if I weren't there.

"This man and woman start out making love once every two weeks, but now they're seeing each other three times a week with plans to meet on the weekend. This is so exciting for me. I'm having the greatest sex of my life, but I think I'm falling for you, Neil. I just wondered if you're having those same feelings, or am I all alone on this?"

She looked at me, but when I didn't respond, she rushed to take a shower.

I was glad she didn't press me for an answer.

Tonight Anya calls me out of my library and pours a pitcher of icy-cold beer.

I have the sports section clutched in one hand. I study her and the pitcher she places on an end table in our living room. One lamp is on. It's hard to see but I notice a wry smile on Anya's lips.

"What you want?" I ask.

She points to the sofa.

I sit.

Anya makes a triumphant noise and kicks off her pink slippers decorated with gingerbread men. She flops on the couch with a grin so wide, it seems like her entire face is lit up. Anya reaches and grabs the pitcher of beer and sets it on the floor. The liquid sloshes so wildly that some of it leaps over the sides and splatters the rug.

"Watch that," I tell her, but I'm not scolding.

"Watch *this*," Anya says.

Anya guides her right foot. Her leg wobbles. She plunges her big toe in the pitcher. "Whew." She shivers. "Cold."

"Are you okay?" I ask.

"Yeah. Why? Doesn't seem like me, huh?"

Anya makes a circle in the beer with her toe, then slithers to the carpet, lies on her back, and looks up at me.

"C'mere, Neil."

I glance at my watch.

"Neil, c'mon now. You're spoiling everything."

I bare my teeth but lay the sports section on the couch. The only sound I hear is the steady hum of the air conditioner. I squat next to Anya. My wife, someone who I cannot figure out half the time, is still smiling mischievously. Her quirky ways enamored me when we first met, but sometimes what starts out as an attraction, a "that's so cute" kind of thing, can become the source of annoyance years later.

Anya looks up and raises her foot toward my face. She giggles, extends her leg closer to my cheek. Her wet toe pokes me. I don't move. She slides her toe until it bears down on my mouth. My closed mouth fights to keep her toe from prying itself inside.

"C'mon, Neil," she pleads.

I can tell what she's doing. Anya knows I love to suck different body parts, but she's never stuck her toe in any of my favorite drinks before. Why is she acting like this? Maybe it's because yesterday, for the first time in a long time, I came home late. Past ten o'clock on a weeknight. When I walked in the door and went straight to the library, I didn't bother to call her from my cell phone to say I'd gotten in like I normally do, so she could then go to sleep.

Anya stares at me with a hardened face. "So you won't even suck my toe?"

I look away until my eyes find the sports section.

"Neil, I'd do it for you."

"No, you won't, or at least you haven't before," I remind her. "Why the sudden change?"

"I was reading somewhere about how to combat my little problem"—she nods—"and it said a little sexual aggression could do the—"

"I doubt that," I say. "Because when I've initiated—"

"Sexual aggression on my part, Neil. I was hoping you'd like it, join in . . ."

I shake my head at her like I don't buy what she's saying.

"I think the point is that I'm making an effort. But you—you won't even try."

Wanting to defuse the atmosphere, I'm tempted to grab the pitcher and start slurping the liquid until it's gone, but I sense Anya won't laugh.

Anya leans against the couch and folds her arms tightly across her chest.

"Neil, you never did tell me where you were last night."

I stare into space, wondering if her little seduction attempt is due to my coming home late.

"Oh, so you're gonna keep that info to yourself, huh? Cool." She may say the word *cool*, but I know better. Women say that when they figure the ball is in their court and now it's their turn to devise some strategy that will make a man regret his actions.

"Anya, I don't want to lie to you . . ."

"Then don't."

"But I don't want to tell the truth, either."

"Oh, Neil," she says. "See, all this isn't even necessary. I just wish you wouldn't act so different. I *hate* that you're changing."

"I'm *not* different."

"Get real. A woman knows her man. I can perceive the subtle changes in you. Even the air feels different in this house, as if spirits are lurking about, and we're sharing our living space with unseen forces. Sounds silly but that's what I sense." Anya shivers and rubs her arms with her fingers. She has a sad look on her face, like she's distressed beyond comfort. I feel like an ass. I wish I could blame everything on someone else, but when I think of who that person could be, everything points to me.

"Anya, look, I don't want to get into a detailed discussion. I just think that if your happiness depends on knowing where I am twenty-four seven, you'd be miserable. And as far as sucking your toes, you have some be-*yoo*-tiful toes." I glance at her. "I'm just not in a sucking mood right now."

"You're not in the mood? Ha!"

I know better than to argue. If she accused me of being the mythical Bigfoot, I'd say, "Yep, you caught me." Anything to keep the arguments from continuing.

I scoot closer to Anya, wrap my arm around her shoulder, and squeeze. Usually she leans against me, or puts her head against the crook of my neck, but now she sits stiffly, like a frozen painting, with a frozen, sad smile on her face, like she's frozen in time.

6

Anya

For the third weekend in a row, Sharvette forces me out the house. We wind up at Memorial Mall and visit the Fashion Fair counter in Foley's department store. Vette starts sifting through packets of eye shadow, blushes, lipstick samplers, and begins experimenting on me.

"Could you not do that?" I ask.

"Nooo, I have to do this." She grabs a foundation stick and starts applying it to my cheeks, forehead, and chin.

"Ugh, you're wasting your time."

"Why is that?"

"I don't like getting made up. I prefer going natural."

"If going natural doesn't work," Vette explains, "you need to try something else."

"Why you trying to get me to enhance my looks? I thought you wanted me and Neil to break up."

"Who says I'm doing this for Neil?"

"Oh, I see." I smile and let her do her thing.

Several minutes later, she grins and hands me a mirror. I take a quick peek. Vette hooked me up. My lashes are longer, my eyes seem bigger. I feel like I am glowing, like there's something to be singing about.

"You look nice, Anya."

"Ya think?"

"Do I think? I'm telling you I didn't even have to do this makeover stuff, because you always look nice."

"Well." I set down the mirror, feeling annoyed. "Why can't I see what you see?"

"I think you're too distracted to appreciate who you are, Anya."

"And what's that supposed to mean?"

"You can't let what's happening to you totally define who and what you are. You're more than what you look like, or more than how you feel."

"Oh, really? And how do you know all this, young lady?"

"Well, it's something I read in a book, so . . ."

"Vette, I swear to God."

She giggles and we head out of Foley's and back into the noisy mall filled with babies screeching and waving their arms. A couple with matching T-shirts and jeans pass by. I avert my eyes whenever I see a man and woman walking close together and pushing a newborn in a baby buggy. It hurts too much to look.

"Speaking of God," Vette finally responds.

"Vette, let's not go there. Not today."

"You kill me, Anya. I mean, you don't feel like doing this, don't wanna talk about that. Is there anything you want to do?"

I am walking but I can no longer see where I'm going. Blurry vision. Watery path. I wish I had a tissue in my purse. But I don't. So the big, fat tears have nowhere else to flow except down my cheeks till they reach my chin.

"Hello? I'm talking to you."

I turn away from her. We've stopped outside a Deck the Walls store. A huge Thomas Kinkade print is displayed in the window. I am mesmerized by his artistry: all the rich colors, the emphasis on light, brightness, and images of peacefulness. Looking at his illustrations always gives me the feeling of being transported. But even though looking at the print comforts me, something just doesn't feel right. I raise my hand to my face and let my skin absorb the wetness.

"You all right?"

"No," I tell Vette. "But I will be."

I start walking. I hear her groan at my back. Soon she's at my side.

"Anya, I heard you and Neil going at it last night. When he came up to your room . . ."

"Yeah, well, sorry about that. He called me on my cell from down in the library. I refused to come see him, so he walked up those stairs to see me."

"What happened?"

"He swears that he's ending his relationship with the woman, that if he goes over to her apartment, it's only so he can see his son. And every time he gets excited about visiting the baby, I feel a pang from—"

"You wish that Dani's baby was yours?" Vette says quietly.

"I can't help but think that could be *us* welcoming our newborn, Vette. If I hadn't lost our child . . . our kids." My voice tapers off and I'm instantly back in the past, reliving the butcher-sharp violence that ripped my womb, the pain that stole away our babies, that robbed our future.

"I've never been pregnant, so . . ." Vette says with a sweet smile.

"You do get attached, is all I can say. Even if the embryo is a few weeks old, or when you're in the first trimester, you still talk to your womb, notice the fetal movement, think that you're carrying a human, which brings me to this," I say with my voice more firm. "I'm assuming that Neil is so grateful to have another chance at fatherhood that he isn't concerned about the Dani part. He just cares that Brax is here, that her pregnancy was full-term. Maybe Neil is scared something bad will happen again if he isn't there for the baby."

"Anya, I–I can kind of understand my brother wanting to care for his son."

"But it still feels weird, Vette. I mean, our family has been totally redefined."

Vette leers at me like even so, I ought to let it go, that a father's love is more powerful than what I can comprehend.

I ache inside, feeling happy for Neil yet selfish.

"Mentally, you convince yourself you can do this, but psychologically . . ." My voice tapers off.

"At least you're being true to your feelings, Anya. Shoot, I'm just the auntie—I'm not in your shoes."

I nod at Vette, appreciating her understanding more than she knows.

"And the Reesy factor is another thing," I pipe up. "She notices the bags of little toys that Neil leaves in his car. She's not dumb. She knows she's too big for those rattles and those soft blocks with A, B, C on them. So she starts asking questions, and right now we haven't really told her anything. I don't want her to be confused."

"So what are you going to do?" Vette says.

"I don't plan on doing anything. Let Neil handle it. I don't feel it's right to lie to our daughter, or drag her into this situation."

"Hmmm, well, I'll tell her, then."

I actually crack a smile.

"What will you tell her, Vette?"

"I'll tell her that her daddy's been a bad, bad man."

"Don't say that."

"It's true," she insists.

"Listen up. One thing that would be wrong is to hurt two little kids in the process. So whether I agree or understand it, I know Neil is going to go over there and bond with his baby. As much as I dislike it, how can I interfere with that relationship?"

"Well, all righty, then." Vette sounds done with the subject. But I hope she never gets tired of talking me through things even if it hurts to discuss them.

I pause.

"Did I ever tell you the story about Reesy? Have you noticed that I call her Reesy and Neil calls her Reese?"

"Yeah, I have noticed but didn't think much about it."

"Neil named her Reese—he wanted a boy."

Vette stares at me and we exchange a knowing look for a long time.

We're in the car on our way to pick up Reesy. The day before, she asked to spend the night at my mother's. My heart was heavy with guilt. In times past, I let her go over to my mother's frequently, but shortly after what happened with Neil, when she'd beg to go see Grammy, the answer would be a red-faced no. Although both my mother and mother-in-law know about Neil's child and don't agree with what he's done, they try not to constantly nag about it, figuring it's mainly my job to stay on his case since I'm married to him and they aren't, but still I'm embarrassed to be around them.

Out of the blue, while we're in the car Sharvette scowls and asks, "Why'd you marry my brother? He's sooo freaky looking."

I giggle and respond, "I get what you're saying. He's freaky looking to *you* because he's your brother—he's supposed to be freaky looking."

Vette snickers, then I explain how, when we were engaged, Neil and I attended marriage counseling sessions along with three other couples. In the beginning, all the men and women openly proclaimed how jazzed they were about getting married, and how they were all in love.

"One couple had been dating since middle school. She was two months pregnant and knew she'd be with Tony for the rest of her life, but she still wanted counseling so she could 'make my mama happy.'

"Another couple were staunch Christians, virgins, and there's no way they'd make that move without clearing marital counseling. The third couple were the children of two prominent Houston families. Harvard Law School, prosecuting attorneys, folks rolling in dough, and everyone expected these two families to merge.

"Then there was Neil and me. Neither of us wanted to be there, but as you know, Neil is a by-the-book type. He likes acing tests, is a finishing-an-entire-crossword-puzzle kind of guy, so we went.

"Do you know that by the time the counseling sessions ended six weeks later, Neil and I were the only couple still engaged? The first five weeks were a breeze. We took little quizzes, did role reversals, fun stuff. But the last week, the marriage counselor told all the couples to 'look closely at the person you're about to marry. If he got into a car wreck and had twenty pieces of glass lodged in his cheeks, forehead, and lips, would you still want to be married to him? If your husband lost his job and could never regain employment, had to foreclose on your lovely home, and the car got repossessed, could you still love this broken man enough to stay with him? And guys, if your loving wife all of a sudden becomes depressed, stops eating, stops taking showers, refuses to comb her hair, and starts wandering the streets at two A.M. talking to herself, would you love her enough to stick with her through this crisis, or would you pack your bags and leave because you're unwilling to be with someone who's no longer the same person you married?'"

"Anya, those are some tough questions. I wouldn't even know how to respond."

"Vette, this counselor scared every one of us. I couldn't even look Neil in his eyes. But I didn't want to back out of a relationship with him based on fear. I was willing to give our relationship a try, go through the fire with him no matter how hot the fire was. He told me he wanted it, too. And because we both wanted the same thing, at the same time, on the same day, we felt ready to get married. And I've never forgotten that day, and that's why I'm married to Neil even now.

"I keep thinking this is why I suggested the arrangement to Neil. Maybe the arrangement would give us a guideline, or serve as a reminder of what we want and how we aim to get what we want. If we stick to the arrangement no matter what, we'd prove our commitment to each other."

"That sounds all fine and dandy," Vette says, "but is marriage really worth it?"

"Marriage has its problems, but as long as it's under the proper conditions, I'd much rather be married than single."

"Why?" Vette says.

"Why what?"

"Answer the question, Anya."

I hook a left onto the freeway.

"Sure," I say. "When you're single you don't have to answer to anybody. You don't have to merge finances, but . . ."

"But what?"

I can't think of anything else to say except, "When you get to my age you'll understand."

"I understand without having to be your age, Anya."

"Oh, Vette, you've been married before?"

"Nooo, I know what I know. I know what I want and what I don't want."

Sharvette has a fiery look in her eyes, almost like a bull—strong, determined, not feeling sorry for anything foolish enough to get in her way.

"When it comes to relationships," she continues, "I refuse to be taken for granted. I can't stand it when someone loves me, loves me, loves me in front of my face, but hates me, hates me, hates me behind my back."

"Sounds like a story behind those words."

"There's always a story, Anya."

"I'm listening," I tell her.

"See," she continues, "a lot of guys think they're slick. They know they have the upper hand in relationships. They know that if things go down badly, they can look two feet over, and there's another prospect. That's what trips me out."

"True, there are more available women than men, but I don't think it's that easy for guys, either, Vette. We're conditioned that men can get anyone they want, and maybe that's why they act so indifferent in relationships, but I'm starting to believe otherwise."

"Didn't my brother go out and find this other lady right away?"

"No." I wince. "It's not just about the numbers game. It's about the fact that when things don't work out, men are disappointed and hurt just like women. They get tired of going through the relationship wringer just like we do. And depression? You haven't seen depression until you see some tall, rugged, masculine man lying in bed in the dark for days, not eating, he won't talk, won't come out the house. *That's* depression."

"What? Where? When has a man ever been depressed?" She looks at me like I don't know what I'm talking about.

"It happens, Vette. You got to recognize the signs."

"Ain't no signs."

"Okay, check this out. What about when a man realizes his girl doesn't want him anymore? She's found someone else and has kicked him to the curb. What's the first thing he does?"

"Get a replacement."

"Vette, some get a gun. Load it with bullets. They find the woman, confront her, and start shooting. They shoot to remove their pain, the hurt of rejection. And by the time it's over, she's on her way to the morgue, and he may blast a bullet in his own head. And two lives are lost over something that's hardly ever worth it. *That's* depression. That's scary."

Vette gives me a concerned look.

"So, Anya. You'd never go that route with Neil? I mean, he's my brother and all but . . ."

"You don't even have to ask. I have a mouth that I don't mind using. And that's about the most violent I can see myself getting. No man is worth going to prison over. Not a one."

"Not Brian McKnight?" She grins.

"Not even super-fine Brian McKnight."

Vette and I pick up Reesy from my mom's, jump back in the car, and head home.

"Did anybody call me?" my daughter yells to anyone who'll listen.

"I don't know, silly," Vette tells her. "We were at the mall, not at home, so how would we know?"

"I'm talkin' 'bout on the cell phone."

Vette just stares at me. I shake my head and wonder if it was my genes or Neil's that make my daughter act this way.

When we arrive at the house, I park in the driveway and notice my neighbors little Tamika Dobson and her mother, Riley. I wave hello to Riley as Vette and Reesy head into the house.

"Hey, hon." Riley waves. "How ya doing? How's the hubby?"

Riley always has a genuine smile and is one of the more friendly neighbors on Chatham Island Lane, a street on the southwest side of town. As usual, Riley looks hot. She's the kind of woman men stop and stare at for as long as possible. Riley has googobs of cleavage and doesn't mind showing it. Her wrists dangle with silver bracelets, and she loves to douse her entire body with tantalizing fragrances. Vette calls Riley Lil' Kim behind her back.

"How's Jamal?" I ask. I hope she doesn't notice I ignored her question about Neil.

"Oh, hon, he's tripping as usual."

"What he do?"

"Umm, he snuck in another pair of pants, some of his nasty underwear, house slippers, and a DVD player, like I wouldn't notice all his things lying around the house. And Jamal thinks I'm blind, but I know he's taken over an entire dresser drawer." She waves her arms back and forth. A half-dozen bracelets ring together like wind chimes.

"Why don't you just tell him to stop bringing his stuff over?"

"I have, but he don't listen to me. He's coming in here all of a sudden trying to play Daddy to Mika. I'm like, 'Cool, you wanna be down now, but you weren't hanging around when I was living in that funky roach apartment on the southeast side.' He just wants to be here 'cause it's finally sunk in I can make it on my own, no ring on my finger, and without his last name attached. Now he attempts to block other men from being in my life. I tell him, 'Look, Jamal Gibson, your name ain't on the mortgage, so I can let any man over here I want.'"

"Go, girl." I snap my fingers. "And what he say to that?"

"He tells me unless it's my daddy, he'd bet not catch a man over here, acting like he don't want our daughter to be around any and everybody."

"Well, that's *kind* of admirable," I tell her.

"It's not admirable, it's sickening. That belief has never stopped *Jamal* from creeping around and being with a dozen other hoebags with all they kids by other men. It makes no sense to me, Anya. I'm about to kick his ass out." She sounds serious, like she's been contemplating this decision for a while.

"Jamal has his own key?"

Her eyes enlarge. "But I didn't give it to him. He stole the dupe. And I thought I hid it good. Makes me so mad. He talkin' 'bout he ain't got no place to stay 'cause his baby brother getting married. That's a damned lie. It's just so wrong."

"Where is he right now?"

"He probably be back soon with his horny ass, wanting to do a hit-and-run. I ain't got time for these quickies he likes to pull. I'm telling you, Ms. Anya . . ."

I sigh and rub Riley's shoulder. I guess after so many group therapy sessions, she's felt liberated when it comes to spreading her business. Even though she's very attractive and seems pulled together regarding other areas of her life, I wonder how she can be so stupid about men. But like my mother says, stupidity is one of the few things that do not discriminate.

I pat Riley's shoulder again. "I feel you, girlfriend, believe me."

"See, that's why I admire you and Neil. Y'all don't go through all the BS. Your stuff is righteous, blessed, honorable."

"Mmm-hmm," I say, and avert my eyes.

"I just wish Jamal had come correct and married me when I asked him, but nooo. He told me he loved me but wasn't feeling the marriage thang. He wants the benefits of the legality without going through the legality. That's why I had to do what I did. Fill out the papers, prequalify, and buy this house by myself and place our daughter in a better environment. I can't wait on Jamal. I just hate that I told him our address. I *hate* that I told him."

She bites her bottom lip and I clasp my arms around her shoulders and squeeze. Hearing her woes makes me feel a little better. I can't imagine being on my own raising a child, handling all the bills, assembling furniture, and playing Mommy and Daddy and everything else in between. So as odd as it sounds, I'm genuinely grateful for Neil. Glad he hasn't abandoned us for his other family. Glad that even if he has to go over there, at least he comes back home when he's done.

"Neil, could you come here a minute?"

He follows my voice. I am in the backyard. We have an enclosed patio that has a screen door that leads to a cobblestone path. If you follow the path all the way past the tall trees, you'll end up at a wooden swing that Neil constructed with his own hands.

I'm standing next to the steel-framed picnic table.

"Anya, what're you doing back here?"

"Waiting for you."

I hope my words make him feel warm and special.

"What's all this?" He points to a melamine platter that holds a pitcher of sweetened tea and tall glasses filled with ice cubes. There are also finger sandwiches, pickle spears, and small bags of Lay's. Neil is major weak for anything salty; he'll knock you over trying to get some potato chips.

Neil rips open a bag and starts crunching on some sour-cream-and-onion-chips. I wink, then fill his glass with tea.

"How was work?" I really don't care, but he doesn't have to know that.

"Busy. Insane meeting schedule. Unreasonable expectations."

"What makes the expectations unreasonable?"

Neil sets aside his chips and peers at me. "Anya, you hardly ever ask me about work, especially like what you're doing now. Are you worried about something?"

"No, nooo, Neil. Not worried. I'm—I'm trying to communicate with you."

He frowns and it hurts to watch him make that face. I feel like he's being unnecessarily disrespectful.

"Neil," I say. "We have to start somewhere to get somewhere, right?"

He sighs like there's no good argument left in him.

We eat in silence.

"How was *your* day?" he finally asks. In no time he's finished off three bags of chips. I'm sure he would've eaten more if I'd brought them outside.

"It wasn't too bad. Reesy and I drove to the Museum District. I started to take her to the Downtown Aquarium to see the tropical fish, but I wanted to make sure you're with us when we go."

"Oh yeah, why's that?"

"It's a family-type place. Lots of kids, parents, things like that."

"Oh." Neil picks up an empty chip bag, looks inside, and sets it down. His large hand sweeps across the back of his head, rubbing, and he stares at the sky.

"Neil, what's happening with us? In the past going to places like the aquarium wasn't a chore at all. But now . . ."

He says nothing for a long time. That makes me nervous. I hope we aren't getting like an old married couple who become too familiar with each other.

"Well, there is something happening that is on my mind," Neil admits.

"And what would that be?"

"It's almost time for . . . for Ms. Frazier to come back to work."

I flinch and stand up. "Why are you telling me?"

He says nothing.

"Now that she's returning, are you trying to pick *my* wore-out brain for answers on how to handle this situation? Neil, you've done a lot of questionable things, but this is a bit much." I swing my fist and smack the pitcher of tea. It falls on its side. The brown liquid flows out of the mouth of the pitcher like it's sick and puking. It looks just like how I feel.

The fact that Neil doesn't quickly upright the pitcher says something. Has he gotten to the point where he doesn't care? What can I do to make this man think about me for a change?

I force myself to pick up the pitcher just before it runs totally empty. The grass is now soaked and doesn't seem as green as it was before. I wonder if the tea will kill it.

"Okay, I'm sorry, Neil. I just . . . This is too much sometimes. I mean,

I try. I'm *trying* to—I wish I could understand and be the woman I'm supposed to be, but who can I turn to that can tell me what to do?"

"Go to church, Anya," Neil says mechanically.

"Church? *You* go to church. You were going to *church* when all this happened. If church didn't keep you from screwing up, how in the hell you think church can help *me*?" I question my mental state, and wonder if it's even healthy for us to coexist. Maybe I should ask him to leave. Then I could be free to cry and scream and curse and kick the walls with my bare feet and not feel self-conscious about letting him know how far gone he's made me go. I want him to know I'm hurt—I wouldn't be human if I didn't. But I don't want things to disintegrate to the point where he thinks I'm so loopy that I'm not valuable anymore. Then what would I do? I have to get a grip.

"Want more chips, Neil? I can bring you a few bags if you'd like." My voice is light and airy, like I'm living in Ditz City.

Neil stares at me with such a penetrating look that I stumble back into the house, grab my keys, jump in my car, and drive until my mind is regulated to the point where I know that my mental doors aren't off the hinges.

7

Neil

To establish a strong foundation, Anya and I decide to do two things.
One, I agree to pray every day for ten minutes. Praying should be the
first thing I do when I get up in the morning. I won't run to the kitchen
and put on the coffee. I won't turn on the TV and check out the weather
forecast. Prayer must be number one.

"Jesus, God, Father Almighty. Take me, this broken man, and direct
me in the way that I should go. I know that no matter how things look,
this *is* the day that the Lord has made. I *will* rejoice and be glad in it.
God bless my wife, my—my kids, and help us, oh *God*. Help *me*."

I feel stupid doing this; afraid I'm wasting God's time. I wonder if I
have to be perfect before the Lord will listen to the prayers of a man like
me. But then I think about the robber dying on the cross next to Jesus.
This robber believed in Jesus' goodness, figured that He hadn't done
anything wrong, yet He was about to die. And he told the Messiah, "Remember me." And Jesus said, "This day you'll be with me in paradise."
Well, even though I'm not a crook, I feel connected to the robber, like
I'm being crucified. But because the robber believed, even if it was at
the last minute, Jesus honored his faith. So even if I think my tiny bit of

faith won't warrant much, I hope it will start to lead me to a healthier place. And these days, when I get through praying, I feel better than I did before I started.

The second thing we want to do is continue carrying out the non-stressful, doable parts of our marital arrangement. Maybe if I'm more committed and give a little effort, it will yield positive results. So Wednesday afternoon I call Anya from my office.

"Hey, Anya. What were you doing?"

"Reesy's napping and I started ironing some sheets. Why? What's up?" She sounds tense. I've gotten out of the habit of calling her during the middle of the day; maybe she fears something bad happened.

"I want you to be dressed when I come home."

"Be dressed? You sound like I walk around naked all day or something."

I actually laugh. "No, I mean don't be standing in the kitchen wearing either your sweats or your pj's and house shoes. We're going out to eat."

"Oh, okay." She perks up. "Sounds good. I'll be ready."

"Reesy, too, now."

"Why, of course." Her voice sounds gentle, appreciative.

We talk a couple minutes longer, then hang up. I think I've just increased my stock with my wife. But I don't want it to seem like, *Neil Braxton Meadows is doing something decent for a change; he's actually carrying out one part of his marital arrangement—to take the family out to dinner twice per week.*

Instead I want the arrangement to become so natural that it doesn't seem like an arrangement anymore, but something I'm doing because I sincerely want to. I don't want to have to refer to these papers in order to remember what I need to do. Going out to eat will be a start. Like Anya said, we have to start somewhere to get somewhere.

During dinner, I get to observe my wife and see how attractive she really is. The weight gain that she worries about has never really been an issue for me. Underneath it all, Anya is still Anya. But I have failed to make her see that no matter how many times I've complimented her. She always seems reluctant to accept praise, so after a while I just stopped telling her, "You look good, baby" or "I love how that perfume smells on you." And when my wife noticed the compliments weren't as frequent as they used to be, I'd get, "Okay, Neil, I see you're slipping on the part of our arrangement which says . . . ," and her voice would taper off. I know she was embarrassed to have to say it. She didn't want to have to refer to the things I should automatically be doing—flattering her, letting her know how much I value her. I guess we should have added a clause to the arrangement that says, *Yes, Neil should compliment his wife three times per week, but when he does, his wife should believe him and not look suspicious, like he's doing something wrong.*

Give me some kind of credit. If I didn't love Anya, I never would have married her. I don't need to grab at any old insincere statement to keep her interested and vice versa. I just wish she'd chill out and understand that because I do care about her, being the imperfect man that I am, all this arrangement stuff isn't necessary. All the arrangement stuff could be an old memory.

We are on our way home from the restaurant. I want to stop by the post office and check my mailbox, something I rented even before I got married because I tended to change apartments a lot.

"Why you need a P.O. box, Neil? You got a girlfriend on the side?" Anya would laugh and tease me back when we met. I told her, "Just because you have a P.O. box doesn't mean you have a girlfriend. If that's all it took, every man in Houston would have a P.O. box." She shut up and let me be me.

When we arrive outside the postal station, Reese and Anya want to get out the car. They linger in front of the broken stamp machine while I retrieve my mail: a sales paper addressed to Nia's Gifts and Things, an unsolicited credit-card application, a Foley's bill, and an issue of *Black Enterprise* magazine.

I'm checking out my mail when Anya comes up to me trying to see what I'm looking at. I shake my head at her, smile, and resume going through the parcels.

"Hey, Neil." Anya and I turn toward a friendly female voice.

I clear my throat. "Hey, how's it going?" I say to the woman.

Anya stares at the woman so hard that the woman gives Anya an unsettled look, widening her eyes, then turns more toward me. She has a baby gripping her hip, a precious little girl who's napping. Her face is pressed against her mother's neck and her mom is stroking her back.

"Ah, the little one must've had a long day, huh?" I ask.

"Yep, we went to the mall and I let her rip and run at one of those Playland thingys. You know how kids can be."

Anya steps around and grabs my arm.

My mouth grows rigid, like I can feel my bones protruding outside my face. When Anya squeezes again, I gently remove her claws from my elbow.

"I guess I'll see you at work tomorrow. Bye, Neil."

"Later," I tell her. My face is heated up. I have such an awful distaste in my mouth, I want to spit on the floor, as if that would release me from feeling uptight.

"Daddy, I'm ready to go home."

"Go sit in the car, Reese." I point my remote-access transmitter at my black late-model Explorer. "Get in, I unlocked the door. We'll be there in a sec."

Reese skips off toward the car. I turn to face Anya. Her eyes are blazing fire, which alters her appearance. I don't recognize her anymore.

"What was *that?*"

"Anya, look . . ."

"Who was she?"

"It wasn't who you think it was. Didn't you notice she was holding a two-year-old girl?"

"So that baby's not yours?"

I stare at Anya and resist the urge to smack her across her ridiculous mouth.

"Okay, okay. Well, why didn't you introduce us, Neil? I don't get that part."

She's acting so insecure I almost don't want to be seen with her. Even though dinner was uneventful, was I imagining things or did Anya stare at every woman who came into the restaurant? Maybe she thought I was like an athlete who gets tickets to the game for both the wife and the girlfriend, and they end up sitting one row away from each other.

"Neil, can't you see you disrespected me big-time? That hurt."

"Anya, I didn't disrespect you. You're going to have to learn how to trust."

"Trust?"

"Yes, trust," I say, standing right in her face. "Even if I screw up every single day, if you wanna be with me, you'll have to trust me. You'll have to believe I'm not sticking it in every woman we pass by. I am *not* having an affair with every female on my job. Besides, we're in this situation because of you, Anya, not me!"

"Oh, hell no." She backs away like I've slugged her in the face. She clutches her belly and bends over, but then rises real fast.

"I should've known this wouldn't work, Neil. If you wanna blame me, fine, but at least I can hold my head up in public." Her voice cracks. "At least I'm *trying* to hold my head up." Even though no one sees us, I still feel embarrassed, like everybody knows all the things I wish they didn't know.

I step up to Anya, drop my mail on the floor, and pull her against my chest. I close my eyes and pat her back until her anger subsides and her body stops trembling.

"Anya, listen to me good." I stare into her eyes. "I have a son and it means I'll be interacting with the mother. That's only natural. It doesn't mean that I see her every day, except I will at work, and I can't help that. But we are not out to make you miserable, my dear Anya. I am there because of the child. Think about the child."

She wipes her dripping nostrils and looks up at me. "Okay, cool, the child. But Neil, I find it strange you've never brought him to the house. Maybe you could do that sometime."

Anya removes herself from my arms and heads to the car.

I retrieve my mail from the floor and toss the junk mail into a garbage can.

Brax is squirming in some warm, sudsy bathwater. He gurgles while I take a soft cloth and wipe his forehead and soap up his arms. It feels peaceful and I enjoy looking at my son's features: the nose he got from me, the large doe eyes he inherited from his mom. I wonder if the fact that he has a large head means he'll be superintelligent one day.

We are holed up in Dani's bathroom. Brax is cooing and enjoying the water that fills his tabletop portable bathtub. It's decorated with seahorses and has a large, soft pillow to support his back. He likes sucking on the washcloth sometimes, but Dani always fusses when she sees me pretending to let the baby have his way.

I've finished rinsing my son and call out, "Hey, can you bring me that towel that's on the bed?"

"What you say, Daddy?"

"The towel. Bring it here."

"Okayyy."

Reese runs into the bathroom huffing and puffing like she's worn out. Her eyes twinkle while she stares at the baby. I hoist Brax out of the tub and place him on a large white body towel. He smells so fresh I want to kiss his feet. But they're moving fast, like he's pedaling a bicycle.

"Can I hold him, Daddy?"

"No."

"Please?"

"Maybe later," I say.

We go to Danielle's room. I nearly ask Reese to wait for me in the living room. I hate for her to be anywhere near Dani's bedroom, but I'd rather keep her where I can see her. Moments ago I had to get on Reese because when she was in the kitchen she told me she washed her hands five times in a row, and she'd gotten water all over the place.

"What's that baby's name, Daddy?"

"Call him Braxton."

"Braxton?"

"Mmm-hmm."

"Like your middle name?"

"Uh, yeah." I rub Brax's thick hair with the towel and watch her at the same time.

She stares at the baby, then at me, then at the baby.

"Bring me some baby powder, okay, sweetie?"

"It makes me cough." She starts hacking, clasps her hands around her neck, and rolls her eyes like she's having convulsions.

"You're so silly, Reese. Just bring it."

"Okay, Daddy." The pitter-patter of her feet fades toward the bathroom. I lay Brax on the bed and watch his legs kick. I go to his drawer and fish out a sleeper that has footed pants so his little toes won't get cold.

"Having fun?"

I almost drop Brax's sleeper on the floor.

"What are you doing here?"

Dani smiles at me and winks. I point my head toward the bathroom. Her eyes enlarge.

"Reese," I whisper.

"Oh," she says, and rushes out the room. I'm not ready for Dani and Reese to meet just yet. It's the first time I've brought Reese over, and I asked Dani to wait it out in her car. Once she sees me leave, she knows it's fine to return to her apartment. The baby's only left alone for a brief minute.

Even though certain things appear organized, I still feel uneasy. I have a need to merge my two families in a way that's workable but haven't figured out how to do it yet.

I dress Braxton and place him in his crib, then motion at Reese. We leave Dani's apartment and get situated in my SUV.

"Now," I say to Reese. "You won't tell Mommy about this, right? This is our secret, okay?"

"Okay, Daddy."

"Promise?"

"I promise, I promise, I promise."

The day that Dani returns to work, Anya calls me shortly after noon.

"Yes, Anya."

"Neil, uh, are you sitting down?"

I stand up. "Yes, no, what's wrong? Is it Reese?"

She cackles but says, "No, no, it's not Reese." She pauses. "It's that *ring*."

"The ring I bought you?" I ask.

"Mmm-hmm."

"Three-thousand-dollar one, right?"

"Was it insured, Neil?"

"Uh, no, it wasn't."

"Well, damn," she says.

"What happened, Anya?"

"I—I can't find it. Been looking for an hour. I doubt anyone stole it. It's usually in my drawer but it's missing. Everything else in the house seems to be in place, though."

I wonder if she's toying with me.

"Well, Neil, sorry to bother you. I know you're busy. But I just wanted you to know so you can keep your eyes open. Maybe it's right in front of my face but I just can't see it. You know how that happens sometimes."

"Uh, yes. Let's hope it's just temporarily misplaced. I mean, what else can I do?"

"Three grand is a lot of money, Neil."

I don't know if I should be flattered that she cares about the expense or what. But maybe I shouldn't have even told her how much it cost. Maybe she feels I care more about the cost than the fact that she deserves some jewelry.

"Yes," I agree, "that is a lot . . ."

"But?" she says.

What's up with Anya? Why is she trying to lure words out of my mouth, as if she's picking my brain?

"Anya, we'll talk about this later. I'm gone."

"Tell that woman I said 'Welcome back.'" She hangs up the phone. And I am so stunned, I lose my appetite for the lunch Anya prepared for me. I go to the kitchen and place my tuna croissants, two oranges, and Caesar salad in the refrigerator. When Dani walks in and says hello, I avoid eye contact and tell her I can't talk.

"Okay, bye," Dani says, and walks away. I watch her glide down the hall. Besides her usual work gear, she's sporting four-inch pumps. Her hair is pinned up, styled in a pompadour. The hallway smells like flowers, capturing her sweet perfume. She doesn't even glance back at me.

Minutes later I walk in Dani's office and close her door. I take a seat in a guest chair that's in front of her desk. She looks up from her PC and smiles like she's not surprised. I hate when she knows what I'm going to do before I do it.

"Whassa matter, Neil?" Her voice sounds so sweet. I am grateful just to be in her calming presence. I am amazed she affects me this way.

When I don't say anything, she hops up and comes to sit on my lap. She's wearing a chocolate-colored business suit I love; the skirt comes right above her knees, and her long legs are stretching from underneath the hem, like they're meant to be on a stage. She hikes up her skirt and wiggles her ass around on top of both me and my dick until we fit nicely together. Her body feels hot next to mine. I take deep breaths. Dani places her arms around my neck and hugs me. I motion like I'm trying to stand up.

"Uh-uh, nope. I'm not letting you leave till you tell me what's wrong." She smiles, gazes in my eyes, and kisses me softly on the cheek. I wish I could stay there, just like that, longer than forever.

Dani kisses my cheek again. I feel my heart getting softer. She kisses my lips. Her lips are wet. I don't kiss back. She covers my whole mouth with her mouth, then tries to poke her moist tongue inside. I open my mouth and let her in. Our tongues slide, dancing like strippers grinding against each other. I close my eyes and suck the tip of her tongue desperately, like I'm trying to prevent it from leaving me. Her juices mingle with mine. I love being inside Dani's mouth. It feels like the home I wish I had. My dick is getting harder by the second. She stops kissing me and takes my hand and leads it inside her blouse. My hand is on top of her right breast, which feels soft and warm. She presses my hand against her breast. I squeeze her nipple. It feels unbendable, stiffer than my dick. I slowly rub my finger across her nipple, torturing her. Dani moans and arches her neck. My dick is about to explode. I wish we were at her place. I wish I could control what should not control me.

"If you suck me, milk will come out," she whispers in my ear. "Suck me, Neil, please, any part of me. I want you, Neil. I want . . ." The heat of her breath against my skin makes me want to nibble on her earlobe, then go on to explore her, from her succulent breasts to her manicured toes. I shift in my seat and want to tug at the front of my pants.

"Dani," I say, and press my wet lips against her warm neck. It feels awkward sitting in that chair, but so what. What would happen if I placed my mouth over her plump tits and slurped? What would happen if I unzipped my pants and she sucked and sucked and sucked my dick? What if our boss knocked on her door and walked in the office and caught me jamming my rock-hard penis inside hot and wet Dani? My dick wants to know, but I know I can't do this. I remove my hand from her blouse and gently pat Dani on her back.

"You still haven't told me what's wrong," she says, breathing hard and buttoning her blouse.

"I know but I got to go."

"You sure?" she asks.

"I'm sure." I try to make my voice sound strong and authoritative, but it's about as difficult as telling Reese no when she begs for a new toy. Dani smiles, stands up, and walks to her desk with a showgirl seductiveness that makes me want to rip off her skirt and panties and make love to her till she starts screaming my name. But as much as I want her, I need to show some restraint. Everything insane is rushing at me and I am thinking about how much I need to figure out what to do even though I'm not eager to make any hard decisions.

On Friday Anya meets me at the door when I arrive home. She hands me a glass of wine and takes me by the hand and leads me to the den. She pushes at my chest until I fall back on the sofa.

"Give me your feet," she commands.

I lift my feet and she pulls off my shoes one at a time, then hands me the *Chronicle*. I am dead-dog tired. My bones are aching and popping; they sound like cracked knuckles. So Anya's gestures make me feel so good I want to yell in ecstasy.

"This is what I'm talking 'bout," I tell her, and lean back in my seat against several huge pillows. I left my suit jacket on the backseat of the Explorer, but she waves at me so I can undo my tie. I feel freer than I have in a long time—at home, relaxing on a Friday night after a psychologically challenging week. The weekend is starting out good.

"Be right back," Anya says. She whisks away my shoes and necktie and comes back holding a blue bandanna.

"Now, close your eyes, Neil," she commands, and stands in front of me.

I sigh but close my eyes, hoping she isn't gonna force her toes inside my mouth. Anya wraps the bandanna around my eyes so tightly that light becomes dark. The darkness makes me feel like I am invisible. I try to imagine what Dani is doing right now. But then I quickly wonder what *Anya* is doing.

I hear giggling. Girlish laughter. Maybe Reese is sticking her hands in her ears, waving her thumbs, and making faces at me. I wouldn't be surprised if she and her mom are getting a kick out of making me look silly.

"Okay, Neil, I'm about to remove the bandanna," I hear Anya say.

When my eyes are free again, I see that Reese and our neighbor Tamika are standing in front of me. Reese has on a black leotard, some black ballerina slippers, some huge pink bunny ears, and a pink bushy tail. She bends over, puts her hands on her knees, and starts shaking her butt. I laugh. Tamika is dressed in a yellow-and-orange clown suit with huge balloons on the front. She has on a pointed orange hat and some big floppy red shoes. Each cheek had a big red circle painted on it.

"Ahhh, how cute," I say. "What's this for? Someone having a party?"

The sound of Mika's and Reese's giggles fall on top of each other.

"Y'all go sit on Daddy's lap," Anya says. The girls jump on me while Anya snaps a few photos with a disposable camera she bought from "Small-Mart," our nickname for the little Wal-Marts that are popping up all over Houston.

"Reese, go get the other outfit," Anya says.

Reese hops off my lap and comes back holding a pair of black pants, a green T-shirt, and one of those Dr. Frankenstein monster masks. "Here, Daddy, this's yours," she says, and tries to place the mask on my face. It feels funny on my nose, which is now twitching.

"Hey, no." I fuss and remove the mask.

"Daddyyy."

"Okay," I tell them. "Now I get it. It's the thirty-first of October, right?"

"Nooo, it's Halloween, Daddy. Go get dressed so we can get some candy, candy, candy."

I smile at Anya and raise my hands, defeated. My heart is racing. I haven't done a Halloween stint in a while. It shouldn't be too hard walking the girls for a few blocks within the neighborhood so they can feel the excitement of filling sacks with chocolate bars, saltwater taffy, strawberry bubble gum, and other treats. I head to the library and quickly get dressed, pulling on the slacks, black loafers, and green shirt that Anya left for me there, but hold off putting on the mask.

I return to the den. "Anya, where's your costume?"

She smiles but does not say anything, just runs up the stairs, the floors creaking under the weight of her feet.

"C'mon, c'mon, c'mon," Reese says, pulling at the tips of my fingers. Her hands are cold. When she's excited it seems her body temperature fluctuates up and down.

"Reese, why does everything you say have to be mentioned three times?" I ask.

"I dunno, I dunno—" She quits jabbering, her cheeks filling up with air while she contains a goofy laugh.

"Tamika, where's your mama?" I say to the girl who is hopping around on one foot.

"She at home, just chilling," she says with an uncaring shrug. I shake my head and rise to go open the front door. Darkness has quickly settled. I can already detect several groups of children ambling down the street, followed by parents or young adults. I can hear the chirpy sound of crickets filling the air. The darkness and slight chill contribute to the murky atmosphere.

I stick my head back in the door. Reese and Mika are playing patty cake near the foyer. "Y'all ready to leave? What we waiting on?"

Anya descends the stairs, taking slow steps toward us. She is smiling, head held high, and hair topped by a silver tiara. She is wearing a long beige gown. I blink twice. Does she actually have on the dress she wore to our wedding reception? Surprisingly, it isn't a tight fit; maybe she had the dress altered. But my wife is sporting that dress like it's meant for nobody but Anya Meadows. I want to slink to the floor and cover my eyes. But I keep staring. She glows like she knows who she is. I hope she's happy that her family is doing something fun together.

"Nice," is all I can utter.

"Mommy, you look beautiful and fine and gorgeous."

"Thank you, my princess. Now we can go?" Anya asks. "Won't take long."

"Good," I murmur, and slam and lock the door behind us. I inhale a mouthful of cool air and slip the monster mask over my face. It isn't as difficult to see as I thought it would be. Yet I can barely breathe. It feels like someone is pinching my nostrils. I adjust the mask so my breathing is less restrained.

Most times you can tell when the neighbors are willing to dole out candy and goodies. They'll have some lights on, indicating their holiday participation. Every five or so houses have these lights, which is fine with me. It feels good to be hanging with the ladies, but I am eager to get back home and remove the mask from my face. I wonder why Anya gets to be a queen but here I am a damned monster.

Thinking about the irony of it all, I laugh to myself while Anya and the girls walk up to a two-story house that has flashing orange lights and porcelain black cats guarding both sides of the front door.

My cell phone rings and the caller ID indicates it's Dani's wireless number. I start not to answer but end up pressing the talk button. "Yeah," I say in a loud, confident voice. I have nothing to hide, so why go into soft-voice mode?

"Having fun?" she says. I hear her smile and I want to smile, too.

"I'm all right. Where are you?" I turn my back so I'm facing the street. I can barely hear because the girls are so loud saying, "*Oooo-wee*, thank you, thank you."

"Uh, I dunno," Dani says. "Out and about."

"Is the—" I clear my throat. "Is the little one with you?"

"Yeah, you wanna talk to him?"

I laugh. Sometimes Dani will call and let me say something on the phone to Braxton. As if he understands what I'm saying. Though maybe he does. I know he knows my voice. Because I used to talk to him while he was in Dani's belly, he already recognizes his daddy's voice.

"Sure, I'll talk to the kid."

I feel someone come up behind me.

"Here, say hello real quick," a soft voice speaks.

My hairs lift off my neck. I freeze, unable to move for a sec. A figure steps in front of me, the streetlight glowing above our heads. This creature is dressed in a long-sleeved black dress that reaches the ground. Her hair is covered by a floppy black hat; her cheeks, forehead, and chin painted with green makeup. Even her teeth are green when she smiles at me. I want to run and leave my wife and the girls far behind.

"What's the matter? Did I scare you, Neil?" She's covered up but I know her voice. Dani waves her cell phone at me. She's holding Brax, who's dressed in a sailor suit with a blue hat and a sweater to cover his arms. I want to reach out and graze his sweet cheeks with my lips but he's asleep. I want to ask Dani what is she doing in my neighborhood, how long has she been here, and did she plan on dropping by my house for Halloween candy but just happened to see us come out of the house, so followed us. I have all these questions, but I'm too stunned to ask. I stare at her; she's smiling like this is all normal and appropriate.

"Wow, look at that ugly witch!" Reese yells. I turn around until I am facing the house. My daughter, wife, and Mika are staring and pointing at Dani. She smiles, growls, and waves her hands real slow, which makes her seem even more mysterious. I am getting freaked-the-hell-out with every second.

Damn Dani. What is she doing? Is this her idea of a joke? Maybe we don't share the same humor when it comes to some things.

"Look at the witch's baby," Reese laughs.

Dani quickly covers Braxton's face with a blanket before anyone can see him.

"Ch–Charles is getting over a cold. I shouldn't have him out here," she says in a nasal-sounding voice, escalating to a real high and demonic pitch, like she's slurring her words. I cough and clear my throat. I realize Anya knows Dani's normal voice. I really want to get out of here.

"Hey, you two, let's keep moving," Anya says. "There's this really cool house a few doors down that's totally decorated with Halloween stuff—corpses, vampires, tombstones, and a wolf that sits on top of the roof."

"C'mon, girls, let's go," I order.

Dani shoots me a look, a mixture of longing and apology. I give her one back that pleads, *Not now.* We head down the street. My cell phone rings again. I turn off the power and pick up the pace of my steps, wondering what other things Dani is capable of.

8

Anya

"C'mon, Anya, stop acting so stupid."

I hate when Vette talks to me this way. She barely has any home training, but I sidestep her rude comments and smile.

"Vette, no, I won't take off my wedding ring."

"Then give me your hand, I'll do it," she says, and waves her fingers at me. We're at Boudreaux's, a Cajun restaurant on the West Loop South near the city of Bellaire. It's Friday night. Neil agreed to watch Reesy. Vette begged me to come here so we could escape the house, partake in a major gabfest, and eat something greasy. We've only been here ten minutes and I've already sized things up. Twenty- and thirty-year-old women dressed like they're going to a club. Short skirts, legs slicked with oil, hair done up fancy like they're at a Bronner Bros. hair show. There are more men here than at a college football game.

"Damn, Anya, you've forgotten how to have fun."

"No. And what I also haven't forgotten is that I'm married. I don't mess around, Vette. Period."

"You don't have to get laid. Just see if any man wants to mack you. Don't you miss that?"

I cringe and stir my iced tea with a long spoon. Vette's words cut deep. Sometimes truth is soothing, and it feels good to admit what's previously been denied. Other times when people see your truth, you feel so exposed. Even when you're as tender as me, you still want to appear strong, like nothing ever steals your joy.

"I am not desperate, Vette. I don't need a guy to look at me and ask for my number to make me feel like I'm somebody. I mean that. I won't sink that low."

"You're weird, Anya."

"No—no, I am not. I may not do what you think I should do, but that doesn't mean I'm weird. You are really getting on my nerves tonight."

"What else is new?" Vette giggles and digs into her shrimp scampi and fried alligator. It's so noisy in this joint. Huge TVs are mounted to the ceiling. You can barely hear from the overpowering music. Chaka Khan screaming. OutKast crooning. In a way it feels good to be out and about, but in this crowded environment, I feel like I'm naked and dancing in a cage.

"It's been so long, you've forgotten how to work it, Ms. Married Woman. C'mon, take that ring off. You'll feel like a different person."

"No, I will not. Taking off the ring doesn't make me not married. Marriage is based on more than wearing some guy's ring."

"Aww, okay. But at least if you remove it, just for fun, you might temporarily forget the bad stuff."

"No, Vette. What you don't understand is I've taken the ring off before. When Danielle first got pregnant, I took the ring off."

Vette sets down her fork and places her hand on mine. "You said her name."

"Mmm-hmm, her name is Danielle. She's the mama of Neil's baby. Can you believe I have two kids now?"

Vette snatches her hand back like I've sunk my teeth into her flesh.

"Don't be shocked, Vette. Denial hasn't helped. I can pretend that this hasn't happened all day long, saying a little mantra, 'Neil doesn't have another baby, Neil doesn't have another baby,' but it hasn't stopped my husband from running over to Danielle's to see their son. So what else am I supposed to do? Continue acting like an idiot so my ego won't feel bruised?"

"Anya, I'll be right back. I want to refill my drink." Vette moves so fast that I can barely glimpse the back of her head when she sprints across the room. I shift in my seat. Even though we're inside and the lighting is poor, I get my purse and find my sunglasses. I slide them onto my face like I'm a cool and together sista, just chilling on a Friday night.

Vette returns to our table. She's snapping her fingers to the music and doing the Beyoncé bounce, shaking her butt fast and hard like she's in a real groove. I ain't mad at her. She's young, carefree, and has the energy to be as spontaneous as she is.

"So," she says, sliding into the booth, balancing her glass, "since you seem to accept that Neil has the kid, why do you still act on edge all the time?"

"No, no, everything is straight. Really. Only thing left to do is meet the baby."

"And when's this gonna happen?"

"Neil is arranging that now." I sip my drink even though I'm not thirsty. "Uh, should be soon, though. Can't wait to see him."

Vette throws back her head and laughs. The music is loud enough to swallow the room, but I can still hear Vette's howl.

"Silly, woman, I *am* up for meeting him."

"But—"

"But nothing, Vette. Meeting the baby is just something we need to get over with. I've prayed about it and I think this is the right thing to do."

"So you're doing it because it's the right thing to do? Not because you really want to do it?"

"Vette." I pause and grip my frigid glass between my hands. "Being introduced to him will move us forward. Begin that healing process."

"You ever gonna do a face-to-face with Dani?"

"Whoa, I dunno. I mean, you think Neil would actually initiate such a meeting?" I say. "I can't even see it."

"What if I do it?"

"Girl, please," I protest, making a face. "You haven't even met her yourself yet."

"How you know that?" Vette says.

"I just know."

Vette studies me. "Tell me something. Are you afraid that Dani has the power to snatch Neil from you?"

I shrug and focus on the stillness of my iced tea.

"Just because you have the man's kid doesn't mean you have the man," she says.

My eyes widen.

"Not talking about you and Reesy. I'm referring to Dani and other women like her. All these chicks think they're doing something great by purposely getting pregnant, thinking that's gonna ensure a relationship with the man. They think having a man's secret kid means something. And it really doesn't—except pain, hurt, shame, resentment, and a whole bunch of other wack stuff."

"So, Vette," I say, "if all this is true, who wins? The wife? Mistress? Kids?"

"I dunno. I think for a long time most men would hide their secret kids and the mothers had to play a role. They accepted the payoffs and knew it was the best they could get. But that stuff always gets tricky because the women ultimately want more cash, especially if the man's pockets are deep."

"Oh, like athletes?" I ask. "The Dr. J's of the world? And that basketball player that has seven kids by six different women? I don't remember his name—"

"Doesn't matter. He's just an extreme example of what can happen. But at least he claims the kids. That's a start. It would be a damned shame if my brother slipped his nut inside this woman and didn't have the balls to admit it. Now, that's when things can get ugly."

Yeah, right, I thought. Let's give Neil a big hand-clap.

"Would you prefer if Neil never told you at all?" Vette asks. "At least he told you."

"Yeah," I say, my eyes glazing at the memory. He did tell me—over the phone, which is understandable. Maybe he thought if he told me in person, I'd nut out in public or something.

Dani was seven weeks along when she found out. She didn't want to abort. Neil, of course, didn't want her to abort, either, but he was still stressed.

"Hey, baby," he whispered after he told me everything and I was icy silent. "I am sooo shocked about this. I can't even believe it myself."

Listening to his confession, I shivered like I was freezing, but I was too hot to respond. I was thinking about the fact that he'd put his penis in her after he signed a document saying he wouldn't. I felt like the biggest fool in America. But in a way it was like I placed a kid on punishment, then took him to the mall, made him promise not to play video games, and wanted to start screaming when I caught him holed up in GameStop.com, laughing and playing Xbox—like what we agreed did not matter. So while I felt betrayed, I guess I set Neil up inadvertently by suggesting he not penetrate. Who was I kidding? If Catholic priests can penetrate, surely married men will.

"Yep," I tell Vette. "Your brother seemed pretty typical in some ways, and astounding in others. He could've lied till his teeth fell out. He could've produced a child that I never ever knew about. Plenty of other brothers keep extra babies on the down low, but secrets like that never stay secrets long. They always have a way of creeping out and exposing you when least expected, you know what I'm saying?"

"Sister-in-law, you are not alone. It happens way more than we ever know. We just don't like talking about it. Men are a real trip. And they say women have issues."

"Well, Vette," I say. "Put yourself in a man's shoes. If you hide the kid, you're wrong. If you bring it out in the open, folks might talk about you like a dog. So what do we do? You know, it sounds weird, but I am glad Neil wanted to deal with it."

"Like I said before, my brother shouldn't have been messing around on you in the first place. His common sense should've kicked in, you know what I mean? What an idiot . . ."

"Okay, Vette," I say with a nervous laugh. "Are we male bashing?"

"We're talking about how things are, the good, bad, and ugly. We didn't create this, we're just trying to sort through it all and survive it."

"Girl, I swear you look at too much *Oprah*."

"Nooo, my show is *The View*. I love me some Star Jones."

"Sure you do," I say. We share a genuine smile.

What would happen if I slid off my ring and dropped it inside my purse? Would the ring line still show? And if a guy could detect the line, would he care? There're always some people willing to cross marital boundaries. And as much as the idea of putting out some ego-building feelers sounded intriguing, I am not down for that. Neil is still my heart. True, I want to place my fingers around his neck and squeeze one minute, and pinch him playfully on the butt the next. And to be honest, when I lay awake at night thinking about my life, I try to remember the times when things were better. Long before Reesy came along, Neil would lie next to me in bed and we'd grab each other's waist and I'd tremble just from his warm and loving touch.

But after the second miscarriage, sexually things cooled way off. Neil treated me like I had a bone disease or something, stroking me with timid hands, perhaps fearing I was too distraught for us to connect. But once I convinced him I was hurt but not destroyed by the miscarriages, his sexual fire lit back up.

Every so often I fantasize about the good old days. Would Neil even be interested in some high-energy cuddling after all we've been through?

Besides, fear and dread keep insisting we're long past that blissful period of intimacy and closeness, when it was natural and not pledged in writing. Maybe being married eight years is too long for us to restore the matrimonial foundation. And the thought of that makes me want to curl up and vanish. What would happen if we reversed time? If my husband wanted to have sex with me five times a day, would I do it? Could I turn off that freaking TV, strip naked in broad daylight, and let Neil screw the goody-goody attitude out of me, my chunky legs stretching east and west, my genitals cold, throbbing, and wet, whether I was in the mood or not? What can I do now that would be the equivalent of that? Truth be told, I'm still searching for the answer.

Vette and I just stepped outside of Boudreaux's. The sky is black, the air crisp and filled with a pleasant breeze. I can't believe women are standing around wearing short skirts and no jackets to cover their bare arms. A few loud-talking guys are huddled in front of an Escalade that has spinning wheel rims. The men yell comments to every woman who passes by.

"See, if that's all it takes to make me feel like a woman, I won't be faring too well," I tell Vette. "I mean, does getting whistled at make you feel good, Vette? You like when guys use pickup lines?"

"Sometimes yes, sometimes no—it depends. If the line sounds tired, like something from the nineties, no, I wouldn't appreciate it. They can send that line back to wherever they got it. But if a man steps up to me and is sincere and I haven't noticed him winking at every other woman passing by, then that's cool. But I still wouldn't hand over the digits."

"Why not?"

"I don't like meeting folks on the street." She frowns. "Too risky."

I laugh and bump my shoulder against hers. "Well, Miss Lady, you ready to go?

"Sure, let's roll."

We head east toward a parking lot that is one block away, passing by a store that sells hip-hop clothing. A bright light shines from inside the display window, spotlighting throwback jerseys and low-rider jeans. A longhaired man with twisted shoulders stands bowlegged in our path. His nylon jacket and pants are wrinkled. He's as thin as Clay Aiken. His vibrating shoulders make him look cold, maybe hungry. I reach for my wallet.

The man wobbles up to me and says in a raspy voice, "Jesus cares about you." I stuff my wallet back in my purse, laugh, and quicken my steps.

"Loser," Vette says under her breath. We don't stop walking fast, our heels slapping hard across the pavement, until we reach my car.

One Saturday afternoon, Neil and I agree that he will pick up Braxton from Dani and allow me to meet him for the first time. Since Houston's mid-November temperatures are still in the seventies, Neil suggests we expose the baby to the nice weather at a nearby park. While he's gone, I slam kitchen cabinets, wash my hands twice, then stand by the living-room window and wait for him to pull up in front of our house.

When Neil arrives, I open the front door.

"Mommy, I wanna go, go, go!" Reesy yells behind me, tugging on my shirt.

"Go where? You don't even know where I'm going."

"I still wanna."

"Stay here with Vette. I'll be right back."

My tiny, stiff steps guide me to the Explorer. The tinted window is rolled up. Ten-week-old Braxton is strapped in the back in a car seat. I am not able to get a real good look at him just yet. I am fine with waiting until I am able to freely observe him. The park we're going to is at the intersection of Airport Boulevard and Beltway Eight, several minutes away.

Neil concentrates on driving. I haven't initiated conversation, but he keeps mumbling, "You say something?"

"Umm, no, I didn't. You're hearing things, Mr. Meadows."

Soon we pull into an empty parking lot, the sound of gravel popping underneath the tires. Neil parks the car and I wait for him to remove Braxton from the car seat.

"Here is my son." Neil cradles Braxton against his chest and I fix my eyes on the baby's plump cheeks, which are the color of a cardboard box. His lips are pinkish red and pressed tightly together like you couldn't shove anything in his mouth even if you wanted to. He boldly locks eyes with me and doesn't look away, like he's the one checking me out instead of vice versa. I am startled by his confidence, humbled that this two-month-old boy seems to know he belongs on this earth even if I don't.

His beautiful, long eyelashes and the noble way he looks lying in his dad's arms steal away the envy I attempt to reserve for this child.

"Ahhh, he's a cutie," I say, and lean into Neil's free arm. I want to say more, but my throat tightens. I simply receive Braxton into my arms. He's not heavy at all. This feels way better than holding Reesy when she's acting spoiled and slips in my arms, or when she falls asleep in the den and I'm forced to haul her upstairs to her room.

I nuzzle Braxton's cheek with my cheek and moan. He stares at my eyes, nose, face. I feel silly and embarrassed but stare back. His tight lips curl into a smile. He has on a cute blue-and-white knit outfit, with huge blue buttons on the bottoms of the pants. As silly as it sounds, I'm ready to head out to the children's department at the nearest store and add to his wardrobe.

"Well," Neil says, "let's strap him in this buggy." He secures the belt around Braxton and we begin walking on an asphalt path that weaves through the ungated park. There are dozens of towering trees, picnic tables, a red-and-blue sliding board, and a sandbox at the far end of the grounds.

"Hey, this pathway is so lopsided and crooked," I say, "you sure it's okay, comfortable enough?" I can't stand to feel hardened stone underneath my feet. Even though I have on gym shoes, the granite is so rigid I feel shoeless.

"It'll be all right. We won't be here long. I just want him to get some fresh air."

Grabbing Neil's arm, I feel my cheeks flush with shame. Prior to this I could contemplate my situation behind the walls of my home, where no one could see or know, but now that we are outside, I feel like I'm standing in the middle of a busy intersection wearing just panties and a bra, as if my secrets are not my own.

"Neil," I sputter, my eyes suddenly latching on to his. "Baby, he—he's adorable. He is." Get your mind off yourself, Anya, I think. The world exists for more than you.

Feeling a little awkward, I rub Braxton's cheek with my finger several times, noticing the softness of his skin. His huge brown eyes sparkle and he coos softly.

We continue taking lazy steps along the narrow path, then come to a stop when a wig-wearing woman dressed in a velour JLo track outfit smiles at us. We smile back.

"He is sooo good-looking," she says. "What a fine boy you have there. Is this your first one?"

"No," I snap, and stop smiling.

"Well, he looks just like you," she says, and points at me.

I burst out laughing and clutch my stomach. Neil mutters, "Excuse us," and abandons me, pushing the baby buggy over the rocky pathway. The wheels are turning and spinning and making ugly noises while clanking against the granite.

"Hey, wait for me," I say. I catch up with Neil and grab his rigid arm until he comes to a stop. "You want me to push the baby? Even better, I'll hold him." I undo the straps and lift Braxton from his seat. "Hi, Brax." He smells fresh, young, innocent. I can't hate this baby. I can't hate him. Instead of seeing him as a threat, why can't I see him as the opposite, a miracle, which is what he seems more than anything? Braxton grabs my finger and squeezes. I surprise myself and giggle. It's like he's saying I'm cool with him. And that's cool with me.

9

Anya

It's the next weekend. Friday night. I'm in bed. Thirty minutes past midnight the phone rings. I lean over and place the receiver against my ear.

"Hello," I mumble.

"Uh, hi, this is, uh, Dani. Uh, I was just wondering . . ." Her voice sounds frightfully fragile.

I sit up in bed and flip the switch on the lamp. "You were wondering . . . ?"

"Is, uh, Braxton there?"

"The baby? Or is that what you call Neil?"

"Nooo, I'm talking about the baby."

"Uh, look, Danielle. I don't know why you'd call here asking about your own child. I mean, why don't you *know* where he is? Wouldn't he be with you?"

"I think there was a mix-up. Maybe it's not . . ." Her voice drifts away, like it's trying to catch up with her foggy mind.

"Are you all right?" I slide my warm feet to the carpeted floor and stand. I hear mumbling. She sounds as groggy as me.

"Danielle," I say louder, "you want me to get Neil on the phone?"

She's breathing heavy, grunting. Listening to her makes my heart pound violently, like it's beating its fists against me and wants to lunge through my chest.

"Oh, no, no. Uh . . ."

I toss the phone on my bed and stomp loudly down the stairs, race through the hallway, and stop at the library. I knock once and open the door, which squeaks and moans.

"Neil, Dani's on the phone. She's talking crazy. She's talking *crazy*. Pick up the line down here and see what's wrong."

Neil bounds off the couch, almost falling back down as soon as he gets to his feet. He blinks a couple times. I grab his hand and lead him to the den. It feels odd to touch his fingers. It's like I accidentally reached out and held a stranger's hand. First I turn on the lamp, then press a button so that the speakerphone is activated.

"Here." I point. "Talk to her."

"Dani, what's wrong?"

"Neil." Dani's shaky voice crackles through the line. "Braxton—is he with you?"

"Yes, didn't you know? Didn't Audrey tell you?"

I cast a sharp look at Neil. He averts his eyes.

I hear silence, then a swear word. "Nooo, Neil. No, she did not. Oh gosh, I feel like such a fool. Well, what happened? Why didn't you tell me?"

"Audrey was baby-sitting, like you arranged, but she called me and said she had an emergency. I rushed over there and picked up Brax. Audrey promised right then she was going to let you know. She was almost running out the door when I got there. Maybe she forgot."

"Oh, God. Maybe I need to forget she's my baby-sitter. That's what I need. That fucking bitch is sooo pathetic."

I walk a few paces, my arms folded across my chest, past Neil, past our wedding pictures, which sit in several frames on a square glass table. In one eight-by-ten, we'd just been pronounced husband and wife. The photographer had taken all kinds of shots: Me and my four bridesmaids embracing one another in a solid hug. Neil sitting down surrounded by his family, who are standing up. Another one with me spread out on my new hubby's lap, squeezing his neck, and both of us grinning so wide you'd think we'd just won a $200 million Super Lotto.

"Well, yeah, uh, the baby's here with us." Neil glances at me. "Been asleep a few hours, since nine-thirty or so. You want me to bring him back to you?"

"Right now?"

"Yeah, Dani, I could get dressed and—"

"That's not necessary," I hear myself say. "Go back to bed, Dani. We'll take care of the baby. He's safe here."

A hush falls over the room.

"Dani, y–you still there?" I find myself saying. "I can imagine how scared you must've been. Hey, I didn't even know the child was here, thanks to Neil. But it's cool." I say this with gentle sarcasm. Things do happen, and God knows the outcome could've been much worse.

"Well, that's kind of you. Thank you, Mrs. Meadows. I guess it makes more sense for Neil to bring the baby back in the morning. Give him a kiss for me."

"Give who a kiss for—"

She hangs up the phone while I'm talking. We are released from a dazed moment. I swallow deeply and press the button to disconnect the speakerphone.

"You know, you could have told me, Neil."

"I know, I know."

He looks at the wall. I look at and talk to the side of his face.

"It takes, what, ten seconds to tell me that the baby is spending the night? I'm actually okay with him. I was hoping that this wouldn't be a big deal anymore."

Why couldn't he just tell me the baby was here? Do I scare my own husband that much?

"Is he in the nursery?" I don't wait for Neil to respond. While he slumps in the chair, I turn off the lamp, leaving him alone in the dark-ened den. I rush back up those stairs, eighteen in all, go to Reesy's old room, and walk in. I smile a bit, excited at the prospect of seeing a little baby in our house. Brax is resting on his belly. A blanket covers his back. I smell milk; some of it must've spilled from the glass bottle lying near his hand, which is curled into a fist. Dear God protect him, I cry inside. I rub his soft brown hair and hear a deep sigh escape from his open mouth. No way can I blame Neil for wanting to share his life with this precious little soul. But something has to happen so we can make sure this situation is workable.

If my husband wants me to trust him, he also has to trust me enough to share vital information, so we can all breathe easier at night. All of us, including Dani.

"No, no, triple no."

I've never heard Neil so adamant. So strong-willed.

"Too late now, hubby."

"Not too late. I can un-invite her. All it takes is one phone call."

We're at home in the kitchen, Thanksgiving Eve, cooking our butts off. Oven-baked turkey, duck, and cornbread, yams, dirty rice, green beans, and Watergate salad. Neil and I are standing near the stove. Sharvette is leaning against the fridge, arms folded.

"I told you, Neil," Vette starts in. "Anya be tripping sometimes. But under the circumstances—"

"Nobody asked your opinion, Vette. Don't you have a mall to hang out at?"

"Malls close early today, Neil, remember?" Vette walks in a circle and comes back to face him. "Shit, ignant Negro. I'm trying to help your ass. I'm siding with you for a change."

"I don't need you to side with me, Vette. I just need some peace and quiet and some control around here."

As bad as I want to say something, I remain quiet and take it out on the stove, wiping away messes with a wet rag that singes near the burner, almost scorching my hand. Please tell me what the hell is control. How do you control what's not in the script, let alone the rewrite? It frustrated me that my efforts to try to ease the situation were met with ridicule. So what if Dani comes by for Thanksgiving? What's the big deal?

This morning when I called to invite her, she gasped but quickly responded with a yes.

"That is so nice of you, Mrs. Meadows. You know, my family's in California . . ."

"I know." I wanted her to know Neil tells me things. Not everything, but enough to play with.

"And around the holidays it's good to go somewhere for a change, instead of being alone—like usual." Her voice sounded dreamy and distant. Did this woman expect me to feel sorry for her?

"You want me to bring anything? Neil tells me you're a fabulous cook. I can't cook worth a damn," she laughed. "Microwave boxes are taking over my freezer."

Ah heck, I was thinking. My homemade-loving hubby has hooked up with a noncooking hooker? I had to witness this up close.

"Hey, no problem," I gladly told her. "Just bring some sodas or a—"

"Oh, oh, I know what. I know. I'll run over to the northwest side real quick and stop by the Flying Saucer pie shop and get Neil one or two of those strawberry cream pies. He loves those sooo much," she laughed. I removed the phone from my ear and mouthed, *Fuck you, bitch,* then pressed it back against my ear. "Oh, you don't have to do that, sweetie. I threw together a homemade apple pie, plus a triple-layered German chocolate cake, Neil's favorite. So just bring a case of Mountain Dew."

"Okay," she said. "Diet for you?"

I cocked my neck and stared at the phone. "Umm, Danielle, not for me. I am not on a diet. See you around oneish?" I slammed down the phone, cursing myself for rising to the bait of her last catty comment. As nutty as it sounded, I was eager to see this woman up close, assess the competition, show her a thing or two, let her know that it ain't over until the fabulous-cooking fat lady sings. Except I am *not* fat. I'm *fine*.

"Neil, trust me," I finally respond to his objections once Vette has left the kitchen. "We are adults, not totally ghetto, so I hope we can pull off a funky little dinner. I know Reesy wants to meet the baby, since she's seen his picture and stuff."

Neil's eyes widen.

"Oh, you didn't think I knew about the picture, did you? I know a lot of things you don't know." I turn back to the stove, take a wooden spoon, and stir my mouthwatering roux for the giblet cornbread dressing. As silly as it sounds, I'm forcing myself to run toward my fears. If you face what scares you, it's not as intimidating. Kind of like how you dread studying for an exam, but once you pick up those books and get into it, the task isn't half as bad as it seemed.

Plus, Thanksgiving is a time to be thankful, to know that as bad as things are, they could be worse.

I respond to the doorbell after four insistent rings that sound like *The queen is now here, let me in, dammit.* I want to meet the whore as much as she wants to meet me, but I cannot stand when people ring my doorbell all crazy like they ain't meant to wait for nothing in life. Don't get me started. I don't want Ms. Frazier to think just because she rings my bell, I gotta toss everything in the air and come hopping. I want her to know that she's merely an afterthought in my otherwise busy and important life.

Dani is waiting on the other side of the screen door. She's wearing some snug jeans with two pockets stitched in the front, a brown clingy short-sleeve shirt, and a tan vest with a white furry collar. A basket filled with fruit, nuts, and other goodies sits on the concrete next to her feet. And her little bambino is strapped in a plastic handheld carrier.

"Hey, uh, hello there," she says, looking me up and down. "Could you take Braxton? I have a few more things to get." I peer beyond Dani's head. A gold Toyota Tacoma pickup is in our driveway, with a customized license plate that reads DANIF. I am a little shocked. It's not like I expected a Hummer, but I definitely was thinking of a more expensive, feminine ride.

She starts singing an Alicia Keys song. I just gawk at her. Dani sets the carrier on the ground and runs toward her truck. I shrug, open the screen door, and pick the baby up, carrier and all. He smiles at me first, so I decide to return the favor. Babies are so naive. What's he got to smile about? Whatever he has, I want some, too.

Once I get Braxton settled, I walk back to the foyer, watching Miss Thang from a distance. She's actually holding a conversation with Riley, who is standing in front of our house.

Dani waves bye to Riley and returns to our door. She notices me staring at her and smiles like she enjoys being observed. "Neil here?" she asks, letting herself in. She's struggling to hold her oversized purse, a case of diet sodas (damn her!), an Eddie Bauer diaper bag, and a portable play gym.

"Uh, sure, he's here. Taking a shower." I smirk at Dani and reach for the portable gym. We walk side by side. I lay the equipment on the floor of the den. "This portable gym is nice," I say.

"Neil got that—Uh, never mind," she says, blushing. That makes me mad.

Dani walks around the room, taking in the sofa with the matching pillows, the entertainment center complete with stereo, DVD, and CD player, the Oriental rugs, the matching tables, and the framed photos on the mantel. She doesn't look at the pictures for long. I wonder what she's thinking. I hope she's torn up inside. If she isn't, she ought to be. Dani sniffs and follows the aroma to the kitchen. Several pots cover the burners on the stove. The shelves are lined with spices, and there are cutting boards with the residue of green onions and garlic that I haven't had a chance to throw away.

"Wow, reminds me of home." I barely hear Dani's voice. "But home is where your heart is, huh? I can't volunteer to cook anything. Well, I do okay with some long-grain rice and gravy, but if you'd like, I can help set the table."

I kinda feel sorry for her. "Dani, relax, everything has been taken care of. You're a guest."

She looks puzzled, like maybe she should leave while she still has a chance.

"Hey," I say and step up to her. "I want you to feel comfy, so make yourself at home. You know, I appreciate your willingness to come by. I mean, I, well, you know, this shouldn't, uh . . ."

She places her hand on mine and squeezes. She has a French manicure. I've never had a French manicure. "I think I understand, Mrs. Meadows."

I blush. "Please, I'm Anya, okay? I mean, I *am* Mrs. Meadows, but you know what I'm trying to say."

Dani nods and blushes again. She still has her hand on mine, so I untangle myself from her and nicely ask her to go sit in the dining room. The family will be joining her shortly.

Neil, Vette, Dani, and I are gathered at the table getting our grub on. Reesy fell asleep before we could begin eating and is now resting in her room. I made a plate for her to microwave once she wakes up. Little Braxton is in his sleeper on the floor next to his mom. He's slurping on a bottle, not paying us any attention.

"So, Danielle," I say. "You told me you're from California. How'd you end up in Texas?"

"Long story short? A dartboard."

"What she say?" Vette frowns.

"No, let me put this in a way that makes sense. When I was a sophomore in high school, a girlfriend told me she was going to Pratt and asked me where I was going to college."

"Oh, so you've been to college?" I ask her.

"Yeah, barely graduated, but anyway, I set up a dartboard with eight or so names of various colleges—Spelman, Eastern Michigan, USC, some others. I threw the dart and it ended up on Rice University."

"Rice? But didn't you attend U of H?" I ask.

"Yeah, I didn't get in to Rice, but by then I was curious about Texas. And on a whim I applied to U of H and they accepted me, so . . . Sounds silly but that's how I came here."

"I hear the West Coast is great. Why'd you want to leave?" I'm full of questions today.

"I like to get out in the world. I mean, sure, I packed my junk and planted myself in Texas, but after messing around in school a couple of years, I hightailed it to Chicago, stuck it out for a solid year, then doubled back to Houston. I love the people and everything, but I'm cold-blooded and Chi-town winters had me going nuts. I don't see how Oprah can stand it."

Neil finally finds the guts to talk. "Oprah has millions of dollars' worth of real estate all over the country, so I'm sure she can escape Chicago's winters whenever she wants to," he says with a tense chuckle.

"Must be nice," Dani says. "Anyway, I needed to get away from crazy Long Beach, meet a different brand of people. Hey, for all I know, Texas won't be the be-all and end-all. I may venture over to Georgia or Florida eventually. Just not sure."

I am amazed that Dani can look so relaxed. It's like she's accustomed to potentially explosive situations and is able to just chill out and take it all in stride. And even though one side of me says having this gathering is a good, mature thing to do, my inner she-devil is screaming to emerge.

"Incredible story," I murmur. "But now that Braxton is in the mix, you probably aren't gonna be hopping up dashing around here and there, or are you?"

"Oh, I haven't thought about that. All I know is I do *not* want to go back home. That would be so humiliating. A lot of my cousins have moved out of the house just to come back and split the rent with their mother. We're talking about thirty- and forty-year-olds. And hey, I've had tough times before here in H-town. When I was living close to downtown, my roommate stole my debit card out of my purse and then abandoned me. She left me in a real nice place that I could not even afford, especially after she charged a few expensive items off my account. Some friend, huh? And all I could think of was, Sink or swim, sink or swim. I had to either figure out what to do to survive or hightail it back home to my mama like a failure. I wasn't about to end up on her doorstep."

"So I assume you swam and—" Vette asks.

"I treaded water, backstroked, you name it," Dani explains. "And fortunately, Sharvette, I am still here."

"And so is Braxton," I say with a sullen look, and glance under the table.

"Right, so is Brax." Even though we spoke his name, he didn't seem to care. All he needs is his bottle. A damn bottle filled with nasty-ass milk. I'm jealous as hell.

"And what about, uh, how can I put this, boyfriends?" Vette says matter-of-factly.

Uh-oh. Here it comes. My sister-in-law has never backed away from speaking her mind.

"Hey, Vette," Neil scolds, knowing she likes mouthing off. "When Dani wants some shit from you, she'll squeeze your head. Lighten up."

"What?" Vette asks, playing innocent. I am energized by Vette's boldness and want to laugh, but I'm dying to see how Dani handles the inquisition.

"No, Neil, it's cool." Dani shrugs. "I'll answer Sharvetta. I don't have a boyfriend right now," she laments, and looks at her plate. "Haven't been looking. No one has approached me. Haven't had time to even notice."

I can't believe she's telling us this, and that Vette hasn't corrected her about mispronouncing her name. But since Dani seems sincere, and I'm confident I have Vette's support, I sweetly ask, "Dani, do you normally date a lot of men?"

Dani's face falls and she looks about wildly.

Vette jumps in, "And do you *want* someone to approach you?"

Neil narrows his eyes at his sister.

Dani glances quickly at Neil. "I don't know. I–I just . . . Can we talk about something else right now?" She picks up her fork and slides it around on her plate, making a loud scraping noise.

I don't know how old Danielle is, but after hearing her comments, I figure her to be about the same age as Vette. More innocent and more vulnerable than I first thought, like she's mature but can crumble under pressure.

"Okay, Ms. Frazier," Vette says, easing up after seeing Neil's disapproving look. "What *you* wanna talk about?"

Dani blushes, relieved. "Well . . . I haven't noticed a tree. Are you going to put up a Christmas tree?"

I tell her, "We traditionally go and get a tree the day after Thanksgiving—buy new ornaments, garland, throw it all together, light it up that night."

"That sounds great. I love the magic of Christmas trees, the twinkling lights, presents underneath. Did you know I love decorating, too?" She smiles and lifts her head high. "See that huge gift basket over there? I assemble those all by myself for extra cash. I just love dressing up things, so it would be great to see your tree."

"Yeah, it would be great, but didn't you hear my sister-in-law say the tree will be put up *tomorrow*? You'll be out of here by then." I guess Vette couldn't resist one last dig.

Dani looks genuinely surprised by this, then peers at her half-empty plate. I try to put myself in her shoes and realize she's in my house only because she accepted my invite; I can take the lead here.

"You'll have to excuse Sharvetta," I say, and laugh. "Sharvetta is still in training."

Dani grimaces. "I think we all are."

Thanksgiving after dinner. With the exception of Dani, who picked at her food, we all go back for seconds and settle into "niggeritis," a condition that can happen to almost everyone who eats a heavy meal. Eyelids droopy. An automatic "No" to dessert. Vette starts yawning so much she finally tumbles upstairs and says she'll see us later. The rest of us relocate to the den. Neil slumps in the La-Z-Boy. Dani and I plunk down on the couch in front of the TV, sipping on tiny mugs of hot apple-and-rum cider stirred with cinnamon sticks, and taking turns flipping through channels.

Neil holds Braxton and plays with him for a while, but around five P.M. the baby is lying facedown on Neil's lap. Neil's leg is gently bobbing up and down. The baby's eyes struggle to stay open. Both Neil and Braxton fall asleep within minutes.

Dani and I glance at the guys, then at each other, and shake our heads.

"Men," she mutters, and laughs.

I hop up. "Dani, I'm going to get us something more flavorful to wet our tongues. Be right back."

I scoot to the kitchen and return holding two ice-cold beer bottles. I hand Dani a bottle.

"Hey now, thanks. Thank you, Anya." She pops off the top, tilts the bottle, and noisily slurps for a good minute.

"Dani, don't be shy. If you need to burp, go right ahead."

She widens her eyes and stifles a laugh. "I'll have to remember that."

We fully settle on *My Best Friend's Wedding.* Midway through the flick, Dani has used the bathroom twice and is now on her fourth beer. I am still taking small sips from my first bottle.

"You know, Anya," Dani says, her voice slightly slurred, "you not so bad, not like I thought."

I glance at Neil. He's quietly snoring. I grab the remote and mute the TV. "What do you mean by that, I'm not so bad?"

"Oh, I dunno," she says, tucking a long strand of hair behind her ear. "I guess, usually when you think of someone's wife, you picture some miserable, nitpicking hag, an overweight, evil, nappy-headed, bitchy-acting thing that nobody on earth can stand, but a woman everyone's used to because she's been there so long, you know, running the house, buying the groceries, fixing dinner—you know how that can be."

She takes another long sip and wipes her mouth. I don't say anything. Dani's eyes are glassy. She looks very interesting right now.

"But," she continues, "you're actually kinda cute, and even nice, in a cautious way. To be honest, I know you've been checking me out, putting out feelers, but nothing major, so I'm not offended." She waves her hand and swallows more beer.

"Okay," I say, "I think I know what you're saying. I'm not the ugly-ass bitch you thought I'd be."

Dani smiles and shakes her head emphatically.

"Well," I tell her, "wives are wives but they're women, too. Always women. I may not wear it often, but I still have the sexy lingerie in my drawer, okay?"

"Dig that." Dani burps and says, "Excuse me."

"You're excused. And since you brought up the topic, please don't let the big thighs fool ya, Dani. Most men prefer women with meat on their bones. They want something they can hold on to. Something that feels good when they wrap their arms around it."

She stares at her skinny arms, then looks up at me.

"Hey, get up for a sec," I tell her. She struggles to her feet, trying to balance herself by spreading her legs wide apart.

"You could stand to put on a few pounds, sista," I say, and walk around her, staring at her perky but sufficient breasts. "I can't see with that vest on—take it off for a sec." Dani removes her vest and sets it on the sofa.

"Not bad, not bad," I tell her. "I can *kinda* see why Neil would want you," I remark, partly humoring her.

"Hey, Dani. You ever check out that movie *The Fighting Temptations*? It talks about how most black men prefer women with a big ass. I always wondered if you had a fat ass."

She bursts out laughing, then stops. "I don't think my ass is big at all. It's okay, I guess. Not as big as yours."

I giggle out of shocked admiration. "Yeah, and quiet as it's kept, Neil likes my fat ass, my big bones, and my bouncy breasts, too."

She frowns and wrinkles her nose.

Dani may be the other woman with the new baby, but I'm the one who has his last name, the one who wears Neil's rings. Inherently, I know I have power, and I can't help but remind Miss Thang what's rightfully mine.

I smile at Dani and say, "Neil loves sucking things. Did you know that?"

She makes a noise in her throat.

"Is that a yes or a no?" I ask.

Instead of answering, she takes a few backward steps and plops down on the edge of the couch, then clutches her beer and blankly stares into space.

"Anyway, Dani, I adore this movie, don't you? I love the idea of weddings. So many people are getting divorced, but no matter what they've heard about how tough marriage can be, men and women still trying to find someone they can walk with down the aisle."

I am pacing around the room, my hands clutched behind my back, speaking to Dani but also to myself. My voice is firm, assured. I know exactly what I want to say, and how I want to say it. There's zero percent alcohol in my system. I have that one beer bottle sitting on the oblong table, but ain't no beer in there. It's full of water that I poured inside the bottle from the water dispenser on our fridge. It sure tastes good, too. *Real* good.

"Yep," I continue, "even though couples run off to Vegas, the Little White Wedding Chapel, and all that jazz, saying your marital vows ain't nothing to play with. Mmm-hmm. I mean, think about it. You are standing before God declaring what you will and won't do, to the Creator of the freaking *universe,* you hear what I'm saying?"

Dani lets go of the bottle. It falls to the floor, topples onto its side. Beer spills on my purple-and-tan Oriental rug, soaking it. I don't even care.

"Eight years ago Neil and I got married in front of one hundred people on July seventh. Lucky seven. Ha!" I say, still pacing.

Dani's quivering on the couch. Her hands, shoulders, and head wobble like a ceramic bobble-head toy.

"We stood in front of that preacher and all those folks talking about how we'll stick together, through sickness and health, riches or poverty, forsaking all others, till death us do part." I flash a look at Dani, eyes blazing into hers. "But that ain't even the best part, Ms. Danielle Frazier. You want to know what is?"

She shakes her head.

"I think you do. The best damned part of the whole damned ceremony is when the preacher made everybody in that damned church say, 'What God has joined together let no man put asunder.'"

I walk up to her.

"Stand up."

She stands and the way she's trembling, you'd swear she's at hell's entrance, the devil waving at her to join him.

"D—do you know what that means?" My voice breaks. I am so close to this woman, my breath humidifies her nose, her cheeks. "What God has joined together, a man and a woman in holy damned matrimony, nobody better not ever, *never,* come between that. That's what it means. And God is serious, Dani. We may forget our vows and blow them off when things don't go our way, but he ain't forget." I place my finger on her chest, between her breasts, and poke with every few words. "And I don't want *you* to forget, either. Because even though *you* were not there with *us,* standing in that *church* on July seventh, repeating what that *preacher* told us to say, you're *still* a part of my *freaking marital vows.*"

"Shit, shit, ahhh shit!" Dani shrieks. Tears flood her cheeks, racing like water squeezed from a rag. "I swear to God, Mrs. Meadows, I swear I won't—" She bends, clutches her stomach, and groans, a guttural sound that even I feel. I gasp, pull her back up, and hug her so tight our breasts mash together. She's trembling, hot, shrieking, sobbing hard against me. "I'm sorry, I swear to God. I won't, I won't—"

"Shhh." I wipe my forehead, which is now beaded with sweat, and I think about this young foolish girl who needs to understand where I'm coming from. "Don't take the Lord's name in vain, Dani. Just do what you know is right."

I release her, retrieve every beer bottle, and walk away—trembling, panting, and feeling as drained as I've ever been in my life.

Last night, as soon as I left Dani, I walked upstairs and went straight to bed, exhausted, headachy, and knocked-the-hell-out. But I set my alarm for six A.M. and I wake up before the beep starts beeping. It's Black Friday. I'm ready to race off to Super Target, the one near Reliant Center, and find my tree, some fabulous decorations, umpteen rolls of cute foil wrapping paper, important stuff like that.

I shower, finger-comb my hair, and run downstairs. And that's when I remember. I tiptoe into the den. Dani is spread out on the sofa. Neil is gone. Maybe he woke up last night and went back to sleep in the library.

I start to just go on to the store and let everyone sleep in while I brave the shopping crowds, but looking at Dani, I suddenly decide that bitch has to get up and go with me.

I fall to my knees next to her and poke her shoulder. Her face looks calm, like she thinks about deep stuff while sleeping.

"Hey, Dani," I whisper in her ear. "I'm about to go shopping. Why don't you join me?"

She frowns in an ugly prune-face way, eyes still closed, gumming her mouth and making smacking noises. "Uh, sure." She coughs without opening her eyes. "I can ride with you. Where's Brax?"

"He's being a little sleepy-head today. Don't worry. Neil's got that covered. We'll be gone less than three hours."

Dani sits up, clears her throat again, and traces her fingers across her throat. It's still dark outside, but I know the sun is gonna rise within a half hour. It amazes me how, if you're outside in the morning and you stare up at the sky, within seconds it seems to go from darkness to light. Like there's not much difference between the two.

"Piss on me," she complains, staring at her wrinkled shirt and vest. "Maybe I should stay behind. I don't have a fresh change of clothes."

"And my clothes are too big for you, so don't even ask. I want you to go with me," I insist, knowing I don't want to leave her and Neil in my house.

"W—why do you want me to go?" she stammers.

"Well, we can talk some more . . . , Besides Vette is still asleep and I want you to help me out, if you don't mind."

She struggles to laugh. "Uh, okay, more talking, huh? I guess I can wash up, put on some deodorant."

"You do that."

After she freshens up we quietly head out. A long line of old ladies, starry-eyed kids, and a few cheap but good men has formed outside SuperTarget. I am not surprised. Those fools'll do anything to save ten cents.

Dani follows me around the store. She rarely smiles. Doesn't talk much. Every time I ask, "How does this ornament look?" she says,

"You're in charge, it looks great," or something along those lines. I grin to myself. I have a need to know that she acknowledges my power.

Before we head to the checkout lane, I ask, "You need anything? Anything for Brax? You?"

"Well . . ." She shakes her head. "I don't—"

"Tell you what. If you're not opposed to getting clothes from here, go grab yourself a shirt at the minimum. I'd love for you to stay around the house till tonight. You might feel more comfy with a fresh shirt."

She widens her eyes. "Buying me a shirt isn't necessary. I live near here—"

"No, no. I do not want to go where you live, Dani. I just don't. Now, this is my last offer, so you better run and grab something. Or if you're too scared to do it, I'm not. I have great taste and—"

"Okay, okay." She gives in. "Be right back." While she runs toward the women's department, I wait in line and wonder what else might transpire to make this a momentous holiday weekend.

Part 2

Anya & Dani

10

Dani

"*A man that already has someone is more appealing than a man that* doesn't have anybody."

"Oh yeah?" Anya says.

"Well, sure," I tell her. "It makes you feel like you're getting something of value . . . if you know that someone else wants him, too."

"Oh, so are you telling me Neil isn't the first married man you've been with?"

Hmm, risky, risky conversation for sure. But, well, maybe it's time for me to *try*, to even *suck up* my nervousness, and be a little forthcoming with Anya. I know she isn't done with me yet. Insisting I stay over her crib all night is so unexpected, a bit *Twilight Zone*–ish. And I feel a bit, well, should I say it?

The S word. Okay, my hands are sweating, they won't stop moving, my legs and feet are bouncing around like I'm listening to a thumping hip-hop song and I can't keep still. Here I am sitting next to this potentially psycho woman. I'm in the passenger seat of her very neat-looking Honda. Too neat. No Burger King bags dumped on the floor, no empty

Smoothie King cups stacked in the cup holder. Her ride looks nothing like the inside of my whip, which at times tends to pile up with trash until I can't stand it anymore. Anyway, we've just left Super Target. Not that I was gung ho about shopping that damned early in the morning, but she dragged me along for the trip, probably thinking if she didn't keep two eyeballs stuck on me while we're at her house, I'd morph into this bad girl the second she turned her back. As if I'd put my hands on Neil in her house. And they think I'm the crazy one? Anyway, here we are. We're bobbing along the Southwest Freeway on the biggest shopping day of the year because Mrs. Wifey claims she's not in the mood to go home. Not yet. And because I've been abducted for this little trip, it's not like I have any other choice. It's not like I really am yearning to sit next to Neil's wife. Sitting so close I can smell her perfume. So much perfume I want to cover my nose with both my hands in an effort not to sneeze. Why'd she spray herself like that? Is she firing subliminal messages at me? Hmm, maybe subconsciously competing or something? I know how some women can be. Sooo insecure. Hateful. Their fragile minds clicking away, sounding like fingers tapping a keyboard. I really don't have time for this. I'd much rather be chilling out at my own crib.

But in spite of how uncomfy it is, here I am agreeing to talk with this lady. Maybe the entire scenario is so bizarre I feel mentally trapped, emotionally obligated, like I have no choice but to go along for the ride, letting her ask me whatever she wants to know. Me trying to explain myself. Picking the right words. Putting out my own feelers to meet some of her feelers.

But I am sitting in her ride, and she's driving, what, seventy-five miles an hour? Speeding like it's nothing. (Hey, where are the police when you need 'em?) What if I try to be forthcoming but end up saying the wrong thing and pissing Mrs. Wifey off, what could stop her from growing horns on the sides of her head, yanking the steering wheel, ramming her car into a concrete guardrail, so my head smashes into the windshield, blood pouring out? I'd be totaled like a tiny hybrid car, and get permanently removed from Neil's life. From life, *period.*

Of course, that scenario isn't likely. I mean, I doubt that! But I'm not a complete fool. I read the headlines and watch CNN. I can't pretend as if awful, unbelievable things don't happen every day. Who can forget the Houston hubby who got trampled by the irate wife and her pricey Benz? So I'm thinking about all these things, and here we go. Mrs. Wifey's asking me oddball questions. Demanding answers. Expecting me to say this, that. *Something.* I could be wrong, but I'm sensing that if I don't BS Neil's wife, if I let her in on some things I'm sure she's desperate to know, maybe she'll view me as less threatening. I don't know where our conversation will lead us, but I am willing to give truthfulness a bit of a chance. God knows I've already been through enough hell to know I can survive hell again, if our discussion comes to that.

"Anya, what I'm saying is this. No, I—I've never been with a married man before. Yes, I've fallen for guys that were already in relationships. But"—I raise my voice before she can say anything—"I didn't do it on purpose. It was like . . ." I squirm in my seat and scratch my scalp. "I mean, a lot of times I'd meet men who didn't admit they lived with someone until it was too late. We'd gotten to know each other a little better by then. I knew he was digging me and I would have feelings for him and, well, because of the attachment, it was hard for me to just . . . walk away at that point." I swallow deeply and lower my voice. "And so we'd be in the middle of the mess and I'd just wait it out. Wait out the relationship, you know . . . Plus, I've never dumped a guy. Ever."

"You've got to be kidding," she utters.

"I wish I were," I comment, my heart feeling strangely heavy.

Anya gives me a dubious look. "Why not?"

"I—I don't know. I preferred to part as friends, and I didn't want to hurt them, I guess."

"Oh, so you're not willing to hurt the man, but you don't care if he hurts you? That doesn't make any sense, Dani."

"I know, I know. But so far that's the story of my life. It's like I just cannot initiate a breakup. The man has to."

"You have problems," she remarks.

I hold my tongue, letting her declaration, something I already know, float inside my heart for a minute.

I tell her, "Even if you're not like me, wouldn't make the same decisions as me, I think we all have problems, right?"

"What? Well, yes, of course we all have problems, but it doesn't mean we should look bad, awful, and gloomy in the face and still go out of our way to make things worse."

Even though she's as blunt with me as I am with her, her words rattle me. It's like we make excuses for what we do, how we are. *That's just how I am.* But if we come face-to-face with someone who reminds us of ourselves in some aspect, well, it's unsettling. Like, for the first time we can really see ourselves as we are, the "self" we are unable to see when we're simply looking in the mirror.

"True, yes, sure," I remark. "But how do we know if the things we choose to do are gonna make things worse? I mean, sometimes you choose things because you're hoping they'll get better."

"Ugh, what? *Jesus.* Some things are common sense, Dani. I mean, getting preg—" Anya stops herself.

Aha. So *that's* where she's going with this. I swallow deeply.

"*That* . . . that was an accident." I say this firmly, loud. I don't want Anya to think I purposely got pregnant. I mean, I know some women trap men, but why would I? How would that benefit me? I don't have the best-paying job in the world; it's not the worst, either, but I definitely don't feel like I'm in a position to add more bills to my life. I love Brax and everything, but hey, he costs! Plenty! Plus, you know how kids can change things between a man and a woman. Casual-sex relationships are not the strongest foundation for starting a family.

Besides, I've been knocked up before. By a guy named Fred. He already had a live-in girlfriend, but my being pregnant didn't automatically make Fred ditch Ethel, or whatever her name was. All I remember is she was a grossly overweight, green-haired, four-eyed, mean-spirited, phony-ass bitch. Meaner and uglier than a junkyard dog. And I couldn't believe he chose *that thing* over me. I liked Fred because he was attractive, comical, and had cheeks full of dimples. Ethel had no kids with him, which left me scratching my head trying to figure out how she got so huge. And here I was—spirited, decent-looking, employed, fun-loving, supportive. I'd buy Fred clothes that he said were the bomb, and the sex was more than adequate (pleasure rating: 8 out of 10), but nooo, instead of running to my side, Fred shoves my pregnant behind out the way just to latch on to that god-awful Ethel thing!

Do you know how dejected Fred made me feel? Don't get me wrong. At first he acted like he was soooo happy I was carrying his baby. Then he begged me, "Don't abort my child." And when I did it anyway, he shook my hand and thanked me afterward. He confessed that asking me not to abort was the easiest game he ever won. Then he told me to get lost and slammed the door in my face. I heard the double bolts click, too. The next day, I contemplated driving to his minimum-wage, shitty piece of a job, whipping out a pistol, and blasting the rotten guts out his soul, but I left stupid-ass, cowardly, horrendously-poor-taste-in-women Fred alone. No cursing him out, no stalking him, no putting sugar in his gas tank. If he would've owned a decent car, maybe I could've considered *that* piece of revenge. But after I murdered our baby, I vowed I'd *never* go that route again. I still get pissed just thinking about it, and it happened years ago. I am pissed that I was so naive to think that taking on a man as a project was something he'd be grateful for, and it would be a task that would fulfill me. Taking on the project is easy, but making it successful is a whole other story.

And although memories of what happened between me and Fred are real and significant, I don't think I'll let Neil's wife in on that part of my background. I've already beaten myself up a million times for that sorry chapter in my life. I've beaten myself up until my heart was raw, but then I've forgiven myself, promised from now on I'll only sleep with quality men, and I'll never do that pro-choice, horrible-choice thing again. And I damn sure don't want to make a confession just to be judged by Mrs. Wifey.

I continue, "What happened between me and Neil was an accident in that we got caught up—"

"Spare me." Anya gazes out the driver-side window even though she's whipping around a curve on the 610 Loop with a million other vehicles passing by us. She doesn't look away for long, thank God. Have you ever wanted to laugh even though nothing is funny? Have you ever found yourself in a terrible, awful, insane spot and wondered how you got there? I mean, what the hell am I doing? Why try and talk frankly to a man's wife like if I do, we'll be best friends within minutes? That ain't realistic. Makes me look—I dunno. *Piss* on *me*.

"Hey," I tell her, "I don't mean to—"

"No," Anya says back, "it's cool. I mean, you're only doing what I've asked you to do—to set the record straight. How can I ask you to do that and then punish you for doing it? That's like setting a trap, isn't it?"

"Sometimes traps are necessary, aren't they?" I remark. "If that's the only way you feel you can find out what you need to know, set the trap." At this point, I'm close to feeling like I don't care anymore.

"Hmm, th–that's shocking."

"Well, to be honest," I say, "I'd rather you hear some of this from me. 'Cause I don't like when someone thinks they know something, and all they know is the A, the B, and the C, but they don't know the D through the Z. I mean, I guess I'm trying to say your knowing a little bit can't really qualify you to judge me. I don't wanna be judged, but maybe you can understand my side."

Anya gives me a sidelong glance.

"I *do* have a side," I mumble, again feeling like an idiot.

"We all have sides, Dani."

I don't say anything.

She shrugs. "You know, Dani, what's done is done, that's for sure. Some days I feel like this messy situation is doable: other days I'm so angry, I'm not in the mood to deal with any of it. But I read lots of magazine articles and hear stories on the radio about black women who are in our situation. And the women are acting out, showing their ignorant, violent sides, their personal business spilling all out into the street, and someone ends up getting handcuffed and driven away in the back of a police cruiser. And I tell myself, That won't be me. I can rise up, do better than that."

Let me be the judge of that, I think, wondering if her taking me on a joyride can be considered "rising up."

"So," she continues, "I really hope we can put our heads together, work with one another, and at least *try* to do this the best way we can. I feel for you, not in an entirely sympathetic way, but if I were in your shoes, I'd want to work things out. The person I really feel sorry for is little Brax. He's the victim."

"Well, I'm glad he's too young to know what's going on." I say that because I don't know what else to say. I have trouble thinking about what's going to happen two hours from now, let alone trying to picture five years down the road into my son's future.

"And then there's Reesy," Anya says. "She's calling him her little brother." She sounds bewildered. "I never told her to do that. Did you?"

My face reddens and I shift in my seat. "No, never. Maybe Neil told her to call him that. Or maybe she's doing it on her own."

"I saw her kissing his cheeks the other day," Anya continues. "I told her don't do that anymore because she sneaks and puts lipstick on sometimes and I don't want his skin to get infected. But she went ahead and did it again. I caught her when she thought I wasn't looking." Anya shakes her head and her eyes soften. "Everyone is falling in love with that baby."

I feel happy yet awkward. Maybe the presence of this child will steer all of us in the direction we're supposed to go. 'Cause some days I don't know where to go, how to be. I am trying to take this new and over-whelming part of life one scary little step at a time.

Okay, so after we go on a short drive to nowhere, we finally end up back at Anya's house. It's early afternoon and no one else is here, not Brax, not Sharvetta, nobody. Even though I agreed to come back to the house, I feel anxious, but Anya says she needs to ask me some final questions. So here I am again, in a tiny space with Mrs. Wifey. True, her car is claustrophobically small, but even a two-story house can feel like a closet when you're sharing space with someone whose goal is to suffo-cate you. Not that she's entirely disgusting, but she's still putting out these annoying feelers. Just when I think we've gotten somewhere, I question where we are, because the feelers are back again, in my face, waving their thick fingers, demanding answers.

So I've managed to eat some leftovers from Thanksgiving, and then we find ourselves in that same ole den. Thankfully, Anya has lightened up somewhat and is making small talk, and we're actually having fun multitasking. We're casually viewing another movie, *Gone With the Wind,* which she popped in the DVD player when I told her the movie is my all-time favorite, and we've started working on this huge fake tree Anya has set up. She has bags and bags of decorations spread out on the floor. I'm getting goose bumps, too, because I love the texture of things—the little frosted glass ornaments, curly-wire Christmas balls, Styrofoam angels, and soft fabrics full of bright colors like purple and red and green and gold. I want to help dress up that tree, silly as it sounds. I'm on one side of the tree, standing on my toes reaching my arms as far as I can to fluff the branches and make them look fuller. Anya is on the other side stringing garland when she casually asks me if I know what a hussy is. I'm surprised that she's going there. Her question makes me want to roll my eyes, but I say, "Is it a woman who goes out of her way to break up someone's family?"

"That's a good answer."

"Is there a reason why you asked me that?"

"Not really."

I didn't believe Mrs. Wifey. In more ways than one I think she has a lot of gall. But I blame both her and myself—her for trying to lay a poorly disguised guilt trip, and me for letting her do it. I've let her convince me that I owe her something, but I'm not sure that's true. But far be it from me to tell her I've survived much adversity in my life, so I'm confident I can handle this.

"Anya, do you want me to try and guess why you asked me that?" I challenge. "Am I supposed to fill in some kind of long blank that's sitting inside your head right now?"

"No blanks in my head."

I laugh, but it's not from the heart. "I'm sorry, Anya, but I just don't believe that."

Her face grows stony, about as rigid as my heart feels. And the space inside this den seems to become so small that I feel like we're two grown-ups trying to fit on one tricycle.

"Sometimes, Dani, people say certain things because they're hoping to hear other kinds of things."

"Excuse me?"

"Never mind." Her voice sounds as strong as mine. She looks up at the ceiling and drops her arms to her sides, sighing.

"Tell you what. This has gone on long enough. What if we call a truce? I am going to try my hardest to leave this alone. I feel like we're treading the same territory. But from now on we can try to move forward, be progressive, and work on what needs to be done to make this situation doable. How's that sound?"

"Sounds fine," I say, measuring my words. "I'd appreciate that."

"Great. There's just one other thing."

"Okay." I nod.

"Do you feel any regrets at all about . . . ?"

"Yes!"

I pick up an angel ornament and rub its face with my fingertip. "I mean, I can't change what's happened, but sure, I feel . . . I feel sooo yucky, and I don't know if this yucky feeling will ever go away, but since you asked . . ."

Anya whispers, "That's all I wanted to know. Now, let's finish decorating this tree, all right?"

I nod, cross my fingers, and rub the angel's face again.

11

Neil

Early Sunday morning I wake up and hear noises. My wife is listening to "What's Going On" by Marvin Gaye, singing along while she rattles pots and pans in the kitchen. I sit up on the sofa, relieved that Dani has finally made her way home, and the holiday weekend is almost over. I glance at my watch and know what time it is. It's the Lord's Day; time for some much-needed weight lifting.

I run upstairs to the bedroom, close and lock the door. I bypass taking a shower. If I get dressed real fast, I can make the first service, hear the choir sing, bone up on the latest announcements, and see what's been going on at Solomon's Temple.

"Welcome to Weight Lifting 101."

I am sitting near the rear of the church, hearing the compelling words and voice of Pastor Solomon, something I haven't heard in a few weeks. There must be a good thousand folks here today, and 50 percent of the congregation is men. That's probably why so many women come here, too. Light, dark, medium complexion, thin, robust sistas, and all smelling like fresh-cut roses in a florist's shop.

"Now, ya'll knowwww how I am." The congregation nods, some laugh out loud. "You know how hard it is sometimes for me to lift y'all's weights, make your burdens lighter. You know how bad I wanna slap something on ya this morning. Get all up in your Kool-Aid, tell all your business."

I smile and shift in my seat. Even though the sanctuary is packed, I feel like there's nowhere to hide, that I'm butt naked. Pastor Sol's words have a way of making me feel that way.

He continues slowly and thoughtfully. "I can see the anxiety in your faces sometimes. When I take a little survey and ask, 'How many of y'all got your party on at the club last night?' and y'all look at me with that frozen, what-the-heck-you-talkin-'bout face." Pastor Sol laughs. "I know some of you want me to stick to the Bible, preach strictly based on what's in the Word. You cry out, 'Talk about Paul.' But I wanna talk about y'all."

Every time he says this, we laugh. I guess bare-boned truth can do that to you.

"But see, don't blame that uncomfortable feeling you get on me. Don't even credit the good feelings you get on me. When I preach the gospel of Jesus, the good news, well, it's s'posed to make you feel good just like a good woman can do. But do make sure the woman's your wife—"

My eyes widen. I rise up and head for the men's room. It's just too early in the morning to listen to this. But even though listening to Pastor's spiritual instruction feels uncomfortable, I know it's something I need, whether I want it or not.

By the time I make it back to my seat, Pastor Sol is getting down and dirty and doing some good preaching at the same time. He's talking about how he's not the Sin Police. He can't follow his congregation home and spy on us, to see if we're making the right choices. He says the eyes of the Lord are in every place, and his are only in his head. And that's fine with me. I kind of like the fact that the Lord will be my judge—at least He will be fair, and know *why* I do what I do. Maybe He'll understand even if I don't. And believe it or not, after church service ends an hour later, and I rise up out of there and grab a bulletin on the way out, I do feel lighter, like my pastor's words have chased a hundred demons from my mind. My heart is lifted, I am hopeful, more focused, and for that I certainly am thankful.

That Sunday afternoon I convince Anya to go with me to the Mister Car Wash on Hillcroft between Bellaire and the Southwest Freeway. My Explorer is so filthy you can blow on it and a puff of smoke will rise up and cloud your vision.

Anya and I enter the car-wash driveway and pull into the lane closest to the building. Attendants with pad in hand are writing up service orders and trying to convince us to get the Red Carpet special, a deluxe service that can make your wallet fifty bucks lighter.

Anya begins digging around the cup holder and console, picking up soiled snot rags, empty soda cans, and receipts from when I've made trips to the gas station and filled up the tank.

"Oooh, Neil, how can you stand it? All this trash. The second it takes to throw stuff on the floor of your car, you could've tossed it in a garbage can. They do have plenty of 'em in Houston, you know."

"I know." I blush. "You're right."

"What's this?" she asks. She's holding up a glossy color advertisement.

"Oh, I got that from church today. I barely glanced at it myself. What's it say?"

She hands me the ad.

SOLOMON'S TEMPLE PRESENTS

AN OLDIES BUT GOODIES GOSPEL CONCERT

FEATURING SONGS FROM THE 70S AND 80S

COME LISTEN TO SOLOMON'S TEMPLE MUSIC DEPARTMENT PERFORM FAVORITES AS RECORDED BY ANDRAE CROUCH AND THE DISCIPLES, REV. JAMES CLEVELAND, WALTER HAWKINS, THE WINANS, TWINKIE CLARK AND THE CLARK SISTERS, AND MORE

ATTIRE: DRESS IN YOUR BEST 70S AND 80S GEAR
(WE KNOW YA STILL HOLDING ON TO IT)

FRIDAY, DECEMBER 19

7:30 P.M.

Anya laughs and snatches the ad from my hand. "Hey, now this is something I might want to get into. You know I love me some gospel."

"Oh yeah," I say. We pull up to the vacuum cleaner area and an attendant writes up my ticket for deluxe service. I leave my keys in the ignition and Anya follows me inside. We wait in line to pay the cashier.

"If I go, would you go, too?" my wife asks. She's standing next to me, looking up at my face. I'm seven inches taller than her. That makes me feel good. I never wanted to date a woman who towered over me. A woman with great height would make me think she'd be able to step on my head, and pin me to the sidewalk so I couldn't escape.

"Yeah, I might go to the concert, as long as you don't invite Dani along. I still don't see why you kept her around the house so long. Y'all best friends now or something?"

She giggles and steps forward even though the line hasn't moved.

"Hey, you think that's funny?" I ask. "Sometimes I wonder about you."

"That's good, Neil. If you're wondering about me, there's hope."

I don't say anything. I pay the bill with my debit card, then Anya and I go to wait in the lobby. There are vending machines, several metal benches, and magazines strewn around. The other customers have stepped outside, so we're the only people in this small space.

"I wanna go because I've never heard of this type of concert," Anya remarks, "so that would be different."

"Right," I say, "it *is* different."

"Speaking of different, that's how I feel sometimes. When I go to the concert, I—I hope everyone at the church doesn't expect me to look and act just like them."

"They're not gonna do that, Anya."

"Oh yeah? Then why do I feel that way?"

"Since when did you care what other people think?"

"I—I dunno." She shrugs. "Just a question that I wish you'd answer."

"You feel different because you have this phobia where you think that going to a church is going to change you into someone you don't want to be."

"Well, Neil, I don't want to be one thing at home and a whole other thing soon as I step foot in church. Ain't that what you do?"

"What's with the attitude, Anya? You were so happy this morning."

"Neil, I don't see how you can do what you've done and still show your face in church."

"Why not, Anya? I—I go to church because I need Jesus, just like everybody else."

"But don't you feel like a . . . ?"

"No, I do not. Why would I? If the criterion for believing in God is perfection, nobody would be there. That's why you oughta come more often than you do."

"No, nooo. Mentally, I am not ready to roll up in church. When I start going, I want to come correct."

"But see, Anya, that's the wrong attitude. That's why some other certain types don't go, because they're thinking they don't belong. You'll never see Jesus blocking the entrance to Solomon's Temple just because some gang bangers or convicted killers come up to the doorstep."

Anya folds her arms tightly across her chest.

"Look," I tell her, "I don't go because I live perfect every second, I go because I *don't*. I need strength to help me get where I need to be."

"But—"

"What do you think I should do? Quit going? And what would that prove?"

She doesn't say anything.

"Get past my wrongs, dear Anya."

"It's not the adultery part. It's . . ."

"The baby? He's the evidence? If I hadn't gotten Dani pregnant, no one would have to know, right? Are you saying you're scared people at church will find out? And what if they do? Because who says it's okay to single out folks and proclaim, 'Oh, you aren't worthy to be in a church because blah, blah, blah'? Or 'You're the *H* word, which everyone thinks Christians are anyway."

"Well, some of them——"

"Don't judge everybody based on a few people," I remark. "Don't judge me, either. The fact that you have to ask what I'm thinking and how I feel proves you don't know my heart."

"Well . . ."

"Let me say this. Just because I dress the part, act the part, and look like I walk the walk doesn't make me any better than Pastor Sol. But God knows my heart. Even if I do wrong, at least I get the benefit of Him knowing why I've done wrong, which is more than what I can say for you, who only sees my actions and not the motivations behind them."

She coughs and clears her throat and attempts to look out the bay window. I realize that I may have gone too far.

"I apologize if this hurts you." I step up to her. "That's not my intention."

"Oh, here we go. People with good intentions always end up doing the foulest things," Anya says. "Intentions mean nothing. Actions say it all."

"Yeah, but——" I stop short when an elderly man enters the lobby.

Anya grabs my arm and lowers her voice. "Hey, you've had your say. Let me think about this concert thing for a few days and I'll let you know if I want you to get me a ticket, all right, Neil?"

"Okay, Anya."

The next Sunday, I don't quite make it to church. Anya and Reese pay a little visit to her mother. As soon as they leave, I head over to Dani's.

When I get there, Dani's rearranging potted plants on her balcony. I go to Braxton's room and play with him, nudging his chin with my fingers, and making him laugh until his joy spills over into my heart. Once he starts yawning, I lay him in his crib and take my exhausted self to the living room. Dani is camped out on the sofa. She sees me walking in and pats the space next to her. I just stand there but she smiles and pats the space again, moving over a few inches and giggling. She went to the beauty salon yesterday and got these spiral curly ringlets put in her hair, loads of curls that bounce and touch her shoulders. I stare at her hair and go sit next to her.

She's wearing a pair of black workout shorts with white stripes on the sides. I have on an old sky-blue muscle tee and some matching warm-up shorts. Dani's white tank top is clinging to her breasts, which are pointed like they're trying to get my attention. I take a deep breath. Dani sniffs and jams her nose against my bare shoulder. I put my arm around her and squeeze.

"Why are you sniffing, Dani? What you smell, huh?"

"You don't want to know what I smell." She smiles in my face. Using my finger, I reach out and rub the tip of her nose, just like I do with my son. Her nose is oily. I wipe off her moisture on my shirt.

Dani sighs and closes her eyes. She places her thigh on top of mine and starts bobbing her bare feet up and down. I'm a thigh man and I stare at her toned thighs.

I clear my throat. "So, what are your plans for today?"

"Umm, nothing. Just hanging out at home. May go window-shopping later today. And you?"

Her voice is strong yet soothing. I lightly caress her thigh with my fingers. She rolls her eyes and grins.

"When Brax wakes up again, my plans are to hang out with my son."

"Am I invited? Huh, Neil?" She presses closer to me, moving her arm inside my shirt, her hands crawling underneath the fabric until her fingers grip my nipple and squeeze.

"Whoa . . ."

"Shhh, stop tripping, Neil. This isn't a biggie. So don't be getting all hot and bothered."

"Too late now."

She looks in my eyes and brings her mouth closer, pressing her lips against mine. She closes her eyes. But I don't. I just watch her and kiss her, and kiss her some more. I have a strong urge to place my fingers in all her curls, which would probably make her mad. Or would it?

She finally releases me and wipes her mouth. I clear my throat.

"Dani," I say, "can we go back to doing what we used to do a long time ago?"

"Huh? Like . . . ?"

"C—could you . . . will you give me some head?"

"Will you eat me out?"

"I'm ready right now."

Dani moves her hands underneath her tank top, staring at me and massaging her breasts, moving them round and round. "Neil, is oral sex sex?"

"Nooo, nope." I shake my head. I want to pull off my shorts, then remove hers.

"Why you say that?"

"Because," I say, staring at her while she works her breasts, "it's just not. You can't get pregnant from oral sex, th—that's why."

"Jeez," she giggles. "You sound like a high-schooler."

"Dani, can we just—C'mon, please." I grab her elbow and yank it.

"Okay, I'll do it. I want you, Neil. I want you."

"I want you, too."

"Do you?" she whispers.

Dani lifts her tank top, pulls it over her head, and arches her back till her bones pop. She's braless. Her breasts are plump, perfect, ready.

"Suck my titties, okay, Neil? Please?"

She goes to lie on the floor, with her legs spread, shorts still on, hands resting next to her side, fingers thumping the carpet.

I join her, bending over her body and staring at her flat belly until she playfully pops me on the cheek. Wow! A *flat* belly.

"C'mon, Neil. What cha waiting on?"

"Who am I?" I ask.

"You're a . . . fireman . . . and I'm totally on fire."

I snatch one of her nipples in my mouth and suck its hardness. Like reaching inside a purse, I slide my fingers deep into her lavender-lace cheeky pants and massage the moistness between her legs, which is just how I like it.

"Mmmm, God, Neil . . ."

"You ready for the fireman to put out your fire?"

I move down and place my lips against her inner thighs, which have zero cellulite. Lightly kissing her flesh, I notice tears springing in my eyes. There's just something about Dani . . . I tug off her shorts, enjoying how warm her legs feel. I press my lips against her panties, kissing her moistness while her cheeky pants are still on. She writhes and wiggles, makes a contented face, and groans.

"Neil, I–I heard you like to s–suck things." She's gasping. "That include me, too?"

I moan. Dani clutches my head tight between her hands. I nibble on her lavender lace some more and watch her legs shake. I slide off her cheeky pants and my tongue laps her like a deer drinking from a river, sucking, licking her, feeling her buck and squirm and moan underneath me. And for one hour straight I do Dani. I sloppily suck her breasts. I devour her toes, fingertips, and elbows. I suck on her inner thighs, ears, neck, and lips, smearing my entire face against her moist vagina and munching away until she comes, arching her back and crying out, "Ooooooh mmm, damn."

When it's all over, our bodies are slippery with sweat. And her beautiful curls look like she got caught in an unexpected rainstorm, her long strands of hair pressed flat on her head.

Dani makes me feel like a dehydrated man thirsty for water, not satisfied till I drink from her well. So what does it mean if I drink—but still feel thirsty?

12

Anya

*It's almost mid-December. Neil has fled the house for the weekend, em-*barking on his customary fishing trip where he treks down to Galveston with a few of his buddies. I have never wanted to accompany him—besides, he wouldn't allow that, anyway. He says men need to get away and bond sometimes, and because he only does this twice a year, I have nothing to whine about. Besides, he says, it's in our arrangement.

"Oh, yeah, right, the arrangement," I said to him an hour ago. "Funny you mention that whenever it's convenient and will benefit you, Neil."

He chuckled in his cell phone.

"Sure, laugh at me now," I told him. "You're probably halfway there, so my little arguments aren't gonna change a thing."

"You said it, Anya. Anyway, take care. I'll be back home Sunday night."

It's Friday afternoon. Miss Reesy has succumbed to the lure of sleep. She's spread out on the floor of the den. I need to nudge her so her body won't be too stiff when she wakes up. I hear no sounds in the house, not the splashing dishwasher, or the knocks and taps of the hot-water heater. Peace at home is incalculably divine, isn't it? The quiet is rare and I need this time to think, ponder the future.

I place my rump in a rocking chair. But the phone rings before I can get good and settled.

Caller ID says *Unavailable*. So who is it this time? Pushy telemarketer who just got to work? Determined bill collector who pays his bills by harassing broke women?

"Hello," I mumble.

"I, uh, I didn't know what else to do."

"Huh?"

"It's, uh, Dani. I didn't want to call you but . . ."

"What's the matter now?" She calls every few days wanting something, wanting nothing. I try to be patient but . . .

"Brax won't stop crying," she tells me. "His forehead feels hot. I've done everything—"

"You call a doctor?"

"No, no, I didn't. The co-pay is sixty bucks." She sucks in her breath. "And we just went to the doctor a week and a half ago. Turned out to be nothing major and I don't have money to—"

"I thought you were earning money from your gift basket—"

"That doesn't stop bills from piling up," Dani says. "Look, Anya, please tell me something." I hear Brax wailing in the background. I wonder why this girl doesn't call her family, but then I remember she probably considers *us* her family. I stand up and begin pacing.

"Uh, tell you what," I respond. "Bring him over here so I can figure out the problem. I can't tell what's wrong if I can't see him. If it's urgent, I can take him to the doctor."

She whimpers and agrees. I want to spit. I want to scream. Even though I pat myself on the back for wanting to face the reality of this situation, at times the pressure closes in on me, especially when I'm forced to hear from Dani on days when I'm just not in the mood. So I hang up, say a quick prayer, and wait for Neil's problem to come over here and become mine.

Once Dani arrives and brings Brax in the house, the first thing I produce is an ear thermometer. Every mother in America needs to have one.

"Dani, this won't take long. Let's go up to my room."

Hearing Dani walk up the stairs behind me is strange. Her footsteps sounds light and sophisticated compared to my hard stomps. Moments later, I can't believe she's in my and Neil's bedroom. It feels awkward, but she needs to be here.

Dani sets Braxton in my arms and I place him on the bed. Puddling tears cloud his eyes. Through his wetness I notice him seeking his mother. That stings. I take his temp. Within seconds the reading says a hundred degrees.

"Dani, this is a tough call. I can see if he were a hundred and two or higher. Then we'd have to go to the ER. But maybe if we get him cooled off, give him lots of liquids, and pat his face and chest with a lukewarm towel, his temp might go down."

"Yeah, all right. I'm guessing he's still recovering from the virus he caught last week. He was really suffering, and I sure don't want it to flare up again."

Within an hour, and after lots of TLC, the baby's restlessness and tears subside. He clutches two of his mom's fingers, until sleep takes over and she's able to pull away from his frightened grip.

Now Dani is sitting on the edge of the chair bending forward, her head sunk in her hands, strands of long, wild hair falling about her face. I lift the baby and press him against my breast, walking a few paces, and patting him gently on his back. He smells like newness, his skin is so soft. Holding Brax reminds me of when Reesy was his age. I take him to the nursery, lay him in his crib, and notice my arms trembling right before I close the door.

When I return to my room, Dani is peering out the window.

"What are you thinking about, Dani?"

She speaks but doesn't face me. "How good and exemplary you are."

"Save it."

She turns around slowly. "Seriously. I'm sure you're cursing me out inside your head." She laughs, then stops. "I really shouldn't be here, right? Under the circumstances, I don't know any other woman who would let me in her bedroom." Her voice is a whisper, a stunned acknowledgment that, yes, I am married to her guy.

"I don't want to claim that I'm good, Dani. That would be stretching it. I have my days, you know, when I don't feel like a good person, when I don't think good thoughts or say good things. But that's beside the point. What I wanna know is, why'd you do it?"

Her eyes enlarge, crammed with bewilderment. "Do what? Call you about Brax?"

"Why'd you sleep with Neil?"

She lowers her head, stares past my voice. "Anya, didn't we already have this conversation? Don't say anything. I know the an—"

"That was then, this is now. I'm nobody's fool—not for long, any-way—and I want you to explain what possesses you to continue lying down with my husband after we've had our talks. I've welcomed you into my—"

I swing around and tightly close my eyes. If a wall was near enough, I'd either slap it with all my might, or lean against it for support.

"Anya, you don't know . . . what you're talking about. W—we don't do that. Not anymore. I can't remember the last time . . ."

I turn back around and face her while she's still yakking, unim-pressed by the way she wildly swings her arms while she's explaining.

"You're a terrible liar, Dani. I know what you've done, and all I have to say is this: Brax is business, and business is business, and I'm fine with that. But please don't sleep with Neil anymore."

"Didn't you hear me? W—why are you—"

"I'm sure Neil never bothered to tell you this, but a little while ago, on a Sunday night, he came home smelling different. Acting peculiar. And when I sat next to him, we ended up holding hands and, to be hon-est, one thing led to another. We ended up here, in the bedroom. Imag-ine how I felt when I started kissing my husband's body, my lips are on his thighs, and a piece of long, curly hair ends up in my mouth."

Dani's eyes flicker with the hurt of betrayal. She takes wide steps to-ward the bedroom door. I rush next to her and put my hand on the door-knob. Her fingers fall on top of mine and feel as slippery as raindrops.

"Look, Dani. You don't have to explain anything to me, but you'd better hope I never find your hair on his body again."

Dani tries to pry my fingers from the doorknob. I pull my hand away, wiping off her guilty sweat. She leaves the room mumbling, headed toward Braxton.

Truthfully, even though that's my husband's kid, a kid he loves more than life itself, I hope it's a long time before I see Brax or his mama again.

Sometimes hope rewards us, and gives us what we've wished for. Other times hope remains hope, not yet fulfilled. I guess this is why Dani shows up at my house the next afternoon unannounced. I go to the front door and peer through the peephole, noting her wide eyes, which are crammed with worry. She is pressing my doorbell, wearing out her welcome with her constant ringing before she's even slipped into the house.

Knowing it would be wrong to pretend I'm not home, especially with Reesy standing next to me yelling, "Mommy, open the door," I swing the door open.

"Yes," I say.

"May I come in?"

"What do you *want*?"

"I'm sorry, Anya, but I—I think I left something important here yesterday."

I let her in, actually relieved that she's standing in front of my face. The way I put her on blast yesterday, she could've headed straight for Galveston. Screw me and my warnings. Every whore doesn't scare easily. That much I know.

"Is what you left upstairs?" I ask. "What is it? I'll look."

"Well, may I go? It's in the baby's room."

I flinch. "Where is he, by the way?"

"I begged Audrey to give me some free time. Literally," she laughs. "I needed to do a little grocery shopping and run out to the ceramics store. Told her I'll pay her when I get the chance. I have some things lined up—more baskets to tend to, actually. So she came and got—"

"Okay, okay, never mind. Go on upstairs."

"Thanks, Anya."

"Mommy, where's my brother?" Reesy grabs and tugs at my hand, pulling me toward the den.

"Reesy, I wish you wouldn't call him that. Just call him Braxton."

"I do call him Braxton. I love Braxton. That's my baby brother."

"Who told you to call him that? Dani?"

"Auntie Vette did."

"She did? What a bitch."

"Mommy!"

"Oh, God." I kneel and cover my daughter's ears with my hands. I kiss her on the cheek and squeeze her tiny frame, feeling the hardness of her bones. "I'm so sorry, Precious. That slipped out."

"Ooooh, Mommy, you said a bad word, you gotta put a dollar in the jar."

I stand up and take a breath so deep it feels like I'm about to disappear. I go to the kitchen, find my wallet, and hand over a dollar to Reesy. She removes the lid from a pickle jar and adds the bill to the other ones. Recently, I promised to stop using so much profanity. I feel tremendous guilt when I forbid my daughter to watch certain TV shows and movies that have tons of curse words I use myself.

"Thank you, Cursing Police Woman." I smile and pat the top of Reesy's braids. "You're doing a great job. You are, you are."

"I know, Mommy."

"Thanks, kiddo."

"Love you, Mommy."

I want to say "I love you, too," but suddenly Dani is bounding down the stairs, beaming.

I give her the eye. "I am assuming you found whatever you were looking for."

"Yep." She waves a credit card. "I always put these in the pockets of my jackets, and yep, my jacket was here, and so was my card, thank goodness."

"Good. Where was the jacket?"

"Lying on a chair in Brax's room. But guess what else I found?"

I freeze.

"What?" I ask, annoyed.

"Is this something that you've seen before?"

She opens up a closed fist. In the center of her palm is my diamond ring. I yelp and jump a foot in the air. "Give me that. Oh my God! Where'd you find this? I gotta call Neil."

I run to the phone, heart joyfully lifted, and dial up my husband on his cell.

He sounds relieved and tells me, "Some things you lose you find them again. Other things you lose are lost forever."

I have no idea what he's talking about, and I just laugh and hang up the phone.

"Whew, Dani, you just don't know . . ." I place the ring on my finger and the corners of my mouth draw upward.

"It *is* gorgeous," she says, eyes flickering with admiration.

"Well, I guess I must've taken it off one day," I tell her, and glance at my hand. "I was cleaning the walls up there. God, I almost had given up."

Dani smiles, nods absently.

"Well, uh . . ." I frown. "Hmmm, jeez."

"Oh, I better be on my way. I'm sure Audrey is counting the minutes till I come back. She does that, you know."

"No, I didn't know. But I'll let you go. Thank you sooo much. I mean it. I don't know what else to say."

"You've said enough, Anya. Good-bye. And bye, Miss Reesy."

Solomon's Temple.

I cannot stand bell-bottoms, but that's what Neil decides to wear. Bell-bottoms that are part of one of those seventies ugly Angel flight suits. It has the tan jacket, vest, flared pants, and silk shirt with the pockets. Pure D ugly. Then there's that huge, floppy Afro wig. Ridiculous. I can't talk, though. Check me out with my button-down shirtdress, complete with a wide metal belt. I'm sporting some black fishnet stockings and these short black boots with a two-inch heel. I feel silly yet wild. There's a disposable camera in my purse, and I can't wait to see what everyone else looks like. Then I want to settle in and listen to the concert.

Neil and I haven't been out together in weeks. His fault, not mine. Whenever I suggest we go somewhere, he's not up to it. But tonight, we'll see what happens tonight.

"Anya, look over there." Neil is talking to the back of my head. He is a few steps behind me trying to keep up. I am walking fast trying to locate our seats.

"Anya!" he yells louder. But the pre-concert music is louder than he is. A great excuse to continue walking, huh? I am gripping this big old purse, clutching it to my side while it bangs against my thigh. I'm partly trying to get away from Neil, and peeking at the other concertgoers' outfits.

Platforms. Long-sleeve flowered shirts. Dashikis. Some kids are wearing Afro wigs covered by apple hats, looking just like the Jackson 5, but not as adorable. I don't feel as silly now that I know there are other self-possessed people here willing to dress the part.

Lights are flashing across the room like we're at a nighttime football game. This oughta be fun.

Neil stands next to me. Stares. "Whatcha think so far? You feel like running out of here screaming?"

"Not yet, silly," I tell him. "I'll be all right. It doesn't even feel like church. I don't know if that's good or bad. Hope nobody starts stripping."

"Don't even worry about that. Nothing that crazy is gonna happen in here."

As soon as the concert begins, I sneak out my mini tape recorder and turn it on.

"You know you aren't supposed to have any recording devices in here," Neil says, pressing his mouth against my ear.

I smile at him and shrug, then bob my head and clap my hands to the music. A woman is singing a Tramaine Hawkins favorite, "Change." The music takes me back years, makes me feel nostalgic about all the fun Neil and I had attending other concerts. Stevie Wonder, CeCe Winans, Kirk Franklin. And now that we're at this concert, I am focused on enjoying the singer perform "Change." I love this song, even though I'm not sure what's so great about change.

After the concert we head out to China Bear, a popular Chinese-food joint off the Southwest Freeway in the city of Stafford. It is so packed, you rub shoulders with people whenever you get up to walk somewhere. When we were at the concert and had settled in, I didn't feel self-conscious about my clothing. But now?

"Jeez, Neil, people are staring at us."

"What? No, they aren't."

"Yes, they are," I insist. "I think we're scaring the Chinese people. They might think we belong to a gang or something."

"People in gangs get hungry, too. Don't worry about it."

"Easy for you to say," I huff, and lower my eyes, avoiding all eye contact with the people who are filling their plates at the buffet. I get some shrimp fettuccine, octopus, sushi, rice, and fried clams.

Neil gets four times as much food as I do. His smiling and waving at people makes me want to slink to the floor.

"So, did you like the concert?" he says.

I nod. My mouth is too full to respond with words.

"I'm glad." He nods. "I enjoyed myself, too. The music was banging, the singing was top notch. It felt kind of good being there with you. You need to get out the house more."

"Would that keep you at home more?"

Neil stares at me.

I squirm in my seat and lower my voice. "I want you to do something."

"What?"

"Promise me first."

"Anya . . ."

"C'mon, c'mon, c'mon. I *really* want you to do this."

"Do what?" he asks.

I retrieve the mini tape recorder from my purse and hold it up.

Neil grins. "You want me to start singing? La-la-la-la."

"No, silly," I laugh. "Wait a sec." I fast-forward the tape a little bit. "Okay, Neil," I say, getting serious. "I am recording right now. This has to do with our arrangement. I want you to verbally promise me you will never sleep with you-know-who again."

Neil lays his fork on his plate, which is half-filled with shrimp and veggies.

"Neil?" I prod. I feel like a snake with feet and big breasts, but maybe this effort will trigger vital changes in our relationship. Maybe in this regard, change can result in good.

"I don't do that, anyway," he claims, and resumes eating, "so why are you trying to make me promise not to do what I don't do?"

Lying punk. I want to rise to my feet, but hesitate.

"Neil, if what you're saying is true, then you won't have a problem vowing on tape not to do that, right?"

Neil stops chewing. He peers far beyond my head and plays with an imaginary piece of paper. I want to place my fingers around his neck and choke him. What's wrong with him?

"Neil, remember the first time we had sex after I had the second miscarriage?"

"Not really."

"I remember . . . the bleeding, the pain. I thought I was having another miscarriage even though I wasn't pregnant anymore."

"Well, uh . . ."

"I'll never forget how you didn't look directly at me, you kept your eyes closed."

"Isn't that what people do when they have sex?"

"But this was different, like your mind wasn't on me, but on something else. And it took too much of my energy to get in the mood. It was like you let down the curtain during the middle of the act, and it fell on my head. Kaboom, all over. So I felt like . . . like I failed you. Again."

"But Anya," he protests, "you didn't fail—"

"Ah, back then you probably wanted me to think that you weren't affected, probably because you knew how much I was." I pause and suck in my breath. "Neil, you might not realize this, but your attitude grew a little cold toward me, even though you tried to act like everything was the same. But everything wasn't. You changed."

"No, Anya, *you* changed. You acted like an anaphrodisiac, and you somehow thought I didn't want sex, even though that wasn't true."

"But Neil, remember the first time we argued a few weeks after the loss? You felt like enough time had passed, and you didn't have to be so polite anymore? Y—you told me you loved me, but you would have loved to have another baby even more. I mean, that was very insensitive . . ."

"It's not like it sounds," he remarks, lowering his eyes.

"If it wasn't how it sounds, then why'd you say it? I took you at your word, Neil, whether the words came out wrong or not. I mean, for God's sake, you might as well have chopped off my head, or threw acid in my face. I never told you how I felt, but I never forgot. Your words hurt, Neil. Yet your drive is always strong, and sexually you were able to rebound. But me? Whether you realize it or not, words like that don't exactly make a woman want to start doing a lap dance."

"Okay, that was so long ago I barely remember." He rubs his eyes like the ceiling lights have suddenly become brighter. "I thought we were trying to eat."

"Nothing stopping you from eating," I say, jaw firm.

"And what does all that have to do with right now?"

"The fact that you refuse to do what I'm asking you right now doesn't make me want to run and do a lap dance, either."

Neil simply stares at me, lips pressed tight.

"Now, can you just make a little effort," I say, and gesture at the recorder, "so I know where you're coming from?"

His eyes are blank and his stare drifts right past me. "I–I'm s—," he mumbles.

I turn off the recorder and throw it inside the purse.

"I'll be waiting in the car," I tell him. And this time, when I walk past all the booths with all the curious people, I could care less that they're staring at me.

13

Dani

I'm at home. Neil is about to come through my apartment door, a door he hasn't walked through in several weeks. I am dressed in a lilac-colored loose-fitting long-sleeve shirt that extends over some flimsy old navy sweats. They're somewhat funky-looking, but I am too in love with them to pitch them just yet.

I haven't had a chance to take a shower. I've been diligently cleaning up, something I hate doing. I'm so pissed right now that I'm scrubbing areas of the apartment I didn't even know existed. Sticky scum on the window ledges. Puffs of dust behind the TV units.

The doorbell rings and I hear a few light taps. I look at myself. Patches of dirt are dotting the front of my shirt. And I've run out of laundry detergent.

Another light tap. Why's he doing that?

I open the door. Neither Neil nor I can muster up a heartfelt grin.

"Can you hurry up so I can come inside?" he fusses.

"Come inside—"

"In your home, Dani. Stop acting silly."

"Fine, okay, all right, Jesus," I say, and let him in.

Neil is carrying two large Dillard's shopping bags. When he just stands in the middle of the room acting like he can't do what he normally does when he comes over, I tell him, "Have a seat, you," and point to the couch.

The stereo is on. A Minnie Riperton song plays softly in the background, talking 'bout "Do you wanna ride inside my love?"

"So," I say, "I suppose all those things are for the baby?"

He nods and starts pulling colorfully wrapped gifts from the bags.

"But Christmas was yest—"

"Dani, she wouldn't let me out the house, so . . ."

"I don't believe that. Anya is big but she's not *that* big. You could've pushed past her. Wrestled her to the floor . . ."

"Look, I didn't think getting here was that critical. Brax is only a few months old. He doesn't even know it's Friday, let alone that yesterday was December twenty-fifth."

"I'm sorry, Neil. I am. I—"

"Don't." He stares at all the gifts. "Let's get this over with."

I rise to my feet and help place the goodies on my dining-room table. There are eight boxes in all. Seven are wrapped in silver metallic paper. One is wrapped in gold paper. It has *DF* on it. I'm shocked he had enough guts to write my initials on the gift card.

"I jotted that on there on the way over here."

It's like he's reading my mind. Well, since he can read minds, does he know how freaking pissed I am? Sure he does. Neil knows me. He knows.

"Where's Brax?" he says.

"Leave him alone. I'm happy he took his nosy butt to sleep finally." I smile, thinking of my son and how he enjoys sitting in his swing staring at me while I prance around the room mumbling to myself and wanting to pull out chunks of my hair some days.

"I can do the honors," I say, and begin ripping gift wrap off Braxton's presents. Two sweaters, a baseball short set, striped sleepers, cotton rompers, and an adorable denim outfit with matching hat. Quality things that Brax will outgrow very soon, but of course, that doesn't matter to Neil.

"Awesome, Neil. You are too good." I am grateful for Neil, realizing that some kids wouldn't get this much attention from their father.

"I—I didn't get you anything." I shrug.

"You didn't?"

"No."

"Why not, D?"

I laugh. "What you call me?"

"Look, I don't care that you didn't get me anything, Dani. Go ahead and open your present."

He doesn't have to plead. I pick up the gold box. Shake it. "Hmmm, it sounds very light, Neil. And it's too big to be something small and expensive. What you get me? House slippers?"

"Yep, you are tooo smart, Dani."

"Stop lying. This big ole box isn't even shaped like . . . whatever. You're insane, Neil. And you're a liar, too." He steps up to me again, looking down into my eyes. I lift up my face and he kisses me quickly on the lips, then turns and looks cautiously at my front door.

"Look, if that's how it's laying now . . . I don't know, Neil."

"Me either. I don't have long, though. Anya probably has me on a timer. I told her I'd—"

I cover my ears and shake my head.

"Let's get to my present," I tell him, ripping the paper off the box. Inside the box is another box, and another box, and another box.

"You are *insane*, Neil."

I am giggling with hysteria by now. Whatever he bought better be worth all the trouble I'm going through.

"Ahhhh!" I scream when I open the final box.

Seven sets of lace cheeky pants. One for each day of the week. Orange, turquoise, lemon, black, leopard, crimson, and a scandalous hot pink. Mmmm.

Neil looks at his watch, then at me. "I'll race you to the shower," he yells, and takes off running. I follow behind this solid hunk of a man, removing my soiled shirt and sweatpants, and giggling like a fool while he strips off his clothes and gets the shower working: steamy and hot . . . just the way we like it.

It's one hour after our shower episode. My phone has rung three times within that hour, and caller ID indicates that all calls are coming from Neil's home. But Neil's not at home, he's with me. Brax is being held by his dad. Cuddled and fed a bottle of juice. The baby fluctuates between screeching and humming. And his mouth keeps opening and closing because he's so greedy he wants more.

I'm slumped next to Neil, my head pressed against his shoulder.

"What we gonna do?" I mumble, the question I've not wanted to ask. Neil gazes into his son's piercing eyes.

"Something's gotta give, don't you think? She keeps calling," I complain. "I'm not answering . . ."

"Turn off the ringer, Dani."

"I want to take that phone and rip the jack out. Does she want anything important or are these social calls?" I'm yelling by now and my face is no longer pressed against my baby's father.

"Dani, let's go back, okay?"

"Nooo." I shake my head furiously. "No going back."

"But we have to," Neil says, and kisses Braxton's lips. "We gotta. If we understand how we got here, maybe it'll help us understand what we need to do." He looks me square in the eyes. "Because we do need to do something."

"No, we don't. We can go on like this. I don't mind. I don't. Really."

He groans and stands up, still holding Brax. I watch father and son. A mixture of feelings settles inside my heart. I have no regrets about giving birth to my precious child. I realize that even if the baby wasn't planned, and the circumstances surrounding his birth weren't perfect, he has a right to exist and have a proper upbringing with supportive parents holding him up. I feel thankful Neil loves Braxton, sacrifices for him.

"You may not wanna hear it," he warns, "but I'm about to recount our history."

I hear a car horn screaming outside my window and sit up with a jolt.

"Does she know . . . where I live, Neil?"

"No, we've never discussed that. I don't have your address written down anywhere, except mentally."

I lean back. "Good. Let's keep it that way. I mean, I feel somewhat safe, but you never know. You won't let Anya hurt me, will you?"

Neil keeps pacing and rocking the baby. I spring to my feet, rush to his side, tug his elbow.

"Promise me you won't let her—"

"Look, I can promise till you're sick of my voice. The Secret Service can promise to protect the president of the United States, but the president can still get hurt, right?"

"Oh, really. Hmmm, so should I start wearing a bulletproof vest or something? Hire a private security firm?"

Right now is the most frustrated I've felt in all the time I've known Neil. And I do not enjoy how that feels. I don't want things to get any worse. I'm open to them getting better . . . but she's the wife. She has what I wish I had—not that I want to be the second Mrs. Meadows. Even if he were to divorce her, it's not as if I'd immediately demand an engagement ring and the promise of a ceremony. Not at all. I don't have to be married. I just want to be happy. I want a strong, good man who cares about me so much that he aches to be a significant part of my life. A man who shows me he loves me by the things he does, not by the words he says.

Neil's voice interrupts my thoughts. "We knew each other from work, but began hanging out during the lunch hour. Solid friends. Nothing romantic lurking in our hearts. At least not in mine."

"Oh, really?" I smirk and sit down on the sofa, crossing my legs and staring at Neil, who is now sitting next to me with Braxton lying comfortably across his lap.

"Yeah, Dani. Remember how I was telling you I had a serious gap in my bed? That I was in a relationship but we were celibate?"

"Right. And you didn't mention that the woman holding out was a wife."

He shrugs, frowns. I wonder if he regrets keeping that info from me.

"I mean, you were still wearing your band, Neil, but you never talked about her, and I didn't want to pry, so I assumed you weren't married, or you were divorced, or maybe separated. I really didn't know what to think."

"Anyway," Neil says, raising the volume of his voice, "I was actually coming to you for advice, suggestions." He's referring to the time when we started hanging out during lunch, and he'd ask if I knew anybody with whom he could hook up. His approach was interesting, to say the least. Like he was out of practice. As a matter of fact, his exact words were, "I haven't been in the game in a while, and I'm kind of rusty. So could you help me out?"

Back then I laughed inwardly, but admired him at the same time. He was a tall, rugged man who seemed so strong, but his vulnerability intrigued me.

"Right," I say, "and I kind of pointed you to a woman on the job. Vivian, remember?"

Neil laughs. "How can I forget? She wore thick glasses. Talked real proper."

"Yes," I admit. "But underneath all her layered clothing was a nice figure. I can tell. I know that women who sometimes hide their body can be something else in the bedroom. A lot of pent-up sexual energy can be hidden inside her."

Neil shrugs and shakes his head like it doesn't matter because Vivian wouldn't qualify.

"And you never thought about getting with me, Neil?" I pouted. "That kinda hurts my feelings."

"No, no, no, it wasn't like that. I—Well, Dani, you were so fine, I assumed you already had a man."

"That's where a lot of men miss out. They think because a woman is attractive, she's unavailable. A lot of times those women are some of the loneliest people on the planet. It's sad. Beautiful-people discrimination should be outlawed."

"Well, I didn't really think of you in that way at first, Dani. You were just a good friend. A woman I could talk to."

I nod. "That's why it surprised me that . . . well, it was so exciting to learn that underneath all our friendship, we had the hots for each other."

"Dani, you know what I liked about you? You'd wink, smile a lot, made me blush a lot."

"I remember. You were sooo adorable, Neil. It was becoming more difficult for me to keep my hands off you. Until the day I admitted to myself I wanted you, and I planted that seed."

Neil stares into my eyes, then leans forward and kisses me on the lips. I love his kisses; they make me forget about all the unpleasant things that exist in my life. He completely takes me there. Although our being a couple seems unlikely, how can I not yearn for our possibilities?

"Okay, back off," I command, wiping my mouth. "I remember saying to you that I was available, and it was like you started looking at me differently . . . as a candidate. And then we did it and, oh my God, it was sooo good." I gasp at the recollection, all the rolling around on my floor, me and Neil horny and naked, underneath my dining room table, screwing each other's brains out.

Neil nods and starts massaging my rigid nipple. "I liked you because you wanted to do the things I wanted to do. So fearless. You'd take it from the rear, you'd do it anytime, anyplace, from the bedroom, to the bathroom, to the kitchen, in every position I wanted, even if it sounded weird or impossible."

"Oh, so you like freaky women, huh Neil?"

"Yep . . . well, no, I want her uninhibited."

"Same thing, you dope."

Neil shrugs and removes his hand from my breast. "If it weren't for you I might never know about these kinds of experiences. And I love how you dress. Classy yet sexy, the best combo."

I beam and lean my head against his shoulder. His musky scent makes me fantasize about what we could be getting into.

"So given our history," I tell him, "I respect the fact that you never wanted to spend the weekend over at my place, or even all night. You always go back home to her," I say. "It's not like you outright dogged your wife. You respectfully dogged her out."

Neil pulls away from me. I feel alone, like he's taken away our special moment.

I cough and clear my throat. "So I've been thinking . . . If you don't want me and Brax in your life, or if you can't be with us, I'd definitely relocate. It would feel too weird to live in the same city as you and not be able to be together."

"Say what? No way I'd let you take my son away from me." Neil rubs Brax's back.

"Don't do that, Neil," I scold. "The baby's gonna be so spoiled."

"This is my little man. My son."

"Oh, that's right. You got your son, didn't you?"

Neil pauses. "I probably shouldn't be telling you this, but after Anya miscarried twice, we never tried again. She got her tubes tied—her decision, not mine. But she blamed me. Then she wanted me to go to this mock funeral for the baby, but I wasn't feeling that."

"Anya had a funeral?"

"Yes! She was emotionally broken down. So I offered her a shopping spree, sent her on a getaway to visit her closest friends, helped out around the house. She doesn't remember all that; she blocked that part out. Everything grew so odd. And so I–I . . ."

I swallow deeply and rub Neil's hand, which is still rubbing Braxton. "I understand, Neil. I do."

"So, Neil, I, uh, wanna ask you a question before you go." His hand grips the doorknob. We've kissed twice already, lots of tongue wrestling and spit action, and he's been unable to just go on and go.

"What you want to know?" he says. Huskiness layers his voice.

"I heard something about you."

"What?" he says.

"You still do things with her?"

"Like what?"

"You know . . . things."

"Not the kind of things you're thinking."

"Whatever." I shrug. "I hope you aren't just saying that, trying to spare my feelings. I'd understand if you gotta go deep-sea diving every now and then. Make her feel good sometimes."

Neil looks like he wants to say something, but swallows a lump instead, a lump that I can see pressing against his throat. That scares me. I want him to be able to talk to me about anything. Sure, his having to service his wife may cause me to feel a twinge of jealousy. But then again, I have no legitimate reason to be jealous. As long as Braxton is around, I imagine that Neil will be, too. That's pretty much a given. I don't know what I'd do if I couldn't see Neil anymore. I wonder if it's his being truly unavailable that makes him so attractive. I've known women who wanted a man as long as someone else wanted him. And as soon as he cut his other women out, the man's appeal was cut out, too. And the women who were once hounding and sweating him like he was a superstar, well, all that running behind the man ceased.

I hope that isn't our case. I feel a strong pull toward this man. I've shared men before but this is different. Neil is committed to me in his own way, and that makes me very special. And when I feel special, I feel happy, like I have a reason for breathing each and every day.

"You know what?" I say, and stand on my tiptoes to cover his cheeks with some final kisses. "You ain't gotta break it all down to me. Do what you need to do, baby."

I blush. He does, too. It's my first time calling him that. I wonder—no, I *know* he likes hearing me say *baby*. I wave bye to Neil. Close and lock the door. Peek out the window. He doesn't look back at my front door. That's okay. I know he'll be back.

14

Neil

"God, forgive me, forgive me, forgive me. Please. I repent. Okay, I'm not sure I can . . . Give me strength, oh Lord."

I'm in the Explorer talking to myself because I don't know if the Lord is going to take me seriously right about now. Is mine the type of plea that gets God's attention?

I say another brief prayer, then hush my mouth. Pastor Sol taught us to do that. He said if we talk to God, we gotta shut up eventually so we can hear if He talks back. After a few moments, a sharp, low voice disturbs my quietness: "You are making a big mistake." I don't know if that's my own uneasiness convicting me or if it's Him, and I squeeze out the voice until it's no longer heard.

Still rattled, I try to level my breathing. I'm sitting in my SUV with the engine running in front of Dani's place. My heart is tugging, yearning, at the same time that my cell phone is ringing. I hear it screaming, *Answer me, you asshole,* but no, I'm not in the mood to answer right now.

I know it's pointless to come up with a lie to tell Anya. She's not down for that. Why would I put myself through that, anyway? I have the right to visit my child. I know I do. Whether Anya has a problem with that or not doesn't matter. I just need her to care about me enough to understand.

I glide into the house from the garage. First thing I see is Anya. She's in the hallway with the closet door open. She's pulling out some winter coats and spreading them on the floor. Lately Houston has been experiencing a warm front, but this week the weatherman predicts cold.

"Hey . . . what's up?" I say with a hopeful voice.

"Hi, Neil. Nothing much." She stops what she's doing and leans her face over to kiss me.

Hmm. Cool.

"What you cook?" I ask.

"Go look," she yells over her shoulder.

I head toward the kitchen. I see one pot on the stove and raise the lid. A half-dozen weenies are floating in some boiling water that's whistling and emitting steam.

Hot dogs?

Is this a joke?

"Anya," I yell louder than I intend.

"What, Neil? I'm kind of busy right now."

"Anya, stop what you're doing for a minute and come here."

I hear loud sighs that ask *Why me?* She walks straight into the kitchen and looks at me, then at the pot, then at me.

"Oh," she laughs.

"Where's the rest of the dinner? Rather, where *is* dinner?"

"Neil, you're so silly. Don't tell me you're too good to eat a hot dog now and then."

"Anya, you know those things don't agree with my stomach."

"Then I suggest you cook something that does. Reese and Vette said there's nothing left in the refrigerator to eat except Oscar Mayer."

"Vette's here?" Lately she's been ducking out, hanging out with her friends. We've barely seen her.

"Yes, she's here. She tried to call you several times on your cell, to ask if you could pick up a few groceries on the way home, but you didn't answer, so . . ."

Anya swings around and struts away from me. As if pulling old funky coats out the closet is way more important than me having something tasty, filling, and edible to eat.

I want to yell at her to come back right now, but then the three musketeers bound into the kitchen. Vette's the ringleader, followed by Reese and Tamika.

"I cannot believe you get your kicks these days hanging out with little girls."

"What you say? Shut up, Neil."

I shrug and reach over to the bread bin to pull out a package of hot dog buns. Vette slaps my hand so hard it stings.

"Why you do that?" I ask.

"Because those dogs are for us." She points at the girls. "I didn't stand up here for fifteen minutes making this meat boil just for you to roll up in here and eat some of it. You got big money, Neil. Go order takeout or something."

"You . . . you." My voice sounds as ridiculous as I feel. I just . . . It's only hot dogs, but that's beside the point. What's going on here? I smell conspiracy. Or is it stupidity?

I start to run up the stairs to take a shower, but suddenly remember that detail has already been taken care of. So after going outside and spending ten minutes watering the lawn, I venture into the kitchen and abruptly stop in my tracks.

Puddles of water are on the counter. Some of the liquid is spilling off the sides and looking like a thin waterfall that cascades to the floor.

"Reese!" I yell.

I go get some paper towels to sop up the spill. The soles of my gym shoes make squeaking noises when I walk on the tile. This isn't good at all.

"Reese, get in here right now. Don't make me have to come after you."

My daughter races into the kitchen; her face is haunted, shoulders stiff.

"You do this?" I ask.

She shakes her head. Her widened eyes never leave my face.

"Reese, don't lie. I know you did this. I just need you to tell me the truth. You won't get a spanking if you tell the truth, but you will if you tell a lie."

"Nope. I didn't do that, Daddy."

"Then who did, your mama?"

Reese nods emphatically, but her lips are quivering. I stoop in front of her until we're at eye level.

"Reese, I love you no matter what you do. So even if you go over-board playing with water and make a big mess, that won't change how I feel. Remember, I got on you two weeks ago about the same thing, but it hasn't changed how I feel about you." My fingertip pushes in her nose like it's a doorbell. Reese stares at me like she's trying to decide if I am lying to her like she lied to me. When it looks like she can't make up her mind, I wrap my arms around her and squeeze her tight. God, she's growing so tall. Where was I when that happened?

"You love me, Reese?"

She nods.

"Were you playing in the water and made this mess even if it was an accident?"

She nods again.

I squeeze her tight. "I'm so proud of you, sweetie."

"You are?"

"Yep."

"What is 'proud'?" she asks.

"It means that I feel happy about you, something you've done. Does that make sense?"

"Yes, Daddy." She looks confused about what to say next.

"Good girl."

"Daddy, what is 'choke the chicken'?"

"Where'd you hear that from?"

"I heard Mommy say she wishes you'd go back and choke the chicken. It sounds sooo gross." She puts her fingers around her neck and pretends to squeeze.

"It *is* gross. Okay, clean up the rest of your mess and go on up to your room."

"Okay, Daddy."

"And don't forget—I love you, Reese."

"I won't forget."

Reese takes one wide step forward, then stops. "You're not going to choke any chickens, are you, Daddy?"

"Believe me, Reese, if I choke anything, it won't be a chicken. Now go on and clean up. I'm tired."

She runs one way. I run the other.

It's the second week of the new year and I have just gotten out of my car and am walking from the parking lot to the building where I work. I pull my coat collar close to my neck. I blow air in the center of my hands and rub them. Houston definitely is getting a reality check this morning. No heat, no comfort.

But I do feel better shortly after arriving in my office. I glance down the hall and see Dani from a distance. I imagine that even with layered clothing—a knit shirt, sweater, and long leather skirt—she still has something special underneath her outfit.

I wince inside. Need to get my mind in the proper place. Lots of work to do but little time to do it.

I'm in my office only fifteen minutes when I look up to find Dani standing in my doorway. She's grinning and has her arms folded across her chest.

"Got a minute?" she says. Her voice is full of elation.

"Not really. What's up?"

"I–I just wanted you to see something."

I glance at my watch.

"Oops. Sorry, Neil. Well, don't mean to bother you, but if you get a quick second, come on down to my office, okay? Only a few doors down from you in case you've forgotten. Bye."

She swings around and disappears from my doorway.

Her perfume lingers. I sniff without much effort and find her in my nostrils. Dani is still here. She's always here.

Soon I back away from my desk and walk down the hall.

Before I reach Dani's door I hear several voices, squealing animated females. I stand a few inches from her door, out of view.

"Dani, he is getting sooo big," I hear someone say. "What a precious one you have. But why'd you take him out in the cold today?"

"Right," Dani says. "That's why I'm pissed. My sitter Audrey had a little emergency. So I brought him to work with me. She's supposed to pick the baby up. Hmm, shouldn't be too long now. I didn't think it would hurt for him to see Mama's job for a quick minute."

What's wrong with this woman? Why does she get into this rattled behavior sometimes? Jaw rigid, I slip back down the hall, reach my office, close and lock the door, and refuse to answer any incoming calls.

I'm not avoiding. I really do need to finish a complex spreadsheet.

But looking at my watch every minute and thinking about what's going on elsewhere keeps me from getting as far along as I'd like.

An hour later, when I step out my office to go to the men's room, I'm happy to take a leak and relieve some tension.

I am headed back to my office when . . .

"Hey there, Neil."

No, no, nooo, get away from me, you.

"Dani told me where your office was and I stopped by but you weren't there." Audrey, a petite redhead with blue contact lenses and dark skin, smiles broadly. She's bundled in a decorative scarf and floor-length black coat, and is holding Brax in his carrier. He gasps and stares at me like, *Don't I know you?* I break eye contact.

"You need to be getting on, right, Audrey?"

I don't wait for her to answer, I just head back to my office. I feel her eyes boring into my back. I close and lock my door again. I'm two seconds from kicking my desk, but I guess I ought to be kicking myself. How many times do I have to go through something to understand I don't control everything? Even with careful planning, why does the unexpected, the unwanted, come threaten what I try to do?

I stay holed up in my office until a little after noon. I deactivate automatic voice mail and I have to call Kyra for any messages I may have missed.

"Uh, yes, you have one from . . . from Danielle Frazier, actually."

"Oh yeah, what she say?"

"She said . . ." Kyra pauses. "Hmm, maybe I should bring this up to you."

"Kyra, just tell me."

"She said she wants you for lunch. Well, that's what she said at first, but then she specifically told me to write down she wants to *meet* you for lunch. Well, ain't none of my business, but that's what—"

"Okay, I–I see. Thanks, Kyra."

Grabbing my coat, I leave my office and go stand in front of Dani's door, gesturing for her to follow me. She nods. I continue down the hall, then ride the elevator to the first floor. Coworkers' voices are weaving in and out of my hearing. I barely see them; I am trying to reach my Explorer without cursing out loud.

I wait until Dani gets into her truck, and then I drive toward Holly Hall Street.

Dani arrives at her apartment two minutes after me and springs from her car. I get out my vehicle and follow her, not saying anything until after she opens the door and steps inside her place.

I remove my coat, slowly. My feet hurt, so the shoes go, too.

When I turn around she's looking up at me, grinning.

I grab her. She tilts her neck and tongues me. The heat is on. I fall into her arms. She weighs much less than I do but is strong enough to bear my weight.

We kiss and I press my hardness into her, pumping against her until she moans. She throws one arm across my back in a slight hug. I close my eyes and enjoy the feeling of her cold cheek against mine. But the inside of her mouth is far from cold. Dani steps away from me, breaking our kiss, and tugs at my necktie.

I open my eyes. She has this piercing look. Breathing hard. Hair disheveled.

"No," I say. "Don't. Can't. Can't do this."

"Oh yeah? Then why'd you have me come over here, Neil, huh?"

"I—I don't know."

She steps back from me, a dubious look on her face.

"You expect me to believe that?" she asks.

"Dani, I . . . you know. You . . . I don't know."

"Say what you have to say, Neil."

"I'm trying."

"You're not trying hard enough."

"Well, Dani, w—why do you act the way you do sometimes? You do a lot of things that make no sense."

"Oh, as if everything you do makes sense." She smirks.

"Stop acting like you don't know what I'm talking about. Dani, you know we agreed that you would not ever bring Brax in to work. I just don't think it's necessary."

"To hell what you think is necessary."

"Dani, what you say?"

"You heard me, you prick!" she screams. "I'm tired of this. All you care about is protecting yourself. You don't care about me."

Oh God, this is not what I want to happen. I reach out for her but she escapes my arms. I hug the air and watch her bail out of the living room.

I grab my coat and get out before I can hear more painful words come from her mouth.

I call my boss to say I need to deal with an emergency and take the rest of the afternoon off from work. My emergency finds me driving to the mostly empty parking lot of Solomon's Temple.

I know that some of the staff is there, but I can't bring myself to go inside. Instead I retrieve my cell phone and dial *67, then the church's twenty-four-hour prayer line. I know the church has caller ID, and even though there are so many members they can't possibly know everyone, I still don't want them to know the call is coming from me.

"Praise the Lord," a recorded voice answers. "You've reached Solomon's Temple's twenty-four-hour prayer line. We'll be with you in a moment."

"In a moment" lasts three minutes—three long minutes that beg me to hang up. What's the use? Who exists who understands the pain I feel inside? Surely no one else knows the battles I fight on a daily basis, feeling split into many pieces, wishing I could please everyone and make myself happy at the same time.

A live female finally answers the line.

"Is there a man available?" I ask.

"No, just me, Sister Zaire. I hope that's okay with you. What's the problem, brother?"

"I—I am doing something that's hurting my family."

"I see." Zaire pauses. "Do you want to go into more detail?"

I—I have a problem, I admit in my mind.

I take a deep breath. "I have a problem being faithful to my wife."

"Ahh, okay, well, you aren't facing anything that the Lord can't handle. Even if it doesn't feel like it, there is a way out, brother. And even if you can't understand it, God loves you just the way you are."

"Hmmm . . ."

"He loves us," Zaire continues, "but He wants to help us with those issues that prevent us from having the most complete relationship with Him. Not to be preachy, but may I share two Scriptures with you, please? I think they can help you."

"Go ahead. I need all the help I can get."

"Brother, I just want to preface this by saying adultery is an indication that our relationship with the Lord is not what it could be. Is it okay for me to surmise that about you? I don't want to judge you, but I need to know where you're coming from."

"Yes," I whisper. I close my eyes and feel a shameful yet sad release within my soul.

"Well, Jeremiah 3:8 says, 'And I saw, when for all the causes whereby back-sliding Israel committed adultery I had put her away, and given her a bill of divorcement.' You know what that means?"

"What?"

"It just means that you do belong to the Lord," Zaire explains. "He knows that you're His, He's jealous, and He wants you back."

"O—okay."

"Does that make sense? Any loving husband would want his wife back, and vice versa. It's not because you agree with what they've done; it's just that you know that you two belong to each other. See what I'm saying? God loved the children of Israel, no doubt, and He took a whole lot of mess off of them."

"Right," I murmur. "I've seen *The Ten Commandments* a million times."

"Good for you." Zaire laughs. "But I also want to share another Scripture. Ephesians 5:25 says, 'Husbands, love your wives, even as Christ also loved the church, and gave Himself for it.'"

"But I do love my wife."

"How do you know that you do? By working every day?"

"Yeah."

"You buy her nice things?"

"So much stuff she forgets sometimes," I tell her.

"But do you give her you?" Zaire asks.

"What?"

"Brother, one thing that might help is if you remember all the things Christ did to show that He loves the church. Study those Scriptures. Examine yourself. And if you fall short in those areas, follow the Lord's example. Sacrifice. Give the deepest parts of yourself. A lot of married couples don't know that—that it's the husband's job to cover his wife with love. And loving her is about the only thing that's going to help you."

"Didn't you hear me?" I ask loudly. "I try my best to love my wife. She knows I do. She doesn't have to work or pay bills. I handle all that. If she asks that small renovations be done around the house, I see that it gets done. And I'm a good father. All that proves how I feel."

"But does all that make her happy, brother? And are there other things that she wants but you refuse to give them to her, simple as they might be?"

"I—I don't know." My face burns. "Could be. I haven't really thought about it."

"Well, regardless, I'm glad you've called here today. I think that based on that action, you are expressing a type of love, so that's a positive thing. And we'll take this issue to the Lord in prayer, but you're going to have to remember to apply what you've heard through the Scriptures I gave you."

I tell Zaire okay, but I'm not totally grasping her recommendations. And if I don't fully understand, am I capable of fulfilling what's expected of me?

15

Anya

It's a Friday evening in late January. I've decided to do something rare—go major grocery shopping by myself, without my kid or sister-in-law tagging along. I decide to take Neil's vehicle this time. I rarely drive his car, but the Honda is a little too small for the amount of groceries I hope to buy.

The minute I find myself deep inside the store, I wonder why I felt I had to come here. I'm in Stafford, Texas, at the Super Wal-Mart. It has groceries, shoes, health and beauty aids, clothes—it has *everything*. Including screaming little people. Lots of them. Knowing there's nothing legal I can do to get these kids to stay quiet, I tune out their energetic voices and head for a quieter part of the store—the fresh fruits and veggies section.

I bag some oranges, green onions, tomatoes, broccoli, and yellow squash.

"Hey, hon, you sure have a serious look on your face today."

I look up to find Riley, who's standing in front of the turnip greens. She's wearing a cute lavender warm-up jacket and matching pants, and her jacket zipper is zipped down far enough so you can see her cleavage. But I am so not in the mood to talk to Riley and I merely wave. I grab the handle of my shopping basket.

"Hey, Ms. Anya, don't leave yet. I haven't seen or spoken to you in weeks. Remember?" She smiles that beautiful smile of hers. I sigh inwardly and wait for Riley to do her thing.

"I just wanted to tell you what's been going on with me." Her eyes twinkle with enthusiasm. "I finally did it."

"'It'?"

"Got rid of Jamal. I thought about how he claimed he wanna be a good daddy to Mika, and that's why he feels he gotta be able to enter my premises at all times." She rolls her eyes. "Well, that's all fine, good, and wonderful, but I figured just because Jamal fathered Mika doesn't give him the right to roll up into my house all times of the day and night. He only did it when it was convenient for him, you know what I mean?"

"Yeah, I know," I say, thinking of Neil.

"So . . ." Riley leans near me and lowers her voice. "I waited until I knew he'd be gone for a couple days and I changed the locks on the door." She laughs. "Jamal was sooo pissed and couldn't believe I'd go there. He started banging on my door yelling and stuff. Did you hear it?"

I shake my head.

"Thank God you didn't," she says. "Anyway, he kept trying to get me to open the door, but then he called me from his cell phone, and I broke it down to him. My voice was strong. I wouldn't back down on what I decided to do. And, Ms. Anya, finally, things are going the way I want them to."

Her triumphant voice crackles. "It's not that I'm trying to be a mean bitch." She covers her mouth. "Oops, pardon me, I meant *witch*. I'm trying to implement positive changes in my life, so the profanity has to go."

"What kind of positive changes are you making, other than Jamal?"

"I wanted to enter the new year with a whole new attitude. I've been attending this great church and it's making a difference. But I still have a long way to go." She examines her cleavage and pulls up the zipper. "I mean, I love to look hot, but I'm finding out maybe that's not the best way to attract a quality man. I always attract men who are interested in me only for one wild night in the sack. It's meant some good loving but that grew old, too, so, hey, gotta try something different. If you do the same old thing, you'll keep having the same old thing. And these days I've been hitting the gym, drinking more bottled water, reading . . ." She laughs. "Me reading something other than hair magazines—can you imagine that?"

No, I can't, I think to myself, and stare at her. Besides the warm-up gear, I do perceive something different about Riley. She seems relaxed, no worry lines decorating her forehead. She's glowing like someone excited about her fantastic future. I wince and swallow the lump in my throat.

"So, as I was saying," she continues, "no more hit-and-runs. I plan to be celibate." She stares at me conspiratorially. "You don't know how hard it is to stitch up nookie, lock it up so long it gets rusty and you're forced to do a rain dance just to raise it from the dead the next time you feel horny. But I gotta do it, Ms. Anya." She pauses. "It's not so bad once you get used to it. I miss having sex, sure, but it's the emotional baggage that comes with it that I don't miss. Anyway, I've talked your ears off. Just wanted to holler at you. How's the hubby? I trust that he's fine. Hey, gotta roll. It was good to see you. Feel free to stop by my place if you want, so we can chat. I have some great books I could hand off to you. Self-esteem stuff. Really good reading. Well, I'm outta here."

"Hold on." I grab Riley's arm. "Do you feel guilty about changing the locks?"

"Umm, no. Not when Jamal would violate me constantly. I don't feel bad at all. And now he seems to respect me more. But I still gotta watch him closely, make sure he's not playing a role until he thinks I'll give in and hand over a dupe, which I won't do. I barely let him in the place anymore. Just the foyer. Not in my kitchen and definitely not in my bed. Uh-uhhh, them days long gone. Mmm-hmm. Oh, well." She shudders. "Gotta run. Time for Pilates class. They offer free day care, too." She grabs me around the shoulder and gives me a solid hug. She smells outstanding. An aroma that matches her attitude. An aroma that stays with me long after I leave the store.

It's midweek. Reesy is in the den looking at a rented video that's due in two days. I tiptoe to the library. Open and shut the door. I look around at dozens of books shelved on oak bookcases. There's a wooden coatrack and a wooden trunk. Neil even has a wooden newspaper rack. I see a *USA Today* spread out on the floor next to the sofa. It has a crease in it and is turned to the crossword puzzle. I slump on the couch and let my hand droop over the sofa, tracing the newspaper with my fingers. There's a slight bulge underneath the paper. I pick up the crossword section and stare.

There's a glossy, smelly mag. Maybe he's not exactly trying to hide it. The magazine is turned to the centerfold. Let's see here. She's Asian. Oh, great! Looks like Kimora Simmons, the wife of Russell Simmons. This centerfold is sitting naked on a horse, out in a grassy field somewhere. How brave she must be to smile for the camera and rub herself against a horse. She's gripping her jumbo breasts. And I thought mine were a mouthful.

I continue turning the pages. All the girls possess the kind of beauty that makes other women feel ugly, invisible, unwanted. But these beautiful women look innocent for some reason, like they're happy about what they're doing and proud of themselves. I think of the irony of how even though I do not agree with them publicly displaying their bodies, they themselves seem satisfied with who and what they are. And if that's the case, the world is going to hell in a handbasket.

I place the magazine back where it was. Why confront Neil? I've known about his habits for a while. I've seen the *Girls Gone Wild* videotapes that show up in our house. It's not like he has hundreds of these tapes that he can't stop watching. But that doesn't matter. What matters is I have failed to keep my hubby aroused. I've been looking for him to do his part, but maybe he's waiting on me.

Deep inside I know he's been waiting for years, since long before we even agreed to a marital arrangement. But the two miscarriages made me view myself differently. Neil specifically wanted a Neil Jr. I wanted to give him a son, but when my body couldn't sustain the two pregnancies,

I felt empty. I shut down. And if I went to the grocery store and saw mothers with infants, I started weeping uncontrollably. After a while I didn't want to go outside anymore. So I stayed in the house—in fact, quite near the refrigerator. The more I ate extra helpings of food, the less I cared about intimacy, especially after Neil shut down, too, for a while.

But all that was so long ago. Nothing can change the past, but I have the power to affect the future. So maybe it's time to switch gears. If a woman feels threatened, fear can force her to do something different.

Feeling silly but determined, I growl, "Rrrrrrrr," and bat my eyelashes. Does that sound or look seductive or do I look like a fool? I have on a long-sleeve shirt. I pull it down off my shoulder, and the air flows and tickles my skin. It does feel kind of sexy. And I am wearing shorts today. My legs, hmmm . . . I remember when Neil would worship my legs and thighs. He liked to trace his fingers against my skin until I shivered and giggled and begged him to stop. I feel like I need some of that right now. I need—

I pick up the phone and dial. Kyra, the receptionist, patches me through to Neil's line.

"What were you doing?" I ask him.

"Who is this?"

"Don't even try it."

He laughs. "Just testing you."

"Don't do that, Neil. You might flunk *my* test."

He clears his throat. "What's going on, Anya?"

"Oh, nothing. I'm bored, Neil."

"You're always bored. I warned you that you'd get tired of being around the house all day."

"I don't wanna go back to work, though. I don't really know what I want to do." I feel silly. I know my husband doesn't have time to listen to this kind of conversation, but isn't that the point? If someone loves you, won't they put up with things that get on their nerves?

"Why don't you go to a movie?" he says.

"Yeah, right. Don't forget I have the little one here. That means I'm only eligible to view flicks like *Finding Nemo*. It was a cute movie, but hey . . ."

"Tell you what. I promise to watch Reese this weekend. You go out, do whatever you want to do, relax."

I bite my bottom lip, appreciative of his generosity. I know it's his way of making up for what happened that night at China Bear after the concert at Solomon's Temple. I know Neil showed remorse in his own way, but I walked out the restaurant before his apology could take root.

"My taking time to relax sounds quite heavenly, Neil, but I have a different plan. There's something I'm thinking of doing, but you may have to drop Reesy off at my mom's."

"Oh yeah?" Even when I can tell my husband is distracted due to work, I love hearing his voice. Deep, resonating, and husky even if he's not trying to sound that way.

"Yep. And on that note, let me go," I tell him. "I'll get dinner started."

"We're supposed to eat out tonight."

"That's okay. I don't mind cooking. I have nervous energy and I—"

"You're too much, Anya, I tell ya."

Don't I know it, I think, and hang up the phone.

That Friday I personally whisk Reesy away to my mother's house. She's gone even before Neil arrives home from work, and even Vette is away for the weekend. So, a couple of hours ago, I called him and told him to come straight home and that he should stop by the foyer as soon as he gets in.

I'm wearing a black negligee. The only light on in the house is the glow that comes from seven lit candles. A Gerald Levert CD plays in the background. I've taken a moisturizing vanilla bubble bath and it feels good to smell fresh. I am in the house all by myself, laughing every few seconds.

Now I am perched on the couch in the den. I press my hand against myself—against, you know, down *there*—and I know I shouldn't do this. It feels like the hardest task I've ever had to face in my life, but I need to see, no matter how scared I am, if my efforts will be rewarded.

What's that noise? I hear the garage door opening, closing. Hurry, hurry up, you fool, I think to myself. I stroke myself again and exhale.

I listen to Neil open and close the front door. Hear his footsteps in the foyer.

"Hmm, okay," I hear him say.

I hear paper ripping; he's found the note card I left. *Hurry up, dog-gone it.* I move my hand to my mouth and bear down on it hard enough to leave a teeth imprint. I sit back on the sofa, cross my legs. *Please hurry, Neil, please.*

I hear other movement, and a soft chuckle. Good, he must be following my instructions. I sit on my hands and wait. Five, four, three, two . . .

"Anya?" he calls out.

"Over here."

Yep, he got undressed, like I instructed. He's wearing a black silk robe, untied. I see his dick dangling like it's looking for me. I block out everything—miscarriage, marital arrangement, all the issues that have interfered with our ability to connect sexually—and I recognize that it's my duty to try something different and expect the best. I know I love my husband in spite of everything.

Neil walks slowly toward me, his enlarged eyes fixed on my outfit. The candlelight flickers and I'm hoping it makes me look like a thick Halle Berry. I want to giggle but remind myself to stay cool. Sexy. In control.

Neil gasps and drops to his knees in front of me. He stares at me, at my hair, which is actually a weave. Today I got lengthy human hair sewn into my natural hair. He reaches out and touches the long strands. I kiss his hand. It's too close not to kiss.

"Anya," he says. It sounds like a question that is insulting yet I understand.

"I'm yours, Neil." I begin removing the negligee, untying each strand while I watch him. His eyes are bigger than I've ever seen them; they are so big, it looks like someone is pulling the skin from the back of his head. Yuck. I slowly pull the negligee off my shoulders, slide it down to my waist. Then I stand up and let it fall to my ankles. Neil stuffs his face against my jumbo breasts, kissing one, then the other. I want to shout but I have to hold it in. Instead I coolly dab at a tear that's developed in one eye.

"Mmm, mmmm . . ." Neil is sucking my breast so hard I feel like a newborn baby. I want something to suck, too, so I move his head gently away and lower myself in front of his body until his magic wand is staring me in the face.

"Hey there," I say to it. "Remember me?" I stroke the head, kiss and lick it, then swallow the entire shaft.

"Damn, oh shit . . ." Neil jerks and sways. I want to laugh and scream. I take my man and work him like I'm a veteran ho with benefits. Neil is moving his hips back and forth, shoving himself farther and deeper inside my mouth. I want to gag. It feels like someone has stuffed a huge, dry bath towel in my mouth. I can think of other things that would feel more comfortable than this, but that's irrelevant right now.

Once I finish up on Neil, I lie back on the Oriental rug. Gerald Levert's commanding voice continues to serenade us in the background. An intense rose fragrance from burning candles saturates the air. I steer Neil's big hand to my private parts and he traces his fingers inside the silkiness.

"Is this for me, Anya?"

"It's all yours, Neil," I murmur.

He smashes his face against me, eating me out, slurping, licking, lapping at my surprised but delighted vagina. I'm holding his head between my hands, squirming, grimacing. He pecks at and licks me until I shudder under the loving weight of his skillful tongue.

Neil has thrown his robe to the floor. Now he's lying on top of me. The air conditioner makes choking sounds, as if it's shocked at what we're doing. Our bodies feel like mass and liquid and heat, pressed deeply against each other. Neil bites my shoulders, and I nip on his arms. I feel his lips gnawing on my nipples and I take his dick and lead it where it oughta be.

"This is it, D," he says. "Let's do this."

Why'd he say D? Am I hearing things?

Even though Neil is heavy, I dig my feet in the carpet and scoot back.

He scoots up, urgently pressing himself against my opening. I scoot back some more. He scoots up, trying to find my hole.

"Anya, stop that. Now, c'mon," he pleads, unaware of the pissed-off look on my face.

"Oh, so you *do* remember my name?"

"Yes, I remember . . ." He glances down at me and pauses. "Oh, okay, what I, uh, I–I meant to say didn't come out right. That was just . . . I'm s–sorry, baby," he murmurs, and starts up again.

I can't believe Neil's fumbling around trying to stab my coochie with his dick. I think about how long it's been since I've felt him inside of me, but I'm torn between keeping my legs open and furthering our relationship, or slamming them shut and gaining some self-respect.

I'm lying on my back and my toes feel frozen, as if I'm standing on a bag of ice cubes. He looks down with pleading eyes and whispers that he's sorry. Neil admitting he's wrong makes him look too fine, like he's a precocious little boy.

"You still want to do this?" he asks in a subdued voice.

I nod and let him gratefully kiss me on the lips.

I wonder if I should get a reality check and make him go find a condom, a balloon, some cling wrap. But I'm sooo horny. And it's been sooo long. Besides, he is my freaking husband. I have a right to this. I have a right to . . . to shove my foot up his butt. He can't call me D and expect me to stay in the mood.

I start scooting back again until I'm sitting up, my behind tingling from the sting of carpet burn.

"What you trying to do, Anya? You think this is funny?" He's rubbing himself but I have zero sympathy for him or his thing.

"Nothing's funny, Neil. I take this very seriously. Why else would I do all this?"

My voice sounds as mechanical as an automated message that you hear when a woman instructs you to press 1 for customer service.

"Hijacking my dick?" he squeals. "That's for me? Or for you?"

"I know you've always hated when I shift gears, but this time I didn't shift them without provocation."

"I apologized more than once, Anya. What more you want me to do?"

"Why don't you watch me closely—while I get the heck away from you?" I stand up and scratch my itchy scalp, eager to rid myself of these new strands of hair. Five wasted hours of sitting in a beautician's chair; five hours of pain—for this.

I turn to walk away but Neil grabs me around the shoulders. He squeezes me tight and silently rocks me. I feel his hands patting me softly on my back. His eyes are closed and he continues to mumble more apologies than I've ever heard in my life.

"Neil, you say that a lot, but 'sorry' grows old after the fifth time."

"But I'm trying, Anya. You have to believe that. Whether you know it or not, these kinds of things are . . . hard for me. I feel like I'm out of touch . . . and I feel like I need help, *your* help, to push me in the right direction. So even though you're mad, why can't we talk about this?"

I am shocked by his serious tone. Neil's actions resemble those of the man I used to know when we first met, the one who refused to fall asleep with the sun going down on our wrath.

"I don't want to wake up with this issue hanging between us," Neil continues. "Now, if I ask for forgiveness, and I plead with you to understand me, what else can I do to convince you I'm for real? Baby, I can't help but see how hard you're trying, and I know you want things to be different. Have you considered I might want that, too?"

Because Neil's expressing words I seldom hear, he captures my attention.

"You forgive me?" he begs, sounding like the young and the desperate. I nod.

"That's what you claimed the last time," he says.

"Well, I'm going to try to do better this time," I promise him. We embrace each other again, and my heart feels a little uplifted from knowing that my man came after me, instead of letting me walk away.

Fifteen minutes later we're in the kitchen. Lights on. Rose-scented candles blown out and thick, smoky scents choking the air. We're hyped and kinda hungry after some almost-but-not-quite ravenous sex.

"Anya, what's this?"

"Spaghetti and meatballs. I made the meatballs myself."

"But it's beef." He sniffs, like *beef* is a four-letter word.

"Oh, please, Neil. Don't tell me you're scared by those news reports. I always pray over everything I cook or eat. Mad cow. Deliriously happy cow. We're still gonna eat this food, so pick up that fork and disregard what you've seen on the news."

I try to stab a fat, slippery meatball with my fork. It flies over the table like a volleyball and lands on the floor. I pick up the slimy-looking thing with my fingers, try to cram it in my mouth, but end up plopping the meat on a napkin.

Neil snickers. I roll my eyes. He puts his hand over his lips and I see his shoulders shaking. Then mine start shaking. I began screeching and clutching my naked belly. Neil comes to sit on my lap, placing one arm across my back, plastering my cheek with a gentle kiss.

"Why doesn't everything go perfect?" I say.

Neil just shakes his head. "Tonight wasn't so bad. You tried. I did, too. And for the record, D stands for 'Damn, this pussy good.'"

"Neil, that sounds so gross, plus it's not even true, you lying liar."

He makes a noise of protest. I move my leg back and forth until he's forced to slide off and returns to his seat.

"What else you have planned for this evening, *Anya*?"

"You don't have to pronounce my name so diligently. It's cool."

"Th–thanks."

"I know what. Let's return to the den. Sit on the floor in front of the couch and . . ." I begin to describe what I want us to do. Neil nods and raises his eyebrows. We hastily finish dinner and head back for a second chance.

Neil and I meet in the den underneath a wool blanket. He pitches the blanket so it resembles a tent. It feels like we're outside at a campsite, underneath the twinkling stars, both afraid, with only each other for protection. We keep it simple. We're closed in together, sitting on the floor shielded by the blanket. Now Luther Vandross is crooning in the background. We're eating some cold white grapes. There's lots of sweet kissing, a little feeding each other here and there. Neil insists on placing grapes on my thighs, navel, and in between my legs, then he slowly eats them off me. I wonder if he learned that from a video, but it doesn't matter because it makes me moist. And I love that I'm able to feel wet again.

When the foreplay/foodplay winds down, a condom is ready and waiting for us. Neil gets me even more ready by massaging my neck, arms, breasts, thighs, ankles, and toes with oil. Then I spread my legs and gasp when he thrusts continually inside me. In, out. In, out. It feels good, rubber-glove tight, so I close my eyes. Suck in my breath. Suffer heated pain. And remember why I initially hooked up with this man. His love-making is tender, raunchy, patient, and complete. And I make a mental note: We definitely should pull out all the stops to regain what we've had; whatever difficulty we must endure to save our marriage is worth the effort.

"Neil." I hear Dani's voice. "You never take me anywhere."

"And I'm not gonna," Neil tells her.

"Hmm, I just think it's weird that I can have an experience like having a baby with you, but you can't even take me to, shoot, to the Piggly Wiggly."

"There is no Piggly Wiggly in Houston."

"Oh, you know what I'm trying to say."

"I know, but no, not gonna do that, Dani."

I smile to myself and quietly hang up the telephone. I'm upstairs in the bedroom. Neil's downstairs. I am organizing my underwear drawer. I didn't mean to listen in, but the phone rang and Neil and I picked up at the same time. It was her, so . . . I've never heard them talk directly to each other without an audience. I think it's natural to wonder how someone will act if they're not aware you can hear what they're saying.

I am curious about what Neil does, but one thing I've learned is a woman will never be content if she's constantly checking on her man. He'll either become more creative or she'll grow more insecure. I believe no matter what a man promises, he'll do what he's gonna do, and if I have to try to control my husband and eyeball him and force him to love me, then that's not love, that's manipulation. So I told myself don't

listen in anymore. I am pleased that he told Dani he won't take her anywhere, and hope he means what he says.

It's Friday night, a week after our rendezvous. We've all eaten dinner,
and Neil, Vette, Reesy, and I play a few rounds of Monopoly Junior until
eight-thirty. The girls then run upstairs, sounding like a stampede of
buffalos. Neil tells me he'll probably sip a glass of wine, read the newspaper, and go crash on the sofa as usual. I've dressed down to a night-
gown and am about to grab a few fashion magazines and read in bed,
when suddenly I remember I left something—a grocery bag—in Neil's
SUV the last time I used it to go shopping. So I go out to the garage. The
door hasn't been let down yet. I open the latch at the back of the Explorer. The green Wal-Mart bag is still there with two tubes of tooth-
paste and a box of cotton swabs. I grab the bag and, for some reason,
decide to sit down. The night air is cool, there's nobody else outside, no
cars driving down the street. I scoot back until I'm further in the vehicle,
then I reach up and close the door. I'm in Neil's Explorer and it's dark
and lonely, but I feel adventurous.

I meditate for a while, then I'm ready to go back in the house, but I
hear footsteps. I lower myself in the small space so that I'm not visible.
I'm pressed against the backseat that's closest to the driver's side. The
driver's-side door opens. I freeze. Neil coughs and slides into the car.
He starts the ignition. I suck in my breath and close my eyes. Even
though the engine is loud and the radio is playing, it seems like Neil
may hear me just because I can hear myself. There's a ringing sound in
my ear and I'm trembling while Neil backs the car out the driveway,
then heads down the street. I try to memorize the turns we're making
but soon give up. Neil has stopped listening to the radio and is now
singing along with his CD player. He's listening to the R&B group Jagged
Edge and singing loud like he's in the band. My hip gets banged every
time he rides over a bump. I feel like I'm at an amusement park on a
tiny roller coaster that jerks a lot. I have to pee and I press my legs together. My feet are bare. I'm listening for specific sounds, like Neil talking on his cell phone, but that hasn't happened.

We travel along the freeway, engine sputtering and tapping. When we're not driving as fast as we were, I figure Neil has exited and we're back on the surface street. I see streetlights every time I'm brave enough to open my eyes and look up through the window. We stop several times, probably at intersections. Then I feel us going up a slight incline like we're entering a parking lot.

The driver's-side window rolls down. Neil punches some buttons. I hear a beep. A gate screeches open, sounding like Godzilla. We roll and dip over a few speed bumps. My toes are curled. Lack of saliva has dried my mouth. I look around and notice the tops of buildings, more streetlights.

Neil parks, turns off the ignition, opens and shuts his door. I raise my neck and watch. He walks upstairs to the door of a three-story brick apartment; he doesn't knock. Neil removes his key ring, inserts a key. He opens the door and disappears behind it. I rub my neck to soothe the cramp that's developed from my attempt to stay unnoticed.

I check the time. I have a Guess watch that glows in the dark. It's 9:28. I wish I had my purse and the extra set of keys; if I did I'd drive off and make Neil think someone stole his ride. Wouldn't that be radical? I laugh at the thought, but get sober real quick. I have no time to play tricks on him. Playing tricks can get you killed, and I'm not down for anything like that.

If only my husband could offer me a fair explanation. No promises. No signing papers. No vowing to do this or that on tape. Make me understand. Let me know what to expect. Is it going to be me? Or her? If I know for sure, I feel I can handle whatever comes my way. Who says life has to be logical? And right? And fair? I am willing to go through the fire, so I told myself years ago. The fire is now raging hot, stinging, and I bleed from its burns. But it's my fire, my truth, and that's where I am right now. As unbelievable as it is, this is my life!

I wait until thirty minutes pass. That's long enough. I sit up. The lights are on in Dani's place. Maybe they prefer screwing where it's bright enough that they can see each other's grimaces or something. I take a deep breath, steadying my chest with my hand. I get on my knees and crawl over the backseat of the car, then move over to the driver's seat. I sit behind the wheel for a sec. Thank God Neil forgot to lock the door. If he didn't and I tried to escape from the inside, the car alarm would go off.

I cautiously open the door and check my surroundings. A few people are lingering by vehicles near the front of apartments. Praying they don't see me, I step on the asphalt, which feels hard and gritty underneath my feet. I wobble toward Dani's apartment, raise my hand to ring the doorbell, but instead press my ear against her front door. I don't hear anything. I wrap my arms around my body and rub. My hands grope the fabric of my outfit. I forgot I was wearing my housecoat, a housecoat that has two pockets—one that has my cell phone in it. My knees vibrate like gelatin; I want to collapse to the ground. I quickly move away from Dani's place toward a main street. I dial my house. I have to call back three times before Vette answers.

"Vette, do me a huge favor."

"A—Anya? W—where are you?"

"Go to my room. My purse should be on the floor next to my bed. I need you to find my car keys and come pick me up."

I'm walking down a busy yet recognizable street. Housecoat, gown, bare feet, staring at my destination. A Citgo gas station that has adequate lighting, a public restroom, and a street address that is readable.

I walk with my head up, pretending no one is staring.

My jaw firm, I give Vette directions on how to get to where I am.

"Sister-in-law, you aren't making any sense whatso—"

"Shut the fug up and come get me, okay? Can you just do that for me, please? Just do something for me, for *me*, no arguing, no smarty mouth, just come get me."

16

Dani

Saturday afternoon. I'm in the kitchen tossing bags of coffee, miniature jars of fruit, and packages of nuts inside several plastic bins that I use to store items for the gift baskets. I hear Neil open and slam my door. I know it's Neil. We decided he should have a key in case of an emergency. He's only used it one time—last night, actually—when he unexpectedly stopped by to check on Brax, who had a fever yesterday afternoon.

I stop what I'm doing, ready to wave at Neil and resume working. I'm sure he's here just to make sure Brax is feeling better and all that, but he keeps repeating, "The hell with this." I wonder if he's referring to me. That would be a bit odd, though, wouldn't it?

Neil is walking toward the sink, cracking his knuckles, walking back across the kitchen floor, mumbling. I just gape at him like he's a man standing on the edge of a tall building. He stops walking. We exchange wide-eyed looks.

"She changed the locks," he exclaims. "Did you know that?"

"Huh?"

"I can open the garage door with the automatic opener," he continues, "but the door that lets you into the house, my key won't fit that.

Front-door key don't work, either. All my stuff is . . . My money pays for that damn house. I hope she—"

He swears loudly and starts pacing again.

"It's my fault, Neil."

"What'd you do, Dani?"

"I mean, overall. Isn't this what this is about? Maybe Anya is sick and tired . . . maybe her line has been crossed. Obviously."

I don't feel like working anymore. I take a seat at the kitchen table. Neil sits down next to me.

"Uh, baby, have you tried calling her?"

"No response."

"When's the last time you two talked?"

"This morning. I was about to go to Home Depot. Last thing she said was 'See you later.'"

"Hmmm. Well, Neil, you can hang out here for a while. Till you figure out what happened." I pause. "Has she been acting standoffish? Noncommunicative?"

"Nope."

"She's been avoiding you around the house?"

"No!"

"Don't yell at me, man. I'm trying to help . . ."

"Shhh." He stands back up. Stares intently at the floor like that holds the answer to his questions.

"Neil, you want me to call her?"

"No, Dani, no, can't you hear well?"

"Well, you know, I guess I can't. And since I can't hear well, I don't care anymore. Do what the fuck you want. Leave me out of it."

I'm not used to Neil snapping at me, so I zip off to my bedroom, crawl underneath the covers. My body is stiff like fear has taken root. I yank at strands of hair. Some of it gets entwined in my fingers. I love my hair, my glory. My mother said to never cut it. Others say women with short hair are more intelligent than women with long hair. I figure that whoever believes that is stupid and I've kept my hair long.

Sometimes I wish Mrs. Wifey would just fade away. No, that's awful to think, isn't it? But sometimes awful is true, ugly reality. And it's a true and ugly reality that if I wish for her to vanish, then Anya may wish the same thing about me. But fate has entwined us and deposited us in similar positions.

Like yesterday at work. The head of our department, Mr. Duntworth, called me into his office. The last thing I want to do is get called into the Big Man's space, unless it's to hear that he's going to pay me more money. But when I went in there and he had this unfriendly look on his face, I started wringing my hands until he asked me to have a seat.

I sat. He asked if I wanted coffee and cream. I said no, I don't do coffee.

He said you might want to get some this time, Danielle.

I gripped the edge of my seat. But I thought how odd that might look to Mr. Duntworth, so I released my hands and started making small talk about the Super Bowl, the crummy weather. He never responded to anything I said, just sat and stared at me till I grew so uncomfortable I clamped my mouth. And the silence between us was some of the most unbearable I've ever endured.

And the person who broke the silence was the one I didn't want to see.

Neil walked in and stopped when he saw me. He avoided my questioning eyes. And he stood motionless until Mr. Duntworth asked him to sit down.

My throat felt dry, my hands were clammy, but I forced myself to chill out.

"I've called you two into the office," our boss said, "because I need to ask you something. This is very difficult to ask but, uh, last year, Ms. Frazier, you became pregnant."

Oh God, Oh Jesus, Oh Mary, no, what does he *want?* I dared not look to Neil for help. The man is only strong when he can control the situation.

"And you never revealed who the father was, which is fine—that's not really our concern."

"Then why are—"

"Let me finish, Danielle. I think even though what you do outside this office isn't our business, if things somehow affect the office climate and atmosphere, then it becomes another matter. Now"—he coughed and cleared his throat—"Neil, are you, uh, married or divorced or . . ."

"I–I'm married, sir."

Mr. Duntworth grimaced and shook his head.

"But last year when I asked you something about this, you said you were separated."

"I didn't say that. I said I may be headed for separation, but it didn't happen."

"That's not how I remember it."

"Well, Mr. Duntworth, I'm sorry if you don't remember." Neil's voice had a defensive edge to it, but he looked calm.

"I think it's very awkward for us when you have a high-profile position in this department, and when you are married to another woman and are openly having babies with someone else."

"Mr. Dunt—"

"And because of this awkwardness, I've decided that it's best for Danielle to leave."

"Please, please . . ." I stood up and begged. I hoped he was bluffing. I hoped he would write us up, dock us a day or two of pay, but no, I could not lose my job.

"I don't see why I have to leave," I told Duntworth. "I have very good performance evaluations."

"Yes, you do, Ms. Frazier, and maybe your good performances could help you to get a job somewhere else."

"Are you saying you'll put me down for a transfer to a similar position within the company? Same pay, same everything?"

"I'm saying you have thirty days to find yourself another job."

"Are you kidding? Neil, he can't do this, can he?"

Neil let out a peculiar noise that gave me my answer.

I left the building immediately. I didn't care if they claimed I walked off the job. I needed some mental relief. And I wept all the way home. I babbled like an idiot in front of Audrey and pushed her away when she begged me to tell her what was wrong. I ordered her to leave and I went to get Brax. He smiled at me, gurgling, and drooling long strings of spit from his mouth. I held my baby so tight I could've killed him. But at that moment, I felt like Braxton was the only sure thing I had in the world. And he had no idea how comforting yet scary it felt for me to think that.

But right now I feel somewhat better. Mr. Duntworth called me at home last night and we talked. I told him my kid needs medical benefits, that Brax gets sick from time to time, and carting him to the doctor and forking over the co-pay, plus buying whatever's necessary to help him regain his strength, well, that ain't no joke. I asked him to please have some compassion. Do something that would consider the child. And old Duntworth had a change of heart. He said he'd let me look for another job, take as much time as I want, but he promised not to let me go after thirty days. He said people were starting to talk, and if I could hang in there through the rumors and judgmental looks, then fine.

People can stare at me and whisper behind my back all they want; if they're not gonna pay my bills, they can eat me. The folks on the job are doing God knows what, and have the nerve to spread my business like they have no drama of their own. Pushing petty people to the back of my mind, I started thinking about the note for my late-model Tacoma, the ridiculously high rent I pay just to live near the Med Center. I considered how much it costs to fill up the tank, pay the cable bill, car insurance, and fork over meager dollars so I can try to have everything that matters to me. And for the first time I felt a twinge of regret for giving birth to Braxton. I hated myself for thinking that way, but it's no secret my life wouldn't be like this if I didn't have a child. Then I cursed myself bitterly and repented for ever having such a thought. No matter what kind of messes I get myself into, Brax is gonna be attached to me for the rest of my freaking life.

So piss on me big-time, but that's the choice I've made. And somehow, some way, even with Mrs. Wifey acting out, my choices cannot result in the ruin of Danielle Frazier.

———

It's Saturday evening now. I stayed holed up in my bedroom battling all kinds of unsettling thoughts until I fell asleep. When I wake up, Neil is lying next to me, which is shocking. I never thought he'd want to sleep next to me.

And here we are . . . in my bed, mostly clothed, and together. But don't get me wrong. I am not tripping off this. I know Anya can make one phone call and it will send Neil spiraling home so fast, you'd think my apartment was about to blow up in five different directions. Hmmm. This sucks. It does. But I'm gonna handle it.

Neil's stretched out snugly against my neck. His whiskers are prickling my chin. His warm presence and musky scent make me want to hold him there, in that position, for the rest of my days. I am too afraid to say anything. I just want him to know that I am here for him as long as he needs me, wants me. I am tempted to press my lips against his hair, his skin, but I don't want to push it. I'm just ecstatic he's by my side. I'm glad he didn't leave while I was asleep, leaving me behind with a harsh note that said, "See ya. I can't do this anymore." Hey, it's not like that's never happened before. Not like another man hasn't made a conscious decision that was beneficial for him, awful for me. And most times, after I get the note on the pillow, the note that comes after you experience lots of sweet lovemaking that you imagine will repeat itself, well, you find out *that* particular love was just a temporary thing. The guy was just passing through, like a man who goes to a gas station. He's only there for a few minutes, fills his tank, and heads off on his way.

Neil has gotten filled up by me many times, but he's always come back. Thank God he hasn't handed me one of those corny, awkward lines, like "It was good while it lasted, but every good thing must come to an end." You know how it can be. Men get scared, confused, feel closed in, not sure of themselves, or of who they are and what they want. They leave dozens of women hanging in the balance, women who yearn to release the tension of not knowing, women who want to know for certain that what they have is solid and true. But when you're with someone like Neil, knowing is never a given. That's apparent going in. But it doesn't stop you from wishing, hoping, praying like you've never prayed before, that maybe this time the odds will be on your side, and for at least once in your life, you'll get the guy. Why is it always so damned hard to just get the freaking guy?

I know Neil's not asleep. His eyes are open. He's staring past my face, submerged in thought. When a man gets quiet for a long time, I feel like an elephant coming face-to-face with a mouse. My bones quiver, and I wonder if he is preparing to tell me something that's difficult for him to say, words I don't want to hear.

I squeeze Neil a little tighter, stroke his head with my fingertips. His hair feels greasy yet comforting.

"You still with me?" I ask.

"You still see me?"

"Just because your body's here doesn't mean your heart is."

"You right about that."

"Yeah, but am I right about you, Neil?"

"Now don't trip."

"If you say so," I murmur.

Neil yawns and lifts his head off my neck. "What's for dinner?"

"Uh, I dunno. What you want?"

"What can you scrape up real fast?"

I tug at my hair and twirl it into a circle. "I–I probably need to go shopping, or we can order in."

"I'm sick of ordering in," he hisses.

Ouch, that hurt. The last few times Neil has been here for a couple hours in the evening, I've dialed up Domino's. And when he got tired of that, I hit speed dial and got Pizza Hut, and another time Chinese food.

"If you go on a job hiatus," he says, "maybe you can take time to learn how to cook."

"Neil, please, don't go there, okay? I cannot stand when you say things like that. You either like me for me or—"

"It's not about me liking you because you can cook. It's about you knowing how to do things for yourself. What's Brax gonna eat after he's off milk and baby food, huh? Pretzels and Kool-Aid?"

He's out of my bed now, raising his arms toward the ceiling and stretching. He doesn't have on a shirt, just some brand-new briefs that he's packing with the sexiest kind of muscles. His dick is poking against his drawers. Either he's horny or he has to pee really bad.

"Okay, Neil. Whatever you say."

"Don't pacify me."

"I can't pacify you when you're telling the truth. I—I'll get right on it, okay? I'll TiVo the Food Network or something. Buy a dozen cookbooks. Sport a new apron. Whatever it takes."

"Sarcasm isn't necessary. Just think about what I said."

"Right. Sure. Absolutely."

"Plus, you're not gonna find too many men who'll put up with a non-cooking, water-boiling, twenty-something female. Not these days."

"Neil!" I shriek. I jump out of bed, run up to him, and pummel his chest with my fists. "Don't take out what's happening at home on me. This is not about me, okay? My inability to cook is not the freaking issue, and you know it. You are almost homeless, and you have the nerve to crack on me about dumb, irrelevant shit."

He stupidly grins and removes my hands from his chest. "Don't touch me, Dani."

"Oh, okay, let me read between the lines. Unless I almost kill myself trying to suck your gargantuan dick or squeeze your deformed nipples, I have no business putting my hands on you."

"That's not what I mean. You're getting things twisted, and I'm not about to listen to this."

"Go on then, punk-ass coward. Why do men run away? Running won't change a thing. It just won't." I hate screaming and letting the neighbors hear my personal business, but sometimes hurt is too hard to contain, and you just can't care what others think.

"C'mere, Dani," he says, extending his hands toward me. "We don't fight. This isn't us."

"Then why are we doing this?" I say, and wipe my eyes with my hand. Neil wraps his big, strong arms around me and hoists me up. He flings me around in a circle several times until the room spins and I feel like lying on the floor. I slap him on his back so he'll stop. He throws me over his shoulder, like I'm a knapsack. I mash my cheek against his back, kick my legs, and scream. Neil tosses me on the bed like a rag doll. I scoot into a corner of the bed and grab a pillow. I squeeze the pillow on my head, still nauseous and dizzy. Neil snatches the pillow and falls on top of me. I wriggle under the weight of his body. He grabs me and twists around on the bed until I'm on top of him. I writhe on his dick, which is so stiff it's nearly bursting out his pants, like a missile headed toward Mars. I hump on top of him, rubbing up and down, creating a wild back-and-forth friction until waves of pleasure calm me. I collapse on top of him, my legs straddling him, his arms wrapped across my back. He unclamps my brassiere. His warm hands rub me up and down, stroking my thighs, digging in between my legs. He slides his fingers inside my cheeky pants, pulling and tugging on my vagina.

"Don't do that so hard." I squirm. "Hurts."

He doesn't say anything. He keeps playing around down there. I fidget, my butt wobbling back and forth, trying to get out of his hands' reach. He reaches for my butt cheek and slaps it a few times and then says "Ouch," like he's the one getting hit. I giggle because his silliness breaks me down.

"Dani, give me some head, okay?" He pleads like he hasn't had sex in months.

"No, baby," I say sweetly. "I'm not in the mood for that right now." The air chills with deafening silence.

"L—let me go brush my teeth, baby, or maybe you should wash up first. Then I'll be happy to do it."

"You're so full of shit, Dani."

"Why you say that?"

"Do I ever tell you to go wash up? Douche it up before I eat it out? Women are a trip."

"Why do you say 'women'? What women? Huh? You trying to tell me something? Are you cheating on us?"

Neil sighs like my question is too stupid to answer. That makes me mad. I wonder what the hell is happening tonight. Is an excellent piece of dick worth drama? Is this really good for me or am I kidding myself? But I quickly kill these thoughts. Drama or not, the dick is definitely worth it. No two dicks are created equal, and I know Neil's is rare.

I straddle Neil, kissing his neck, chest, nipples. I lower my head until my mouth finds him and I suck him, lick and devour him like a fiend, until he moans, shakes, shudders, and tells me, "I l–love you." It's something he's never said before, and in spite of not knowing if he means it or not, his words replay in my head, and comfort me all night. I think of his words while we make passionate love three more times— in the bed, on the floor, in the chair—screwing each other's brains out . . . until the sun shows its face. I think of his words until I realize this is the first time Neil has stayed an entire night with me. And make no mistake—I don't want it to be the last time.

The next morning I scoot off to Kroger and pick up a few groceries. After I get back, I scramble eggs, pan-fry bacon, cook a pan of runny grits, and pour Neil a glass of ice-cold orange juice.

"I can't believe I did all this," I say proudly. "You should be cooking for *me*." I pick up a thick, crispy slice of salty bacon and wave it in front of him. He opens his mouth and chomps off little pieces until the meat is all gone.

"You're spoiled, Dani. How many men you say you've been with?"

"I haven't said."

"Tell me."

"I'll tell you if you tell me. Wait, don't. It doesn't really matter, does it, Neil? I feel weird talking about my past relationships with you."

"Why?" he asks.

"I don't want you to use that info against me one day. Believe me, it's happened."

"If it has, you've been with some sorry men."

"Like I don't know that." I laugh. "Well, they all weren't awful. I don't really regret the experiences. It helps me to find out what I want and don't want, and that's not so bad."

"Guess so," he says in a monotone voice.

"Uh, Neil. What do you usually do on a Sunday morning?"

His face looks ashen. "I go to church. Not going today, though."

"Oh, okay," I reply, and scratch my ear vigorously. We've never really talked about God or religion or spirituality.

"Uh, you like your church?" I ask for lack of anything better to say. He shrugs and sips his juice. "You got a newspaper around here?"

"I'll go check," I say. I'm dressed in a lime-green T-shirt and my usual sweats. I open the door and see the thick Sunday *Chronicle* wrapped in clear plastic sitting outside. It's very brisk this late February morning, and patchy clouds shift across the gray sky. I step inside to get my running shoes, which are sitting near the door, and hand Neil the paper.

"Where you going?" he says as I start lacing up the shoes.

"I didn't check the mail yesterday. I want to go take a quick look."

I grab my tiny metal key and race toward the mailbox, which is a few hundred yards away. I pass by a gated built-in swimming pool. The property is very quiet right now. I locate my mailbox, stoop to insert the key, and remove a stash of mail. City of Houston water bill, *Country Accents* magazine, a department store circular, and a Ludacris CD I ordered from the Columbia House Music Club.

I am walking back to my apartment when I hear footsteps behind me. I walk faster, not wanting to look back. The footsteps get louder. I drop the JCPenney circular on the ground but keep going.

"Hey, Dani."

I spin around. It's Neil's sister.

"How'd you get in here?" I'm referring to her getting inside the apartment complex, since we have a gate that's opened with a security code, and I'm certain she doesn't know the code.

"I followed behind a car that was coming in the gate. Hey, I'm not trying to make trouble."

I don't say a word. Don't know what to say.

"Is he here, Dani? Someone is asking."

"I doubt that," I say firmly.

"You doubt someone's asking?"

I turn away from her and start heading past the pool. I keep walking beyond my apartment. I hear her footsteps behind me. I hike around the perimeter of six buildings and even pass Neil's SUV. He parked it far away from my unit, just in case.

My ears feel chilled, and when I cough, smoke drifts from my mouth. But the cold doesn't seem to bother her. I wish Neil's sister would get lost like a three-year-old.

"Hey," she says, "I'm not going to follow you all around this place. You ain't slick. I know what you're trying to do."

"Then go on and go, Sharvetta, please."

"I go by Vette or Sharvette. And I will leave. I never wanted to do this, anyway. But this is what family gets caught up in sometimes. Always something."

I slow down, let her catch up. She doesn't look too intense, but still . . .

"I understand," I say, almost whispering.

She stares at me. "Well, if you hear from Neil today, please tell him to call home."

"Oh, really?"

"Yes, really. They have some unfinished business."

I watch Vette walk away, then I hug myself and rub my cold arms for another ten minutes, praying Neil doesn't come looking for me. When I sense she's no longer a threat, I run back to my apartment and slam the door shut, wondering if I can survive this state of existence much longer.

The phone rings.

Area code 562. Long Beach.

"Hi, Ma." Gosh, it's been so long since I've heard her voice. I miss that connection.

"How you know it was me?"

"It isn't hard to figure out, Ma. I knew my sisters weren't calling me." I go to my room and shut the door. Neil is in the kitchen getting ready to bake a thick apple pie he discovered in the freezer.

"What's going on with you, Dani?"

"Nothing much. Everything is fine, Mama."

"And my schnookums?"

"He's getting so big with his greedy self."

"He's still on the breast?" she asks.

"No, never really was."

Mama laughs. "I can't picture you washing all those bottles and stuff."

"Well, I'm doing a lot of things you can't picture me doing." I murmur my response, talking more to myself than to my mom.

"You need anything?"

"No, Mama, we're doing okay." I pause. "Well, will you ship me a double-double from In-N-Out Burgers? I could use a great-tasting burger right about now. Something that reminds me of home."

Mama laughs but I get distracted when I suddenly hear Neil's voice.

"Dani, you got any potato chips in here? That pie won't be ready for another forty minutes," he says, then bursts into my room, sees me on the phone, and hushes.

I cover the mouthpiece with my hand. "Look in the bathroom."

"The bathroom? For chips?"

"Don't ask," I say, and wave him away.

"Dani, who was that? You got company?"

"Uh, yeah, Mama, but we can still talk."

"That's your sitter, what's her name, Audrey?"

"No, Mama, it's, uh, Neil."

"I thought you said you weren't seeing him anymore," she says, anguish in her voice.

"Well, we aren't really seeing each other. Brax wasn't feeling too well and I called Neil and he swung by. He's just doing daddy stuff, that's all."

"Mmmm-hmmm. Dani, I told you to leave that man alone." She sounds disappointed, which makes me feel bad.

"Yeah, well . . . leaving Neil alone isn't as easy as it seems."

I stand up, then sit down again and recline clumsily on the bed.

"You love him?"

"Mama, you already know the answer to that. I mean, my feelings for him are kind of complicated, and I don't think you'll understand."

"Don't assume I'm some dried-up thing that was born at the age of sixty. I've seen lots of things in my day."

"Hmm, looking at soap operas and reading a bunch of romance novels . . ."

"No, no, real life, too, Dani."

She's scaring me. I don't ever want to think of my mother as someone who knows the pain that I've known.

"Well, Mama, it was good to hear your voice, but I don't want to hold you. I'll call you next time, okay?"

"Don't be rushing off the phone now that the talk is getting juicy."

I laugh. "No, really, I got some things to take care of, but thanks for checking in with me."

"That's a dangerous situation, so you be careful, Dani. I'm praying for you."

I bite my bottom lip. She's such a mom . . . and I don't know what I'd do if I didn't have that.

"Go home to your wife."

It's Sunday evening. Hard to believe it, but I'm tired of looking at Neil's face. Even Brax is staring at his dad like, *Why are you still here?* You know something's up if a baby can sense when things are off center.

"What if Anya doesn't want me there?"

"You won't know what she wants unless you go back." I see the lines of tension in his forehead.

Brax, Neil, and I are all sitting on the love seat. God knows I love having this man here, but sometimes I just want to be by myself and not have anything or anyone to deal with. So I decide I need a break, and I'll be getting Brax ready to leave with his father.

"I think going back is the best thing to do. Anya's just annoyed with you. Women get that way sometimes."

"Oh, yeah? I'm surprised to hear you say this. It's like you're defending her." He challenges me with his eyes. "You really want me to do this, and if so, why?"

"It's the right thing," I say, thinking of my mother.

"You sound like you're lying, Dani."

"Not lying. I'm *tired*. It's been a long, exhausting weekend. And don't forget, shoot, I don't know if I should go in to work tomorrow, or hit the pavement with a fresh résumé."

"Hmmm, yeah." He sighs, stands up.

"Go on and go. It's gonna be fine, Neil. I believe that. You have a good woman over there. All that goodness isn't going to evaporate overnight."

"I hope you're right."

"I know I am." I continue reassuring him, offering emotional support while I finish dressing Brax.

A moment later, we're standing in the open doorway and I hand over Brax and some of his things, which I quietly packed.

"Take him with you, Neil."

In spite of Neil's widened eyes, I close the door behind him and wait to see what happens next.

17

Anya

"*'Hit the road, Jack, and don't you come back no more . . . don't you* come back no more.'"

I ask Vette, "Where'd Reesy learn that song?"

"I think from *American Idol.* She sure didn't get it from me." Vette playfully cuts her green eyes at me, then watches her niece sing and act the fool. It's Sunday afternoon and we've decided to try the new Metro Light Rail System just so we can get out the house. This was Vette's suggestion, and at first I rolled out the house kicking and screaming, but now that we're out and about, things don't feel as agonizing as before.

"See, told you riding the rail is cool," Vette assures me. "Too many damn kids up in here, but still I love being around all the people."

"That's nice," I say, trying to act noncommittal, but my eyes soak up the scenery. Vette and Reesy are in the same row as me, but I'm sitting across the aisle gazing out my window. Some parts of Houston look fantastic—especially when we approach the Med Center and the Museum District. The streets are swept and litter-free. I almost feel like I'm in another city. The thought of this makes me excited.

"Mommy, can we go to the zoo and see the monkeys?" I look out the window on the girls' side and watch women and children riding on the Houston Zoo's tiny yellow-and-red train.

"No, we're just gonna stay on the rail for now. Maybe next time." I know there'll be a next time. I know that life is changing right before me.

At the next stop a man wearing tan Dockers and a thick navy sweater sits down next to me. I stare out the window and lower my left hand into my jacket pocket. I feel a mixture of freedom and shame. It's amazing how if you want to pretend like you're not married, all you gotta do is cover up the ring; as if that gesture cancels every vow, or every shared experience, between a man and a wife.

I sneak a look at the man's left hand. No ring. I breathe easier and smile. I think I'm smiling because I finally realize this man looks at least seventy; he's got a cane with him, and his dreadlocks are so gray, long, and twisted, he looks insane. Totally not my type.

After Old Dude departs the train, this wig-sporting, false-boob-toting, fake-eyelash-wearing, six-foot-tall person sits next to me. This man applies lipstick, throws on a dress and a wig, and he believes he's a female? I want to pull him to the side and give him the real deal. By the time I finish telling him what it's really like to be a woman, I'm sure he'd toss that wig off his head and ditch his four-inch pumps.

This little trip on the train makes me think of Neil, and how much of a man he is, and how favorable he looks when compared to those two guys.

Jeez, I cannot wait to get off the train.

An hour after our ride ends, we spot a French bakery, buy some goodies, and enjoy munching on chocolate-chip cookies. Now we're bobbling along in the Honda, taking a casual drive home.

Vette clears her throat and glances back at Reesy, then turns to me. "So, Ms. Meadows . . ."

I laugh. "I'm not sure I like the sound of that."

"You're aching for him, aren't you? I know you've pretended like you're having fun, and I hope you are, but I see that distracted look in your eyes."

"Bless you, Vette. You're just trying to help. I can't get angry about that."

She shrugs and quickly glances at Reesy, who's nodding her head and singing to herself.

"Whatcha singing, niece?"

"'Your love's got me looking so crazy right now, looking so crazy in love . . .'"

"Ahhh, I thought that's what that was," my sister-in-law laughs.

Vette turns back to me. "So you told me you and Neil, uh, ahem, changed oil one Friday night. How was the oil change?"

I smirk. "It was slick, got my engines roaring again—at least for a hot minute."

"And did that oil change fix everything? Y'all plan on getting another tune-up?"

I glimpse at Reesy, who's in her own world. "I dunno. May be closed for business."

"Oh yeah? Why y'all shutting down the shop already?" Vette asks.

"Gotta make sure Neil isn't servicing any other cars."

"Would this car be a gold pickup?"

"You got it," I confirm.

"Ya think?"

"I dunno. I can't get him to admit— I mean, I don't know if he's still giving that truck any jumps. He might still charge those batteries here and there," I admit to Vette, "but I can't find any receipts, ya know what I'm saying?"

"Hmmm," she says. "If you had to do it all over again, would you, you know, get him to sign that piece of paper?"

"At this point I question my judgment. I wonder how I think it could have worked. So naive . . . . But to be honest, he was naive, too, right? He must've thought the arrangement could work."

"Oh, we know what he was thinking . . . or maybe he wasn't thinking," Vette responds.

"Tell me something. How was Neil with his former girlfriends? I know there was one he used to rave about for a minute when I first met him. What was her name?" I snap my fingers a few times, trying to get my brain to cooperate with my mouth. "Uh, shoot, starts with a K, I think."

"Kashmire Andrews?"

"That's it. I knew it was something unusual sounding. She was his last torrid romance before he and I hooked up." I wait a minute and concentrate on driving. "Vette, you haven't said anything . . ."

"I'm trying to remember," she mumbles.

"Oh, don't give me that. They were so long ago. It's not like I can do anything with that info today."

"Exactly."

"Why are you being protective of Neil all of a sudden?" I wish I didn't feel so resentful. I know so much about Neil already, why can't I know a little more? Maybe it will help me to understand him better.

"Okay, okay. Let me think of something I can tell you. I was young when he knew Kashmire, but from what I remember he was obsessed with her body."

I giggle but still feel uneasy.

"He would stare her down, which is really annoying, but I think Kashmire liked the attention—it flattered her. And I saw some old photos—she used to be a little heavy but apparently went on a super health kick and got in shape. Hired a personal trainer. Drank lots of juices, water, became a vegan. So Neil met her when she was slim and trim, and everything fell in the right places."

"So what happened?" I ask. "Something always happens."

"Neil said she wasn't marriage material. I think she had rotten credit and couldn't even qualify to buy a VCR."

"Stop lying, Vette."

"Okay, it wasn't that bad, but there was something about her that turned him off, something that took his eyes off Kashmire's body and made him notice the other characteristics he didn't notice before. I believe he called it off. Said she grew depressed, of course, but eventually she let it go."

"Hmmm . . . I wonder if I should be happy or scared?"

"Now, one thing I can say about Neil is he isn't the most unstable man I've ever seen. He's consistent, not acting like Jekyll and Hyde from one day to the next."

"Is that what you think? Easy for you to say."

"Well, you know what he does moment by moment better than me. I ain't checking him out that tough, but I just tossed that out to you. You can do what you want with it."

"One thing I know is this situation can't go on forever. I'll bet my life that it won't," I say in a measured voice.

"But what if it does?"

"There is no *but*, Vette, I'm telling you. Men get tired eventually. I am just hoping he'll get tired before I do."

"Now, that doesn't sound like a proactive attitude."

"Oh, you think it sounds passive, huh? Well, it's not."

"I'm just saying that most wives aren't like you."

"Oh, really?" I say, insulted. "Well, as far as I know, there is no universal textbook that instructs wives about how to feel or react in every situation. And whether I'm married, single, or whatever, one hundred percent of women will never feel exactly the same about a situation."

"Yeah, but—"

"Let me finish, Vette, since you started this. You claim most wives aren't like me—most *people* don't think alike, let alone wives. Example: One mother stops breast-feeding her kid when he turns one, another keeps breast-feeding her son even though he's thirteen. The point is no two people think alike, period, Vette. And guess what? Everybody still assumes they're right. So with my situation I'm doing what feels right— for me."

"Anya, but the things you put up with lets me know Neil's got you all cubed in."

Her remark makes me think she's not listening. And I almost regret having told her certain things.

"Like I said before, Vette, you just don't understand. Women like you, women who don't have a man, are always quick to give advice. So it's easy for you to judge me because it's not your heart that's in the middle of things."

"Okay, then, if that's the case, why even tell people your problems, and ask someone else's opinion? You're still gonna do whatever you—"

"Because, Vette," I say loudly, "women have to talk about our drama or else we'll go crazy. So even if we get awful advice from no-man-having girlfriends, we feel like we're sharing the pain. We need someone to shed a little light, even if the 'light' isn't any more far-reaching than a flashlight."

Vette laughs. "Oh jeez, great, thanks for letting me know all this. I mean, woo, where would I be without your life-altering wisdom?"

I smile and swat her and my frustration subsides.

"You know what I'm thinking about doing?" I say.

"What's that?"

"What if I enroll in whore college? See if I can get over like some of these women out here are doing. Oh yes, go to college and earn a Ph.D. in whoreology. I can even do an internship—"

"Mommy, you going to college? I wanna go. Can y'all speak up? I can't hear you."

For an embarrassing minute, I've forgotten my daughter's in the car. Mortified, I exchange a look with Vette, then yell, "Hush, Reesy! Don't talk. Keep singing, okay?" I smile at my daughter. "I'd rather hear you sing."

"Okay, Mommy." And she starts to belt out a Christina Aguilera song.

I laugh, thinking about how accepting kids can be. They possess boundless energy and are quick to believe something just because they're told it's so. I wish I could be childlike sometimes—to believe elephants can fly, and all that jazz. And if I continue hoping that my marriage will survive all its challenges, then faith will be worth holding on to. But I'm not always naive; I've lived long enough to know that hope can make a fool out of you. You can wish for something your entire life, and it never materializes. I don't want that to happen. Instead I plan to make a fool out of hope. I want to prove that my hope isn't in vain, and that every crooked thing in life has a way of righting itself.

"Hi," I say to my husband.

"Hey."

Us females march into the house chuckling. We glance at Neil, who has Brax sitting on top of the kitchen table in his infant seat. Neil is shoving a spoon toward Braxton's mouth, making loud engine noises and gliding the utensil up and down like it's an airplane. Brax is grinning up at his dad like he's the most adorable thing on earth.

Even though I question my judgment, I walk up to Neil and softly squeeze his cheek.

"Thanks," he tells me. "Thanks for keeping the front door unlocked for us. I appreciate that."

"Well, I just wanted to get your attention, Neil. But I see you have better things to do, so we'll talk later, okay?" I don't give him a chance to reply. I run up the stairs and am gasping for breath once I reach the top. I enter my bedroom, eager to know if things still look the same. I swing open the door. Everything's the way I left it. I feel relieved knowing you can never predict how someone will respond when they're frustrated.

What would've happened if Neil came home when I was changing the locks? Would it have caused an ugly scene? Would we have screamed with bitterness and cursed each other out? Would Reesy have caught us fighting and started crying, too?

I watched my parents argue and fight countless times when I was a kid. I never wanted to be like them, acting out in front of neighbors. My mom would chase my dad around the front yard, pink sponge rollers bouncing loosely in her hair. She would scream like she was doused with scalding-hot water while Dad struggled to hold her off. She'd aim a firearm at him and I'd see my father stone-faced, daring her to do it. Trembling, Mom would put away the gun, curse at Dad, and threaten to throw him out. She'd change the locks on the door, declare she was through. But five days later she'd hand my father a new set of keys. And like many women of her era, my mom put up with his ways until he became bedridden and died a slow, agonizing death. Watching Mom, I vowed to never do foolish things on account of a man. But it's incredible how circumstances can cause you to repeat everything you've seen and hated. It's learned behavior—something I wish I didn't know, but can't deny knowing because at that point it might be *all* I know.

Sunday evening, the temperature is pleasant, so Neil and I agree to meet in the backyard. We sit across from each other at the steel picnic table and gaze directly at each other no matter how awkward it feels. When I get tired of looking, I sip on a glass of lemonade, then clear my throat.

"What's up, Neil? One day you're swearing you want to make things up to me, next day you're back over there."

"Well, if you didn't act the way you do, maybe I wouldn't do what I do."

"So this is my fault?"

Neil just stares at me.

"I'll let you in on something," I tell him. "To me your having Dani's key signifies an open-door policy. First it's the key, then it's pajama parties, or splitting a bill, then you two could be staying together. Is that the road you're planning to walk?"

"No," he claims.

"No?"

Neil nods real slow, like I ought to be ashamed for asking.

"You don't have anything to add to that?" I ask.

Neil shakes his head.

"You don't even want to say if you understand where I'm coming from?"

"Well, Anya, I don't understand, yet I do. You're looking at this way more deeply than you should."

I bare my teeth and want to bite my fingernails. Men are so hard to understand that it creates an enormous gap between the genders. My stuff is like A, B, C, a five-year-old should be able to understand. But with men giving hints isn't enough, and sometimes being a straight shooter doesn't help, either. It's like no matter how many angles you describe, sometimes they still don't get it.

"Neil, you have a mom, a sister, other females in your family. Haven't you ever listened to their woes about relationships, the stuff they go through with men? Do you ever sympathize with what they tell you?"

"Sometimes. It's still different, Anya, because I'm not those guys. I'm me. And you're gonna react the way you do because you don't know the entire story. This whole weekend . . . totally unnecessary. All over a key? I didn't ask for the key."

"What difference does that make?"

"No, nooo, listen, Anya. Dani is thinking about what's most important to her. Now, sometimes that eclipses what's important to you."

"And so, I mean, what about you? What do you want, what is important to—"

"Everything most important to me clashes big-time. That's where my head is now, what I'm trying to reconcile. It's not about me trying to run and be with her. It's all about Braxton, in case you've forgotten. His birth has changed everything. I wonder what he's doing right now."

"Oh, don't worry about Braxton. He's upstairs either sleeping or sitting on Reesy's lap."

Neil stands up. "I hope she doesn't drop him."

"Have a seat. She's not going to hurt that boy."

"Y—you don't like him, do you?"

"What? Why are— That has nothing to do with anything."

"You pretend like you care about him, but I'm not sure I buy it."

"Well, Neil, let me ask this. If I was still married to you and got pregnant by a neighbor, and brought the baby home, told you this is a new addition to the family, would you be in love with that child?"

Neil downs the remainder of his lemonade and pushes the glass toward me.

"Just as I thought," I say with firmness. "Maybe for once you'll understand how it feels to be me, because up till now very little has shown me you do."

"Anya, do you know how split I am? I—I feel like I have to be in two places at one time. I want to be here with you and Reese, but I want to go over there and see Brax, too."

"I've never seen any father spend as much time with their other kids as you do. I just don't think it's all that necessary. I mean, if you skipped a few days, you think this baby would notice?"

Neil's eyes flicker with coldness and he stares till I break eye contact.

"Neil, may I propose something? What if I go over there and pick up Braxton and bring him back here each time you want to see him? You and Dani would have no contact, except over the phone."

"Hello? She works with me."

"I know, but I'm not exactly worried about that. What can you do while you're at work, anyway? I doubt you'd screw her on the desk." I laugh, hoping he'll laugh, too. When he grins, I don't feel much better. I've heard of women who go up to their hubby's job his first week of work, then go around introducing themselves to all the women, getting in their face, making themselves known. I've never done that. Besides, you can go up to the man's office, walk all around the building thinking you've met each and every temptation in the joint, and there's always one you don't find out about until after the divorce papers are final.

"Give me that key, Neil."

Neil makes a face but ends up handing me the key.

I am perched on the edge of Dani's love seat, watching Dani, who's sitting on her living-room floor changing Brax's clothes.

"I spilled some grape juice on him " she explains, "and I can't have him going out the house looking like any old thing."

She doesn't have to give me all those details. I just want to grab the kid, his diaper bag, a teddy bear, and get out of there. I feel proud of myself for sticking to my end of the deal—pick Brax up from Dani at two o'clock on a Saturday afternoon, and resist saying anything too sarcastic.

Reesy is singing and hopping on one foot.

"Sit down, girl," I fuss. "I told you twice already."

"I wanna stay here, Mommy. I don't wanna go home."

I clear my throat. "That's an idea . . . Dani, while you run and do whatever, Reesy and I can hang out here. Brax doesn't even have to go out. I know you couldn't be gone for more than a few hours."

"Say what? I'm not down with that. I–I . . ."

"You what? I don't mind doing it."

"That's what I have Audrey for," she explains.

"The Audrey you talk about like a dog behind her back?"

Dani smirks and continues stuffing Brax's bag. "Just take him back to your place and I'll pick him up when I'm done. Plus, doesn't Neil want to see him? I thought this whole idea was really about Neil, or have things changed?"

I stare, trying to bore an intense hole in the side of Dani's face. She picks up her child and straps him in his car seat. "You know, Anya, I do realize the sacrifice you're making. If you do this for me, I'll be your friend forever."

"That's okay." I shiver. "With friends like you . . ."

Dani laughs heartily and finally looks at me. "Don't say it. I'm not a bad person. You just don't understand me. You haven't given me a chance."

"I think I've given you more chances than is reasonable."

"Well . . ." She pauses and stares at Braxton. "If that's the case, why do you do it? If cooperating isn't what you sincerely want, why—"

I stand up. "Don't get me wrong. I'll give you chance after chance, but it doesn't mean I'll let you run over me. You don't want to see what could happen if you try to do that. All I ask is that you respect me and I'll respect you. I know I can do that much."

"Hmm, I get 'cha. Nothing wrong with that." Dani sighs, yet she looks so relaxed, like nothing is a big biggie for her. I've always wondered about people like that. Are they assets to society or perpetually dangerous and us normal folk should take a hint and run for the hills?

"One more thing," I tell Dani, and grab Braxton's diaper bag. "Not that you've asked, but I think you really need to get out more. Hey, if you call me on a Thursday night and say you're going out to party, I wouldn't mind watching Brax for you. There are lots of popular clubs out there, and I'm sure—"

"Look, I hear what you're saying, but I haven't really thought about all of that lately. My life is work and Brax, work and Brax." She bites her bottom lip. "To be honest, not too many guys have been taking serious looks at me. I mean, they talk noise a lot but I'm not hearing it. I don't have time for casual relationships. Next time I do something, it's gonna be serious. And right now I just can't see that happening."

I've never thought about how Dani might want to be with someone else but just doesn't have any solid prospects. I guess she's in that dilemma—the one where a woman becomes a single parent and gets more selective about who she dates and lets her kids be around. It's sickeningly amazing how women acquire so many new values once kids are thrown in the mix.

"You know what, Dani? Having a kid doesn't automatically make men any better or any worse. Men, are men period. You'll attract the same types whether you have one, two, or zero children."

"Don't say that," she says, sounding alarmed.

"Well, you won't know this unless you go and see for yourself."

"I'm not doing that. Whoever I'm meant to be with is gonna have to find me. I'm not going to go search for him. I have an awful track record when I try and choose a guy. My jerk radar is way off at times." She laughs. "Does Neil have any brothers or male cousins?"

"Even if he did, none of them would be Neil, now, would they?"

Open-mouthed, Dani watches while the kids and I quietly leave her apartment.

18

Neil

I am standing on the sidewalk in front of my house waving to Anya. She's backing out the driveway in the SUV. It's packed with suitcases, a makeup bag, an orange cooler filled with waters, sodas, sandwiches, and fresh fruit.

"Why you got that messed-up look on your face?" Vette is standing in the doorway, her arms folded across her chest. She's smirking.

"I don't have a messed-up look on my face," I tell her.

"How would you even know? You can't see what I see, Neil."

"Whatever you say." I ignore Vette's rude stare and brush past her so I can go in my house. My spirit is a mixture of joy and anxiety. I am happy Anya was determined to go on her weekend getaway, but I hope she doesn't get any spontaneous ideas while she's out trekking through the state of Texas. She's driving up to Fort Worth to hang out with some girlfriends and will be back Monday.

When she first told me she was going away and asked if I'd watch Reese and my son, I smiled and told her, "Sure, I'll baby-sit for you." She rolled her eyes. When I asked why she did that, she said, "It's amazing that when the mother is caring for the child, she's doing her natural-born job, but when a daddy watches the kids, he calls it baby-sitting. Baby-sitting? Are you not the daddy?"

Flabbergasted, I told her, "Have a good weekend."

She said, "No, I will not, and you can't make me." But then she burst out laughing. And I knew right then Anya Meadows is one of a kind—*most* of the time. She's the type of woman that if you aren't cautious, you won't realize what you've got until it's gone.

Vette trails me into the house. When I walk to the den, she's there. And when I am craving potato chips and some Snapple and go to the kitchen, she's right there again.

"I thought I was the baby-sitter," I told her.

"What? You paranoid. I ain't spying on you, trying to keep up with what your scandalous ass is doing."

I grab two bottles of Snapple from the refrigerator.

"Thanks," Vette says, and places her hands around one of the bottles.

"That's mine, get your own," I snap.

"Oh, I thought you were being thoughtful and sweet and kind—"

"Remember the hot dogs?"

I grip both Snapples and a few bags of chips and head back to the den.

"So what are you gonna be doing, Neil?" Vette asks, following me down the hallway. "Bumming? Eating, watching TV, and scratching your butt all weekend?"

"What if I do?"

"The front lawn is looking mighty raggedy out there."

"If you care so much, you know where the lawn mower is," I tell her.

"You are one self-centered, lazy—"

"Hey, hey, Vette, what have I done to you?" We're now in the den. "Why are you always up on me? I am not married to you."

She waves her hand, as if to say *Whatever,* and takes a seat on the floor in front of the TV. A Chris Tucker flick is on. She's sitting so close to the screen that if she moves any closer she'll be costarring in the movie. Vette starts snickering.

"Hey, Vette, do you mind? I can't see with your head in the way." I am beyond irritated. I imagined myself spending time mostly alone, a rarity, and hanging out with the kids this evening. Dani will bring Brax over later. Riley took Tamika and Reese to the zoo and they should be back soon. Great time to do nothing, but with my sister here, following me with every pace, it's like I have no justice, and no peace.

"Why are you here, Vette?"

"What?" My sister lowers the volume and looks up at me. "You let me come stay with you, remember? You didn't want me living on the street, living with some guys or even girls, for that matter."

"I thought once you got yourself together, you'd be . . . doing something else."

"Oh, am I wearing out my welcome here? Going to school isn't enough? You want me to get a decent job, right? Or do you feel I'm like your conscience, and if I'm here, you can't do what you want to do?"

"Vette, I'm a grown man. I don't answer to you. I don't even know why you'd say you're my conscience. All I have to do is throw you out and all that talk would end, right?"

She averts her eyes and runs her fingers through her hair.

"I just wonder whose side you're on, that's all, Vette. You're so wrapped up in my business—"

"Okay, from now on I won't be," she exclaims. "You can do whatever you want, which wouldn't be anything different. I won't say a word. Let the chips fall where they may."

I sit up in my chair. "You meant that? You won't go tell Anya any- and everything you think she may want to know?"

"Nope, never. You're on your own, kiddo."

"Good, thanks. Now, get out so I can watch this movie in peace."

"As you wish."

She leaves the den, runs up the stairs. I hear a door slam and I laugh to myself. I sip on my juices, eat my chips, break wind as loud as I want, and feel freer than I have in a long time.

When the doorbell rings a few hours later, Reese runs to open it. I frown, get up, and stagger toward the front of the house.

"Hey, there. She's gone, huh? You feeling okay?" Dani smirks and rolls her eyes. "Come get your mini me."

I look at the Tacoma. "Why'd you leave the baby in the truck by himself?"

"Hey, I can't carry Brax and everything else. Just go get him, please. I think I hear him crying."

I go and get the baby. Dani is waiting for us in the foyer. She looks relaxed. She has on some cropped pants and a flowery-looking short-sleeved shirt. And it looks like she's recently been to the beauty salon—her hair is full of bouncing ringlets that make her look even younger than she does normally.

I gesture, so she follows me. We retreat to the den and I remove Braxton from his baby prison. I bounce him on my knee a few times, until he gurgles and giggles, and when he starts slobbering, I ask Dani to go to the kitchen and get some paper towels and a bottle of juice.

She comes back and sits next to me on the couch. Our knees are touching. She reaches across my body to caress Brax softly on his cheek. Then she puts her arm around me and squeezes.

"Thanks, Dani." I cough and scoot away. She slides closer to me. I look at her sternly. "Do you mind?"

She pouts and rolls her eyes.

"Do you have any limits at all, woman?"

"I don't know."

I laugh. "I hope you aren't trying to find out if you have limits or not. Not right now, anyway."

"You're just whipped, that's all you are."

"Don't go there, Dani. Can we just, uh . . . never mind. It doesn't even matter."

"Say what you wanted to say, Neil." She looks in my eyes and we stare at each other for two full minutes. She leans up and tries to press her lips against mine. I move my head away and continue playing with Brax.

Dani leans against the couch pillows and folds her arms across her chest. She stares around the room. "You're acting like Mrs. Wifey has surveillance cameras installed in this joint." Then she yawns and stands up. "Hey, I don't care that you're acting weird. I need to go, anyway. I'm supposed to be hanging out with some friends at Club Max's."

"What friends? Why Max's?"

She laughs and shrugs. "I don't know why they chose that club. Maybe to do something radical like, um, having fun with friends."

"I didn't know you had any friends."

"Don't be silly. Everyone has friends, Neil."

"Why haven't you told me about them? Are they males or females?"

"They're *friends*, Neil. Hang-out buddies. To be honest, I haven't seen these folks in a while, so it'll be like catching up. Don't worry. They're legit."

"Legit meaning females?"

She laughs again and blushes. "You want me to stay here with you?"

I bounce Brax on my knee.

"Hey, I'm talking to you, Neil."

"Is that why you got your hair done all fancy?"

"Mmm-hmm, you like it?"

I stare at her hair and lay Brax on the couch.

"Don't do that," Dani scolds. "He'll roll over and end up falling on the floor. Strap him in the seat."

"He'll be all right. C'mere, Dani." I pat the space next to me.

Dani glances at her watch. "Damn, I gotta go, Neil. Maybe I'll see you tomorrow afternoon."

"Tomorrow? Afternoon? What about tonight? When will you be back from hanging out?"

"I have no idea. But I'll see you tomorrow, okay?"

I watch her walk away from me, leaving the den, hearing her heels click against the tile in the foyer, and then I hear my front door shut.

It's two in the A.M.

As soon as I see Dani's truck pull up, I slip through the front door and walk briskly to it. She rolls down the window. "Hop in," she commands.

I run to the passenger side and slide onto the fabric-covered seat. The engine still humming, she backs the Tacoma out the driveway.

"Where're you going?" I ask.

"Shhh," she says. "You worry too much."

We drive down my block, up a few more, and end up still in the neighborhood at the end of a block that has inadequate lighting. Dani kills the engine and everything goes quiet. Soon I hear crickets chirping. It's difficult to see and I wait for my vision to adjust. The wind is whipping around us and causing tree leaves to flutter and swirl.

I ask her, "How was the—"

Dani lips devour mine. I hesitate for a minute but open my mouth. Her tongue explores me, pressing deeper and sliding on top of my tongue. She smacks my lips several times, pecking me. I squirm and want to caress my dick. My knees are smashed against the instrument panel. I wipe my mouth.

"Are you crazy?" I ask her.

"Are you?"

"The kids are upstairs, Dani. Four blocks away."

"They'll be all right. I want to be alone with you."

I moan and passionately kiss her again. When I'm done, I tell her, "I haven't made out with a girl in a car since my college days."

"You didn't have any money for a hotel room?"

"I was a student earning minimum wage. We laid the pipe wherever we could—dorm rooms, the back of a van, in the library between the shelves . . ."

"Mmm. I believe it. Was it fun?" She smiles.

"Yes and no. Yes, because it was adventurous and sneaky. No, because I was never able to maneuver myself into the right position. If I'd taken up yoga, something different might've happened."

"You're so naughty, Neil. Don't change, okay?" Her voice is sooo soft, sexy. I look at her and unlock the doors and command her, "Get out the truck."

Dani wastes no time opening her door, and I follow her out. She leans her back against the driver side of the Tacoma. I rub myself against her like we're teenagers in an empty school yard. She arches her neck and I kiss the skin underneath her ear. She smells sweet, edible. I grab her head between my hands, press my lips on hers, and slob her down. She lets me. She's mine. She has on a black strapless form-fitting dress. Dani lowers the top of the dress and grabs her breasts between her hands like she's holding two oranges. I suck her nipples, giving each one three seconds apiece as I go back and forth, rolling my tongue across them.

"Dammit, Neil," she gasps. "Let's do it, now. C'mon." First she grabs a large scarf and completely covers her hair, tucking loose strands underneath the fabric. Then she clasps her hand in mine and pulls me to the back of the truck. She steps on the rear bumper and hops in the cab.

"We can lie on these quilts that are in the corner," she tells me.

"Why you have quilts here?"

"So I can fulfill a fantasy."

"Stop lying, Dani."

"Stop asking, then."

She spreads out the quilts, pulls her black dress above her hips, removes her cheeky pants, and lies down with her legs spread open. I collapse next to her warm body, unzipping my blue jeans. Getting on top, I plunge my rigid, throbbing dick inside her. Dani is soaking wet and squishy sounding. I clamp my hand over her mouth when she begins to wail and tremble. I sex her hard for ten minutes, then we straighten our wrinkled clothes and hop back into the truck. She quickly drives off and drops me off at home.

While showering and wiping Dani off of me, I feel convicted and weakly ask the Lord to forgive me. I wait and listen and stop soaping myself when a voice whispers, "You are not sincere."

The phone rings at four A.M. It's my cell, which I customarily leave on all night.

"Neil."

It's Dani. She's crying.

"What's wrong?"

"I'm sorry," she sniffs. "I hate this."

"Hate what? What happened?"

"Why didn't you stop me?" she cries.

I sit up on the sofa. "Dani—"

"We did it without protection, Neil. Didn't you notice, or did that not matter to you?"

"I thought you were on the Pill."

"Sometimes they make me feel sick, so I stopped taking them."

"And when were you gonna tell me that, Dani? After you take a test and find out you're pregnant again?"

"I'm sorry, Neil. I don't want that to happen again. I wouldn't be able to handle that again. What are we gonna do?"

Hey, I was happy to have one baby with Dani, but two?

"Dani, if you're pregnant, you might—"

"No, nooo. No."

"Well, you should've thought about this." My voice is tight. I am pacing across the library now. I recognize that, sexy as she is, Danielle Frazier can be sexily stupid. But I feel dumb for dealing with her. I wish we'd used our brains and I'd worn protection, 'cause these days having sex without protection is like eating barbecue ribs without a napkin. Doesn't make any sense.

"You still there?" she sniffs.

"I'm here."

"Well, I asked you a question twice and you didn't respond. I thought you hung up on me." She pauses. "Don't abandon me, Neil, promise me."

"Dani, look." I don't know what to do, say. "I—I'm not gonna do that."

"Promise?"

"I don't make promises."

"Neil!"

I pull the phone away from my ear. I feel like ending the call, silencing her voice. But I calm myself down and speak into the mouthpiece.

"Dani, look. Worrying about this won't change a thing. Say your prayers. Take a long bath. Scrub yourself real good. And let's wait and see what happens."

"Awful, yucky, sucky advice, Neil. You could never be a psychoanalyst with a hot column."

"Thanks for sharing that, Dani. Just be cool, okay? I'll try to come see you tomorrow."

"Are you going to church in a few hours?"

"I don't do church anymore," I say with sorrow, and hang up.

Do you know what it's like to love a woman so much that she makes you feel weak, as if you possess the strength of a flimsy piece of tissue? The woman you love is that one-of-a-kind, God-broke-the-mold-when-he-made-her type; she walks the earth and can affect you like no other. One woman can have the hots for you, ask you to call her, and you keep on stepping, acting like you don't speak her language. Another woman tells you to call, says she needs to hear your voice, and you add her number to speed dial, wishing there were more than twenty-four hours in a day, so you could talk to her and be with her all the time, as if the day had no beginning and the night had no end. You stare in this woman's eyes whenever you're together. And when she's not with you, you whip out her ever-present photo, look at her face, smile, and talk to her picture even though you know she cannot hear you.

But then there's the other side. The same woman who causes you to stagger after her like a happy drunk is the very one who tires you out, making your legs collapse underneath you. You're the dopehead resisting rehab. Your soul cries for her, and you're willing to steal from your own mother—anything to pay the price it takes to be with that woman. And you love how love feels, yet you hate the feeling that love gives you. You've fallen into a deep well that has no walls, into relationship purgatory. You're dropping, descending, wailing, grinding your teeth, so horribly tormented you feel no one, not even God himself, can hear your cries and rescue you.

That afternoon, Dani calls and asks to come by. I say, "Don't bother." She screams at me and says don't tell her what to do. Flustered, I explain I'm not telling her what to do, but I wish she'd lay off me for once. I promise I'll bring Brax to her early the next morning before I go to work. I know Audrey will get to Dani's place around seven. I can be there at six-thirty.

"Why are you acting like this, Neil?"

"Acting like what?" I snap. "Saying no for a change?"

"I wish—"

"The things you wish always get me in trouble, Dani. I've only gotten a few hours of sleep in the past twenty-four. I have two kids in my care, and so far none of this has been the most peaceful experience."

"Oh, and I suppose all of this is my fault. You know what, Neil? You're terrible at taking your share of the blame."

"I know, and that's why for this one day, I want to be by myself. Let me care for the baby without any impromptu visits. I need to concentrate more on being his father than being your crutch . . . and, well, that's all I have to say."

Dani is disturbingly quiet, which causes me to whistle. I'm in the kitchen trying to fix a Sunday afternoon meal. Brax is in his infant seat. Reese is sitting in the corner, with large yellow, green, and blue crayons spread on the table. She's trying to color in the lines but isn't doing a good job of it. I've promised her that I'll help, but I have to put a honey-baked ham in the oven. I am rinsing the broccoli so it can be steamed, and I want to make some hollandaise sauce, and strip and rinse a few stalks of corn.

"You know, Neil, you're totally right about this. It's not like we cannot function if we aren't in each other's face all the time. Besides, I need to get a life. I'll be twenty-six in a couple of weeks. I have no real boyfriend. I want to find someone who is serious about me, who loves my son and appreciates and values both of us. So you go right ahead and play Daddy. I'm going to do what I have to do. Let's just be best friends, okay? We'll freeze the sex and be good friends, Neil. What do you think of that?"

I close my eyes and tell her, "I think since we're so-called best friends like this, you have no damn reason to call me again." And I hang up.

19

Dani

There've only been two times in my life that I've wanted to kill myself.
The first was when I was a nineteen-year-old college student. It was a
Friday night and I was invited to a frat party. These types of parties went
on all the time. We'd see flyers about the event at the University Center on
the UH campus. Me and my girls would get dolled up and head out. We
danced till it was so hot our clothes fastened to our skin. And we'd gulp
beer past one in the morning, then ask around about the after-party.
This one time, some guy I never heard of was having a get-together at
his home in Third Ward. Since that wasn't too far from campus, we girls
thought, Cool, let's close down the night by making this one last stop.

It was me, my roommate Samone, and our friend Nikki. Nikki
claimed she knew the guy, had been to his place before. We went, par-
tied, and drank till our tongues were silly and satisfied, and I ended up
in the arms of a guy I never formally met—a handsome but short, hy-
peractive dude I'd seen around campus who flirted and called me
"cutie." Hype took me by the hand and led me to the privacy of a dark-
ened room. It felt weird to press my lips against the mouth of someone I
barely knew, but the heat was on, so we kept the heat going. I didn't or-

gasm, and I don't know if Hype did or not. The only good thing is that he wore a condom. But the worst thing was to return to campus on Monday and experience hearing a noisy cafeteria grow quiet as a golf course when I entered. All these guys, my classmates, were smiling and giving me knowing looks. It seemed like a hundred pairs of eyes monitored me while I was walking and grasping my tray of food, searching for a seat. When I passed by the table with the guy who saw me naked that weekend, I heard laughter, saw fingers pointing. I blinked several times, wanting to eradicate these heartless fools from my vision, but their stares and judgmental smirks kept hanging around. That's the first time I'd been called a whore, obviously, and I didn't enjoy how that felt. I wondered if those loose-tongued people ever stopped to think that I was someone's daughter, someone's sister, someone's grandchild.

Even though I didn't own a gun, I wanted to find one, then find the hyper guy with the big mouth, press the steel between his eyes, pull the trigger, and take my pain away. I wanted to torture the man who only cared about me as long as he could hit it and run. Then for him to go tell what happened, as if I fucked myself by myself and he had no part in it at all . . . or maybe his part didn't matter as much as mine. I never understood how guys could hound, beg, and promise, then kiss and gleefully, stupidly, loudly tell. These guys make themselves the heroes of sexual conquests, and the woman is the clueless, stained villain.

Unable to see clearly, I got sick of the cafeteria's laughter and whispers. I abandoned my tray of untouched meat loaf at an empty table. I ran to my dorm and searched around until I was holding a bottle of my roommate's white pills. I didn't think about it, I just started popping them. One, two, three, four . . . I quit when I got to five. I slumped to the floor of the bathroom, leaned my head against the hard wall, with the plastic bottle clutched in my hand—a bottle with the power to terminate my life. Even though at first I yearned to end my life, I hoped my efforts wouldn't succeed. I figured that if I tried to kill myself because someone said something vicious about me, then I was weak and deserved to die. But I knew better. I knew there was no way I'd let people like that steal my breath away. If I made a mistake, okay, I've blown it, but why should I go before my time, before I find out if there's more to Danielle than the mistakes she's been proven to make? Fortunately, Samone soon came home. She screamed when she saw me, then made me stick a finger down my throat, and remained by my side until I could pull myself together.

But today, when Neil hangs up on me and I tremble and stomp and scream at the air, and fling a glass against the wall and watch it shatter into dozens of pieces, I'm taken back to that day in college, revisiting the pain, hurt, humiliation, and lowliness tugging against my spirit, the haunting whispers that declared, *You are a worthless fool.* Today I am tempted to find another bottle of pills, but before that temptation takes root, my inner strength counsels me, "No, don't do that. His ugly words can't take your breath away. You're worth more than what someone else thinks about you, good or bad." And I listen and I agree . . . and I listen and I agree. I listen until my heart is persuaded to do something different. I pay attention and say yes to something positive instead of agreeing to beat myself up and take the pathetic way out. I don't want to live inside the pain anymore, the pain that says I'm not worth the dirt underneath my feet. I tell myself I *am* worth something. And even if I haven't any means by which to prove my worth, I know the end of my life will not consist of someone stumbling upon my cold, soulless body sprawled on the apartment floor. No way. No way.

Besides, that would be so unfair to my son. It's no secret I'm not the best mother in the world, but I'm not the worst, either. I realize I could do much better than what I've been doing, but Brax knows me and accepts me the way I am. He knows I'm Mama even if he can't yet form the word. I can tell by the way he pats, smiles, and strokes my cheeks. And I'm sure of his unconditional love when his toothless grin brightens his face every time I enter a room.

I have to get myself together for the sake of Brax. I want him to know me, to be with me long enough to remember me, to always know he has a place in my genuine but confused heart. I want him to know that even when I mess up big-time, we still have each other, I'm still his mama. So let me shake the fear within, begin again, and do something I should've done months ago. It's something I've half-heartedly thought of, but maybe I should try to put my *whole* heart into it.

Dear Anya Meadows,

Not long ago you asked me to do something for you. To re-spect you because you planned on respecting me no matter what has happened in the past. I haven't done a very good job of respecting you, not when I keep having intimate rela-tions with Neil.

I put down the pen and read my words. My hands are shaking and I'm tempted to tear the paper up into tiny bits. I want to burst into tears, but don't. Confession may be good for the soul, but isn't it risky for my safety and welfare? Even if you know the right thing to do, what if you're not quite ready?

I pick up the phone and dial. When Neil picks up, I feel relieved.

"Hi, Neil."

He pauses. "Didn't I tell you not to call me anymore?"

"Actually, I don't want to talk to you. I want to talk to Anya."

"For what?"

"Neil, could you please give me her cell number?"

"Dani, why are you tripping?" His voice sounds hoarse.

"Give me her number, please, Neil."

"For what?"

"I—I need to ask her something."

"Tell you what. I won't give you her number, but I can call her for you on the three-way."

"O—okay." I give in.

"But will you first tell me what you want to ask her?"

"I'd rather not," I mumble. "It's hard enough as it is."

Neil sighs but clicks over to make the call. My hands are sweating so much I have to wipe them on my slacks.

"Dani, I have Anya on the line. Go ahead."

"Um, hi, Anya. I, uh, I just wanted to say that I am going to make a real effort to do better than I've been doing. It's not my intention to come between you and your family."

"What? Dani, have you been drinking?"

I hear a smile in her voice, which surprises me and makes me wish I could smile, too.

"No, ma'am. No drinking. No nothing."

"Well," she responds, "I'm not sure what this is all about, but I'll tell you one thing. What you just told me— I'll believe it when I see it. Good-bye." The smile in her voice is gone. And she hangs up.

I wait a day, and call Neil again. After some awkward small talk, I ask him, "What's going on with us? What is our bottom line?"

When he doesn't respond, I ask, "Then answer a yes or no question for me."

"Okay," he says.

"Can we start again, can you give me another chance? Because in my heart I don't believe you meant what you said; that you don't want me calling anymore."

He laughs. "That doesn't sound like a yes or a no question."

I laugh, too, and I know his reply is his way of saying he wants to give me another chance.

All drama ascends to a climax just to come to a stop so it can gear back up again. Two weeks later after our drama subsides, my March birthday arrives, on hump day. It's sun-drenched in Houston, hitting sixty degrees as early as eight in the morning. I go to work and am surprised but pleased to find huge helium-filled balloons dancing outside my doorway. Inside the office, a huge white envelope with my name scribbled on it is leaning against the framed picture of Braxton. Inside is a beautiful card, fifty bucks, and my coworkers' birthday greetings.

"Don't make plans for lunch," a woman tells me when I pass her in the hallway. Other coworkers are friendly while some offer me their customary aloof vibe.

After falling out for a hot minute, Neil and I made up and are on somewhat regular terms. He calls me thirty minutes before lunch.

"How's your day going, Dani?"

"So far I've received three hundred e-mails, and two hundred ninety-five of them were spam. How's that for being productive?"

"What about projects?"

"If a project includes zapping two dozen pop-ups, I've done quite well."

"Did you do what I advised you to do?"

"Yes, and it hasn't done any good. My workload has dwindled drastically. Mr. D has been doing this stupid stuff for going on two weeks. What, is he trying to break my spirit or something?"

"Don't start me to lying," Neil says. "I thought if you talked to him, he'd work with you, but it sounds like that isn't the case."

"Well, what do you expect from a bastard? Bastards sure are good at being bastards."

He doesn't say anything, maybe realizing I need to vent.

"Neil, I dunno. It seems like so much is coming at me. My you-know-what test came out negative and that's great, but I'm still having some feminine-type problems and will be going back to the doctor this afternoon. I get off at three."

"Why didn't you tell me the test was negative?"

"Get that smile out of your voice, okay?" I snap at him, then lighten my tone. "I mean, I was relieved, too, but lately if it's not one thing, it's another. I'm forced to be strong even when I don't want to."

"Hey," he says suddenly. "Someone's in my office. I gotta go. Let me know how your appointment goes."

"Right, sure, no problem." I hang up, eager to see this day come to an end.

The only good thing about today is I know I look hot. I'm wearing a gray-and-black pinstripe suit with a skirt that comes a few inches above my knees. My black patent pumps click with authority every time I walk down the hall. So when a group of us go to lunch at Pappadeaux's on the South Loop and I drink two margaritas, I don't feel guilty.

But when I get back to work around one-thirty, I see a pink envelope on my desk.

"He did it, that bastard." He promised not to let me go after thirty days, but technically it hasn't even been thirty days.

A minute later I look up and see two uniformed security guards standing in my doorway. They instruct me to pack all my belongings, and they say they'll accompany me out the building once I'm done. I slowly stash Brax's photo, a few potted plants, my Rolodex, some books and magazines in a cardboard box that a guard hands me, and twenty minutes later, when I leave work, I know that the fifty bucks I got as a birthday gift will hardly make a dent.

At the doctor's I am trembling and feeling insecure. I wonder what will happen in the future if Brax or I get sick. Maybe Neil can add Brax to his insurance, but what about me?

I leave the doctor's in a daze. I don't remember passing by South Braeswood, or Fannin Street, or any other spot I typically notice when driving home.

As soon as I get there, I pick up the phone. It's times like these I wish I had a long-distance calling card. But I dial the area code 562 and the remaining seven digits.

"Hey, Mama, it's me."

"What's wrong?" she says, alarmed.

"Can you call me right back please, here at the apartment?"

"Why can't we just talk now?"

"Please call me, Ma."

"Okay, okay, give me a minute."

I hang up and dab my nose with some tissue. I check the time. Audrey probably took Braxton on an outing, and as soon as she gets here, I'll have to figure out what to tell her.

I kick off my stupid heels and slide my useless two-hundred-dollar suit off my body. I slump on the couch, my hand clutching the portable.

I let the phone ring twice, even though I want to pick up when it rings once.

"What's the matter, Dani?"

"Ma, how are things going with you?"

I lay back on the couch wondering if I should speak louder or something. "Ma, did you hear me?"

"Yeah, I heard you. I know you didn't ask me to call you long distance just to talk about me. So what's going on?"

"I, uh, I'm so scared . . ." My voice catches.

"Scared of what? What happened, Dani? You want me to fly down there?"

I sit up. "No, no. Well, not yet, anyway. As of today, I–I'm jobless . . . I believe I'll get another gig, but right now I'm trying to absorb the shock."

"How'd you lose your job? Does it have to do with that guy?" Mama's voice is filled with disappointment, which makes me feel worse.

"Kinda, sorta."

"Why haven't you filed for child support? Much money as he makes, you could be getting a good thousand dollars a month to help take care of that baby."

"Aww, I just don't want to do that. Neil is very good to Braxton, and takes good care of him on his own. I don't want to burden him—"

"This is not about that piece of dick, Dani. This is about you and that baby. Now, what's done is done, and I hope you aren't still sleeping with him. . . ."

"Nooo, no way. I've wised up." I cross my fingers, close my eyes briefly.

"Well, that's good to hear. Just don't panic, okay? Maybe you can draw unemployment, or you could sign up with a temporary agency."

"Ewww," I protest. "Heck no, temping is the worst."

"Ain't nothing wrong working contract."

"They always treat you second rate, like they need your ass to do the job yet you don't belong. I always feel like a piece of toilet paper, and everyone is about to wipe me against their smelly butt."

"It's not that bad. And don't be worried about how the employees act, not when you got bills to pay."

"I know, I know. Thanks, Ma. I just want another great job," I told her, *one that I won't blow the second time around.* A good lesson can never be learned until a person goes through hell just to find out what *not* to do.

"Well, I'm listening real well right now," I say out loud.

"What you say?"

"Nothing, Ma," I say, my face turning red. "I just need you to walk me through some things. I believe everything will work out. Hey, I'm a great employee—at least I think I am. I just hate when wrenches are thrown. It takes me a while to bounce back and get focused."

"Dani, someone's banging on the door, so let me get off this phone. Call me if you need anything."

I hang up and wince after hearing her words. I feel rotten burdening my mother with my problems, but at the same time I'm glad I even have a mother to talk to. God knows I need someone to talk to. Need someone to hold my hand. And this time around, Neil just isn't the perfect fit.

20

Anya

"As you know, I am a Christian, and I believe in God and Jesus and all them, but some things about the Bible just puzzle me. Am I the only person who feels that way?"

Reesy and I are sitting next to Riley and Tamika. It took three non-pressured invitations to convince me to visit Riley's church. I am enjoying the words of Pastor Solomon, who tends to look out at the congregation like he's personally talking to you.

"Yep, the Bible is a great book, but have you ever wondered about something? Like, Noah and some of those folks living to be five hundred, six hundred, seven hundred years old." Pastor Solomon scratches his head. "Now, I'm trying to figure out, when Noah turned five hundred, how'd they fit all those candles on that cake? And where did they find a birthday card that said, 'Happy Five Hundredth Birthday'? I don't know about you, but those are just some of the things that I sit around and think about. It's like, you got me straight tripping, Boo."

I sit back and relax. Reesy squeezes my hand and I squeeze back. When it's drop-dead quiet she says, "I like this church, Mommy." I tell her to hush, but you know what? I am totally feeling what my baby is feeling. I squeeze her hand again.

A couple of days later, Neil is sitting at the dinner table. We've eaten baked fish and steamed veggies. He's reading the newspaper and sipping raspberry tea, a drink I'll make for him but won't sip myself because of the odd aftertaste.

"Anything good in there?" I say, and turn my back to load the dishwasher with plates and glasses.

"If 'good' means war casualties, corporate heads being exposed for criminal acts, and the price of gas skyrocketing, there's all kinds of good in the paper."

"I hear ya," I reply. I rotate the knob on the faucet and begin rinsing some of the dirtier pots.

"Hey Anya, could you please do something for me?"

"Okay," I say without turning my head.

"When you're done with the dishes, could you pour a glass of water from the fridge? Make sure it's totally full."

"No problem," I lazily reply. I feel worn out and want to go upstairs, run a bubble bath, then maybe read and get some sleep.

I fill a glass with water and sit next to Neil.

"Here, take these," he says, and slides two blue-and-white capsules near me.

"Take them for what?"

Neil is turning the pages of the business section but says, "Just do it."

I laugh. "Just say no."

Neil doesn't laugh but I sense he's waiting on me.

"Okay, I'll do it but you'll have to explain what this is about." I pick up the pills one at a time and wash them down with the entire glass of water. "Happy now? Okay, what's up, Neil? Are you trying to tell me something?"

"Like what?"

"I've gained five pounds. Is this some type of diet pill? You're ashamed of me?"

He lowers the paper. "No, Anya. You look the same to me."

"'The same' could be interpreted 'fat as always.'"

"I don't mean that and you know it. You're the one who feels self-conscious about your weight. You know I never ride you about that."

"But if you had your choice, you'd want me slimmer, wouldn't you?"

Neil resumes reading the newspaper. He's reading the death notices section, and I know there's nothing in there that could possibly concern him.

"You don't have to say it, Neil. It's cool."

We lock eyes and both laugh. I hop up. "You want dessert? I can whip up some strawberry shortcake real quick."

"No, I'm good. I'm about to tuck myself in."

I stand up, "Okay, see ya."

"Anya." He coughs. "I'll need you to take these pills twice daily for another eleven days, okay?"

The next morning after Neil leaves for work, I burst in the library and start pulling out desk drawers, search under the couch, running my fingers all over his desktop. I un-shelve and re-shelve books, and remove sofa cushions. Nothing there, either.

When he gets home that night, I behave like everything is normal, but when he goes to use the bathroom on the first floor, I wait outside the door so I can ask him about the pills he's just given me. They're resting in the center of my hand. Neil told me to go drink some water while he went to relieve himself. I hear him in there—it sounds like a gallon of liquid is being poured in the toilet. He makes moaning sounds, hissing and groaning at the same time. When he opens the door and sees me, his eyes are red, and he gives me a skeptical look.

"Neil, you are not going to give me pills and not explain why I'm taking them. All I have to do is go to my pharmacist and she'll tell me what these are."

He bristles but walks past me. I follow him to his library.

"I see all my things look messed over," he says. "Why'd you ransack my room? I may have to pull an Anya and install a lock on this door."

I throw the two pills on the floor and crush them with the tip of my pumps. White powder is now smeared on the rug.

"Anya, you're stupid, you know that? You have no idea what you're doing. But don't say I didn't warn you."

"What's wrong with you, Neil? I can't be with a man who talks in riddles, who only wants me to do what he says. It's not right and I won't stand for it."

Neil sighs and lies on the sofa. When I sit next to him he doesn't scoot over to make more room.

"Think about this," I say to him. "You have a daughter who's going to develop into a young woman one day. How will you like it when she begins dating and having sex? What if she hooks up with a man who acts just like you? You won't like it when Reesy comes home crying because some brother dogs her out, has sex with multiple partners, and she gets emotionally damaged in the process."

"The multiple partners idea . . ."

"What can I do to change that, huh, Neil? I've done things because I loved you."

"Loved? As in 'not anymore'?"

"It's not feeling like it used to."

"And when were you going to tell me all this?"

"I'm telling you now. But . . . I don't really mean it. I don't want you to think I don't care. If I didn't, I wouldn't still be with you. I just wish you'd talk to me. Sometimes we go days without saying one word to each other. I don't get it because it's not like I'm angry like I used to be. I'm not totally angry, just frustrated."

Neil is lying back with his hands tucked underneath his head. His eyes are closed. It's the classic shut-out move; he's being a hypocrite, and it's wrong. To me communication involves talking things out even if you're arguing. But if Neil refuses to say anything, I know I'm on the losing end.

"Neil, either tell me what these pills are or I'm going to my pharmacist."

"Okay, give me a sheet of paper and a pen."

I walk over to his desk and grab a memo pad and a pen and give them to him. He jots down a few words, then hands me the paper.

"Don't read this until you are out of this room," he tells me. "Once you read it, I don't want to talk about it, Anya. I just want to go to sleep."

"Everything always goes your way, right? The world revolves around you for some reason."

I close the door to the library and walk up the stairs to my room. And when I look at the paper, I see that it says:

Antibiotics. Doxycycline. Take every single pill. Your health depends on it.

I Google "doxycyline" on the Internet and get some info on chlamydia. I recall how a few weeks ago Neil and I had some spontaneous unprotected sex, and coupled with the vaginal discharge I've been experiencing, my worst fears are confirmed. I run down the stairs screaming and stop at the library door. Neil's standing there blocking my entrance and he closes the door in my face. He keeps holding it so I can't come in. So I sob like a wounded animal and curse him out from the other side; I'm too upset to care that Reesy has come downstairs and is crying, too.

Then I calm down, remember the bigger picture, and realize I have no choice but to take the rest of the pills. And with or without antibiotics, Neil better not touch me with his diseased double-dipping dick again.

All while I was taking the meds, I didn't initiate any conversation with Neil and barely looked him in the face. He had to cook his own meals, wash his own laundry, and clean the kitchen for a change, and he had the nerve to complain the entire time.

But now it's a couple of weeks later in early April, on a Saturday afternoon. Vette, Riley, and I are in the mood to see a movie at the Alamo Drafthouse Cinema in West Oaks Mall. This is the only theater in town where you can watch a flick while being served food and drinks by waiters. We find our seats and order grilled chicken salad, vegan pizza, blue-cheese hamburgers, and sodas. Then we settle in, eat good food, and laugh at Adam Sandler's antics for an hour and a half.

"Mmm, that was fun, ladies," Riley says afterward. "Let's walk around the mall and look for shoe and purse sales."

After examining lots of merchandise but not buying much, we order ice-cold kiwi smoothies and relax at a table in the noisy food court.

"I wonder how Neil is making out with the kids," Riley says. "I was very impressed he agreed to watch the girls."

Vette and I just glance at each other.

"The Bible says a man that finds a wife finds a good thing. I'm gonna sit back and let the man find me," Riley says. "I want to be like Ms. Anya and Neil."

"Uh, no you don't," Vette says. Then, turning to me: "Sister-in-law, it's time you schooled this woman."

Riley looks from me to Vette, then to me again.

"You are a sweetie, Riley. But I hate when you think Neil and I have a perfect marriage. We're not exactly Will Smith and Jada. In fact, the only thing Neil and Will have in common is first names that rhyme."

"Awww, it couldn't be that bad," Riley says.

"You don't know the half," Vette offers, and I'm sure she's dying to disclose all the juicy details.

"I'm sorry, Riley, but you put me and my husband on that pedestal, a place I never wanted to be."

"I apologize for assuming, Ms. Anya. It just seems like whenever I see you two, you look fairly content."

"We're like any other couple, Riley. We have our moments. But don't despair. I think you deserve a good man and I hope you find someone much better than Neil."

"Well, anybody's better than Jamal." She laughs, her eyes sparkling. "There're some good men at Solomon's Temple, but seems like most of 'em are already taken. I don't want any man that's always attached to someone else. Talk about drama."

"Let's talk about it," I say.

Riley lets slip a sharp laugh. "I can tell you some stuff, hon. These chickenheads out here don't care. You tell them that's your man, they'll say, 'Well, he's mine when you turn your back.' And they'll be grinning and proud of themselves. I don't understand this generation at all. Back in the day, we wouldn't think of taking someone else's man. Or we'd at least be a little more discreet about it. But in the new millennium, no shame in the game."

"You got that right," says Vette. "But what goes around comes right back the fuck around, so . . ." She has a gleam in her eye. "Like what happens a lot of times in the movies—the bad guy can raise hell the first three-fourths of the flick, but by the ending, everyone knows what's going down. And when it does, we never even feel sorry for his dumb ass. Everyone gets their due in the final scene."

"That's all good," I tell Vette, "but in the real world sometimes things have a strange way of dodging fate. Because I'm a witness that everybody doesn't get what's coming to them. Everything doesn't always work out for the bad guy. Haven't you heard of getting away with murder?"

"Anya, if you could see the look on your face, hon."

"That's okay. I don't need a mirror to see what I already know."

The people you hate tend to inhabit your mind. So when we get back from the movies and I notice Neil sulking around the house, I ask, "Where's Dani?"

"Huh? I dunno. Home, I guess."

"You look so depressed. Why don't I go pick up the baby? Dani can come, too."

"I'm not in the mood for your games."

"I'm serious, Neil. I think they both should come over here more often."

"Why would you think something like that? I don't want both of them over here."

"Okay, tell you what. Let's flip a coin. Heads, I'll go get Brax. Tails, Dani has to come along, too. How about that?"

"Whatever."

I go to my purse and pull out a shiny quarter. "You flip the coin, Neil."

"Anya, you need therapy," he says in a tired voice.

I smirk and press the coin in Neil's palm. He flips the silvery piece of metal and looks at the results of the toss. I laugh and pump my fist. Neil walks away.

"Why'd Neil leave so suddenly?" Dani asks. We're in the kitchen. I've cut up pieces of banana. Reesy is mashing the fruit with a spoon, and Brax is trying to grab the spoon with his fingers because Reesy isn't feeding him fast enough.

"Hmm, your guess is as good as mine," I tell her. "But that's okay. We don't need him to hang with us all the time, now, do we?"

Dani's sitting down with her eyes fixed on the kitchen table. She's acting like she can't hear. I know it's because I'm making her nervous. She's hip to the fact that, on the one hand, I treat her nasty-nice, but then on the other, I turn around and request that she come over. Both she and Neil think I'm losing it. But I'm losing nothing. Haven't they heard about keeping your enemies close? Keep them so close that they feel too awkward to try anything?

"Now finish what you were telling me," I say, and take a seat next to her. When I offered her a beer a few minutes ago, she just stared at me. I think she wanted to roll her eyes but thought twice about it.

"I was saying that my boss was really acting like an ass."

"What was he doing?"

"What wasn't he doing?" she says.

"Be specific, Dani."

"Okay. Duntworth would stand over my shoulder even though I really didn't have any serious work to do. And sometimes he monitored my personal calls."

"That sounds like something every boss does."

"Remember a month ago when it was storming really badly? Well, while I was outside battling the weather, my stupid thirty-five-dollar umbrella broke. So I go to the ladies' room and have to blow-dry my hair, 'cause it's all wet and stringy looking. My hair took a good thirty minutes to dry. And when I got back to my office, Mr. D hands me a personal-leave request form. And my time spent in the ladies' room? He forced me to charge that to vacation time."

"Hmmm," I say, suppressing a smile. "Whatever did you do to piss off your boss?"

Dani frowns and avoids eye contact. She's not her usual spirited, happy-go-lucky self. She's more sullen today, like she has serious issues on her mind. And from everything she's been telling me, I'm thinking maybe the bad guy does get what he deserves—even if the bad guy is a woman.

"You know, Duntworth has always been an all-out bastard, it's just that lately, His Royal Asshole really lived up to his title. So, you know, I don't know. I—I . . ."

She looks at me like she's studying me, assessing what's in my eyes.

"Anya, what time do you get up in the morning?" Her voice sounds sweet yet edgy.

"Uh, usually at six, sometimes a little earlier. Why?"

"And you're here every day with Reesy?"

"Get to the point."

"I'm thinking about doing some serious hustling trying to find another gig. It'll look bad if I walk into a potential employer's with Brax strapped to my back. Or do you think they'd even notice? I'm sure I can bring him with me just to fill out some applications—No, no, that wouldn't work. Too unprofessional."

"Audrey?" I finally find my voice.

"Uh, no. I feel like I can't depend on her to do a good job every single day."

Dani leans toward me and whispers, "One time, when Audrey gave me the slip, I had no choice but to take Brax with me to work. I put him in the truck, drove to the job, and was about to leave him in the car while I worked half a day." She leans back against the chair and calmly gazes at me.

"Dani," I say firmly. "Now, I hope you didn't do that one time, but even if you did, ain't no way I'd let you do something so foolish a second time. It's getting so hot in Houston and you cannot leave that precious baby in your car. Brax would be dead by the time you get back, and CPS would be after you." Brax looks up. I guess he's like most other folks. Whenever we hear someone speak our name, our ears prick up.

"Hey, you," I say, and go lift him up. Looking at me with wide eyes, Brax places his head against my chest. I tap his back with my fingers, then kiss him on the cheek. He takes in a loud breath and sighs. Content. Secure.

"Anya, can I let you in on something that I swore I'd never tell you?"

"What?" I freeze, my gut stiffening into a tight ball.

"I know what it's like to lose a child."

I stare at Dani, perplexed.

"I've never had a miscarriage, but you can lose a baby without having a miscarriage, if you know what I mean." She takes a deep breath. "I know what it's like to carry a man's child yet never get to see the baby's face. The father's name was Fred. And Fred didn't want me anymore, which I automatically interpreted as him not wanting our child, either. So . . . I made an appointment, went to that stupid abortion clinic all by myself because I had no one to go with me. I—" Her voice catches. "I saw all these silly-looking young girls waiting in the lobby—black, white, you name it. I kept my face buried in a magazine, though. I pretended like I didn't see them and I hoped they didn't see me. I–I rubbed my belly over and over and kept saying to my baby, 'I hate you, I hate you,' but I was *lying*." Her voice is a shattered whisper, and her head shakes in wonder.

"Oh, Dani," I mumble, and reach over to stroke her shoulder.

She sighs. "The doctor asked me if I was positive I wanted to terminate, and I said, 'Hell, yeah.' He probably asked because my face was all wet. I looked a mess. But he went on and completed the procedure. Got it over with. And I lay there in that cold room, scared for my future, thinking about what could have been."

"My God," I say, shuddering.

"The nurse issued me a prescription for these pills I needed to take for two weeks. She told me no sex for six weeks, yada yada. So I called a cab and went outside to wait for my ride, and I started feeling dizzy. A thick amount of bile rose up my throat and I puked right there in the bushes, seconds before that cab drove up. I hopped in and chatted with the driver as if everything in my life was absolutely perfect." She stares at me with haunted eyes, stares at me with eyes I recognize from when I stare in my own mirror.

"Dani, I'm so sorry . . ."

"I guess I'm trying to say that it may not seem like it, but I know what it's like to be you in some ways. Except you have such outstanding motherly instincts, and I'm trying my best to make a good life for my son. I just need to get the right gig, so . . ."

My throat swells so much I can barely talk, but I tell her, "You know, I don't mind watching your baby for you . . ."

Dani quietly gazes at me as she ponders my offer.

I tell her, "Just bring an ample supply of clothes and toys. We'll handle buying his food—at least Neil will."

Dani's watery eyes lock with mine, and for once I detect genuine appreciation in her. It's amazing how common experiences have the power to transform.

"You know, Anya, I haven't always made the best decisions in life. But know this: I truly long for a sane, good life. I want normalcy. Don't want to be poor, barely making it, and trying to raise a child. I've seen mothers struggling here in the city so many times. Life is hard. So while I transition, I . . . Well, I hope you know what I'm trying to say."

"Sure, I understand. We all want happiness, huh?" I reply, and pat the top of Brax's head. He squeals and squirms in my arms. "To quote the late Ann Landers: 'The poor want to be rich, the rich want to be happy, singles want to be married, and the married want to be dead.'"

"And my starving ass wants something to eat," Dani says, and rubs her belly. "You hear my stomach growling? What's on the stove?"

"Hmmm, well, Dani," I say, struggling to hold Brax, "we got some rice, smoked turkey, pinto beans, cornbread, and collard greens."

"I'll take a little of each, please."

I just look at her.

"And I'll be happy to make my own plate." Her face reddens and she breezes to the stove, lifting up lids, which make clanking noises. I ask Brax if he wants any more bananas, but he just makes a face and laughs. I pick up a spoon filled with banana and direct it toward my mouth. Brax's little legs start moving.

"Oh, so now you want some, now that you think I'm about to eat up your food, huh?" I press the spoon into Brax's mouth and listen to him gurgle and baby-talk and say whatever it is he feels he has to say. And I pray this situation is doable. It's so strange, painful, and challenging, but will it be doable?

"I don't care what you say," Vette tells me, "you are weird, weird, weird."

It's the first day of my playing stepmom/baby-sitter to Brax. Vette is standing in my face watching me dress Neil's love child. We are in my bedroom. And I don't appreciate how loud Vette is talking. It's only seven-damn-thirty in the A.M.

"Don't you have to be at school, young lady?"

"I'm going later on. I'm trying to figure out what's up with you. I thought you said you hate Dani."

"It's not hate. More like love-hate. There's a difference." I shrug and pull a sock onto Brax's fresh-smelling foot. He balls his hands into fists and is baby-talking to himself.

"You have a love-hate relationship with Dani?"

"We're polite because it helps us to get through our situation. We do what we need to do even if we have to push ourselves," I admit.

"And you're satisfied with that?"

"People in struggling relationships sometimes play a role until sincerity takes over. That's just how it is. The almighty Danielle Frazier is no exception."

"Shhh, you shouldn't say things like that around the baby."

"Vette, he's only seven months."

"So what? He knows his mother's name. He knows by the scowl on your face that you're saying negative things."

"I'll cover his little ears with my big hands," I say, and make a face. "Weirdo, weirdo, weirdo." Vette walks out the room.

"I'm glad she's gone, aren't you, sweetie?" I rub my cheek against the baby's. "Mean ole Auntie Vette don't know what she's talking about. She's an evil demon and she must be destroyed."

I carry Brax downstairs and prop him in his carrier. After I feed him some cereal and hand him a bottle of juice, I pray that Reesy stays asleep for another thirty minutes. I am breathing hard and my back is starting to hurt. All this weight I'm carrying, plus hoisting Brax around all weekend, well, I need some rest.

I go pick up a book that's in the den. Written by Lisa Bevere, it's called *The True Measure of a Woman: You Are More Than What You See.* Riley loaned it to me—or, rather, *gave* it to me. She said, "Hon, you can keep my copy. That's how bad I want you to read this. Tell me what you think when you get a chance." So I took the book and promptly laid it on a table somewhere. I've glanced at the pretty orange-and-yellow cover, read the back-cover copy, but haven't wanted to get deep into the material. But its laid-back, conversational style is now drawing me. The book challenges me to be open and honest with myself, and to not be afraid of what I find. I need that. It's important to know I can develop to be the woman God created me to be no matter how I've started out.

I'm skipping around reading, based on chapter titles such as "Escaping Your Past" and "You Are Not What You Weigh." I read for a while, then go upstairs to my room. I walk straight into the bathroom and close the door. I'll only be a minute, I say to myself, thinking of Brax. I take a deep breath, look in the mirror, and appraise everything that physically makes up Anya Meadows. My eyebrows are neatly arched—that makes me feel good. But my nose is bigger than I'd like. It's so big I wonder if it's the first thing people notice when they see me. My hair—I still have the weave. It itches a lot and I'm tempted to ask Phyllis to remove the extensions so I can feel more like myself. When I look in the mirror and notice my neck, it's like my eyes refuse to go any farther south. I'm not in the mood to view my wide shoulders, huge breasts, and puffy belly. I pat my stomach, wishing that it could flatten just by the stroke of my hands.

I don't always appreciate how I look. Sure, I've seen much uglier women. But still . . . I wonder how it would feel to be a truly beautiful woman, someone with perfectly shaped cheekbones, wide, expressive eyes, sensual and even-toned lips. I wonder what it would feel like to wear low-riders. Show my belly button without feeling the need to cover up my love handles. I wince and sigh. I have to catch myself because even Tyra Banks admits that all the hot cover models have flaws. All women have defects, even the alluring Danielle Frazier. So I smile at myself, wave good-bye to the mirror, and know that in spite of how I look, the real measure of a woman is more than what the mirror shows her.

Although my true measure is based on the inside of me, I still find myself on the University of Houston campus. I feel I need help with the spiritual, the mental, and the physical. Vette has convinced me to try out the treadmills at the Campus Recreation and Wellness Center. As a student, she gets a free membership and it cost six bucks for my one-day visitor's pass. This $52 million facility boasts two levels and includes basketball courts, a rock-climbing wall, steppers, elliptical machines, NordicTracks, and weight-training equipment. When we walk up the stairs and locate a locker, I hear the radio playing loudly. The ubiquitous 50 Cent is rapping over the airwaves.

"Anya, the reason why you stopped going to those other gyms is because you had no one to go with you. Now that I'm here, it'll be more fun. I'll help you."

Now, why Vette is working out in a gym in the first place is beyond my level of understanding. She doesn't have the perfect body, but she's as svelte as they come. Folks like that make me sick. When I glance around, I see that most of the people (make that *kids*, because they look twenty-five and under) are shapely, toned athletes.

"They look this way because they work out," Vette explains, like she's reading my mind. I guess she can read me because I'm openly gaping at everybody. Vette has on this cute, cute, cute yellow workout shirt that emphasizes her perky breasts. And her purple biker shorts display beautifully toned thighs, curvy hips, and long legs. She has no problem moving from the treadmill to the stationary bike to the thigh abductor machine to the track.

At first I feel self-conscious, especially when the treadmill asks for my weight. Should I lie? I punch in a number, having subtracted three pounds off my true weight. One hour later, when I'm sweating and the moisture is making my hair feel curly and nappy, I am smiling. I feel invigorated, alive, and *sexy*. Working out makes me more aware of my body than sex ever did.

"I want to come back," I say to Vette when we're finished. "Let me know when you work out again, okay?" She nods and rolls her eyes. We pat the moisture from the back of our necks and go downstairs to toss our used towels in the bin.

"You looking good, sister-in-law. I see a little strut in your step. You exude sexiness. As usual, you're just too blind to recognize it. But I see it in you big-time." She grabs me around the shoulders and squeezes. I nod my head, beaming, feeling good and energized.

Vette motions with her arms like she's swimming. "Next time let's jump in the outdoor pool."

"Humph. The only part of my body that swims is my head, okay? You can go in the pool. I might do the hot tub."

"You do that. I'm so proud of you. And even if Neil doesn't notice, I'll bet other people will. You'll be fighting guys off. Watch."

"You're a silly dreamer, but I appreciate your kind words. I don't know what I'd do without you, girl."

"Good, because I don't know what I'd do if I couldn't be here for you."

Vette ignores the stares of the young bucks who pass by on the way to the parking lot. And I look forward to the day when guys stare and I enjoy them staring, when Neil notices me like he's never noticed before, when Dani sees the changes and feels threatened, and when I can't deny the changes myself.

Part 3

Anya & Herself

21

Neil

"Okay, let's do this," I say to Dani. "We'll have the U-Haul truck all day. That should give us enough time to move the bulk of your things to storage, and we'll bring only your essentials back to the house."

Dani is slumped on the couch, which is pissing me off. Time is money.

"Dammit, Neil. I hate Mr. D. People like him have a special suite in hell, I know that much."

"Look, you need to get focused, and think about what needs to be done. So get off your lazy ass and start wrapping all your dishes with this newspaper. I thought I told you to do that yesterday."

"Yeah, yeah, yeah." Dani's blasé attitude makes me want to shake her by the shoulders. But I suppress my frustration and head to the balcony. I'm waiting on one of her neighbors to come help me move the couch, the queen-size bed, and other furniture out to the truck. It feels like a sizzling July day on this early May morning.

"Neil, where's my gift basket stuff?" Dani shouts out to me.

"Already on the truck."

She steps out onto the balcony. "Is it? Okay . . . well, what about my CDs and DVDs?"

"They're in that crate by the door. Since you have nothing better to do, why don't you carry some of the lighter boxes outside?"

"Okay, okay, sure." Dani's hair is pinned up. Her ponytail is bouncing around as much as her breasts. She's braless and wearing a tank top. I've warned her about doing stuff like that.

"What are you doing out here? Taking a break? You want me to get you something cold to drink?" Dani steps farther onto the balcony with me. She looks me up and down and her breathing seems to settle, like she's calming down and accepting that she has to move. Even if she can't visualize it now, I believe a woman of strength is inside her and she can get through this.

"I love you," she whispers, and then strokes my cheek. I shake my head, firmly stopping her with my eyes.

"Follow me." I walk toward the hallway.

She slinks behind me, right on my heels. I turn around and grab her tight by the shoulders.

"The past is gone, Dani. We're shifting into a whole different gear. You're going to have to get control."

"Oh, like you have so much control?" She smirks. "Weren't you the one who tried to slob me down three nights ago? Didn't I have to force your horny ass to go back home?"

"I wasn't horny, I was delusional. I'm sorry about that. It was just a tiny kiss."

"Kisses are never tiny kisses. They always imply something. So, if you want me to keep my hands off you, you're gonna have to keep your big, strong, sexy hands off me." She pouts and blows me a kiss. Even though I know better, I want to grab her and toss her over my shoulder, whisk her off to the bedroom. But the bed is leaning up against the hallway wall. Erotic visions cloud my mind as I try to imagine us making love against a bed that's leaning on—

The doorbell rings.

"Hey, you," Dani says. "That must be my neighbor George here to assist you, so go on and leave so I can get back to being *fo*-cused. Take the crate out for me while you're at it, will you, sweetie?" She talks loud, like I'm deaf. I want to swat her butt, but it switches away, so I can't get to it like I wish.

For the next few hours we pack Dani's and Brax's things and make a few trips to the self-storage facility on West Bellfort. That's where she'll be storing most of her furniture. I'm somewhat angry at myself because I volunteered to pay Dani's monthly costs—told her I'll do it as long as she aggressively looks for another job, as long as she doesn't file for child support.

A few days ago when we had this conversation, I said, "You never have to file. I'll always take care of my son."

"I know but my mama says—"

"Don't listen to her. She's old, bitter, and lonely."

"Neil, stop lying!" Dani shrieked. But then she covered her mouth with her hands and giggled. And I knew I was relatively safe.

"Keep the state of Texas out our business and we'll be cool," I told her. So far I feel she has no reason to doubt me. It's not like she doesn't know where I work and live. It's not like I've denied I am the father of her child, or demanded a paternity test. I've been there long before day one. I love my little man and will do what it takes to make sure he's secure and well taken care of.

After all the furniture and other belongings are totally cleared away, we head back to the apartment so we can clean it well enough for Dani to get back half of her eight-hundred-dollar deposit. As we drive toward Holly Hall Street, Dani pulls up the bottom of her tank top to wipe sweat from her forehead.

"You lost it finally?" I yell. "Dani, cover yourself."

"What?" She looks down. "Oops," she laughs. "I'll bet my life ain't nobody trying to look at me." She finishes drying her forehead, exposing herself while we drive through the streets of Houston. I grit my teeth and imagine my mouth covering her breasts, sucking them. I curse myself, order myself to get a grip. I know that her living under Riley's roof for the next couple of months will present a challenge like no other.

A couple of weeks ago, when Riley was at our house and heard about Dani's dilemma, she offered the spare bedroom in her home on a temporary basis. I felt nervous about the situation, and so did Anya, but Riley assured us that she'd be on top of things, and what better place could Brax be during this transition than close to his dad. Since we had no other fast fixes, we all said okay and crossed our fingers. And though it might be challenging, I think I can make life workable until Dani is out of my neighbor's house and things settle down again.

We're back at Dani's. The room sounds hollow with all the furniture gone. I have a bucket, some Pine-Sol, sponges, and other cleaning supplies situated on the breakfast bar.

"Dani!" I yell.

"You rang?" she says, and enters the kitchen.

"Where were you just now?"

"Peeing, if you don't mind."

"Okay, anyway, don't forget I'm gonna give you a hundred dollars out of the tax return when I get it in a few weeks."

"You're one of a kind, Neil. I appreciate that." She smiles, then abruptly frowns. "But still, I don't like living junky, you know? I'm pretty independent and this . . . this is something different for me. But then again, I've never had a kid before, so . . ."

"Kids change everything."

Dani looks thoughtful. "Is Reesy excited about having her baby brother come live next door to her?"

"She's excited, but then again, she'll probably barely notice. He's been at the house so much lately . . ."

"Ah, I gotcha. But Anya isn't Reesy, and probably won't share her excitement. And Vette, yuck . . ." Dani shakes her head. "She's the one I gotta look out for. I notice her eyeballing me every time I'm over there. I feel like she's my probation officer or something."

"Don't worry about her. Vette has mental problems."

Dani laughs. "Only a brother would say that about a sister."

"Well, it's true." I tease, "I just gotta remember to always come to Riley's with a baby bottle." I wink. "Trying to feed you, and bathe you, right along with Brax."

She looks surprised, then smiles sexily. "That would be nice. You've never bathed me before, Neil." Her eyes widen. "Hey, if I still have some body wash here, can we take a bath together?"

"No, Dani. Nice try, though."

"You are no fun, Neil Meadows."

"Then why are you with me?"

She's silent, assessing me. "*Am* I with you? I mean, are we really together?"

"No, we aren't. I was just kidding," I pause, eager to change the subject. "Let me start wiping these walls. You vacuum."

"But if I vacuum, it'll be too noisy for us to hold a conversation. I–I feel like with me moving closer to you, we won't be able to talk anymore. I don't work with you . . . and I'll miss that, Neil."

I walk over to her and give her a quick hug, then back away. "Well, Dani, what if we still meet for lunch now and then? How's that sound?"

She beams up at me like a little girl. "You think of everything, don't you?" She dreamily rubs her shoulders. "Yes, that sounds good. We can meet every now and then and discuss raising our child. We can debate whether or not Bush is doing a good job running the country, and whether or not gays should be married. We can chat about the plight of the world economy, and if the Astros will go all the way and win the World Series."

"Stop it, Dani, shut up." She's making me laugh. Her ponytail has become loose and her hair is now falling all over her shoulders. I feel myself getting aroused.

"Hey, Dani," I say, "come to your bedroom for a second."

"Okay." She shrugs. "I'm really gonna miss living here."

"Why's that?" I am almost in her room.

"Because so much happened here. Braxton was conceived here."

I turn around and face her. "Oh, you remember that?"

"Of course." She looks at me without smiling. "People never forget things like that. Making love for the first time, the first kiss, the first dinner together, first argument."

"Why don't you have a man, Dani?"

"Huh? Where'd that come from?"

I plop down on the floor and motion at her to join me. "You're a true piece of work, but I still think you're the girlfriend type. If I weren't—"

"Don't say it. Doesn't even matter, because you're never, ever leaving that woman. She has you wrapped around her fat fingers."

"Dani."

"Okay, sorry. I shouldn't have said that. Anya is cute, actually. She can be way too bitchy, though."

"You're one to talk."

"I have a right to be a bitch. I've been through hell in my life, and going through lots of shit sometimes makes you act a certain way, Neil, so don't judge me. Plus, I think you're attracted to how I am. That's why I like you."

"Like?"

"Ooooh, the male ego is at work. Okay, that's why I *love* you, Neil. Because you put up with my mess, and I know whenever I look around you're going to always be there. That means a lot to me. God, I wish you hadn't imposed that get-under-control rule on us, because if I had the chance, you know what I'd do to you right now?"

I lean closer, touching her shoulder with mine.

She says in a low voice, "I'd take you by the hand."

"Take it."

She gently grabs my right hand.

We're sitting on the carpeted floor of her bedroom. It's dark in here because I flipped off the light when we first walked in, and it's very quiet, like we're cut off from the problems of the universe.

"And I'd—"

"What, Dani? What would you do?"

"Oh, never mind. You don't care, you're not interested. You're such a Boy Scout."

"I've never been in the Boy Scouts," I say. "Now tell me what you'd do."

She giggles, voice low. "I'd pull off your T-shirt and pull down your shorts."

"Keep going."

"And I'd start licking you from head to toe. I'd suck your nipples, run my tongue up and down your beautiful thighs, and place my entire mouth over your big, long weapon of mass destruction . . ."

I begin to lie down, still grabbing her hand, and find myself with my back on the floor but she's still sitting up, yakking, and my dick is poking its way outside my shorts. Can't she see this? Maybe I should turn the lights back on.

" . . . and we'd make love, one last time. Because once I start living next door, I know there won't be any more making love. That pisses me the hell off."

I hear her voice, like she's talking to herself. She sure isn't talking to me. Her voice is too low, and I'm alone on the floor. She untangles her hand from mine, stands up, and disappears into the other room. I hear the vacuum cleaner being turned on. And I'm amazed that an inanimate object can be turned on, but I'm abandoned on the floor of an empty apartment. I'm a few feet away from one of the most beautiful, sexy women I know, yet something that should be big and erect is shrinking on me right now.

Midweek while I am at work, Kyra forwards a call to me.

"Neil, I need to find a job . . . fast."

"What happened?"

"I made the mistake of going over to your place unannounced this afternoon," Dani explains. "One of Mrs. Wifey's main rules is to call first, but I popped over, and I guess she didn't like that. I get the feeling that if she had access to a gun, the woman might pop a cap in my ass."

"Anya wouldn't do that, Dani. Don't be so paranoid. Stay focused."

"Easy for you to say. If you were in my situation, you'd know what it feels like. Sometimes our interactions feel tense."

"Well, what do you want me to say? What more can I do? I'm out of answers."

"I'm sorry, Neil, you've been great, and it won't be long before I'm far away from Anya's comfort zone, but, uh, I just needed someone to talk to. I'll let you go."

She hangs up abruptly. And I get pissed. I don't like being clowned on. I'm tempted to call her on her wireless but resist the urge. Dani has to grow up, stop dodging the fear, and do what needs to be done. Quiet as it's kept, I don't want her next door, either. But if it has to do with my son, I'll do whatever I have to do. I know people at work are still giving me disgusted looks, and I sense they can't wait to get in my business. But I wave hello and keep moving. I have to work twice as hard, making sure my position is safe. I don't have time to socialize, to give them the dirt about my personal life. I need to be concerned about two kids, two women, plus my own damned self. And with all the power within me, this is what I plan to do.

22

Anya

Vette and I have been hitting the gym twice a week for one-hour workouts.
I'm feeling good, sexier. It's apparent that I'm losing inches. And I get
excited when we go shopping and I fit into smaller-size shirts and pants.

Today is Saturday and we're in Foley's at Memorial Mall. I'm in the
dressing room trying on summer outfits. I have on this flowery two-piece
yellow-and-orange outfit with a skirt that emphasizes my legs.

"Hey, Vette!" I open the dressing room door and yell. I see her walking down the hall toward me.

"Let me see you."

"Okay," I say, "but will you zip me up in the back?"

"Sure." Vette stands behind me and struggles a little to get the zipper
closed. The fact that she has to work at it makes me bite my bottom lip.
When she's done and orders me to turn around, I make a slow circle.

"Oh, cheer up, it's not so bad. You look cute."

"Don't lie, Vette."

"I'm not lying. You're losing, Anya."

"Yep, twelve pounds, which is awesome, but I still want to lose at
least another twenty." She follows me into the dressing room and begins

to unzip the top without me having to ask. "Thanks," I say, and pull the blouse over my head and place it back on the hanger.

"Damn," she squeals, "your boobs are as huge as pineapples."

"Shhh, do you mind?"

Vette shrugs and giggles.

"That's not funny. I don't want the whole world to know about my double D's."

"At least you're no Queen Latifah," she says.

"Hey, she's looking good these days. She got surgery."

"Well, sister-in-law, surgery is one thing you do not need. Just keep going with me to the gym, and in four months you'll have to replace your entire wardrobe. Wouldn't that be awesome?" Vette says, beaming.

"What's awesome is the fact that I've set a goal and I'm reaching it," I tell her. "I feel like screaming and I don't care if anyone hears me."

Once I finish dressing, Vette and I leave Foley's and wander over to the California Pizza Kitchen. We find a booth and sip on Arizona iced tea until our order arrives.

"So, how've you been holding up?" Vette asks with a serious look. I know what she's referring to. I insist that Dani bring Brax over to our place instead of Neil going next door. So with Dani around so much, Vette and I lack the opportunity to talk like we used to. That's why I'm glad she dragged me away from the house today. If she stopped doing things like this, I wouldn't know what to do with myself.

"It's weird, Vette. I mean, it's like the air feels and smells different. It's a little bit awkward, and I don't know how much more of this I can take. I'm tempted to look through the *Chronicle*'s employment section and help that girl find a job myself."

"How's Neil acting?"

"Normal, like it's not that big a deal. I don't understand men. They are so emotionally removed from things, it's unreal."

"Neil's a trip, that's for sure. But for what it's worth, I haven't noticed anything scandalous going on. It's been three weeks now and he's never gone over there. And when she's over at our place they don't even brush past each other's shoulders. No lusty looks. Nothing."

"You're so silly, Vette. You don't have to spy on them. I'll be all right."

"They'd be fools to act stupid now. You watch and feed her child almost every day. She owes you, sister-in-law. You're practically doing her damn job. Trick ho!"

"Vette." I giggle, but get a kick out of what she's saying. "I don't know. Neil is trying his best to treat me right, but he insists on treating her decent, too. He's doing something unprecedented. We should be on a reality show, huh?"

"Right. Be like Paris Hilton and Nicole Richie. Get paid to look like fools."

I wipe tears from my eyes, giggling like there's no tomorrow.

"I guess I'm realizing I'm not totally alone," I respond. "You know I've been going to Solomon's Temple lately, right? Well, I found out there's a woman there who has two kids by two different men, and both men attend the church. I was shocked to find out this threesome manages to get along. I guess once the members got over the scandal, they fell in love with those two adorable boys. So watching that situation makes me feel like perhaps this generation is trying to handle these kinds of things in a direct manner. It's nothing like how things used to be when you secretly sent away a single pregnant girl. She'd quietly give her baby up for adoption and would return home, making up excuses for her absence."

"Well, as bad as it sounds, you aren't alone, sister-in-law. I know while you're home all day you have to be watching Springer, Montel, or Ricki Lake. That stuff happens all the time. All kinds of twisted love triangles and dramatic baby triangles."

"Oh, yeah?" I say.

"I saw one show where they had a man with three kids by three different women and another one on the way," Vette says. "And the women all got pregnant at the same time, so he's almost paying for triplets except he's dealing with three mamas instead of one."

I raise my hand. "My brain is getting twisted. I can't even think now."

"In a way you're fortunate," Vette replies. "Dani is a drama queen but she could be doubly worse."

"How so?"

"Girl, she could still be having babies with him. She could act slippery and convince Neil to dump you and marry her. She could try to move inside your house, take your car, or abuse Reesy, although I've never seen her do that. She could—"

"Okay, okay." I understand what Vette is saying but I still don't feel lucky. I hardly want to break into a victory dance for being the chosen one.

"Well," I say, "one eye-opening thing I've learned lately is there's nothing new under the sun. We were in church one time and Pastor Sol preached on Genesis 30, the story of Rachel and Jacob. Rachel couldn't bear children, so she thought she'd help out and told her husband to go have sex with Bilhah, the concubine, so they could have a child. Goofy Jacob was game. No argument whatsoever. So . . ." I swallow deeply, realizing how slightly parallel my situation is to a family predicament that happened thousands of years ago.

"How does it feel to know that you're a drama queen just like Dani *and* Rachel?" Vette jokes. "But enough of all that. Let's finish our pizza."

We go home. Reesy is over at my mom's, and Neil isn't home either. Vette soon gets picked up by a friend who's in the mood to ride down to Galveston. She says she'll be gone the entire night. I tell her to have fun and I wave her off.

I am puttering around in my kitchen, feeling free and lighthearted knowing that I have my house all to myself. There's a little room near the front of our home that's rarely used. We refer to it as the parlor. It has French doors, a tiny desk, a chair, a two-drawer file cabinet, and some bookshelves lined along the wall. I settle in there and resume reading *The True Measure of a Woman*. Lisa Bevere's book speaks to the marrow in my bone:

> *The past has been set up as an excuse or a justification for our present behavior. When we make excuses for ourselves by drawing from our past, it is idolatry.*

I read those two sentences and burst into tears. The razor-sharp words were written just for me. And just like in a surgical operation, something must be cut out in order to be healed. Shaken, I try meditating on the book but end up falling asleep in the chair. I wake up when the phone rings.

My mother wants me to pick up Reesy, who's crying to come home. I tell her I'll be there soon. I grab my purse and keys and jump in my Honda.

I'm headed for the Greenspoint area of town, about thirty-five miles from here. Ten minutes after leaving my house, I get onto I-59, traveling north. I'm making good time and am approaching the West Park Curve, which is a wide arch of slanted lanes on the Southwest Freeway. Driving on this curvy stretch of road can make you feel like you're zooming around a racetrack. But traffic is building and my speed is forty-five miles per hour. I am in the right-hand lane just past the Chimney Rock exit when I see a gold Tacoma truck on the side of the freeway with the emergency lights flashing. I manage to slow down and pull up on the shoulder. I get out the car and hike toward the front part of the truck, seeing the DANIF vanity plates. Our Ford Explorer is parked behind the truck a few yards away. Dani's carrying Brax on her hip, and she and Neil are walking toward her vehicle. I glance at the ground near the side of her truck. Flat tire. Okay, fine. But then I look again. There's a used condom on the ground. I smack my hand over my mouth. Dani's clothes are wrinkled. Neil's zipping his pants. Who were those two kidding when they claimed they don't have sex anymore? And where was the baby while they were getting their freak on?

I turn back toward my car and start scrambling. And even when I hear Neil yelling, "Anya, wait," my feet don't stop moving until I reach my car. When I pull out into the traffic, my tires screech like they're back on the racetrack.

It's the next afternoon. I missed church altogether, and as soon as Vette returns from Galveston, I whisk her off in my car. Now we're traveling down South Main Street near Reliant Stadium.

"Vette, there're more than a thousand divorce attorneys, family law counselors, and arbitrators in Houston. You think I can find someone out of all of them?"

"While you're at it, why don't you locate a psychiatrist, too?"

"Why would you say that?"

"An attorney?" Vette says. "Isn't this serious enough to discuss with Neil first?"

"I don't want to hear anything he has to say."

"But Anya, how can you witness what you described and not confront him?"

"Well, after I got home from picking up Reesy, Neil tried to talk but I stayed locked in my room all night, and I wouldn't come out until I heard him leave. I don't give a blankety blank anymore."

"Oooh, I see." Vette frowns. "But you haven't been crying, have you?"

"Hell, no. What good will it do? Neil and Dani are not worth my tears. I just need some money, bad." I glance at the ring Neil gave me. "Maybe I can pawn this and retain a lawyer, get Neil served on his job, and apply for alimony."

"Anya, please slow down, damn," she says, rubbing her temples. "You're getting on my nerves."

"Well, you're getting on mine. And since I'm wearing you down, why don't you get out and catch the bus home?"

Vette is wise enough not to respond. She lets me continue to drive and vent. "God, forgive me, but I hope Neil gets hit by a truck and dies on impact. No," I gasp, "no, I take it back. I didn't mean it. I wish Dani would just go away. He just loses his mind around her, and for what? It's not like she's the cutest thing in the world."

"I would comment but won't."

"Vette, I don't want to hear it," I snap, not wanting to admit that Dani is a looker. "You don't even have a man, so—"

"How you know what I got, huh?"

"Well, if you have one, you can never seem to bring him over to the house. Why you always gotta go meet someone somewhere, anyway?"

"I'm not the one with the relationship problems," she remarks, sounding incredulous, "so get off me, will ya?"

I zero in on her tense expression and mumble, "Sorry for taking it out on you."

The air swarms with friction. We ignore each other while I drive through the downtown area, observing the immaculate streets and the newly constructed Toyota Center.

I want to say more but frustration is a thief that runs away with my words. I long for Vette to side with me, or give me solid direction about what to do. But everything I want is nothing I have. And I drive back home concluding that leaving Neil is debatable, but facing Neil and Dani is inevitable.

We are having a powwow. Dani shows up in her Tacoma. I take my Accord, and Neil drives the Explorer. We decide to meet in a public place, the huge parking lot of a strip mall at the intersection of Fondren and West Bellfort. There's a Fiesta grocery market and a Cingular store; a busy gas station occupies the corner. The air chokes with the smell of fried shrimp and egg rolls from the Timmy Chan restaurant that's across the street. We're standing by a U.S. mailbox that sits squarely between the parking lot and the sidewalk.

"I feel embarrassed, so violated," I begin, "and Riley's being here is pointless."

"I'm here because Vette asked me to come. She thinks I'd make a good mediator. Plus, I *want* to be here. Regardless of your situation, God loves each and every one of you." Riley makes an effort to look directly at all of us. I just want to get this over with.

Riley continues, "Neil, you start. Anya needs to know exactly what she saw."

"I had just left the car wash on Saturday when Dani called. She got a flat and asked me to come help. Brax was with her, whining in the background. So Dani described where she was and I drove over there. I brought along a jar of food so she could feed the baby while I changed the flat. We were in broad daylight, Anya."

"That's why it's so sickening—"

"Let me finish. I get the jack but realize I need to take a leak," Neil explains. "I ran out the house before taking care of that, so that's what you saw."

"I didn't see any men's rooms on the shoulder of the freeway, Neil," I protest.

"Right," he says. "I asked Dani to cover me so I could take care of my business. Men do that sometimes, you know. It only takes a few seconds. So when you noticed me walking back toward the truck zipping my pants, that's all that you saw, Anya."

"Thanks, Neil." Riley looks at Dani. "You want to add anything?"

"Hey, look, I'm sorry for making a mess out of everything. I am. Maybe I should have called a tow instead of Neil, but the price they charge is such a rip-off. In spite of all that, nothing happened. I had my baby with me! But even if I didn't, nothing would've happened, I swear to God."

"Woman, please," I say.

"Dani's right," Neil agrees. "I wouldn't disrespect you like that."

"Ha!" I say, and walk in a circle. "Neil, you need to let me know where you stand. Do you want to be with her?" I nod at Dani. Her eyes widen and she steps back, shaking her head.

"This isn't about that, Anya," Dani insists. "Neil clearly loves his family. I've never, ever tried to come between that. I don't even want to. That would be one big mess now, wouldn't it?"

"Then what do you want?" I ask.

"I—I dunno. I need my own place, a new gig. I want to take care of my child and live my life in peace and security. And yes, I'd like to have a good, solid relationship one day. You just don't know how badly I do, but so far it escapes me."

Dani's voice is quivering. Thick lines stretch across her forehead; her thin lips are turned downward. She looks like how I feel. Emotionally I am so drained, I feel like I haven't slept in months. I figure that if Dani is going to successfully find a job, she needs as little stress in her life as possible. The quicker she gets a job and moves away, the sooner Neil and I can resume a sense of normalcy.

"And, please listen," Dani continues, "I want you and Neil to go out tonight, spend some time together. I'll watch the kids. You go to a movie or a comedy show, and just laugh and be with each other. I don't mind."

"Gee, thanks," I say. It's like she's giving me permission to go out with my husband.

"May I say something?" Riley interjects. "Anya, don't you find it strange that you, the wife, would ask Dani what she wants?" Her voice is gentle. "Dani is correct about one thing: This is not about her. So what do you want, Anya?"

I gasp and lean against Neil, my knees nearly crumbling underneath me. Someone asking *me*, Anya Meadows, what *I* want . . .

"I want my freaking husband. I want my life back," I say firmly.

Neil stares at me. Dani stares at Neil. I take a deeper breath. "I want Neil to want the same things I want."

"And what would that be, Anya?" Neil says.

"Church. Will you attend prayer service with me tonight?"

"Uh, I don't know about that," he protests. "I'm not ready for that."

"I just don't believe you, Neil," I say, appalled, "and I'm not sure why I ever did." I glare at him and advance a few steps closer to my car while still facing him.

"Neil, what's the matter with you? Why won't you go to church with your wife?" Now Dani's shrieking, and that's the last thing I want.

"Neil won't go because Neil's a coward," I answer, and stop. "He begs me to go to church but he won't go. I hate that about you," I tell him, wanting to gouge out both his eyeballs.

"Anya—" Neil says.

"Don't Anya me. I'm so pissed right now, I–I . . ." I close my eyes and wish I could go away to a better place. And as I tune out Neil, Dani, and Riley, mentally I am transported to another time. Saturday, May 12, 2001. I'm thirty-four. Three-year-old Reesy is wondering what happened to the little brother or sister we told her was on the way. I'm not quite sure what to tell her, so I say nothing.

It's mid-morning on this day. The sky is overcast. Neil and I are in our bedroom. I'm rolling sheer black stockings up my thighs. Neil is standing in the doorway glaring at me, but I continue getting dressed. I'm wearing a long black wool-blend dress. My pumps are black, and so are my dangling earrings, and the string of beads that loop around my neck. A black mourning veil covers my face.

"Anya." Neil steps up to me. "Are you sure . . . ?"

"Of course. If I did it for the other baby, I'm doing it for this one, too."

Neil shakes his head. Despair swims in his eyes.

"You can come with me, Neil. Not too late."

He doesn't utter a word, and I slowly walk downstairs and out the back door, my heels clicking on top of the cobblestone walk until I'm in the middle of the backyard. I'm clutching a Bible in one hand and a white lily in the other.

I lower myself until my knees are touching the coolness of the dry, hardened ground. I wince staring at the mound of soft dirt that I prepared one day ago, two weeks after the death of what would have been my third child.

"Good-bye, my sweet baby," I mumble to the little shoe box I buried in the makeshift grave, the box whose contents contain my heart, my dreams. Inside the box is the first pair of baby booties I bought for this baby. Right next to the booties is a yellow-and-blue rattle that Reesy loved to bang against the table when she was younger. A mass-market baby-names book is there, too, a book I wanted to thumb through but never did. And there's a copy of the little white appointment card for the ultrasound scan I would have had had our child lived long enough.

"I didn't know you that long, but you're my child. And I love you. And one day I'm going to see you again. See you for the first time." I bow my head for a brief moment of silence. And for the second time in two years, I find myself questioning why life is brought forth but always dies inside of me.

Even though Neil couldn't be here, your daddy loves you, too. Those were my thoughts, but the words stopped short of coming out my mouth.

Then I set the Bible and the lily aside. I place the lid on the shoe box and lower it into the ground. Instead of using a shovel to cover the box, I grab handfuls of dirt and layer it on top until the box disappears. My fingers now caked with grime, I insert the root of the white lily deep inside the dirt, right next to the memory box, patting the mound firmly to secure the flower. I say a quick prayer and whisper a final good-bye.

A voice within me urges, "Say good-bye again, this time to your past." My body trembles and I know my fixation on my sorrows must one day take its last breath.

Releasing memories of May 12, 2001, I find Neil, Dani, and Riley arguing with one another.

"This is your chance, Neil. Do something for Anya, just for her," Riley urges.

"Yeah," Dani pipes up, "don't be such a tight ass."

"But why can't we do something else?" Neil says. "I know church couldn't be the only thing Anya wants."

"It's okay," I remark, and re-approach the circle where everyone's standing.

"Let's just go have a nice quiet dinner and have a serious talk, okay, Anya?" Neil says. "How about some seafood, sweet margaritas—could we do that? I think this would be better than being around all those people at church. This way we can focus on us."

Tired as I am, I muster up a response. "I'm okay with that. Now let's go home and get dressed."

Riley beams at me with a smile that makes her face look even brighter than normal. I turn toward her, falling into her curvy arms. We hug for a long, long time.

We go home to get dressed, and I make arrangements for Vette to watch Reesy. We're not really saying much to each other, but during dinner at Little Pappa's Seafood Kitchen, I decide to initiate our "talk." The restaurant, thankfully, is scarce of people and we're seated at our preferred corner booth.

"You know, Neil, sometimes I wonder why others can see the things in us that we can't see ourselves."

"Like?"

"Like Riley taking a stand for me. I ought to be standing up for myself."

"Oh, but you do it, you just aren't aware that you do. When you know what you want, you don't seem too shy about speaking it."

"For the most part I believe that, Neil," I tell him, "but I'm starting to figure out why I sometimes hesitate to speak up. I want to know one hundred percent that I can have what I want. But if I feel something is going to block it, I deny those wants and urges. I'll admit I hate being disappointed."

"Oh, Anya . . ." Neil's voice is gentle.

"And sure, I'm almost forty, but everyone still wants their dreams to come true. Hoping isn't reserved just for the young and inexperienced. But now I'm at the point where I am able to let go of a certain dream that I had—blessing you with a son."

"Don't beat yourself up about that. It's not a big deal."

"But it is a big deal. And I'm struggling to accept my destiny. In a weird way, if it weren't for Dani, you wouldn't have that son, would you, Neil? And because I encouraged you to hook up with another woman in the first place, it's like I inadvertently gave you . . ." I wince and bite my lip.

"Anya," Neil says, incredulous, "please tell me you're joking."

"No, no, no, think about it. My pregnancy didn't survive, but hers did? Maybe her pregnancy wasn't accidental since I couldn't . . ."

I know my reasoning sounds unusual, but at this point what else could I reach out for and grab on to? I want to bring closure to this issue in any way possible.

"Anya, there's something you need to know." Drops of sweat spread across Neil's forehead. "Baby, part of this is my fault because even though I didn't act like it, I was torn up by the miscarriages. I blocked out the pain by staying busy with work, going on fishing trips, buying you almost anything you wanted, but deep inside I was devastated about our not being able to have another kid or two."

"Neil, you never told me this."

"I'm telling you now. And so when Dani and I hooked up, at first, I swear to God, she meant nothing to me. But we got carried away, and when she got pregnant . . . Anya . . ." He can barely look in my eyes. "I—I had no idea that I . . . when she found out and got the sonogram and it was a . . ."

"Oh, Neil, please. I don't want to hear this anymore." Truth sure hurts. But truth is what we need to have to get us through and beyond this.

"I can't believe you have the nerve to tell me this," I finally say to him.

"I won't ever talk about it again. I'm done."

"Sounds typical," I tell him, "but can I ask you something and then *I'm* done?"

"Go ahead."

"Do you know what today is?"

Neil scowls. "No."

"Our other kids would have been three years and four years old this week."

"Oh yeah?" he replies, staring at me like I'm a goner.

"I loved them enough to know this, Neil."

"Sure you did."

"And back when we lost the kids . . ." I squirm in my seat. "Why didn't you come with me to say good-bye to the babies?"

"Anya, you have a right to think I was being insensitive during that time of our lives, but you were a complete wreck."

"I wasn't that bad."

"Anya, be honest. Don't you remember how you'd cry all the time, you wore the same clothes every day, you didn't cook for weeks, laundry went undone? And don't you understand that both of us couldn't fall apart? One of us had to be strong for the other. I was being strong, not being a jerk, as you accused me of back then."

"Neil, I did that? It sounds too bizarre."

"Anya, you may not remember, but I cared about you enough to put on the strong front, but sure, I was as upset as you. I just don't show it the same."

"Oh God, all this time I thought you didn't care about me, the babies . . ."

"No, not true, Anya. It hurt me to see you hurt. But life has to go on no matter what happens. And that's what I was focused on. That's what I'm still focused on."

I stare at my husband, debating whether I should let his truth become mine.

"Thanks for being honest, Neil," is all I can say.

Neil and I manage to enjoy a civilized dinner, then we leave the restaurant and head for the parking lot. He opens my door for me, starts up the Explorer, and says, "I want to take you somewhere."

"Where're we going?" I ask.

"Not home." He's heading east, in the opposite direction of our house.

"Neil, stop playing. I'm ready to go home."

"No, not going."

He's irritating me but I shut my mouth. We end up at the Comfort Inn on Westheimer Road. Neil checks in and gets us a room with a king-sized bed. With a huge grin, he holds both my hands and leads me inside the room. He hoists me up and plants me gently on top of the bed. He removes my pumps and then my skirt. He stares at my legs while he yanks his shirt over his head. I sense he's happy to be in control.

"First, Anya, I want you to know how good it feels to be out with my wife tonight. And thanks for going to dinner with me."

"Okay, fine, Neil."

"And I'm so proud of you for letting Riley convince you to resolve that issue with Dani and the truck and all that while it was still fresh. It's so important for us to talk things out instead of staying mad and not talking."

"Look, I appreciate your words, but I'm not in the mood to hear all that."

"Listen to me, please." He takes a deep breath. "Me going to help Dani . . . I want you to know I could have handled things better. But I was thinking about Brax, not her. And I really am sorry, Anya," he says and kisses my hand.

"Oh, Neil," I choke. I feel conflicted. It seems Neil's trying, but should I trust him again just to possibly get my heart broken? I don't know if I can withstand another broken heart.

"So, Anya, we've had our talks. I feel we're in a good place." He looks around the room, then focuses back on me, his eyes gleaming. "I want to know if you're all right with being here with me like this. And most of all, do you forgive me?" Neil pleads, his eyes never leaving my face.

I take a while to answer, thinking about all we've been through, knowing that forgiveness is like medicine—it's a restorer of health, and the foundation of a clean slate, which I desperately need.

"You know I forgive you, Neil."

"You sure? I don't want to pressure you, Anya. Take whatever time you need to get some peace inside. I won't have peace until you have it."

"Y—you mean that?" I say, impressed.

He draws an imaginary X over his heart.

"Ahhh, okay, that settles everything, huh?"

We both laugh and I feel a lot better.

"Now," he says, and slowly looks me up and down, "will you let me get up in that?" Neil's words shock me and make me hot. He clutches my left hand and kisses it and I want to smack his wrist, but I smile at him, blushing. It feels like we've just met and are getting acquainted.

"You're looking fine, Anya. Always have."

"Oh, so you've noticed." *Finally.*

"Can't help but notice. Don't work it off too much, though. I'm crazy about your big thighs. Love squeezing them." He falls on top of me. I squirm underneath his warm body. I adore the attention, but I wonder whether I should give in or give him a hard time.

"Neil . . ."

He hushes me before I can say anything further, stealing my words away while he kisses me deeply, sensually. It's been a while since we've kissed with genuine passion. I want to forget all the craziness that's happened and enjoy the moment. I let the tension flow out my body, and I relax while Neil stamps wet kisses on my cheeks, lips, and neck. I grab his head and pull him closer to me, against my skin. I want him. I want this man. I can't imagine leaving him. And I'm afraid to break up my family, the only family I'll ever have.

I cry when Neil makes love to me, nice, slow, taking his time. We use

K-Y Jelly and a condom—make that three condoms, since the sex gets so slippery and sloppy that we have to keep trying. Neil calls in sick the next day and it's the first time in a year that he's done that. I wake up with my husband cradled in my arms. He assures me that he does love me, and I confess that yes, I love him, too.

The next weekend, Neil and I are in his library. He's standing up, arms folded across his chest.

"Neil, could you just do this, not just for me, but for yourself, too?"

"But how's it hurting anything?"

I wave the slick porno magazine in his face. "Do you even have to ask? Even though being with you has been good the past couple times, sometimes while we're doing it, I wonder if you're fantasizing about the women in these—"

"Anya, I won't lie. Most of the time when anybody's making love to *anybody,* they imagine they're with someone else. For men it might be Beyoncé. And for women, shoot, probably that Denzel dude."

"Please. I've never fantasized—"

He shrugs like he doesn't believe me.

"But it's not the fantasy," I tell him, "it's the addiction. I know you're not the only man drawn to this stuff. Quiet as it's kept, apparently a lot of churchgoing men have their *Kama Sutra* stashes—preachers, deacons, it's not like you're alone. I just want one less man that's addicted. And I can't see why it's so hard for you to simply throw this junk away."

Neil opens his mouth but doesn't say anything. I stoop and begin gathering up porno magazines, at least a dozen of them, flipping through the pages, my eyes widening at each graphic image. No, I don't resemble any of these women—never have, never will—yet Neil insists I'm attractive. If that's true, wouldn't my beauty, my body, be enough for him?

"Would you want me looking at photos of naked men?" I ask.

"Look, do whatever you want to do."

"You mean that?" I ask. "Does that include throwing this stuff—"

"Yeah, I–I don't trust myself enough to . . ."

I immediately collect magazines in an empty cardboard box. The

awful *Girls Gone Wild* videos go, too. When I've discarded every piece
of material I can find, I wrap a tight ball of string around the heavy box
and load it into the backseat of my Honda.

I can't allow myself to place this box out on the curb with the rest of
the garbage. I get in my car and special-deliver Neil's addiction to the
nearest trash compactor myself.

23

Neil

Midweek Anya calls me at work to remind me that today is Wednesday.

"Anya, I really don't want to go anywhere. I'm tired from working hard."

"Don't care. No excuses," she says.

"Anya . . ."

"Neil, we all get tired, but if we really want to do something . . ."

"Yeah, but—"

"Quit whining and butch up. I'll be dressed and ready when you get here."

I would've protested more but she hangs up. After I get home and wash up, Vette agrees to watch the kids. Anya and I enjoy a relaxing dinner at the Olive Garden, where we eat spaghetti and meatballs that rival her own.

After we walk out the front doors and reach the parking lot, Anya says she wants to show me something. We hop in the SUV. Although I am in the driver's seat, Anya tells me where to go, giving me detailed directions. Her hands rest on her lap while I drive. It's twilight, the time of night that hides you from the day. We travel east on North Braeswood.

Anya instructs me to turn left at a street where several apartment buildings are located.

"Park on the side street," she says in a soft voice. I pull into an empty space near the end of the corner. She gets out of the car and I follow her lead. We walk down Braeswood past the Nob Hill Apartments complex.

"Remember this?" Anya asks, her voice quivering.

I glance at her, then at the building. We're standing in front of a two-story brick structure that has lots of windows with green shutters.

"This is the first place we lived when we got married," I remark.

She smiles and nods.

"Before Reesy, before the craziness. This was our beginning, Neil." Anya shivers and rubs her shoulders even though it's warm on this early-summer night. "You carried me over the threshold once we got back from Cozumel. And what's the first thing you did after we got home?"

"Did I turn on the TV?" I ask.

"No."

"Go use the bathroom?"

"No, silly."

"Uh, I give up," I tell her.

"Neil, you told me you were happy to be finally living with your best friend."

"I said that?"

"Neil! Why don't you remember?"

"I—I dunno. Maybe I was feeling so good that night I couldn't take it all in."

"Okay. Fine," Anya says. "I may not remember everything, but that's one moment I haven't forgotten. I know we were very happy that we did things right. We didn't shack up until we felt we could handle the marital thing. We insisted on having trust, *true* trust, to forge ahead without first giving our commitment a trial run."

"Yeah," I tell her, allowing her words to lift me back to where we used to be.

"We started out with so much trust. But why does time change every-thing, Neil? Sometimes I wish—"

"Don't. Won't do any good, anyway." I can understand her yearning for the past. It's something everyone wishes for once they don't have it anymore.

"These are our good ole days, Anya. Right now. Remember how we used to trip out over that? The times we were living in back then? We'd reminisce about when we first met, the first few dates and all that. And we thought our past was the good old days, not our present."

"Yep," she says. "No one can re-create the past. And based on some things, I really wouldn't want to repeat it, anyway. I just want to guaran-tee that we don't commit the same mistakes, so we don't keep going through useless mess day after day. How can we prevent that, Neil?"

"Well," I tell her, "maybe what you did tonight is a start. Anya, you made me come with you, do you realize that? When we first met, you were the same way. You didn't take no for an answer, and that got my at-tention. I felt you were very decisive in those days. But years later it seemed you were content to go with the flow."

"Not necessarily," she replies in a snappy voice. "I do what I have to do because you don't listen. You don't take me serious. And I get sick of screaming and hollering, trying to convince you—"

"Man, you know, I'm sorry about that," I say, seeking peace.

"There you go again saying 'sorry.' How many times you expect me to forgive you, Neil?"

"As many times as necessary."

"Is that so? You can make mistakes over and over again and you ex-pect me to just accept them, no matter what, time after time?"

"Yep," I tell her matter-of-factly. "I do."

"But how—"

"Anya, that's the only way we're going to make it. The only way any couple will make it. If you want a marriage to survive, you have to let things go, big or small, no matter what."

"Hmm, so what if I started doing these Neil-type mistakes? Would you feel the same way then?"

"Anya, let's get one thing straight. The state of our marriage is a reflection of both of us. Not just me. Yeah, you're a great cook, loyal, a caring and committed mother, but think long and hard. You weren't fulfilling every part of the arrangement, either."

Anya fails to respond. She seems to enjoy playing the victim, but is unable to admit I've been victimized, too. Denying a man sex on the regular makes him function differently. At least it's like that for some men. I just want her to realize that every bad patch a couple experiences starts with a few wrongs that lead to greater wrongs. And if Anya pays me back for my wrongs, she's just as guilty as me. And if and when things go there, the mistakes aren't all about me anymore.

A couple days later . . .

"You son of a bitch."

"Hey, hey." It's Dani. She's calling me on my lunch break. She wants to tell me how her interviews have been going. I haven't had time to take her calls or see her the past two days.

"Neil, I don't believe you don't have time for me. You've always had time for me."

"Yeah, well, things change."

"No, no, I don't want change. And didn't you tell me it wouldn't ever be that way?"

"Calm down, Dani." She sounds like she's trying to keep her composure. I hate hearing her cry. She's a pro at making me feel like an ass. "You know how things have become lately."

"And so? I still don't want you to forget about me. I will *not* be abandoned, Neil. I'm so tired of this shit. What's the matter with me that I can't have a good relationship?"

"Dani, w—we can't really be—"

"Yes we can, Neil, we can. I—I love you." Her voice breaks. "Don't you know that?"

I can't speak. I feel twisted inside. As much as my head steers me to do the right thing by Anya, there's something about Dani that makes it hard to give her up 100 percent.

"I said I love you, Neil," she sniffs, "and I know you love me."

I stand up with the phone pressed to my ear, thinking about her words.

"What are you wearing?" I say in a thick voice, my eyes glazing.

She moans. "A pink miniskirt, white cowboy boots."

"Mmmm, that's enough, be quiet."

She laughs, then gets serious. "You gonna answer my question? I just want to hear you say you don't love me, and if you don't, I'll leave you alone."

"Oh yeah? N—no you won't. I don't believe that."

"Do you love me, Neil?"

Who am I kidding? I don't lie to Dani. She knows me too well. She's like my twin, and we're too connected. Sometimes I wonder what would've happened if I'd met her first. Would we be deep into a satisfying, compatible relationship? Would we be making love every day and she'd be stroking my ego like I need it to be stroked? Or am I wasting time thinking about this 'cause it's never going to be reality?

"I'm listening." She catches her breath, the sound of fear stealing her volume.

"You know I do, Dani."

She starts weeping again, and for a rare moment I'm tempted to cry with her.

After Dani and I indulge in some sweet talk, I manage to take a break and dial the twenty-four-hour prayer line. I ask for Zaire, the same woman who prayed with me last time. I say to her, "What if I do the right thing but keep backsliding? I know it's wrong, and I try to resist, but . . ."

"Do you put yourself in these situations?"

My silence provides Zaire's answer.

"Brother, listen to me. Don't be like Adam and Eve in the Garden of Eden. Protect your boundaries."

24

Dani

It's Wednesday night during the week of Easter. I'm going next door to pick up Brax, but before I do, I change into my casual gear—some tight jeans and an Usher T-shirt that's tied into a knot so my belly button is showing. When I enter the house, Neil is upstairs getting the baby ready, and Anya and Reesy are watching *American Idol.* But me? I have the pleasure of being cornered in the kitchen by Neil's sister.

"Are you afraid of going to hell?" she says, staring at my clothes. I've never been asked anything so rude in my life.

"I don't believe in hell," I snap back. "It's the figment of someone's imagination."

"If you believe that, you're more stupid than I thought!"

She looks at me likes it hurts to look at me. I can't believe she and Neil are blood-related. Being loud and ignorant is not an admirable combination.

"All I'm saying is," Vette continues, "you should take your hot ass to church sometime. I'm sure Anya wouldn't mind if you join her and Riley."

"Uh, last time I checked, you haven't joined them for church, either. So why are you so concerned about the state of my spirituality?"

"I dunno." She stares me up and down. "Seems like some folk need more help than others."

"Oh, and I'm supposed to believe that you actually care about me? You sincerely want to help me?" She has some nerve.

"I don't really care about *you*. I care about my brother."

"That's not how he describes it."

She's now up in my face. I don't back away or blink. I won't allow her words to scare me.

"Oh, I guess he talks about me to you, huh?"she asks.

"Sometimes."

"Not surprising since he also tells me things about you—like how you gave him that nasty disease."

"What?" I widen my eyes. I can't believe he'd tell her something like that; it was so long ago. "Well, Neil says worse things than that about you, like how you're probably still a virgin, and that Michael Jackson can get more men than you."

"Not funny, not true."

Neil has never said that, but I want to hurt her like she's hurt me. "Whatever, I just don't see how you can get in my face about him when you two don't seem all that tight. Always going at it."

"Don't fool yourself. We may fight," she admits, "but Neil has my back, and I have his."

"That's wonderful," I say. "But Neil's grown. He can take care of himself. Your brother is an awesome man, a great father. Anya is lucky to have him."

"Right, she *does* have him, and don't you forget it."

"Forgotten."

"What?" Vette looks shocked that I'm hanging with her insult for insult. But I'm not in the mood for her. Not today.

"You don't have to remind me to behave myself," I inform her, "nor caution me about hell, or any other thing. I've been in the world a lot longer than you, and I've done all right so far. I'm not planning on staying in this situation forever, so keep your advice to yourself, because I do not take orders from you, Sharvetta."

She doesn't correct me. She leaves me alone. She watches me walk away from her. She hears me running upstairs so I can see what's taking Neil so long. What she doesn't hear is when I stop off in the bathroom, sit on the toilet seat, and cry. I plead with God to change my life, if only He'd listen.

The next week, I go on another interview. I make sure not to act too cute or get personal with this man. I dress conservatively. I maintain eye contact and note my strengths. When it's over, I'm not sure how it went but my fingers and toes are crossed. On my way home, I go to the Hallmark store and buy a blank card that has roses on the front. Damned card costs four bucks, but I hope the expense is worth it.

I sit in my car and write:

> *I'm sorry if I said anything that offended you. I really want us to coexist peacefully. Truce?*

I seal the envelope and write *Vette* on the front.

The next day, I check in with Neil by phone and he tells me, "Vette said you almost made her cry."

"She didn't *almost* make me cry, I *did* cry. She's tough."

"Not any tougher than you. Ya'll need to chill."

"I extended her an olive branch, but I just want her to stay away from me. I mean, not be so intense and all. I remember when I was young, when girls would get all up in my face sweating me just because I was eye candy, and light-skinned with long hair. It's not like I asked to be born with these features, so when they'd come at me swinging, I always did what I had to do. They'd corner me, shove me against the wall, pull out blades. We're talking seventh grade here. I didn't enjoy fighting but fought, anyway. Luckily, some of my brothers and sisters would jump in. But I handled these girls on my own real good to show 'em they couldn't treat me any way they wanted."

"You Long Beach girls are so ghetto," Neil jokes.

"It's not about the ghetto, Neil. Survival is everywhere. You *have* to be hard. Being soft doesn't get you far."

"You're a combination of soft and hard, so . . ."

"And that's how I should be. I just wonder if it gives the wrong signals. I want to be feminine but let people know I won't be treated bad—not for long. I think I tend to take more mess from men than women. I don't know why that is."

"Because you love us," Neil exclaims.

"Yep, I do. I'm strictly dickly. Love me some nice, masculine hunk of a black man."

"You've never dated outside your race?"

"I've had the opportunity," I say, and yawn, "but never went there. I don't know. Not against it, just haven't tried it."

Neil laughs. I wonder if he's happy about that little disclosure.

"Well," he says, "as soon as you hear any good news, be sure and call me."

"Oh, you know it. You'll be the first one. And if something good happens, I'd like to treat you, Neil. Maybe we can do lunch. Anywhere you want to go."

"Anywhere?"

"As long as it's a spot where you gotta get decked out and spend a grip. Wendy's, KFC, Whataburger—anyplace where we can go all out. My treat."

"You're so bad, Dani."

I laugh. "That's not true and you know it. I'm just . . . I'm the way I need to be, and I hope that's acceptable. I need to know you're with me, ride or die. Once I get a job, I don't want you to do a disappearing act. I want to stay in touch, you hear?"

Neil doesn't say anything. Maybe he's imagining what will happen after we've rid ourselves of the madness. Maybe he knows I can't be up under him forever, that I will sincerely want a man of my own, because as much as I act like he's mine . . .

But if things were different, if Neil were free and available to hook up, I believe we'd be happy. We'd be normal. That's all I really want . . . in my perfect world. Can you imagine? He and I living together in a wonderfully furnished house in one of Houston's master-planned communities? I'd want everything on one spacious floor. Me and Neil's master bedroom would be in one wing, so when we made love we could scream as loud as we wanted. And we'd have a floor-to-ceiling shower with a Jacuzzi. And we'd amorously christen the Roman tub, the veranda, and the top of the breakfast bar. We'd have one more child, a girl hopefully, who'd run around the house joyfully playing (or fighting) with her brother. We'd manage our lives together, of course, allowing Reesy to be a part of it. I'd never have to worry about finding a good man, and Neil would never stray within our marriage, because I alone would fulfill him.

We'd shop for each other. I'd buy him nice gear, and he'd buy me lots of jewelry so I'd know what it feels like to be Jenny from the block, back when she had Ben Affleck. And whenever we could, we'd fly to San Diego or the Poconos, Switzerland or Brazil, and lounge about in luxury suites. We'd be deliriously happy, crazy in love, and life would be so complete.

I am engrossed in my thoughts, fantasizing about what I could have if only my wildest dreams materialized. Then Neil interrupts my daydream and says, "Dani, there's something you need to know. My wife and I have been making a few strides in our relationship. She wants us to go hang out tonight and I told her I'll do it. Make sure to pick up Brax early."

His *wife*?

And the dreams, yearnings, and visions of love, hope, and happiness are gone . . . just that quick.

25

Anya

It's mid-morning on a Sunday. The brightness of the summer sun fills the sky and the excitement of a new season electrifies the atmosphere.

The final morning service at Solomon's Temple has just ended. Hundreds of men, women, and teens are chattering away, hugging and rocking one another, and enjoying some last-minute fellowshipping before scattering for the exit doors. Riley and I are loitering inside the sanctuary, still tingly from the afterglow of an empowering church service. Besides, I'm much too preoccupied to rush off and round up Reesy and Mika from children's church just yet.

"I want to ask you something," I say to Riley, who has just grabbed her purse and flung the strap over her shoulder. "Let's sit down for a few minutes, okay?"

Riley and I settle into a pew in the rear corner section and I pause, trying to form the words I'd like to say.

"I just want you to know that I really admire the changes you've made in your life, girl."

Riley smiles so wide, I can't help but offer her a warm smile, too.

"I've been praying that people see something different in me, Ms.

Anya. I'm a witness that the Lord can turn your life around for the better."

"Good, that's exactly what I need to know," I tell her. "But before all the good stuff happened, did you ever get tired of the bad?'"

"Hon, don't start me to lying," she exclaims, her eyes marked with sincerity. "There was a time in my life when I despised waking up. I was sooo scared of what the day would bring. When Mika was little, my life was a stinking mess. Me and Jamal would be getting into it day and night. He was so controlling and would demand my paycheck even though he didn't have a job." Her voice catches. "And like a fool, I'd cash my check, give him money. And he'd take my car, leave me stuck at home with the baby the entire weekend, and sometimes I would be left with no way to pay the rent. Don't ask me what he did with the money." She shakes her head. "I ended up taking out loans with thirty percent interest, just to pay my darned bills." She laughs. "Thank God them days are long over. I got a nice little raise with my job at the hospital, and me and Mika are doing just fine. I even started socking away ten percent of my salary." Her eyes sparkle and I can sense her relief at being in a better place.

"I'm so happy to hear that, Riley. Now all you need is a man." I giggle.

"Oh no, wait a second, now don't be cursing me." She laughs, too. "Don't get me wrong. I'm not one of them new-millennium chicks that don't need a man and all that. I'm just content to wait on God's timing. His timing is everything. But I didn't always feel that way. Years ago when life was rough, I dreaded the weekend, the nighttime, every single day. And I blamed God, actually hated Him at one point because I felt He had the power to intervene, but thought He flat out refused to help me. I'd see other folks getting blessed and that made me so upset."

"Girl, are you kidding me?" I bite my bottom lip. "I've felt that way, too, but would be so scared to think those thoughts. I actually started looking for lightning bolts to strike me."

"Ha, that's just a myth. That ain't gonna happen, hon. But anger is a process we must go through in order to find joy. You know how they say it, 'Weeping may endure for a night, but joy comes in the morning.' I'm a witness. Especially when I had an abortion—shoot, let me stop lying, two, count 'em, two abortions. I got the first one when I was eighteen, then oops, I did it again three years later. But for some reason it took me a long time to conceive Mika. And I think that's why I hung on to Jamal. After messing around with these other men that I really liked and wouldn't mind getting with, it seemed like Jamal's sperm was the only one that could swim upstream." She throws back her head and laughs heartily. "But yep, I can admit I had issues with the Lord, till He told me something that changed my attitude."

"What was that?" I ask, and lean forward.

"The Lord told me, 'I create life, not you.' See, I was mad at myself, questioning my self-worth because I couldn't get pregnant after having those abortions. But I learned God can open a womb, and He can close it. Sometimes we forget that, but for sure, you can believe I'll never forget it again. Mmmm-hmmm, no way. I'm cool with the life that I have right now, just me and Mika, but it took me a good while to get there."

"But at least you got there," I tell her.

Riley continues, "Yep, Ms. Anya, some things you can't control. You can't fight it, you can't even fix it. Why? Because that's not your job, you just have to acquiesce." She giggles. "Is that a word?"

I giggle, nod, and squeeze Riley's hand.

26

Neil

"You sitting down?"

"I am now, Dani. Just closed my door, too. What's up?" I'm at work, and just now returned from some back-to-back meetings. It's almost six o'clock. I know I won't be home before seven.

"Five thousand dollars," Dani exclaims.

I stiffen. "What about it?" I remember Dani telling me she's let some of her bills pile up.

"Executive administrative assistant. Five-grand increase per year, on-site day-care center, pretty decent health and dental, two weeks' vacation—"

"You got the gig?" I'm standing now, head spinning. It's taken Dani almost three months for her luck to change, but it finally happened.

"Neil, everything is great. My boss is a female, thank God. But there's only one catch." She pauses. "This company is in West Houston. So I'm gonna look for an apartment out there."

"Makes sense to me."

"You sure you're okay about that?" she asks. "I mean, I thought about it. It's way out Highway 6—I mean way out. The commute wouldn't make any sense. So . . . I'm disappointed in that part, but on the other hand, it'll be good to get away from this side of town—like I'm making a brand-new start."

She sounds a little sad, but mostly happy. I can't interfere with that.

"So," I ask, "what will this mean regarding . . . ?"

"I dunno. I gotta figure something out. I guess the baby can stay with you one week out of the month. Damn, I don't like thinking too much in advance."

"I wish it weren't so far."

"Me, too, honey."

Much as I wish they wouldn't, my ears tingle. Her voice drips with earnest sensuality. I close my eyes and move the phone away, but then press it hard against my ear.

"But hey," Dani speaks up, "It's not like I'm moving to Atlanta, silly. We'll still hook up. But I really want to treat you, remember like I promised? We can go anywhere you wanna go."

"Dani . . ."

"I won't take no for an answer, Neil. It doesn't have to be a fancy place. My funds are way screwy, but I'll just charge this to my almost-maxed-out Visa."

"Well, I'll pay," I offer. "Let's go eat crab legs at some point."

She squeals. She loves seafood as much as I do.

"It's a date," Dani says.

A couple of weekends later, Anya and Vette drive down to Galveston to buy fresh fish, and Dani decides to take a "me day," as she calls it, all of which means I get stuck watching the kids for most of the day. No problemo.

Later that afternoon we venture out to Super Wal-Mart. I strap Brax in one of those shopping carts that has its own baby carrier. I grab Reese by the hand and we walk down an aisle that has junk food.

"Daddy, can I have some potato chips?"

"No, Reese. And it's 'May I have,' not 'Can I.'"

"Huh?"

"No, you can't have potato chips. They're fattening."

"You always eat them."

I clear my throat and shake my head.

"What about popcorn?" she asks.

"What about it?"

"Is popcorn gonna make me fat?"

"No, it's not, because I'm not buying that, either."

"You're mean!" she yells.

"I know. Being mean is what mean people do, Reese. They're great at saying no."

My daughter does some serious rolling of the eyes and tries to loosen her tiny fingers from my firm grip.

"No running around the store where I can't find you," I tell her. "Stay with me, we won't be here long."

She pokes out her bottom lip but I don't care. Meanwhile, Brax has been looking at both of us and laughing. I don't see what's so funny, but if he does, I won't argue with him.

"Daddy, I wonder if they have new dolls here." Reese's eyes are sparkling.

"Probably," I murmur. We're in domestics, quite a distance from the toy section. I'm examining vacuum cleaner bags, trying to remember which brand we need. My cell phone rings. I glance at caller ID.

"Hey, you," I answer, letting go of Reese's hand, and looking around to see who's nearby.

"Hi, honey."

I try not to blush and I'm happy Dani can't see me.

"Where are you?" she asks.

"At the store."

"Oh, wow, thanks for being so precise. *At the store.* Hmmm, I'm done taking care of my business. How about if I come to the *store* so I can be with y'all? Where's our son?"

"Right here," I say, glancing at rosy-cheeked Brax. "Wanna talk to him?"

"I wanna talk to you."

"Talk." I cradle the phone between my ear and shoulder and grab a package of vacuum cleaner bags.

"Neil, I can't wait for you to see my new place."

"Oh, so you *do* want me to see it?"

"What you talking 'bout? Of course I do. Not just yet, though. That's why I haven't let you over here. I'm trying to get it perfect." She sighs with contentment.

"When will it be perfect?"

"Once you walk in the door, baby. It'll be too perfect once you're here."

I feel like crossing my legs even though I'm standing up. Brax shrieks and laughs. I plant my lips against his cheek. He gurgles, "Mama."

I lock eyes with him.

"Did you hear that, Dani?"

"No, what happened? Why are you shouting?"

"Brax said 'Mama.'"

"Stop lying," she laughs.

"Dani, I'm telling you he talked."

"Maybe it sounded like he said that. He's too young to be saying it."

"But haven't you been in his face a lot lately, saying that to him? Maybe he misses you."

"Of course he misses me," Dani says indignantly. "But I doubt he said that."

"Wait a minute, ask Reese. Hey, Reese!" I call out, and turn around. I look down an aisle that has only me and a Wal-Mart associate wearing a blue vest.

I turn my head the other way. No one.

I walk a few steps, leaving Brax in his basket.

"Hello," I hear Dani saying, but I'm too distracted trying to look for Reese.

Braxton shrieks. Maybe I've gotten too far away from him. I take a few more steps away from him until I can clearly see the video games.

A few teenage boys are gripping joysticks, but no one else is around.

Brax cries again. I hear him all the way around the corner.

I hurry back and see my red-faced son. He's kicking his legs and tears are sliding down his cheeks.

"I'm sorry, little man." I kiss his cheeks and wipe his tears.

"Dani."

"Don't 'Dani' me. I've been calling your name forever. I thought you lost the signal or something. What's up?"

"It's Reese. She's gone. I mean, she's probably around here somewhere. I need to find her."

"Go to the toy section, Neil. Try that, or maybe she had to use the little girls' room."

"I'll, uh, okay," I answer, my face heated. "I'll call you right back."

I try not to move the basket too fast, but it's making loud noises, squeaking and screaming, sounding exactly like how I feel inside.

I wheel the shopping cart down any aisle that I think would lure a little girl. Barbies, dollhouses, games, anything electronic . . . It's when I realize she's not in any of those sections that I am tempted to dial up Anya. A thick knot develops in my throat, but I concentrate on the need to find a manager and have my daughter paged. I hope no one has snatched her. I hope she hasn't escaped the store somehow. I can't imagine not being able to lay my hands on my child ever again. I want to pray, but praying is for those who have favor with the One they're praying to.

I'm walking past the aquarium section when I hear . . .

"I want one of those," a familiar sassy voice proclaims.

"Me too, me too, me too."

I stop pushing the basket and stare down the aisle. It smells fishy and it feels chilly, but the chilliness turns to warmth when I see the back of my daughter's braided head.

Tamika is pointing at some fish in a twelve-gallon tank. Reese is jumping up and down, waving at some creatures that don't know she exists.

"Reese," I say, voice firm, trying to squeeze back the anger that makes me want to shake and kiss her at the same time.

"Hey, Daddy," Reese says casually.

"Don't ever do that again."

"Hello, Neil." Riley rounds the corner with a welcoming smile. "I wondered where you were. I saw your daughter in the doll section and told her to come with me since she informed me that you must've gotten lost."

"Uhhh, yeah, thanks," I tell her.

"Hi there, Brax. Since Dani got the job and her new place, I've barely seen the baby. He's so precious. May I hold him?"

"Sure," I answer Riley, and let her unlatch my son so she can prop him on her hip and flirt with him and watch him flirt back.

Seeing my daughter again, especially with Riley nearby, makes me feel better, kind of like when you drive through a school zone and see children walking alongside a crossing guard. It's just a good feeling.

I sigh and mumble a quick thanks to the Lord. Right now I want nothing more than to round up my family and embrace them all in a tight hug, squeezing them like I never want to let them from my sight again.

We've just finished shopping and paid for our purchases. We're now in the front lobby of Wal-Mart, where they have vending machines for bubble gum and soda. Of course, Tamika wants a cold drink, and whatever Tamika wants, Reese has to have it, too. While the kids are getting a kick out of inserting dimes and nickels in the machines, Riley stands patiently nearby.

She wears a contented smile on her face. In fact, she's glowing. The more I stare at Riley, the more I want to look away. Her light is too bright for me. Her light reminds me of things I want to forget.

I wonder what Anya has confided to this woman. Is Riley aware of all my personal failures or am I just paranoid that she knows?

I don't care what she thinks, I say to myself. But a lie doesn't lie very well, and standing in Riley's presence makes me feel like Jesus Himself is hanging out at Super Wal-Mart. I'm ready to bounce like a kangaroo.

"C'mon, Reese," I say firmly. "We really need to get going."

"Okay, Daddy. Want some soda?"

"I want you to come on. I have a million things to do."

Riley smiles and waves. I turn from her, heading toward the huge parking lot, which is bustling with cars and people coming and going. I walk away from Riley—and feel like I just walked away from God.

The next Sunday morning, I hear Anya tell our daughter to take her bath. Reese is going to church with Anya, Riley, and Tamika. After Reese finishes bathing and getting dressed, she runs downstairs so her mom can make her hair look fancy. They're in the den. I'm in the kitchen popping two slices of bread in the toaster, and frying bacon on the Foreman grill.

I'm pouring some orange juice in a glass when the phone rings. Anya catches it. I go in the den and smile at my daughter. She's wearing a pretty pink-and-blue dress with patent-leather shoes. She's spruced up in white tights, and her braids are decorated with pink-and-blue flashing barrettes.

"You're coming to church, Daddy?"

"What? Uh, no, not today."

"Why not?"

I don't say anything.

"Go to church, Daddy. God loves you."

My daughter gives me a thoughtful look that suggests I should know this already. I hear the bell ring. The door opens, then slams shut.

My son is upstairs asleep, Vette is MIA, and for once I am a man alone inside his castle. I scrutinize my home, which is sparkling clean, every room tastefully furnished, but sometimes the house reminds me of a bride without her groom. I remember where every stick of furniture was purchased, how much it cost, when we bought it, Anya and I relishing in the joys of home ownership, marveling that we were doing something positive together.

I am tempted to dwell on the past, but I know that will only make me feel depressed, so I wander into my library and shut the door.

I plop down on the sofa, which makes a swishing noise, like it's sighing.

Looking around, I notice my daughter's thick white children's Bible.

I guess she forgot and left it in here one day. A year ago I presented this book to Reese. She enjoys sitting on the couch, turning the pages, and listening to me read while she nods and shakes her bare feet up and down. Observing Reese's pure faith reminds me of when I was a child, the days when I simply believed just like she does.

Again, my eyes are drawn to her Bible. It's not closed shut but is open—like it's expecting me.

The illustration on the page it's opened to shows Jesus Christ of Nazareth looking up at the sky. The background displays a blue sky with white clouds, and a few words are written on top of the clouds like someone is talking.

I read the words: "This is my beloved son in whom I am well-pleased."

God giving Jesus props like that amazes me. Jesus is "the man," something I know I'm not. I ponder my recent behavior, my lack of commitment, prayer, and sincere repentance, and I say aloud, "God saying that about His Son is really impressive. I know He'd never say anything like that about me."

A few seconds later, I hear inside my mind, "Son."

I tremble and blink my eyes several times.

I hear a gentle voice again. "Son."

"But Lord," I cry, "I don't do everything you say. How you can call me that?"

"Reese doesn't do everything you say, either," the voice tells me, "but she's still yours."

"But I mess up and do wrong over and over," I say aloud. "How can you love me, talk to me, still consider me your son?"

"Your daughter does the same things. Do you still love her? Isn't she still your daughter?"

It's Saturday morning. Reese is in the kitchen screaming and running around in circles. This is making Braxton scream, too. I am trying to wash a few loads of clothes, then the front and back lawns need cutting.

Anya is standing in the doorway of the laundry room staring at me.

"Hey, if this is a bad time," she says, "I could cancel New Orleans."

"What? No, you planned this trip a while ago. Go down to the French Quarter and have fun."

She presses her lips together. "It seems too coincidental, though, for me to plan this trip and then Dani finds a job."

"Ain't that something?"

"Oh, well. Whatever. I'm going no matter what. Don't want to lose my deposit on the hotel suite. Us girls are gonna get our party on. Then to-morrow we're scheduled for an airboat swamp tour."

"Good for you, Anya," I say.

"You sure you'll be okay?"

"With Vette gone for the night, and Reesy about to hook up with my mom for a sleepover, it'll be tough, but I think I can manage."

"Hmm, I'll bet you can. I guess you're just gonna watch Brax, huh? Do a little baby-sitting?" She smirks.

"Dani made plans to go to Joe's Crab Shack, I–I told you that. So we'll do that and that's about it," I assure her.

"Well, I'm glad you told me, but you're gonna do what you want to do, anyway, so . . . Don't forget the eyes of the Lord are in every place—"

"Anya, please."

"Well, they are."

"Okay, that's nice to know," I say. "Now, let me get back to my chores."

Later on I wave at Anya when she backs out the driveway, her Honda packed for a four-day-weekend trip. I run and take a shower so I can go drop off Brax at Audrey's, where Dani is waiting for me. She actually sweet-talked Audrey into watching Brax while we go out.

Dani and I hit Joe's Crab Shack, the one near Reliant Stadium, and we have a good time eating steamed crab legs, corn on the cob, oysters, and parsley potatoes.

"I love the new job already," Dani says, beaming "I work ten hours a day, Monday through Thursday. Roomy office, brand-new computer, even a reserved parking space. It feels like my real life is about to begin."

Dani's glowing in her pink spandex shirt, which partly falls off one shoulder, and a white denim miniskirt. It's like she's gained a few years, and a dazzling twinkle has returned to her eyes.

"I'm happy for you," I tell her.

"I'll bet you are, you dope."

I blush and try to stop staring at this woman. Although our having dinner is based on very respectful terms, I hope we can hurry up and get out of here.

When we've finished eating, I comment, "That hit the spot," and whip out my debit card to foot the bill.

"You're about to go back to Audrey's, right?" I ask her. "You need me to stop by anywhere before I take you back?"

Dani frowns. "Hmm, sure. There's one place I want to visit before I go to Audrey's."

"No problem," I say, hoping it won't take long.

When we settle in the Explorer, she commands, "Hop on the South Loop and exit at Braeswood."

I follow her instructions. Once we're on Braeswood, we continue west for a while, then make a left onto Fondren.

When we end up in front of my house, I just look at her.

"Let's go in, okay?" Dani whispers. "I want to finish celebrating."

I gulp and unlock the doors. It's seven in the evening. I imagine that Anya is almost in New Orleans by now. We enter the quiet house. Dani waits in the den and I go to my library and dial Anya's cell phone. Voice mail kicks in. I disconnect the line and turn around. Dani is standing in the doorway.

"I've never been in here before," she says, strolling to one corner of the room. Dani examines the spine of several encyclopedias. She picks one up and her mouth opens wide when a men's magazine falls out. It's an issue that I bought after Anya got rid of the rest of my stash. Various beautiful black women, of different complexions and sizes, are wearing thongs and aiming their huge, round butts at the camera.

"I didn't know you were into this," Dani says, holding up the magazine and eyeing me.

"I'm not," I say, and snatch the magazine. "Let's leave."

"Let's not," she says, and plops down on the sofa, kicking off her heels. Her toenails are painted a shade of soft pink.

"Are you always so color coordinated?" I ask, and point to the pink clutch she's gripping under her arm.

"Not all the time. I felt special today." She sighs and leans back and closes her eyes. I notice her breasts pressing against her pink spandex shirt. Of course, she's braless. I wish she wouldn't do things like this. I wish she . . . I leave the library and head for the den.

"Whassa matter you?" she says, running behind me. When she tries to grab my hand, I shake my head.

"Neil?" She pouts. "Why are you acting like this?"

"Dani, please . . ."

"I'm gonna do that to you, baby. I promise."

She leans toward me, closes her eyes, and puckers her glistening lips. I look at this woman, a woman whose existence has changed my entire life, and I take one step backward. She pops open her eyes; the hurt inside them is undeniable.

"I'm sorry, Dani, but this is where the foolishness ends."

"You mean the sex, doing each other? You telling me you don't want this anymore?"

I think long and hard and tell her, "No, not anymore."

"Are you serious? Why not?"

"I need to do right by my wife. I'm tired of this back-and-forth. I love my son, but we can't keep doing this, don't have a right to do this. Someone's going to get hurt."

"But y–you told me you *loved* me. Did you lie?"

I turn away from her, unable to look her in the eye and speak painful words at the same time.

"I love you so much, Neil, it hurts, it does," she moans, and firmly hugs me from the back, squeezing my waist. "The more you reject me, the more I—"

I take a deep breath and remove her soft hands off my trembling body, a body that wants her so much I wish I could die. I wish I could die to the strong desire, die to myself. But death is so final, so certain.

"At one time your words would flatter me, but now? Dani, why don't you just leave? I'll give you cab fare so you can go to Audrey's and get Brax yourself. I'm not trying to be mean, but maybe we should do something different."

"Neil, I can't believe you. Do you realize all I've been through because of you? Lost my job, my apartment—"

"You made those decisions, too."

"And what difference does that make? Is that supposed to make me feel any better? I don't understand men. I'm giving you everything I have, Neil, every fucking thing, and it still isn't good enough."

"What you want me to do?" I ask, frustrated. "You think we can do this forever?"

"Y—yes." She nods emphatically. "Let's keep doing it."

"But listen to yourself. Why would you even accept this? Don't you want better?"

"I want *you*, Neil, you. Can't you understand that?" She sucks in her breath, and there's so much tension showing in her forehead that I know my words, however daunting, are sinking in. I do not like this, I don't, but what other choice do I have? My feelings can be compared to when I discipline my daughter. I love Reese with all my heart but am obligated to correct her. And even though it hurts her and she thinks I'm mean, I know I have to do what's best for her even if I don't enjoy doing it.

"But I just don't see why things have to change," Dani pleads. "We can do this—you've said it many times yourself, Neil. You said you could make both of us happy."

"That was way before I knew how life would end up. Juggling everything is too much sometimes. As much as I love my son, I can do better. And you can, too. He's starting to notice everything you do now."

"Oh, okay, right, our relationship is *all* my fault." Her voice rises. "Totally my idea. But you're the one that propositioned me at work, or did you forget that little detail?"

"I remember," I say, and squeeze shut my eyes briefly. "I also remember calling you soon after our conversation and telling you I was having second thoughts. I felt that before we even got into this affair, we should slow down, reconsider. But you said it was too late, a done deal, and you pretty much seduced me."

"Ha! Well, you could have changed your mind, too, Neil Braxton Meadows. You didn't say no when I invited you to my place, and I definitely didn't hear any complaints the first time I made you do some serious moaning."

"You know, Dani, I can't deny that. But I still think that if you had listened to me when I had my initial doubts—"

"Oh, I'm so sick of this blame game. What kind of man are you? Do you *ever* take responsibility? You know what? I–I–I can't see myself wanting you anymore. God knows I can do way better than you, you prick."

Even though I can't figure out how she can come up with more to say, Dani keeps screaming. She stands before me, slapping my face with the palm of her hand so many times I stop counting. Yes, I'm a big man, but her punches sting and I jerk and flinch with every hit. It grieves me to hurt this woman, but I'd rather she and I hurt than to continue letting this pain affect my entire family.

The following week I stay strong as far as Dani is concerned, and by the time Saturday arrives, I ask Vette to watch Reese. I tell Anya, "I'm in the mood to go to the mall—haven't been in a hundred years. You wanna go with me?"

Anya shrugs, smiles, and quickly grabs her purse.

We walk through Foley's and end up in the women's department. Tons of colorful summer outfits are displayed all around us.

"Hey, Anya, you see anything here that jumps out at you?"

"No, not really," she says. But I notice her eyeing a lilac-colored dress with a flowery short-sleeve blouse and purple leather belt.

"Hmm, what about this?" I grab the outfit and thrust it at her. "Why don't you go try it on?"

"Neil," she argues, but I hear the delight in her voice. Anya grabs the dress and flees to the fitting room. I hear her squealing after a while. When she emerges from the fitting room and walks toward me sporting the new dress, I rise up from the chair I was sitting in.

"Mmmm, nice," I tell her.

"You like?" She beams, glancing down at the outfit.

"Do you?"

"Shoot, do I? Haven't you noticed something? I'm wearing a belt. I'm wearing a belt!"

I laugh and wink. When she returns to the fitting room and comes back out, I grab the dress from her and head to the nearest register. Anya says nothing. She simply smiles at me for the longest minute, staring like she's just now seeing me for who I really am.

We walk back into the crowded mall and she trips over her own feet and accidentally drops her purse. Everything spills out of it. I bend over to help her pick up the pens, wallet, calculator, and a tube of lipstick. There are still other items, but instead of her waiting on me, she snaps, "Okay, let's go." Her face flushes to a deep red and she twists her back to show we're leaving.

"No, wait, you forgot something." I kneel and sweep into my hands four sealed packets of super maxi pads with wings that also spilled from her purse. People are smiling at me, watching me scoop up the packets, but I ignore their amused stares, and when I finally get to my feet and run to catch up with my wife, Anya's face is still the color of crimson. But her hands are trembling. She's smiling, and I don't mind when she clutches my arm within hers—she latches on to me like she never wants us to be separated from each other again.

Dani

All during my "I hate Neil" phase (which lasts a good two weeks), I fix my attention on getting oriented to my new job and whipping my new two-bedroom apartment into shape. Neil hasn't bothered to come see me yet, but when he does, maybe he'll regret the damaging words he said to me. When he finally makes his way over here and sees how cozy everything looks, I hope he'll have a change of heart. I want him to take a good look at the bamboo wall coverings mounted from floor to ceiling, the bouquet of white lilies, gardenias, assorted tulips, and pink roses accented by baby's breath. And I hope he's impressed with the wicker gift baskets that sit next to the front door—they're filled with all kinds of goodies (wrapped mints, aromatherapy candles, and those cute little cans of Sprite). These are items I am going to dole out to guests to show them I now have a home and some security. At least that's my goal.

Neil and I have worked out a temporary arrangement. I will enroll Brax in my employer's on-site day care. The baby and I will spend Monday through Thursday together, but come the weekend, Neil takes over. Because Brax has spent so much time over at his dad's, playing with his sister and bonding with his extended family, Neil doesn't want to interfere with that routine. It's his suggestion, and I am fine with it.

So on Friday, mid-morning, a day that I know Neil has taken off from work, I find myself in the bathroom, calling him on his cell and attempting to style my hair at the same time.

"Hey, where's the baby?" I ask.

"He's here standing up, holding himself up by gripping the table. He's cracking me up. You need to come see this."

"Hmm, I guess so. Anya there?"

"Not right now."

"I'm in the middle of doing laundry," I tell him. "Maybe I'll come by later. And I wonder when you're going to stop making excuses and finally bring yourself over here?"

He pauses, voice firm. "I haven't decided when or if yet, Dani."

I clamp my mouth and wish he had given me a different answer. This man is so frustrating these days, a mere fraction of what he used to be. And this kind of change frightens me, like he's handed me one of those "good-bye" notes that I've been too scared to read just yet. If only I could get him to return to his former self, I probably wouldn't be so out of it like I've been feeling these days.

I'm happy about the new changes in my life, but I want to feel like Dani again.

"Neil, this is where your son is staying now. Aren't you even a little bit curious about his new home?"

"Yeah, sure, but . . ."

"Okay, are you scared I'm going to rip off your shirt, your shorts, and rub myself against you as soon as you come in here?" I know how visual Neil is. All I have to do is say certain key words and I'm sure his juices start churning.

"Danielle," he protests in a stubborn voice.

I smile. Hearing him say *Danielle* lets me know he's mad. And you can't have anger toward someone if you don't have any feelings for them. I just want to know that he still feels something for me.

"A—are you happy, Neil?"

"Not answering that."

I am hopeful enough to answer for him. Let's get real. Anya Meadows has nothing on me. Sure, she's lost tons of weight—okay, not literally but enough to let me notice that she struts around looking more confident and sexy. I don't know everything that goes on in their bedroom these days, but there's no way she and Neil can share the sexual fire that he and I once did.

I reach down and caress my nipple and stare listlessly in the bathroom mirror.

"Why are you so quiet?" Neil asks. "What are you doing? You got someone over there?" he asks jokingly.

"I wish." I smile. "I wish *you'd* come over here."

"Is that a fact?" he says.

Like times past, I imagine his thick bulge waving at me from inside his slacks. I wouldn't be surprised if he's horny. It's been so long since we've made love that I'm starting to feel like a wife.

"Don't even try it, Neil. You know how much I still want you."

"Hmmm," he murmurs. Maybe his visual creativeness is kicking in.

"Well, after I put the clothes in the dryer, I guess I can pick up Brax. Even though I dropped him off last night, I miss him. Does he miss me?"

"He called Anya 'Mama.'"

"Oh, did he? I'm walking out the door right now," I say. "Can't be having my son calling her that."

I decide to dress in one of Neil's favorite outfits—a white spandex top and a lime-green miniskirt with some three-inch pumps. I put on sheer white panty hose, and the essential cheeky pants that I hope he wants to slide off my hips one more time. I douse myself with six different perfumes. A shot of light spray behind each ear. Body mist squirted on the front of my neck. A fruity aroma between the breasts. Another blast of eau de toilette near my crotch. And two different floral fragrances sprayed on each ankle.

What will happen when I walk in Neil's house, dressed so hot with my curls falling all over my head and every inch of my body smelling like dozens of roses? What will he do if I grab a bottle of honey and ask him to lick it off me, something he's done before? How can he resist when I squeeze him around the waist and cover his cheeks, his forehead,

and his lips with some of Dani's juicy kisses? That's the thing. Once I
put it on him good, I don't see how he can resist. Then his mind will
start clicking and he will give up this nonsense about being with *her*.
Then I can jog his memory about what he's had and enjoyed, and what
he can continue to have and enjoy.

I pull up in the Meadows' driveway and smile when I see the Explorer
parked in front of the house. I look in the mirror again. Makeup is in-
tact, some curls are partially covering my eyes, and my lips are glistening from this strawberry gloss that Neil used to enjoy kissing off me.

I swing my legs out of my whip and take a deep breath. My panties
are moist. It's difficult to walk in these heels, but damned if I'm not
gonna try. I cannot wait for Neil to make love to me like I'm Beyoncé,
Halle, and Janet Jackson all rolled into one.

I step up to the front door. It's partially open, so I just go in. It's like
my man is expecting me. I like that. I walk right through the foyer, past
the den, straight to the library. I tap once, grab the door handle, and
march in. The door makes a light swishing sound. I place my hands on
my hips and stare at Anya's side. She's scooping up a porno mag and
tossing it in a garbage bag.

I clear my throat. "What are you doing?"

Anya swirls around, her eyes enlarged. "How'd you get in here?" she
says. "You scared me."

I sigh heavily and question her with my eyes.

Anya looks me up and down. "Neil's not here."

"Where'd he go?"

"Why you want to know?"

I can't believe the agitation in her voice. Okay, maybe I shouldn't act
so pushy. I need to calm down a notch.

"I, uh, he asked me something about getting tickets to the circus," I
tell her. "And I wanted to follow up."

"Neil hasn't told me anything about circus tickets, Dani. And, uh,
why are you coming over to my house to see my husband dressed like a
whore? Oh, I remember why, its 'cause you *are* a whore."

Anya drops the garbage bag on the floor and leaves the library.

I follow her to the kitchen. "Anya, can you explain why you're being so rude?"

She swirls around, waving her arms. "I don't have to explain anything to you. By now everything should be clear and certain. You, Danielle Frazier, don't belong here. Period. I want you to pick up your son and I want you gone. You and Neil will have to create a different kind of arrangement. And if he's not up to the task, then I'll do it. But this is the last time you're stepping inside my house."

"What—"

"Shut up. Baby mama or no baby mama, you don't have any rights. And you definitely don't have more rights than me. So if it takes deprogramming your little mind and making you understand who is who around here, then I am prepared to do that."

I gape at her open-mouthed. Her eyes are blazing and I see a butcher knife on the counter, so I decide to chill out. I wouldn't want to have to use it on her.

"Where's Brax?" I ask in a delicate voice, and try to smile.

"He's upstairs. I'll get him. You go sit on the couch. Don't go anywhere else in my house. And do not try to call Neil."

I stomp into the den and flop down on the couch, crossing my legs at the ankle, my mind swirling. What the fuck's wrong with her? And why'd Neil take off so fast and leave me to deal with this mess? I hate being blindsided and not being able to figure out what to do.

Anya brings down Braxton, goes back upstairs, and returns with three huge bags of clothes, two more bags of diapers, toys, blankets, every single thing that has to do with my son. I feel discarded. So unwanted. Sure, she's his wife, but do I have to be treated so awful? Like a nothing . . . a pariah . . . or maybe she's giving me what I've often given her. Even so, I can't appreciate how she's acting.

I feel so humiliated. My jaw is rigid and I am this close to falling apart, something I've never wanted to do in front of Anya. But feeling vulnerable, all I can do is grab Brax and give him a strong hug. I wish he would hug me back, but he doesn't. Instead he squirms wildly in my arms, like he's forcing me to let him go. Something has Brax's attention, and instead of fighting him, I let him have his way and allow him to drop to the floor.

While Anya continues to fuss at me like I'm less than a piece of shit, Brax crawls to a table and pulls himself up. He picks up an object, looks at it, and opens his mouth. I want to tell him to come here, but Anya is yelling at me like she's crazy, which makes me want to run to the kitchen and grab that knife in case she really goes off. But then her screaming stops. She points at Brax, who has fallen back on the floor.

I rush to his side. "Brax, what's wrong?"

I look down and lock eyes with my son . . . He is staring at me strange . . . and his face is slowly turning blue. I lift him up and pat his back. He doesn't respond. I slap his back again. "Brax, Brax!" I scream. "Say something." I laugh like this nightmare isn't really happening, then stop.

"Anya, could you? I can't, he's not—" I scream again.

"Dani, I don't think he's breathing. Don't slap—it could make things worse. Let me have him." Anya extracts the baby from my arms, grabs a chair, and sits him on her lap facing away from her. Her index and middle fingers resemble a pad when she places them under his rib cage, then quickly thrusts inward and upward. Nothing happens. I watch her thrusting, and hear her praying, until my baby coughs, sputters, and expels a lime-green button from his mouth. When Brax starts quietly crying, making the same amazing noises I heard the day I gave birth to him, Anya whispers, "Oh God, keep protecting him."

All I can think to do is snatch my purse and head for my truck. I get in the vehicle, turn on the ignition, back out the driveway, and never look back at the door. But in my rearview mirror I see Anya holding and cradling my son, and for the first time ever, I'm glad she's doing it.

28

Anya

It's still Friday afternoon. Dani's just sped off in her truck. I'm standing outside the house near the front door holding little Braxton in my arms. He's leaning his head against my breast, purring. Comfort, protection, peace.

He wants what I want, but how can he enjoy peace when he sees me and his mother at war?

"I'm so sorry, so sorry, so sorry, little Brax, it won't happen again," I say and press my lips against his soft brown hair. He squirms in my arms and sighs. I turn to go back to the house.

"Hey, hon. You watching the baby today?"

"Riley, if you only knew," is all I can say.

My neighbor charges up our walkway dressed in a pretty tan summer dress suit.

"Where you going?" I ask her.

"Solomon's Temple. I skipped Sunday night's Communion service, and I wanted to go up there and drop off my tithe. You doing anything special? Wanna ride?"

Moments later we're entering the doors of the church. Braxton is perched on my hip, laughing uproariously as I bounce him up and down so it seems like he's riding a galloping horse. Hearing him giggle makes me so happy. And it feels wonderful to get away from the house and momentarily forget the scary drama that just happened.

I follow behind Riley, who's walking through some double glass doors into a suite of administrative offices. There's a redwood desk manned by a receptionist. On her right is a row of telephone cubicles complete with headsets.

"What's all that?" I ask her.

A woman has approached us from down the hall and overhears my question. "That's the call center where the prayer counselors sit and answer phones seven days out the week," she tells me.

"Hey, Sista." She nods at me reassuredly. "Anytime you want to talk, give us a call or come see us. We'll cry with you, help bear your burdens—we do it all."

"Hmm, sounds good. Thanks for letting me know," I tell her gratefully.

"My name is Zaire if you ever need anything." Her voice is strong, confident.

Riley signals to me that she'll be right back. Brax bounces up and down in my arms, his hands waving excitedly when he sees a water fountain.

"Okay, partner," I tell him and start walking down the hall past the call center.

"Hey, Sista," says Zaire. "After you get your water, c'mon in my cube. You can rest your feet and let your son sit on your lap while you're waiting."

I take one long look at her. After I get Brax his drink, she stands up and leads us to a nearby private office and closes the door. Within ten minutes I tell her everything: the marital arrangement, Neil's affair with Dani, the miscarriages, and our bedroom issues. Of course, I have to spell out certain words because of Braxton, but Zaire catches on fast.

"Sista," Zaire says, "it takes a lot of strength to tell me all this. But that indicates you're ready for a change. Can't say I blame you." She laughs. "But seriously, as I sit here and listen to the things you've said about your husband, his friend, et cetera, I do get one major impression: The problems you're having aren't about the marital contract, they're not about you. Not about him, that woman, or even this precious little baby."

"What did you say?" I ask, darkness clouding my eyes as I stare at this woman. "Do you understand that I've put up with so much mess I almost lost my mind? I've sacrificed, put my health in jeopardy, and trusted him too many times to count."

"Sista Anya, you may have done the right things, and that's good, but something bigger than you sustained you. So, like I said before, this isn't about you," she says in a slow, calm voice.

"Omigod, omigod, omigod," I say, and rise up out of my seat. I hand Brax over to Zaire, leave the office, and pace the hallway.

"I'm sorry, I'm sorry, I'm sorry," I weep, and finally discern the wisdom that has eluded me.

29

Neil

Yesterday before Dani arrived to pick up Braxton, I got called into work.
I left the house immediately, worked for hours, and barely took a break.
And late last night when I got home, I went straight to sleep.

Now it's Saturday, early. I hear Anya in the kitchen stirring around.
Thirsty and hungry, I walk in her direction.

Bacon pops and sizzles on the grill. A pot of grits cooks on a burner.
The smell of coffee fills my nostrils. Anya cracks several eggshells
against the sink and pours egg into a skillet.

"Hey," I say, "what's all this for?"

"I usually cook breakfast on Saturday," she responds. "Nothing new
about that."

"*Usually* being the operative word. I don't think I've seen you doing
this on a Saturday morning in at least two months."

"Well, things change." Anya shrugs and resumes cooking.

I walk over to the bread bin and remove four slices of wheat.

"You might want to toast a few extra pieces," Anya says.

"Why's that?"

"Brax is a greedy little something," she laughs.

"He's still here? Why didn't Dani come pick him up yesterday?"

My wife grunts and shakes her head.

I run upstairs and find Reese tying Brax's shoestrings into a knot. Once she's done, I scoop my son up in my arms, hold my daughter's hand at the same time, and bring them both downstairs.

All four of us eat in the dining room. Brax screams from his high chair, drowning out Reese, who's trying to talk. She puts up with his shrieking for a while but then runs from the room, covering her ears.

"That girl loves that baby, huh?" I say jokingly.

"Yeah," Anya says in a serious voice. "It's kind of like she has no choice. It's just worked out that way. Life does that, ya know."

I stare at her.

"Neil, I guess now's as good a time as any. We need to talk. I want to propose something."

"Go on," I tell her.

"I want us to make a strong commitment toward our relationship. And I need to know if you want the same. Were you sincere when you recited your vows on July seventh?"

"I was at the time."

"Oh." Her voice is low. "What about now?"

"I still mean it, even if I don't show it all the time. But yeah, I'm committed."

"I guess that's fair enough. But let's move on to something else."

First Anya yells for Reese to come get Brax. Then Anya leaves the room and returns within minutes carrying several sheets of paper. Her hands are trembling.

"This," she says, "is our marital arrangement. I can't believe how much trust I put in these sheets of paper, how much I supposedly valued the words. I want—"

"This?" I say, and grab the papers. Anya and I are both holding the arrangement. Ten sheets in all. Anya goes to a kitchen drawer and retrieves a box of matches. She motions for me to follow her outside. We end up in the backyard next to the metal picnic table and a black garbage can.

Anya lifts up the first page of the arrangement. "This, Neil, is no longer valid."

I strike one match and lower it next to the paper. The yellow fire lights up, cracks and pops. The fire singes the page at one end, making the words of promise disappear, transforming the sheet from one form into another.

By the time we're done, a smoky aroma burns and clogs our nostrils. The odor is so strong, Anya covers her nose with one hand. I grab her other hand and squeeze.

For the first time in a long time, I feel free, like I'm finally in the place I've been trying to get to. I stare at the ashes and my mind is jammed with memories of what tried to be but couldn't. I wonder what the future can give us that the past could not.

"Starting now, we're putting all of this behind us," Anya proclaims. "And I am sooo sorry for the pain I've caused you."

"Anya," I say, shocked, "you haven't done anything."

"Oh, but I have."

She walks back into the house and returns waving another set of papers.

"I'm burning these up, too," she says, "but want you to see them first."

I read the top of the first page: "Petition for Divorce. Petitioner: Anya Taylor Meadows."

"You?" I say.

"Yes, Neil. About six weeks ago, I pawned the ring you gave me, retained an attorney, and was in the process of filing. But you were starting to change for the better and I still had hope. So my going forward with the divorce was placed on hold. Riley and I prayed about what to do, and I heard in my spirit 'Wait,' so . . ."

I just gawk at her, swallowing the lump that has developed in my throat.

"I'm going to be a better wife to you, and I believe you can be a better husband. But the one thing that I demand must change is Dani's presence, you understand me? We have to establish and protect our boundaries. So Dani is no longer welcome here, Neil. Ever. And I don't want you seeing her anymore. I need to know if you can handle that."

"You're serious about that?"

"Like nothing I've ever meant before," Anya responds.

"But since she's—I mean, how else can we raise our son?"

"Riley's agreed to be our mediator. That way we won't have to deal with Dani directly. And I'm willing to give this a try if you are."

"And you're really okay with mothering Braxton?"

"Yep, absolutely," she says. "He can be the son I'll never have, the son I'm supposed to have."

So much hope and strength are shining through her, she's blinding me.

"We're going to make it, Neil. We can do this. And I know you still love me."

"Of course I love you. But it's tough being loved by two different women—"

"And it's tough when you love two different women, right, Neil?"

I wish I could respond, but don't.

"Neil, regardless of how tough things are, I won't play second fiddle anymore. Not when I know I have a God-given right to claim you. The vows we gave to the Lord are still good. He hasn't forgotten the vows, and He will bless this union if we do what's right in His eyes. Not in our own eyes. You up to the task?"

I firmly nod. Again, I know I have to release Dani. It's hard, so hard. And the fact that letting go is hard lets me know it's something I need to do. I try to imagine starting anew. I want to see what Anya sees. Feel what Anya feels.

The next morning, my entire family gets dressed for church. And when we all enter the doorway of Solomon's Temple, Reesy grabs my hand, looks up at me, and says in a loud voice, "I'm so proud of you, Daddy."

Anya

It's mid-September. I'm reclining facedown on a padded lounge chair and wearing a cute one-piece orange-and-lilac bathing suit. A nearby band is jamming, playing "Celebration" by Kool and the Gang. Neil's hands feel soothing as he gently pinches my skin between his fingers. He vigorously rubs jojoba oil on me, squeezing all the tension from my shoulders. We're on the Lido deck of the Ecstasy ship, a four-day cruise that's headed to Cozumel. Second honeymoon. No kids. Just us.

We're spent the afternoon dancing, people-watching, and eating steak and lobster for lunch. I've just finished sipping on a magnificent Bahama Mama and can't wait to order another.

"Okay, that's enough of you groping me," I say to Neil, and sit up. "Now it's your turn."

He happily complies, at first flopping onto his stomach, but then he turns over on the chair so that he's looking up at me.

"Anya," he chokes, reaching out to grab my hand, "if your fingers massage my body, I won't be responsible for what happens out here."

"Neil, don't even try it." I blush.

"I am serious, baby," he insists, deliberately looking me up and down. I want to place my arms around his neck and squeeze real tight.

"Dang, jeez, all righty then. We can go back to the room and finish playing that game you like," I tell him. "This time, instead of you pretending to be a fireman, I want you to be, uh, how about a TV preacher? Think you can manage that?"

"Huh?" He scowls, looking at me like I'm nuts. "You *do* want me to stay in the mood, don't you? Not gonna play a preacher. Let me try playing a good husband, okay? I'll pretend to be that."

Actually, the past few months Neil's behavior has improved. He's managed to keep Dani at bay, and she accepted our decision without a fight. I guess she got tired of the drama as much as we did.

"A good husband, huh?" I comment. "That's funny. Okay, you can try that."

"And if I play like I'm a good husband, who are you going to be?" he asks.

"Hmm," I say, "how about your girlfriend?" I stand next to Neil and lower myself to my knees. I press my lips against both his cheeks and his lips, kissing him deeply, and rubbing his legs up and down. I find myself getting aroused, and I love how that feels, since me getting horny is still somewhat hit-or-miss.

"Who are you again?" he gasps, squirming and grinning, leading my hand below his waist.

"I'm going to play like I'm . . . my husband's girlfriend."

Acknowledgments

I've met quite a few folks during my short time in the biz, so bear with me. Much love to my author crew: Margaret Johnson-Hodge, Marissa Monteilh, Lexi Davis, and Cheryl Robinson. Margaret (Cuz), keep doing your thing. (((Marissa))), my sis in the biz, you are so sweet. My girl Lexi (author of *Pretty Evil*), I love to discuss writing, share experiences, and laugh with you. I'm happy you were brought into my life. Cheryl, I knew you were gonna make it.

Authors: Nancey Flowers, E. Lynn Harris (who encouraged me to write book reviews on a national level), Nina Foxx, Alisha Yvonne, Shelley Halima (my Detroit homegirl), Tina Brooks McKinney, Phillip Thomas Duck, Tracy Price-Thompson, Nikki Woods, Shelia Goss, MBridges, Frederick Smith of L.A., Darrious D. Hilmon, Elyse Singleton, Philana Marie Boles, Pat Tucker, ReShonda Tate Billingsley, Toy Styles (you are a sweetie), Ms. Erica Perry, Keith Lee Johnson, and Brandon Massey—thanks, Brandon, for your generosity and ongoing participation regarding Book-Remarks.com.

Reviewers and Supporters: Brian K. Walley for the excellent feature with Ebony Expressions Book Club, Romance in Color, Looseleaves.org, Tee C. Royal & The RAWSISTAZ Reviewers, ReadinColor, One Swan Productions, Road to Romance, Romantic Times Book Club Magazine, Avid-Readers.com, and Disilgold.com. Toni Bonita, Simone A. Hawks (thanks for checking on me when I was sick), Simone Kelly, Cynthia Holsome, Mr. Robert Pope (for going above and beyond), Joan Havis, Marla Ofor, and Sheila Lindsay. Mega thanks to Chris Pattyn for hanging out with me in ATL and making me laugh. Let's do it again.

Bookstores: B&N, Kiso Books, Soul On Wheels, Shrine of the Black Madonna (Houston and Atlanta), Jokae's, Waldenbooks (in Dekalb Mall, the Houston One Center, Detroit Renaissance Center, and Fairlane Town Center), Cushcity.com, Black Images, and Karibu Books in Maryland (thanks, Lee).

Bookclubs: Cover2Cover Book Club (Houston)—the first club to sponsor me—Circle of Friends Book Clubs in Columbus, Ohio, and Atlanta; Cushcity Book Club; Ebony Eyes Book Club; The African-American Authors Book Club of Palmdale, California; Ebony Dimensions Book Club; Brownstone Book Club of Houston; Kismet Book Club; Divas Read 2 of Dallas; Carol Mackey of Black Expressions Book Club (you are *so* awesome); Sistahood Book Review (thanks for a FUN book club meeting); the wonderfully crazy folks in RAW4ALL; Prominent Women of Color; Soulful Literary Experience; Queens In Pen Book Club; The Sistah Circle Book Club; Black Professionals Consortium of Houston; The GRITS; and all the other clubs around the country and radio stations (including FM-107 in the U.K.) that selected *My Daughter's Boyfriend*.

Web Sites/media: The Black Library, AALBC.com, The MPB Network, Roads to Romance, Sonya Harris of Sayha Pub, Mybestseller.com, PeopleWhoLoveGoodBooks, JeffRivera.com, The Literary Café, *Quarterly Black Review* magazine, *Publishers Weekly, Booking Matters* magazine, Maurice Hope-Thompson of KTSU-FM, and my UH hook-up (Francine Parker, Mike Emery, and Thomas Shea).

Many thanks to Chris Jackson—your editing skills and tough questions made this book a lot better. And thanks to Rachel Kahan, the editor who acquired *My Husband's Girlfriend*. Shout-outs to my cool agent, Claudia Menza, who is so enthusiastic and helps to whip my novels in shape. Thanks in advance to my new editor, Shana Drehs. Much appreciation to my wonderful publisher, Crown Publishing Group/Three Rivers Press. Your support means so much to me.

Shout-outs to my relatives in Michigan (hi Mom), Texas (sis and hubby), Louisiana, Illinois (Aunt Michel), Arizona, and elsewhere. (Thanks to my uncle Reggie and cousin Terri for coming to see me in downtown Detroit.)

Thanks to those who support me at the University of Houston. You are a true cast of characters who force me to constantly listen and take notes. Special thanks to Dilip (who's always raving about my book), Claudia O'Hare (Drama Queen) just because, and all the brothas (you know who you are).

Special thanks to Dawnya Ivey and Kim Floyd for helping me out with reviews.

I can't forget Marvin D. Cloud of Houston, the first person to publish my nonfiction through *Gospel Monthly* magazine in the mid-90s.

I appreciate anyone who bought and enjoyed *My Daughter's Boyfriend*. Your comments make my day. Visit me online at CydneyRax.com or e-mail me at Cydney@booksbycydney.com.

Last but not least, thanks to God for sustaining me through all my trials, tribulations, triumphs, and victories.

If you read *My Husband's Girlfriend*, I want to hear from you. *MHG* is a story I've wanted to do for years, and it's amazing to write about this topic. Keep an open mind while reading and don't forget that in real life some men have babies with multiple women and some women are trying to deal with it. And even if we don't understand or agree with folks' choices, everyone has a story to tell. I truly love this book and I hope you do, too.

If I mistakenly omitted you from these acknowledgments, please forgive me. I'm always touched by your efforts.

Luv y'all.

Cydney (no middle name) Rax
February 2006

About the Author

Cydney Rax was born and raised in Detroit. A graduate of Cass Technical High School, she earned an undergraduate degree in written communications from Eastern Michigan University. Cydney has been featured in publications including *Publishers Weekly, Quarterly Black Review,* and *Booking Matters,* among others.

Cydney is an avid reader as well as creator of Book-Remarks.com, a popular website that is devoted to promoting African-American literature. She has interviewed authors such as Carl Weber, E. Lynn Harris, Eric Jerome Dickey, Kimberla Lawson Roby, and dozens of others. Her author website is CydneyRax.com, and her blog is available at http://cydneyrax.blogspot.com.